THE HIGHLANDER'S
Tempestuous Bride

CATHY MACRAE

Published by Short Dog Press
ISBN-13: 978-0-9966485-0-9

Published in the United States of America

This book is dedicated to Derek—my very own hero.

Prologue

Ard Castle, above the Firth of Clyde, Scotland, 1375

Ten-year-old Ryan Macraig sat astride his horse, struggling to keep his emotions in check. He gritted his teeth, but refused to let his father see him as less than a man grown.

Laird Macraig patted his son's knee awkwardly. "Ye will be fine." His words were firm, though his voice sounded rough. Ryan wondered who he was trying to convince.

"Ye will foster at the MacLaurey keep. The laird's son is yer age and ye will get along grand."

Ryan held back the words he'd already said. He had plenty of friends at Ard Castle, lads he'd grown up with. He had no wish to make new ones. But he knew lairds' sons often fostered with other clans, and his childhood was now past. It was time he became a man.

"Remember yer heritage, Ryan. Remember our ways." Laird Macraig's head turned ever so slightly toward his southern border in a gesture Ryan knew well, but did not understand.

"Learn yer lessons. The Macraigs dinnae always have allies to rely on. Ye must make new ones."

Ryan faced southward, too. Years ago, the Macraigs and the Macrorys had a firm alliance. For reasons left unspoken, that alliance failed, and the never-ending battle against pirating along their coastal boundary now strained the Macraig power and coffers.

"I will make ye proud, Da." Ryan bit back the tears of parting.

1

"I know ye will, lad." Laird Macraig turned and motioned for Ryan's escort to mount up. As the procession filed through the castle gates, Ryan allowed himself one final glimpse over his shoulder.

His last sight of his father seared into his mind. Laird Macraig stood tall and straight, the hem of his kilt swaying gently in the breeze, one arm wrapped around the swollen waist of his leman who leaned against his side.

Ryan wondered if his father would forget him once the bairn was born.

Chapter One

Scaurness Castle, Overlooking the Firth of Clyde, Scotland
Ten years later

*T*heir gazes prickled the hair on the back of Gilda's neck. Though she couldn't see them, she knew they were there. Ruthless and cunning, they would not give up until they got what they wanted. Escape would be difficult, if not impossible this time.

Normal sounds of castle life drifted to the third level from the great hall below. Voices chatted, tables and benches scraped against the stone as servants moved them against the wall after the midday meal. Nothing seemed amiss. Yet Gilda knew better. Somewhere in the shadows of the upper gallery, they awaited her first misstep.

There was no place to hide. She'd outgrown such places long ago, leaving her exposed to their every whim.

By St. Andrew! Can they not leave me alone, even for a moment?

It was an uncharitable thought. As the oldest child, Gilda was expected to help care for her younger brothers. But this was the last straw.

She tried to conceal the basket in the folds of her surcoat, but the scent of warm berries wafted out, betraying her presence.

"She has pastries!"

Six-year-old Finn cackled gleefully as he swung from the carved balustrade, landing on the floor with a jolt before her. Gilda jerked to a halt, startled in spite of the fact she'd known he was near. Jamie, his twin, sprang from behind a hanging tapestry, paying no heed to the costly fabric billowing wildly against the wall. He grabbed at her basket but Gilda swung it over her head, out of his reach.

"Och, no fair, Gilda." Finn's voice took on a petulant whine. "Ma willnae like it if she learns ye've been snitching pastries."

"Nae, she doesnae like the two of *ye* snitching pastries. Cook gave these to me because I helped gather the berries yesterday." Gilda frowned at the two imps. "Ye dinnae help."

Jamie leapt into the air, crashing against her as he swiped upward with one hand. Gilda staggered, but was familiar with her brothers' tactics. Well aware of their trick of pushing her into the other's clutches, she shifted her balance and stood firm.

"Wheesht!" She raised a hand to stop them. "I'll give ye the pastry if ye but wait a moment."

The twins eyed her speculatively. It was clear they didn't trust her to simply hand over one of Cook's coveted pies. Not willing to lose the game now, Gilda kept the burgeoning triumph from her face.

Food was the quickest and easiest bribe known to the young rapscallions. With a mock sigh of surrender, Gilda pried the basket's lid up and peered inside. She waited until the boys were all but drooling as the scent of hot berries wafted in the air. Reaching in the basket, she picked up a pastry, careful not to burn her fingers. She held it out to Finn, knowing Jamie would try to snatch it away.

"'Tis mine!" Jamie cried, seeing his brother reach for the prize.

"'Tis not!" Finn protested. He grabbed at the pastry and Gilda let go. The boys fought over the pie, breaking it open, dark purple berries spilling out with a rush of steam and mouth-watering aroma. Their attention diverted by the near-disaster, Gilda made good her escape.

Her feet beat a rapid tattoo down the stairwell, through the hall and out to the stable. With a pause to set her basket on a rickety table, Gilda grabbed a bridle from its peg.

She flung the leather straps over her mare's head and with a practiced leap, sprang to the horse's back, not bothering with blanket or saddle. Dainty hooves pranced as Gilda gathered her reins, leaning forward to retrieve the little basket. Thumping her heels into the mare's sides, she sent her bounding from the stable.

"Run, Fia, run!" she chanted. The mare took the bit between her teeth and raced along the path to the castle gate. Gilda ignored the guards' stares as she passed through the barbican. Midmorning travel in and out of the castle meant the gates remained open. The guards were too accustomed to her riding to the beach to visit the clan's wise woman, Tavia, to challenge her. To be sure, she bent low over Fia's neck and did not slacken her speed until they were well away from the walls.

The surefooted pony skidded down the switchback trail through the bracken to the beach below the castle. Gilda rode pressed close against the mare's back, gripping her tight between her knees, swaying with her movements.

They soon arrived at the beach and Gilda reined the mare in, mindful of the rocks studding the ground. She dismounted near Tavia's ancient cottage tucked against the stark cliffs. Dropping Fia's reins, Gilda checked the contents of her basket and skipped up the driftwood-lined path.

Lifting a fisted hand, she knocked at the portal.

"Enter."

The pungent odor of herbs filled the little cottage and Gilda inhaled deeply as Tavia glanced up from the leaves she was grinding.

"Ah, lass. 'Tis good to see ye."

From the far side of the room, a goat bleated.

"Wheesht, Auntie, when will ye put wee Agnes outside?"

"She would be at the mercy of the woodland beasts were I to stake her out."

Gilda set her basket on the table and stepped behind Tavia, hugging her waist.

"Ye know there are no beasties in these woods. None that come down to the beach, anyway." Gilda stepped back to the table, lifting the lid from her basket. The scent of berry pastries shouldered past the tang of the herbs and Tavia perked up with interest.

"And how did ye come by those, lass?" Her ancient blue eyes twinkled as she teased Gilda.

"Och, Cook gave up keeping her pastries away from me years ago. Ye know she spoils me," Gilda replied with a grin.

Tavia put her mortar and pedestal aside and wiped her hands on her apron. "Ye have always been a wee charmer." Her lips curved in a smile of affection. "I suppose the more direct question is how ye got these past those two wee *louns* at the castle."

Gilda rolled her eyes. "Jamie and Finn are fighting over the pastry I baited them with. They become more annoying every day." She turned to Tavia, drawing her face into a long-suffering pose. "When will they grow up and stop pestering me?"

Tavia chuckled. "Ye have to give them time. Young boys eventually become young men."

"And still pester me." Gilda frowned, deep furrows forming between her brows.

"Aye?" Tavia peered at her, new interest gleaming in her eyes. "A particular lad pestering ye, then?"

Gilda trailed a fingertip along the back of a chair. "Not sae much," she admitted slowly. "But he seems to show up everywhere I do."

"Tell me." A deceptively mild command edged Tavia's voice.

"Now, dinnae be telling Da," Gilda chided the old woman. "He'd just frighten the poor lad." She managed a grin to allay Tavia's fears. "Gordon is making eyes at me, but I dinnae take him seriously."

Tavia nodded. "Ye are too young to consider a match. And yer da willnae like the lads paying ye too much mind."

Gilda rolled her head on her shoulders. "But, Tavia. I've sixteen summers and my friend Anice has already wed."

"Do ye have yer eye on someone, then?"

"Nae, 'tis not that…" Her voice trailed off uncertainly.

"Then what is it, lass?"

Gilda blew out a breath of frustration. "I'm afraid Da will set me to marry someone I dinnae like."

Tavia gave a snort. "Ye willnae worry about that, lass. Yer da wouldnae ask ye to marry a *wickit* man."

"Not evil, no. But someone I dinnae love."

"Love?" Tavia's eyes opened wide. "Ye are the laird's eldest daughter. He willnae bind ye to a man without honor, but he will ask ye to marry to benefit the clan."

Gilda brushed at her eyes, startled at the tears welling there. "Ma and Da love each other." A petulant snuffle escaped her.

Tavia laughed. "Och, lass, ye dinnae remember the two of them before they wed. The king himself commanded it. Yer grandda, the auld laird, was dead, the castle in contention from several clans and pirates marauding the coastline. Yer ma had a great dowry that attracted all manner of scoundrels as long as she was unwed."

"I know all that. But they act, well…" To her embarrassment, heat rose in her cheeks.

"Yer ma and da acted like cats fighting over the same piece of fish," Tavia announced. "And they still do."

"They do not," Gilda cried, astonishment coloring her voice.

Tavia clucked her tongue. "They dinnae always disagree, and rarely in public. But they do always make up." Her eyes twinkled.

Gilda pulled the chair away from the table and sat. "So, they dinnae love each other when they wed?"

"They resolved to make their marriage work, and fell in love very quickly. Yer da is an honorable man, but he was once a wee *loun* just like yer brothers. I remember him well."

"Not like Niall," Gilda championed her brother, five years her junior.

Tavia shrugged. "Niall is too serious by half." Her lips quirked into a grin. "And he is away fostering with yer uncle's clan. Likely ye dinnae remember his pranks, he's been gone that long."

"Mayhap Jamie and Finn will foster soon," Gilda groused.

Tavia laughed. "'Tis a day we all look forward to, I am sure." She waved to the pastries. "Now. Let's enjoy these before they cool."

Ryan sat astride his horse, Duer, as he gazed across the beach. The land dipped low beneath the cliffs, sand and stones mingling with the soil of the forest, giving rise to dense underbrush and gnarled, stunted trees. He inhaled the warm scent of berries ripening on the bushes, the sharp tang of the salt air, and the musky sweat of the horse between his knees. The corners of his lips curved upward. After ten years away, he was home.

With a nudge of his hand on the reins, he turned Duer down the beach, content to explore the shoreline for a time. Behind him, his retainers unloaded the *birlinn* bearing his belongings, and his best friend, Connor MacLaurey, still nursed a bout of seasickness leaving him tired and irritable. It was a relief to be alone.

He trailed down the beach until he reached a small rise. He knew beyond lay the boundary between the Macraig and Macrory clans, and he would not stray that far. A silent feud smoldered between his father and the Macrory laird, and though the Macrorys would not kill him for trespassing, neither would they send him home with a friendly pat to his head.

Reining Duer to a halt, Ryan dismounted, tying his reins to his saddle, leaving the horse to graze. He climbed the rise and dropped to the ground, settling to gaze over the firth. He plucked a stalk of grass and chewed the stem absently, grimacing at the salty taste. Before him, small boats plied the waters, an invisible line drawn between the Macrory and Macraig fishing grounds.

Ryan shook his head, wondering at the cause of the rift between the clans. His father would say naught about it and as a lad he'd learned little from even the most ardent gossip. He knew only his father had offered for Lady Macrory before she wed, and had been rebuffed. He shrugged. It was not uncommon enough to remark on it further. Something else had happened, it was certain, but he was unlikely to ever know the whole truth.

A whistle from the beach below caught his attention and he spotted a pony trotting lazily along the shore. The horse halted beside a girl, her hair blazing red in the afternoon sun as it peeked through gathering clouds. She waved to someone in the shadowed doorway of a ramshackle cottage tucked beneath the overhanging cliff. Springing lightly to the back of her mount, she kicked her pony into a run up the beach.

Ryan admired her skill. He saw neither saddle nor blanket, yet the lass clung to the beast's back like a burr. They passed before him at speed, hooves kicking up sand. Surprised to see her cross into Macraig territory, he rose to his feet and mounted his own horse to follow.

He caught up with them, and found the pony idly plucking grass near a sprawl of brambled berry bushes, an empty basket nearby on the ground. Curious, Ryan urged Duer cautiously through the underbrush. The clouds and deep afternoon shadows cast confusing patterns among the trees and rocks. He paused, adjusting his eyes to the gloom. Scanning the area, he saw nothing. He grew still. The forest was quiet. Too quiet.

Duer bobbed his head nervously and pawed the ground. Ryan checked the horse, and Duer tossed his head again as he sidled deeper into the bushes, protesting the hand on his reins. Ryan peered into the undergrowth and spotted the girl's pale gown spilled across the forest floor. With a start, he realized she knelt on the ground, a hand outstretched in a placating manner, her red curls tumbling across her shoulder. Ryan's gaze darted past her hand and his blood ran cold.

A young wolf lay awkwardly in the brush, apparently unable to rise.

"There's a good lad," the girl crooned. "Someone left a trap unattended, didn't they? Ye need only be still a moment longer and I will have ye cut loose in a trice."

8

Ryan stared at her in disbelief. The wolf's front leg was twisted beneath him, and the girl would have to get next to the animal in order to free it. Was she daft?

Slowly the girl reached a hand inside her bodice and pulled forth a *sgian dubh*, its short blade winking dully in the sun-dappled gloom. Easing forward, she reached toward the wolf. The animal recoiled with a snarl, exposing his trapped leg. With a swift move, the girl cut the slender length of tether, releasing the beast.

The wolf leapt to his feet, and Duer neighed in fright. With a gasp, the girl startled, losing her balance. She rolled backward, her skirts flying, arms windmilling wildly as she tried to catch herself. Duer reared, front legs pawing the air, squealing in terror.

Afraid the horse would strike the girl, Ryan hauled back hard on the reins. Duer, unable to remain so poised, fell backward with a crash.

Gilda jerked at the unexpected sound of a horse behind her, afraid of a Macraig patrol. Her feet slid beneath her as she tried to rise, and she sprawled hard on her rump before she managed to stop.

She caught a glimpse of the horse as it reared in panic. The poor animal staggered backward and fell, tossing its rider into the underbrush. Gilda rolled to her knees, fingers against her lips, aghast at the sight. Unexpectedly agile, the horse surged to its feet and bolted away. The sound of its escape faded and Gilda stared after it.

A low-pitched moan pulled her attention to the man on the ground. Scurrying to him, she knelt at his side and shook his shoulder, afraid to roll him over after witnessing the force of his fall.

"Are ye injured?" Her voice pitched low and soothing.

The man moaned and rolled to his side. Gilda gasped at the blood smeared across the side of his face. She tightened her grip on his shoulder, willing him to be still. "Dinnae *fash*. Ye took a bad fall."

He eased onto his back and opened his eyes. Gilda stared into their amber depths, shaken by their unusual, pale color. She shivered.

He frowned. "My horse…" He gave a low grunt of pain.

"Has run off, as has mine, I would imagine." Gilda grimaced at the thought of the long walk home.

The man sat, a scowl on his face, and turned his piercing stare on her. "My horse nearly trampled ye. Are ye hurt?"

"Of course not. He wouldnae have landed on me."

The man snorted. "Ye seem to have a lot of faith in animals. That wolf ye set free could have torn ye to pieces."

"Not trapped as he was. And had yer great horse not made such a *stramash*, the wolf would not have been so frightened."

Giving her a narrow look, the man gingerly shook his head. "Do ye always make such a fuss over animals?"

"What is wrong with that?"

"'Tis a good thing there havenae been any bears in Scotland for the past three hundred years or so. Ye'd be eaten for sure." He touched the side of his head. With a scowl, he drew his fingers away and stared at them.

"Ye are lucky I am such a kind-hearted person," Gilda informed him archly as she searched through the bag at her side. "I have just visited with my auntie and have some wych elm leaves." She pulled large, green leaves from her bag and set them on a nearby rock, using a smaller stone to gently bruise the leaves. Moisture welled to the surface and she pressed the dark mass carefully against the deep scratches on the man's face.

He jerked away, a suspicious look narrowing his eyes. "What are ye doing?"

"Be still. They will help heal the wound. It looks as though *ye* are the one who just encountered a bear." Gilda swept a fall of dark hair from his face and reapplied the salve. Her skin tingled as the dense strands slid through her fingers. Her cheeks heated and she dropped her gaze, puzzled by her reaction to this strange man.

Cautiously, she peeked at him from the corner of her eyes and found his head turned away, looking about the forest. She perused his tanned skin, smooth and warm as she'd already discovered. His dark hair just brushed shoulders that were broad and muscled beneath his leine and plaide. He appeared to be only a few years older than she, and she wondered who he was. A Macraig, surely, for Gilda knew she trespassed on Macraig land. She squirmed, uncomfortable to remember where she was.

"Here, let me have that." The man turned his attention back to her and took the crushed leaves from her hand. "I thank ye, but 'twill heal fine."

"At least clean it." Gilda sat back on her heels in protest as he wiped his fingers on his plaide.

"Are ye a healer?"

"Nae, though my auntie is and I have helped her for many years."

The man frowned. "'Tis an honorable occupation. Why would ye not apprentice with her?"

"Because I am..." Gilda bit her lip. She'd almost revealed she was the laird's daughter, though that wasn't the reason she wasn't a healer. "I dinnae like to see people in pain. I can heal, I have healed, but I am too soft-hearted to make it my life's work."

The man's lips quirked. "A soft-hearted healer? So ye couldnae lop a man's leg off if he mangled it?"

Gilda paled and her heart fluttered. "Nae."

"Then all the more reason to seek ye out should I need a healer's touch. I dinnae like someone too anxious to remove an offending limb."

"Have ye had a need for a healer like that?" Her gaze took in the man's well-made form. She saw no evidence of deformity. Quite the opposite, in fact. Heat flared anew in her cheeks.

"Nae, and I hope it never comes to it. I would rather be dead than only half a man."

Gilda tilted her head. "Ye dinnae know what ye speak. Life is too precious to dispose of so callously. What is an arm or a leg compared to a life?"

"Compared to a 'useful' life, ye mean. I wouldnae be at the mercy of others for my daily living."

Gilda leaned back on her heels, nonplussed. "How did we get so far? Ye fell from yer horse and I put a salve on yer wound and ye now swear ye'd not want to live if ye lost a leg." She shook her head. "I think 'tis best we look for our horses."

A stray breeze filtered through the bracken, lifting the curls tangling against her forehead, and she glanced upward. Dark clouds replaced the summer blue sky. A rumble in the distance caused her to jump, and a flash of lightning heralded an afternoon storm as the day plunged into early darkness. Gilda's heart missed a beat.

"Oh, no."

Chapter Two

Ryan touched the side of his face again, glad to discover the blood in the scratches had dried. Cool air rustled through the leaves and he looked at the young girl next to him. Her fair skin blanched white, all color leached from her cheeks as she stared into the distance. A freshening breeze lifted her hair.

"Oh, no," she whispered.

"What is it, lass?"

"A storm."

"Och, ye willnae melt." He grinned and rose to his feet, relieved not to be surrounded by wolves. Or Macrorys. He held a hand out, offering to help her stand. To his surprise, she ignored him, still staring at the coming storm. With a start, Ryan realized she wasn't dismayed at the prospect of a wetting. She was utterly afraid.

"Here, lass." He pitched his tone low, calming. "Let us find a place to shelter. I am sure 'twill blow itself out soon."

She turned her gaze to him, her smoke-colored eyes wide. Her breast rose and fell rapidly, confirming her fear. Ryan stepped close and stooped to pull her to her feet. She stood and walked with him without comment, and he could feel tension singing through her as he held her hand.

"I seem to remember these woods are riddled with caves. Mayhap we can find one before the rain starts."

She nodded and swallowed hard. "There is a shallow one just ahead."

"How do ye know the land so well?"

"The berries are good and plentiful here along the border between us and the Macraigs." She regarded him with a worried look. "Ye willnae call me a thief?"

"For picking berries?" He grinned easily. "Nae. But if ye get a stomach ache for eating too many, ye willnae let me know of it."

The girl offered him a small smile at his jest, but she was still too pale.

Thunder rumbled. A sudden gust of wind bent the trees nearly double. She gasped and stumbled.

"Wheesht, lass. I have ye." Ryan nudged bracken aside. "And here is our shelter. Wait a moment while I make sure one of yer wolves hasnae chosen it for himself."

He released her hand and stepped to the entrance of the cave. Branches concealed the opening and he held them aside to admit the rapidly fading light. As she'd said, it was shallow, only six or eight feet deep, and scarcely tall enough for him to stand upright. The underbrush at the mouth of the cave would shelter them from the worst of the storm.

A flash of lightning split the sky, opening the heavy clouds. Rain dumped in a deluge, blinding him as he turned back for the girl. Blinking his eyes, he barely had time to open his arms before she ran straight against his chest. Her red hair clung to her, wet from the downpour. The top of her head fit neatly beneath his chin. He gave himself a shake.

"Come, then." He gently pried her away and led her into the cool, dry interior of the cave. Within moments, she was shaking.

He gentled his voice. "Still afraid of the storm?"

She shook her head. "Nae. Cold."

Thunder crashed again and she jumped, betraying her lie. Ryan sat on the dusty floor of the cave and unfastened his plaide at the shoulder. He beckoned to her as he unwrapped the woolen fabric.

"Come sit with me, lass. I will keep ye warm."

She did not move and he quirked an eyebrow at her hesitation. "I willnae harm ye. But ye dinnae need to stand about dripping wet and cold." He tried a lopsided grin. "I only bite impertinent lasses."

She almost smiled, but her lips trembled. "Then, sir, I am forewarned, for I fear I am nearly always impertinent."

He laughed. "My name is 'Ryan,' not 'sir.'"

The girl bit her lip and did not reply.

13

He sighed. "Saying it willnae make ye impertinent."

"Ryan."

His name rolled sweetly from her lips, sending a frisson through his veins. He blinked. She was too young. A mere lass. Teasing her was only a way to keep her from being afraid. He gave a reassuring nod. "There. That wasnae so hard. Now ye can sit with me and be warm."

Still hesitant, she lowered herself to the cave's dust-covered floor. He tucked the end of his plaide around her shoulders and pulled it down her side to hold in the heat. They sat quietly, listening to the wind rage outside. Ryan carefully controlled the unexpected storm quivering through his insides at her nearness.

The girl moved slightly. "My name is Gilda."

Gilda waited for Ryan's reply. It seemed only fair after he told her his name to offer hers in return. Just her name. Nothing more. There was no need for him to know she was the laird's daughter. She knew full well she could be kidnapped and held for ransom, but Ryan had done nothing to alarm her, nothing to send unspoken warnings through her. Except for sneaking up and startling her as she tried to release the captured wolf, he'd been honorable. Maybe a bit grumpy about her attempt to help with his wound, but what man didn't make a poor patient?

"'Gilda' is a verra pretty name."

Unexpected heat slid beneath her skin as he said her name, causing her to shiver.

"Still cold, then?"

"Nae." Gilda shook her head. She was far too heated and sure her cheeks were red, as well. This would not do. Whatever caused her to quiver as her name rolled from his lips in a low rumble, it wasn't right. In fact, sitting here in a cave with a strange man's plaide wrapped around her was wrong. Even if it meant facing the storm outside, she must leave.

Later.

Surely, it wouldn't hurt to wait until the storm passed. Who would miss her?

"Will ye be missed, Gilda?"

She jerked. Had he read her thoughts? The plaide slid from her shoulder and Ryan reached around her and pulled it back into place. She barely controlled the tremor this time at his touch, and gave a slight shake of her head.

"Nae. Ma will suppose I stayed at Auntie Tavia's, and she knows I left well ahead of the storm."

"No search party until the storm blows over?"

Gilda hesitated, realizing she'd said far too much. "Mayhap. Ye never know what my ma will do."

Ryan sighed. "Lass, I am trying to keep yer mind off the storm. I have no wish to do ye harm. Ye are safe here with me."

"I thank ye. I have been afraid of storms since I was a bairn. The noise frightens me."

He looked at her askance. "Ye cannae be verra old, now. How many summers have ye?"

"Sixteen."

"Sixteen? That many? Ye look mayhap twelve."

"I dinnae look twelve! And I will be seventeen soon."

Ryan laughed and Gilda basked in the warmth of the sound.

"I only tease ye, Gilda. I am twenty, soon to be twenty-one."

"Truth? I thought ye not much older than me. I was right."

"Nae. There is a world of difference between sixteen and twenty."

"Four years," Gilda scoffed. "What more is there?"

At his silence, she studied his face, now grown serious.

"There is much ye dinnae know, sweet Gilda. Ye must trust me."

"Aye, I trust ye. Tell me."

She saw his frown. Did he think she baited him? She hated it when her brothers taunted her. Lightning ripped the sky and she did not want to leave the shelter. His warmth radiated against her and she shifted, wanting to press closer.

Surely, conversation was better than this uncomfortable silent awareness. She ventured to ask, "Have ye been away for a while?"

"Why would ye say that?"

"Ye said there were caves around, if ye remembered correctly. Why else would ye have to remember if ye hadnae been away?"

Ryan nodded. "Ye are a canny lass. I have been away at the MacLaurey keep for the past ten years."

"Fostering?"

"Aye."

"My oldest brother is away as well."

"Ye have more than one brother?"

"Aye." Gilda couldn't keep the exasperation from her voice, and Ryan chuckled. The low, rumbling sound, so like thunder, and yet so much more compelling, warmed her. "I have two younger brothers, twins. I hope they foster soon, too."

"How old are they?"

"Six."

Ryan nodded. "A truly terrible age."

"Truth?"

"Aye. I was a wee *loun* at that age as well."

"My auntie says all men are the same."

"Well, mayhap not all the same, but I am sure we share a lot of the same vices."

Gilda shifted on the rock floor of the cave, enjoying their conversation. "What have ye learned, fostering? My brother is but eleven years and a serious lad. I havenae seen him in over two years and miss him."

Ryan quirked an eyebrow at her question. "What do ye mean?"

"I mean, what did ye learn? I've seen the lads who foster at Scaurness. They learn fighting skills, lettering, drinking and…" Her cheeks heated again, remembering Gordon's warm, inviting eyes, and she hoped Ryan wouldn't notice her discomfiture in the semi-darkness. But of course, he did. He nudged her.

"What else do they learn at Scaurness, Gilda?"

Gilda turned her back to him. She'd had this discussion with Tavia earlier, and wasn't going to voice her opinion in front of a stranger.

A puff of warm air against the side of her neck tingled across her tight-strung nerves, and she jumped. Ryan's face loomed next to hers, his nose near level with her ear.

"Seems as though ye already know the answer to that question, sir," she replied tartly. "I told ye men were all alike."

"Och, Gilda. Dinnae blame us for noticing such a sweet, red-haired lass as yerself."

Gilda flung the plaide from her shoulder and leapt to her feet, displeasure radiating through her. "I dinnae have to put up with it at home, and I of certain dinnae have to put up with it from the likes of ye!"

Ryan's laugh and rueful smile did little to mollify her, and she continued to glare at him. He rose to his feet and cupped her chin in his hand.

"Ye are the most fascinating mixture of sweetness and fire." His eyes roamed over her face, his other hand gently skimming the hair beginning to dry and curl at her temples. "Ye asked what we learned, but I think ye know."

Gilda's eyes grew wide as his gaze lingered on her mouth. Her breath hitched and her lips parted, her muscles trembling as though they'd forgotten how to act.

"We also learn this." Ryan lowered his mouth to hers, touching her softly. Gilda gasped air into lungs suddenly empty of breath, and nearly shattered as the tip of his tongue gently traced the outline of her lips.

His mouth moved against hers and Gilda fisted the front of his shirt in her hands, clinging to him as desperate as though she'd been dropped from the highest cliff above the firth. Her world spun out of control, and a tiny moan escaped her as she rose to meet his kiss.

Ryan released her and caught her hands in his. Gilda took a step back, shocked to find the earth still beneath her feet. They stood silent for a moment, and the slow, lazy sound of dripping water grew loud.

"The storm is past."

How could he say that? A storm still raged through her and Ryan acted as though he were completely unaffected.

He gave her hands a slight tug. "I think we should go now."

Gilda slipped her hands from his, trying to hide the turmoil inside. "Aye. Ye are right. I must be home." She strode to the cave's entrance and pushed past the rain-drenched bracken.

"I will walk with ye to the beach to be sure ye make it to yer land."

"I dinnae need yer help."

"Ye will get my help whether ye need it or not." A gravelly tone laced Ryan's voice and Gilda bristled.

"'Tis ye who are trespassing now, sir." She nodded her head to a large rock a few feet away. "Yon outcropping is the border."

"My name is Ryan," he bit out, obviously as edgy as she.

Gilda whirled on him. "Leave me alone, *Ryan*." She stamped her foot with all the petulance of a child.

"As ye wish." He gave her a curt bow and turned. Their path a single trek leading to the shore, they hurried down the narrow trail, wet leaves and branches tugging at Gilda's skirts and hair.

Ryan paused as they broke the forest's cover. "Here is where we part. If ye hurry, ye can make it to yer auntie's cottage before 'tis dangerously dark."

Gilda stared at him. *The only thing dangerously dark is ye. And I willnae make the mistake of underestimating ye again.* She couldn't get away from him fast enough.

A shout arrested them. "Ryan!"

Lifting a hand to shield the glare of the setting sun, Gilda scanned the beach. A lean man, his blond hair glinting in the last of the sun's rays, held the reins of two horses. The midnight black stallion tossed his head and neighed. The white-stockinged mare nickered and sidled away.

"Who is that? He has my mare."

"My friend, Conn, has found our horses. Come. I feared we were in for a long walk."

The young man quickly caught up to them, and the assessing look he gave Gilda brought a frown to her face.

He glanced from Ryan to Gilda and back. "I thought ye went for a ride to clear yer head. If I had known there were mermaids about, I'd have left the unloading of the ship to the others and come along with ye."

"Ye were too sick to be in charge of unloading the ship, and this is nae mermaid. This is Gilda, healer and wolf-tamer."

Gilda shot Ryan a narrow-eyed look of disapproval, then turned a gracious smile on the blond-headed man.

"I am pleased to meet ye. I am neither a healer nor a wolf-tamer. Yer friend is a bit addled. His horse threw him and he has a wee knot on his head, as well as scratches on his face where he thinks he was attacked by a bear."

The young man gave a bark of laughter. "I have known for some time Ryan is addled, and his social skills still require polish. I will introduce myself. My name is Conn MacLaurey. Ryan and I have been friends for many years."

"I see ye found my horse. Fia bolted and ran when this big lad tossed his rider." Gilda sidled carefully to the black stallion and offered her palm for him to sniff. The horse shook his head in a show of prideful annoyance but snuffled her hand when she didn't draw back.

Gilda laughed. "Such a temper. A wee bit like his rider, would ye say?" She turned to Conn, a conspiratorial smile on her face.

Conn looked at her askance. "Bonnie and canny," he mused.

Ryan growled. "She is impertinent."

Gilda tossed an innocent look over her shoulder. "I did warn ye," she reminded him.

Ryan nodded curtly. "Mount up. Ye need to be home."

Gilda gave them both a sweet smile. "I thank ye for catching my horse." She mounted with Conn's assistance and smoothed her skirts over her knees. With a thump of her heels against the mare's sides, she rode swiftly away, leaving the two men to stare after her.

Chapter Three

"Are ye daft?"

Ryan broke his gaze from Gilda's retreating form. "What?"

"The lass. Ye were alone with her. Are ye looking to get *marrit* or start a clan war?"

"What the hell are ye talking about? There was a storm and we sheltered in a cave."

Conn's voice turned mocking. "Och, ye sheltered in a cave, did ye? With the laird's daughter?"

"Nae. She's the healer's niece." Ryan motioned down the beach. "Ye cannae see it now, but she lives in a ramshackle cottage against the cliffs."

"I tell ye, she's the laird's daughter."

Ryan's eyes narrowed in annoyance. "Why would ye say that?"

"Her speech, for one thing. The lass doesnae sound like a crofter's daughter."

"Mayhap, but that doesnae mean the laird is her father."

"What about her mare? 'Twas a fine piece of horseflesh and no Highland Pony. Not every lass has such an animal nor the time to learn to ride as she does."

Ryan waved a hand in the air in dismissal and stomped to his own fine horse. He shoved a booted foot into a stirrup and swung aboard the restless stallion. "Mayhap a long walk will clear yer head. I think the *mal de mer* has addled yer brain."

"Ye are a wee bastard, Ryan," Conn shouted after him as he rode away.

"'Tis no' what my father told me," Ryan flung over his shoulder.

"Come on, Ryan. Give me a ride back. I caught yer mangy horse. 'Tis the least ye can do."

Ryan reined Duer in a wide circle and set the stallion to a slow canter back to his friend's side, clods of damp sand flying from his hooves. In a seamless maneuver born of long practice, Ryan clasped Conn's forearm and swung him up behind him. Duer gave a short buck of protest at the extra weight, but settled at a command from his rider and headed up the beach.

Trumpets sounded and bagpipes skirled the return of the laird's son. Torches blazed on the parapets and in brackets along the walls, making the bailey nearly as bright as day under the evening gloaming. Ryan and Conn rode at the head of the procession of guards and servants, their horses shying briefly at the wild sounds of homecoming. The iron-studded, heavy wooden gates opened wide, the creak of the portcullis chains its own welcome as it rose in the air to permit their passage.

"'Tis a verra nice place ye have, Ryan," Conn murmured just loud enough to hear. "I hope they held dinner for us. I could eat a horse."

"Ard Castle bids ye welcome," Ryan returned. "And I would imagine Da has a banquet well in hand."

A tall, gray-haired man strode from the great hall, a large group of people at his heels. They met in the bailey where Ryan and Conn drew to a halt. Stable lads rushed to take their horses as they dismounted, and Ryan stared at the man he scarcely remembered as kin.

"Welcome home, son."

The knot in Ryan's chest eased and he closed the gap between them in two long strides. They clasped arms in welcome and the unexpected joy of homecoming washed over him. It was a long moment before either of them remembered manners or voice.

Laird Macraig stepped to one side, exposing a young girl who hung back, her eyes wide and assessing. Ryan stared. Her near-black hair and startling, amber eyes marked her as kin. His sister? She looked to be no older than nine or ten. Ryan cast his memory back to the day he'd left Ard Castle, his father's arm about his leman's swollen waist.

"Ryan, this is yer sister, Lissa."

Ryan bowed his head in formal acknowledgement. "M'lady."

Lissa's eyes narrowed. "Brother." She offered him no other title, and the lilt to her voice challenged him to remark the slight. It was obvious she did not relish the return of the laird's son.

Ryan allowed a small smile. The lass had spunk. Would she also be a pain in his arse? He let silence linger a moment longer in mild rebuke for her childish behavior, catching a satisfying glimpse of the flush of embarrassment that rose beneath her skin, then continued with the introductions.

"Da, this is Laird MacLaurey's son, Connor. He and I have become great friends over the years." He turned to Conn. "This is my father, Laird Macraig."

Ryan's father inclined his head at Conn's short bow. "Welcome to Ard Castle. Ye are welcome as long as ye care to stay."

"I thank ye, m'laird. I appreciate yer hospitality."

"Speaking of which, I am sure ye lads are famished, and we have a feast prepared for ye." Laird Macraig turned to a man at his side. "Find places for the guards and servants to shelter and wash, and send them in for their share. Call for more lads to care for the horses."

He faced the people around him, a broad smile on his face.

"My son is home!"

Ryan propped his feet on the hearth, leaning his head against the chair's high back. The sharp scent of burning peat filled the air, and embers lit the room with a golden glow.

"I may never move again." He groaned, covering his belly with one hand as he slumped further into his chair.

"If I even catch a whiff of food cooking on the morrow, I think I will be sick," Conn muttered from the other chair. "'Twas the best meal I have eaten in days."

"'Tis the only meal ye have kept down in days," Ryan retorted.

Conn burped pleasurably. "Aye."

Ryan's eyes became hooded, mesmerized by the flickering glow of the smoldering peat. Warm and dry and overfed, still he couldn't help but worry about the red-haired lass he'd left behind, wet and cold on the beach.

"Do ye suppose she got home all right?"

Conn roused with a grunt. "Who?"

"Gilda, ye *amadan*."

"I imagine she knows her way home."

Ryan snorted. Knowing her way home and staying out of trouble along the way were two different things.

Conn shifted in his chair. "Will ye ask yer da?"

"About what?"

"Gilda."

Ryan shrugged. "There is a feud between our clans. I cannae imagine my questions about a Macrory lass would be well-received."

Conn sat straight up. "A feud? About what?"

Ryan shrugged again. "I dinnae know, exactly. My da offered for the auld laird's daughter when I was a wee lad, but was refused. She then married the current laird, and there has been no alliance between us since."

"Is there war between ye?"

"Nae. But neither clan 'tis likely to help the other."

"Ye should forget the lass, Ryan."

Ryan had no answer.

"Will ye let it go?" Conn persisted.

Ryan considered his answer—and lied. "Aye."

Gilda peered around the great hall, searching high and low for the twins' tousled blond heads. 'Twas no surprise she didn't see them, but she greatly preferred knowing where the imps were to happening upon them unawares.

She slipped up the stairs and quickly changed into dry clothes, briskly toweling her hair before the low embers on the hearth. Running a last critical appraisal over her appearance, she headed down the hall to her mother's room and rapped softly on the portal. Cracking the door open, she peered inside. Her mother sat in a comfortable chair before a low fire and Gilda grinned as their gazes met.

"Enter." Riona beckoned with a smile. She wrapped the bairn in her arms in a soft blanket and Gilda took the wee lass with a coo, jostling her gently on her shoulder. Her mother adjusted her gown and rose from the nursing chair.

"God bless ye, wee Sara." Gilda laughed as the bairn burped contentedly. Her ma grabbed a piece of linen and wiped the milky bubbles from the rosebud lips.

"I will take her now."

Gilda handed Sara back to her ma with a wistful tilt to her head.

"I dinnae mind holding her." She plopped down onto the window seat cushion. "She is much sweeter than the twins."

"She will be fast asleep in a moment." Her mother swayed rhythmically as she approached the cradle beside the bed, conspicuously empty with the knowledge the laird was not at home.

"When will Da be back?"

Her ma tucked Sara into her cradle and tweaked the curling silver birch bark trim meant to keep evil spirits, faeries and goblins at bay. Finished, she straightened and turned to Gilda. "I dinnae know, lass. He is away for the king, and he couldnae say for how long."

Gilda tossed her red curls over her shoulder with a sigh of annoyance. "Why must he continually curry favor with King Robert? The Macrorys have always been faithful to the crown."

"Scaurness is of vital importance to the king, ye know that. And since King Robert bestowed the rank of earl on yer da…"

Gilda's deep sigh was full of youthful frustration. "I know, I know. Da is known and respected and well-liked." She listed the well-known litany with a scowl.

Her mother crossed to Gilda's side and gently swept an errant lock of hair behind her ear. "What troubles ye, lass? Did ye not have a good visit with Auntie Tavia?"

The corner of Gilda's mouth quirked in an attempt at a smile, but her eyes remained troubled and she knew her ma noticed.

She motioned for Gilda to make room for her on the window seat, and Gilda scooted to one side. Her mother slid an arm about her waist and pulled her close. Gilda tucked her feet beneath her on the cushioned seat and leaned into her ma's comforting embrace.

"Auntie Tavia is fine, as always." She sighed.

"Then, what troubles ye?"

"Ma, did Da say anything to ye about a betrothal for me before he left?"

Her mother's hesitation was short, but Gilda's heart quickened when her ma did not hasten to reassure her.

"Lass, yer da willnae ask ye to wed without consulting the both of us first. As far as I know, he doesnae have plans for ye yet."

24

"But he will expect me to marry for the clan, aye?"

"Gilda, ye are the daughter of his heart, and he couldnae bear to betroth ye simply for the benefit of the clan. But even though he isnae yer father by blood, ye are still known as his daughter, and ye are expected to behave as such."

"Like ye?"

"Mayhap not like me. There were nae other options for me at the time."

"But there were other lairds ye could have wed. Why Da?"

"Ye know that story. And yer da and I have made a very good marriage of it. I wouldnae change a thing."

Gilda sighed. Her mother's answer only partially reassured her. She couldn't explain why she felt so restless, and to her surprise, her thoughts drifted back to the young man who'd sheltered and distracted her from the storm. Her face flushed and she squirmed as she remembered his kiss.

"Is there a problem, Gilda?"

Gilda risked a peek at her ma and quickly schooled her expression into innocence.

"Nae. One of the lads has paid me attention overmuch, and it caused me to wonder if Da thought me old enough to wed." She gave her mother a bright smile. "'Tis nothing."

Her ma gave her an assessing look, but did not pursue the conversation.

Ryan swatted at Conn's feet beneath the coverlet as he passed by the bed.

"Ye are a lazy lout," he complained, brushing aside the single heavy curtain at the narrow window.

Conn rolled over, groaning in protest. "Leave me be, and get out of my room." He dragged his pillow over his head. "The sun isnae up yet, either."

Ryan frowned in disgust at Conn's mumbled words. "Ye are missing the best part of the day. I am going to explore a bit before breaking my fast. Are ye coming with me or nae?"

"Nae." Conn grunted and clamped his arms around his pillow, burrowing deeper into the soft mattress.

Ryan spun on his booted heel and clumped noisily to the door, ignoring Conn's muffled grumble. Slamming the door behind him with a little more force than entirely necessary, Ryan hurried down the hallway. He made his way down the stairs and out into the bailey where he pulled up short. And whistled in surprise at the thick mists blanketing the air.

Taking a step into the gray fog, his surroundings were immediately lost to view, the candlelight from the great hall reduced to nothing more than a pale yellow beacon. Ryan stepped cautiously forward and the dark hulk of the stables loomed ahead.

A single lantern hung on a sturdy post, its light penetrating a scant few inches into the fog wrapped around the stone building. Inside, the heat from the horses' bodies turned the cold mist into a pleasant steam.

By the time Ryan fed and saddled his horse, the morning sun broke through the misty confines, revealing the new day. He swung aboard Duer's back and leaned in to pat the gleaming neck.

"Double yer oats, lad, after we have had our outing." He urged the horse on and Duer tossed his head as he bounded forward.

Ryan let his horse stretch his legs once they cleared the castle gate, giving the sentry a brief nod. He wasn't willing to submit to the need for guards on his first day home, and knew he would get a lecture if he lingered. He wanted to wander the paths he remembered from his childhood; the freedoms he'd treasured as a lad. There would be time for protocol soon, but now he wanted to wander and remember, and wonder what lay ahead.

He rode to the coast, unconsciously retracing the path he'd taken the day before. As rising sea breezes blew away the mists, he drew Duer to a halt and dismounted. Dropping the reins, he left the horse to graze in the sparse grasses on the semi-barren land near the shore. Ryan climbed the rock that marked the border between Macraig and Macrory land, keeping a watchful eye out for wolves and red-haired lasses.

Gilda inhaled deeply, filling her lungs with the crisp morning air and the scents rising from the waters below. Mists clouded her view, but the lapping sound of the waves meeting the shore was a melody she'd known since infancy, one as familiar as her own heartbeat, and it soothed her.

She turned to the thickets spreading inland, knowing the path she wanted to take. With long experience, she absently twitched her skirts aside to avoid the brambles as she plucked the berries from the bushes and dropped them into her woven basket, humming to herself as she worked at her task, one ear alert to sounds of approach. She was, once again, on Macraig land.

A slight rustle to her right stilled her actions, and a wild, musky odor wafted to her on a slight breeze. She cut her eyes from side to side, searching for the source, but the wind was fickle and died away, taking with it the fleeting scent.

A trill of alarm flashed beneath her skin and Gilda slowly sank to her knees, instinctively making herself as small a target as possible. Was she imagining things? She hadn't slept well the night before, the episode with Ryan repeating in her mind until she'd fled the confines of her room to escape to the arms of the new day. Did someone watch her, or did her imagination betray her?

Her heart pounded in her ears, masking any sound of movement around her. She took a careful, deep breath, willing her heart to slow. On level now with the deepest shadows of the thicket, she peered into the gloom and met the feral glow of yellow eyes.

Chapter Four

$\mathscr{G}$ilda forgot to breathe. Fright pooled like ice in her stomach as she gaped at the wolf's face and its unwavering stare. At last, the necessity for breath filled her lungs with a sudden rush of air, bringing her to her senses as the shaggy animal leapt to its feet.

A snarl rippled across the wolf's features, but he did not run away. Gilda caught sight of its forepaw hovering just above the ground.

"Och, ye are the poor lad I rescued yesterday, aye?" She crooned gently. The wolf tilted its head to one side, his gaze never leaving her.

Gilda carefully lowered herself the rest of the way to the ground, her hands in her lap to avoid startling the large, gangly beast.

"Ye are a young one, aye?" She eyed the lean, disproportionately long legs and body, the wolf not yet grown to its mature form. "And hurt and scared. I know. Ye frightened me, too."

She kept up the one-sided conversation, her voice a low monotone, steadying her nerves as she watched the young animal. The wolf's unearthly gaze pinned her, but after a few moments, he dropped to his haunches, touching his injured paw briefly to the ground as he shifted his weight.

"I wish I could help ye. I know the trap hurt ye." Gilda shrugged, eying the line of raw flesh encircling the animal's swollen foot. "But ye dinnae trust me enough to put salve on it, do ye?"

The wolf collapsed its body to the ground and began licking his paw, his broad, pink tongue repeatedly stroking the injured flesh.

Gilda sighed. "Ye know 'tis best to keep it clean. Ye would just lick off any salve."

The wolf, having apparently lost interest in Gilda's non-threatening form, did not look up. Gilda relaxed, but continued to watch the wolf, fascinated by its actions and lack of concern with her nearness.

"Ye keep massaging it to keep the swelling down, too, aye?" She shifted to a more comfortable position and the yellow eyes snapped to her. Gilda froze and after a moment, the wolf returned to his rhythmic, soothing motions, once again ignoring the human mere feet away.

"I wish I had something to feed ye. Ye look half-starved. A good meal wouldnae go amiss." She glanced at the berries in her basket and frowned. A thought struck her and she slipped one hand into a pocket, searching for the piece of dried meat she'd wrapped and brought with her for her morning meal.

"This might not be verra filling, as 'tis not verra much, but I was going to eat it if I got hungry later." Gilda slowly leaned forward, the hardened meat held out for the wolf's inspection.

The wolf once again ceased his actions and leveled his yellow gaze on her. Gilda swallowed hard, but did not waver. The animal's nose twitched.

"Aye, there are some spices ye are no' familiar with. Ye may like them. Go ahead. Try it."

The wolf refused to come closer. With a gentle flick of her wrist, Gilda tossed the meat to the ground near the wolf's feet.

"There. Try it if ye like. I need to get my berries and head back." She drew away slowly, retreating a bit before rising to her feet. The wolf's gaze followed her movements, but he did not startle. Gilda walked away, her steps measured and sure. She peered over her shoulder for a last peek at the young wolf and her lips curved in a smile as the animal leaned forward and took the strip of dried meat from the grass.

Ryan gazed across the beach, his back to the heat of the early morning sun. Summer was near its end, and such luxuries as being comfortable and warm were to be enjoyed. From the corner of his eye, he caught a glimpse of movement on the sand. Turning his attention to the person crossing the beach, he watched idly as he identified the form as female, her skirt hiked up, exposing her calves, the fabric pulled between her legs and tucked in at the waist to keep the hem out of the wet sand and tiding waves.

Sunlight glinted off the woman's red hair, and a jolt of recognition shot through him. Could it be the girl he'd met the day before? His last glimpse of her had been of sleek red hair darkened by the rain and a gown plastered wetly against a slender form. His eyes narrowed as he sought more detail to confirm her identity. The spring to her step marked her as young, and, despite Conn's earlier warning, Ryan was surprised to discover how much he wanted to meet Gilda again.

She passed scattered boulders on the beach, one hand outstretched to lightly touch each one, a basket swinging from her other hand. Ryan smiled to himself. It had to be Gilda—once again filching berries from Macraig land. Mayhap he should warn her of the folly of trespassing. His smile widened, creasing the scabbed scratches on his cheek, and he remembered her touch. Mayhap his wounds needed tending? He frowned. He wasn't sure he agreed with Conn that Gilda was Laird Macrory's daughter, but any Macrory lass was off limits to him. Whether she was a healer or not.

Realizing he had half-risen from his seat, he settled back on his haunches, cursing the attraction he felt for the lass. It would be best to remember who he was and let his interest in the lass go. Nothing could come from renewing their acquaintance from yesterday. He snorted. A daft lass scairt of storms nearly got herself eaten by a wolf, and he was moved to shelter her until the skies cleared.

And then he'd kissed her.

"Damn!" The curse whistled past clenched teeth. This time he rose to his feet, his gaze focused on a dark, four-legged form slipping from shadow to shadow. What was a wolf doing on the beach? And why was it following Gilda?

Gilda hummed to herself as she wandered across the rock-strewn sand. She needed to retrieve Fia from her tether near Tavia's house, but was aware the young wolf followed her. Though she did not fear the animal, leading it to her horse or, worse, Tavia's young goat, was not a good idea.

She tossed a look over her shoulder and smiled. The beast still trailed her. Perhaps he was curious about the human who had saved him.

A different awareness prickled across the back of her shoulders. Gilda's smile vanished. Was something or someone else watching her?

Without slowing her pace, she turned her head to gaze across the low rise to her left. Familiar views of rocks and twisted vegetation did not ease her feeling of disquiet. Trying to appear nonchalant, Gilda stopped next to a large boulder. She leaned her shoulders against the stone, clasping her basket before her as she let her gaze drift idly from tree to tuft.

A shadow moved, unfolding to reveal a man's form. The sun shone behind him, and Gilda raised a hand to her brow to counter the effects of the bright light.

Gilda gasped and her heart beat quickened. The man's broad shoulders were outlined in gold by the sun's rays, and his hair glinted dark as night. She didn't have to see the color of his amber eyes to know who watched her. Her memory was completely clear. It was *him*.

She gave herself a mental shake. *It doesnae matter how he looks. He is a Macraig, and he is spying on me.*

Ryan leapt easily from his rock to the wiry grass and headed toward her. She smoothed a hand down her skirts, feeling the hem tied around the belt at her waist. She tugged at the fabric, anxious to release it to cover her legs before he reached her, but she only succeeded in tugging the knot tighter.

With a sharp intake of breath betraying her frustration, Gilda grabbed the knot with both hands, letting go of the basket of berries in her haste. She dropped to her knees to retrieve the basket and her gaze followed the clumsy roll of the woven reeds right to Ryan's booted feet.

Ryan stooped to capture the errant basket before it could empty all the berries onto the sand and rocks. His hand shot out to seize the twisted handle, but Gilda's grab was faster, and his fingers encircled her slender wrist instead.

Gilda snatched her hand away with a startled cry, releasing the basket. Berries bounced across the ground, their dew-moist skins instantly littered with bits of sand and debris. Ryan saw the flash of annoyance on Gilda's face, and raised his eyebrows at the word that passed her lips in a hissed whisper.

"Are ye hurt?" He squatted next to her and put his hands to the task of retrieving the fruit.

"Must ye always sneak up on me?" Gilda groused as she dusted the worst of the sand from a handful of berries.

"I dinnae sneak. Ye saw me on the rock."

"After ye stood, aye. Before then I had a terrible feeling I was being watched."

Ryan dumped the last of the berries into the basket and rose to his feet, wiping his hands on his plaide. To his amusement, Gilda remained seated, her bare legs tucked beneath her.

"Ye were. By a wolf."

Gilda lifted one shoulder. "Och, the wolf doesnae mean any harm. I had given him a scrap of meat, and mayhap he wanted more."

"Fresher meat, likely," Ryan snapped, eying the all-too-trusting young woman at his feet. "Ye shouldnae try to make the beast a pet. He would rather eat ye than sniff yer hand."

Gilda glared at him, but did not answer and Ryan felt his annoyance fade.

"Come, then. I will walk ye to yer horse."

"I told ye yesterday, I dinnae need yer help."

A dull ache threatened behind Ryan's eyes. "Then what do ye need?"

"I need ye to turn yer back." Frustration colored her voice.

Ryan remembered the enticing view her hiked-up skirt had given him and he tilted his head to one side in an attempt to recreate the image. Gilda snatched her skirt close. 'Twas all too clear she knew what he was up to.

"Ye are a rogue, Ryan Macraig!"

Ryan grinned. "Och, aye. 'Tis a well-known fact. I could help ye if ye like."

"Hie yerself away, and dinnae look back!"

His look became one of innocence. "Yer horse is nearby? I wouldnae forgive myself for leaving ye to walk the long way back to Macrory land."

"I am already on Macrory land, and my horse is tethered just beyond the bend. Not 'tis any of yer business."

"Then I shall leave ye to make yer way home." With a deep bow, Ryan pivoted on his heel, his plaide swinging about him. He took a few steps then turned back to Gilda who had risen to her feet, intent on correcting her attire.

"Are ye sure…" A quick stride took him back to her side.

Gilda jerked the knot at her waist and the skirt fell free, but not before Ryan got a glimpse of slender ankles. She settled an arch look on him and it was all he could do to keep from laughing at the regal air she portrayed.

"I am fine. I am also certain I will not meet ye here again?" Though couched as a question, her tone indicated she'd rather see anyone other than him the next time she ventured out to pick berries.

Ryan shrugged. "I think the berries are about finished for the year. Mayhap the Macraig cook will send a lad out to pick the rest. We like sweet jams and pastries at Ard Castle, too, ye know."

"Goodness knows the men at Ard Castle need sweetening," Gilda shot back, her cheeks pinking as she clearly regretted her quick retort.

"A kiss from a pretty lass would help sweeten this Macraig's disposition." Ryan marveled at the swirling colors changing Gilda's eyes from silver to stormy gray.

Though a well-trained young warrior, Ryan was not quick enough to dodge the palm of Gilda's hand as it made stinging contact with his cheek. He rubbed his jaw ruefully. He should have remembered though the lass had fascinating gray eyes, she also possessed fiery red hair and a temper to match.

He opened his mouth to apologize, but Gilda had already spun, her back ramrod straight as she marched away, the handle of her basket gripped tight in one hand. The other hand clenched and opened, possibly to relieve the answering sting he felt on his cheek, perhaps echoing a desire to encircle his neck.

Ryan grinned. He would have regretted the apology, anyway.

Gilda stumbled as she swept down the beach, her attention clearly not on the treacherous footing. She righted herself with a jerk and plunged ahead, laying one more grievance at the unfortunate man's doorstep. Never in her life had she been so rattled as to falter on the land that was as familiar to her as the floor of her own bedroom.

Where is the wolf when I need him? Gilda shook her head. *I would be glad to see him devour that man. Slowly, painfully, one annoying piece at a time.*

By St. Andrew's teeth, her hand still stung. In truth, she hadn't expected to hit him. She'd expected him to be fast enough to dodge her. But she'd always been quick, and living with the twins had sharpened her wits and self-preservation skills.

With a soothing caress for the mare, who shook her head suspiciously at her owner's temper, Gilda swung herself onto Fia's back and urged her up the trail to the village. She scanned the crowd of people milling around the market, catching sight of a petite young woman scarcely older than herself.

"Anice!"

The girl turned at the sound of her name, her round cheeks blooming red with pleasure as a broad smile creased her face.

"Gilda!" she squealed, hurrying through the crowd. Gilda slid to the ground, Fia's reins in one hand, and hugged her best friend close. She stepped back, a teasing look in her eyes as she surveyed the young woman.

"'Twould seem marriage agrees with ye."

Anice laughed and twirled about, careful not to spill the items in her market basket.

"I can truthfully say it does," Anice admitted. "Colin is about his work. Can ye come with me to the cottage for a bit? I haven't seen ye in weeks."

Gilda shrugged. "Aye. I can come for a bit." She grinned. "But I willnae linger. Yer husband will no doubt want ye to himself when he gets home."

The girls walked the short distance to the tiny cottage at the edge of the village. Used to the soaring ceilings and open spaces of Scaurness Castle, Gilda was taken aback by the close confines of her friend's new home. But the smell of fresh-baked bread lingered in the warmth of the two-room cottage, and it was neat and clean, obviously well-loved.

Anice set her basket on the table. Gilda added her own beside it.

"Here are some berries I picked this morning. I am sorry they are a wee bit sandy, but I dropped the basket on the beach. I will rinse them for ye and ye can make Colin a pastry for his supper."

"Oh, Gilda! How wonderful! He will love it."

Gilda sat in a chair and watched her friend bustle about, setting mugs out for them to drink from. Anice poured water and they sipped for a moment in silence.

"How are ye?"

"How have ye been?"

They spoke in unison and laughed. Gilda shook her head. "Ye first. Tell me about yer new life."

Anice blushed. "He is wonderful to me, Gilda. We wake up smiling and go to bed well-pleased."

"I can see ye are happy. Is the housekeeping and shopping and cooking not such a burden, then?"

"I know ye are used to castle life, Gilda." Anice motioned around her little cottage, a satisfied smile on her lips. "But everything I do is with love. He would deny this, but when I am overwhelmed, he steps in and helps a bit." Anice's eyes danced. "And as tiny as this cottage is, we bump into each other a lot when we are both moving about. 'Tis worth it, though."

Gilda's eyes widened. "Truth? Do ye not get frustrated, getting in each other's way?"

"Nae. He is verra accommodating. Sometimes we forget the chores completely."

Gilda's cheeks heated. Anice laughed and patted Gilda's hand. "I think I have shocked ye, Gilda. I know I am but a year older than ye and marrit, too. Surely some lad at Scaurness has turned yer head."

"Nae. I cannae give my heart so freely."

"Do ye not wish for even a stolen kiss or a smile from a lad ye feel attracted to?" Anice asked curiously. "Ye dinnae have to marry every lad who smiles at ye."

Gilda sighed. "There is no lad at Scaurness who has caught my eye. I've known them all their lives and they are all scoundrels, gossiping amongst themselves about the lasses they've kissed."

A kiss from a pretty lass... Ye are a rogue, Ryan Macraig...

The words floated back to her and she slid her gaze away.

"There is someone, aye?"

Gilda frowned at Anice's too-accurate perception. "'Tis no one. A chance encounter on the beach. 'Tis why I dropped the berries." Gilda rose to her feet and snatched the basket. She poured water into a small bowl and rinsed the berries, setting them on a nearby cloth to dry.

Anice rose and gently placed a hand on Gilda's shoulder. "I know it cannae be easy being the laird's daughter. I dinnae think yer da would wed ye to a man ye couldnae respect. Talk to him when he comes home. But in the meantime, have a little fun. At least learn to talk to a lad without wondering if ye can best him in archery."

Gilda relaxed at her friend's teasing words. "Aye. Mayhap my husband would prefer I have other talents as well."

"Och, Gilda, ye can do anything ye set yer mind to. Ye are a verra caring person. 'Tis what draws people to ye."

"And I can sew a fairly straight seam, plan a menu—though I shouldnae be trusted to cook water. However, I can provide the proper soothing tea if anyone is brave enough to eat food I have prepared."

The girls dissolved in a fit of giggles, remembering Gilda's almost legendary cooking disasters.

"Oh, Anice, 'tis so good to talk with ye again. Ye must come visit me."

"Aye. I have missed ye, too. Mayhap we could find time to spend together again soon."

Gilda gave Anice a hug. "I must be going. Colin will be home soon, I am sure, and I have chores as well."

"Remember what I said. Talk to yer da. Ye never know what he might say."

Gilda left Anice's little cottage, her attention caught by the air of excitement among the people, spotting their gestures and stares up the sloping hill. Something was happening at the castle. Urging Fia to a fast walk, she guided her around the people thronging the street. The stone towers came into sight, and Gilda saw the banners being hoisted to the top of the main tower. Elation filled her.

Da was home!

Chapter Five

Hastily stabling Fia, Gilda ran excitedly across the bailey. Not even the twins' chatter deterred her as she raced into the great hall. A brief pause was all it took to recognize the tall, dark-haired man amid a group of clansmen.

"Da!"

Ranald, Earl of Scaurness, turned at the sound of her voice. Gilda's heart tripped at the angry look on his face.

"Where have ye been?"

Jamie and Finn skittered out of her wake, determined to share in none of their sire's reprimand. Gilda came to an abrupt halt, bewildered at her parent's rebuke.

Her da strode to her side. "There are pirates on the coast, lass, and no one knew where ye were. Even Tavia said ye'd not been at her house this day." His voice was rough with anger and relief.

Gilda's eyes teared. "I dinnae mean to alarm ye, Da. There are always pirates along the coast." Her attempt at a teasing reminder was met by a narrowed look.

He shoved a hand through his thick hair and Gilda noted the strand of silver at his temple had thickened. She darted a look at the twins. Perhaps they were not the only source of stress in the family.

"Come with me, lass. Let us see yer ma. She was *worrit*."

Relieved to hear his voice soften, Gilda took a deep breath and peered upward. Her mother stood on the balcony, and even from this distance, Gilda sensed her disquiet as she turned silently away.

Her father spoke briefly to the captain of his guard. "Tend to the defenses."

Finlay nodded and spared a wink for Gilda which she returned, happy to know her lifelong protector was not put out with her. She turned and made her way up the stairs to her parents' room.

Her ma gave her a short hug and whispered against her hair. "Dinnae *fash* yerself, Gilda. Yer da isnae angry with ye, only worried."

Gilda flashed a tight smile. "Aye, but it sounds the same."

She crossed the room to the crib where Sara kicked at her blanket, bubbles of concentration pooling at the corners of her pursed lips.

Da closed the door. He raked a wry look over Gilda's sand and seawater-stained dress. Her cheeks burned to remember why she'd allowed her hem to drag across the beach.

"I picked berries and then rode to the village to visit with Anice." *Please dinnae ask where the berry patch is.* Gilda couldn't bring herself to tell an outright lie, and she was in enough trouble already.

Her da shook his head. "I know ye are used to doing as ye please, but ye willnae leave the castle again until the threat is gone."

"I am sorry, Da. I dinnae know there was danger."

"I should have insisted ye keep a guard with ye. I know ye like yer freedom, but ye would be a prize for any marauder who found ye. Even going to Tavia's cottage is dangerous right now."

He paced a few steps. "The king sent me home because there is a new threat to Scaurness. MacEwen's nephew, Acair, has sworn vengeance against me in his uncle's death."

Her mother gasped. "But that happened years ago!"

"Aye. The MacEwens have been leaderless since Morgan MacEwen died, but his nephew has claimed the title, rallying them together to avenge his uncle."

Gilda watched her parents in rapt fascination. This was a story of which she'd only heard bits and pieces. Would she hear it all today? She scarce dared to breathe, afraid she'd remind them of her presence and end their talk.

Riona tossed her head and scoffed. "They can hardly claim revenge on a man killed in battle. Why, he was a scoundrel, a rogue...a pirate!"

"The fact remains, I killed him."

"He kidnapped me!" Riona tilted her head, her suddenly pale skin reflecting the unwelcome memory.

Da's face blanched, and for the first time Gilda understood the fear he must have felt that day. The bottom dropped out of her stomach and she stifled a small cry. Her da did not notice, his attention fixed on his wife.

"Aye. I will never forget, and the MacEwens have a long memory as well. I dinnae regret the man's death. The harm he'd done to ye was unforgivable." He stepped to Riona and folded her gently in his arms, resting his cheek against the top of her head. "I would kill him again if I could."

Harm to her mother? Gilda had heard the story of how her da had set aside his fear of boats to rescue his wife as Laird MacEwen tried to escape the castle with Riona in tow. The storytellers usually made this part into a huge joke even her da laughed about as his tendency to seasickness was well known. Gilda knew her ma had been kidnapped by a cruel and vindictive man. But how had he harmed her?

Sara cried out, tearing the others' attention from their thoughts. Riona pulled from Ranald's arms and smiled as she reached for the bairn.

"Wee lass, dinnae kick away yer blanket. 'Tis chilly to be exposing yer chubby legs." Riona lifted Sara from her crib, wrapping the blanket around her. Ranald moved close, his grin reflecting the beaming joy on the bairn's face. He tweaked a rosy cheek and Sara bounced in her mother's arms, drooling with delight. Gilda felt the sting of tears as she beheld her family. If only the twins were as sweet.

Ranald angled his gaze to Gilda. "Lass, I am sorry I was short with ye earlier. 'Tis said Acair MacEwen is without fear or care for his actions. I know what kind of man his uncle was. I dinnae want ye to run afoul of him or his men. Do ye understand?"

Gilda nodded her head. "Aye. I will stay in the castle unless I have a guard."

"Ye must let me or yer ma know if ye plan to leave." He pinned her with a look. "And if we say 'nae,' ye willnae go."

The walls closed in on her, but Gilda could do nothing more than nod her head in agreement. She thrived on being outside. Riding Fia headlong down the beach beneath the wheeling gulls made her heart soar. She was completely at ease alone in the forest, and restless even within the lofty confines of Scaurness Castle. She twisted her toe on the floor's rug, already feeling the burden of her restraints.

Gilda fisted her hands on her hips and blew a sigh of discontent. "Tell me again why the Macraigs are invited to Scaurness."

Tavia leveled a stern look. "Lass, all the neighboring clans are coming to hear what yer da has to say."

"I thought we were feuding with the Macraigs."

"Wheesht, lass. Where did ye hear such?" Tavia turned to the vegetables on her chopping board.

Gilda stared at the old woman's uncompromising back. Would she never hear the whole story?

"The Macraigs havenae been welcome at Scaurness since the laird bid for yer ma's hand, lass."

Gilda turned to the cook, who slid her gaze to Tavia. The healer woman jerked to attention, waving a hand in protest.

Another woman chimed in before Tavia could speak. "Aye. 'Twas a shameful bargain he tried to make with the auld laird." She shook her head. "Claiming he would take his bride but not the wean."

Tavia whirled on the woman. "Cease yer gossip! I willnae have ye tellin' such tales."

"What wean?" Gilda's voice halted the harangue.

"Why, ye, of course, lass," the woman replied, giving Gilda a pitying look. "Ye know the laird isnae yer real da."

Tavia drew herself up, every inch of her quivering in indignation. "If there is another word said about this, I will see the lot of ye sent to the laundry."

The threat caused a good many narrowed eyes and frowns. Both were hard jobs, but at least those in the kitchen ate well and their hands were not as worn by their labors.

Gilda scowled. "And I shall bring ye right back," she declared, fixing Tavia with a stare. The old woman gaped at her. Gilda's face softened. "I want to know, Tavia. I think 'tis time."

Tavia shrugged and sniffed. "'Tis yer choice."

Gilda turned back to the women. "What did the Macraig laird offer?"

Cook hesitated, obviously torn between her desire to repeat the story and her concern with the power Tavia wielded with the lady of the castle, Gilda's mother.

"Yer grandda was near death and yer uncle Kinnon gone to war in

France. With him missing and feared dead, yer ma was the only heir to Scaurness and an heiress in her own right. Both the MacEwen and Macraig lairds bid for her."

Gilda quashed the desire to stomp her foot in impatience. This much she already knew. Kinnon had returned home injured and too weak to claim the lairdship. He lived at a monastery several hours' ride from Scaurness and visited a couple of times a year.

Cook spared a quick look at Tavia who resumed her task with a quivering hand and a shake of her gray head.

"Yer grandda wouldnae consider an alliance with the MacEwens, as they were reported to be pirates, though none could prove it then. The Macraig laird, however, had known yer ma since she was a wee lass, and she would have accepted his offer."

Once again, Gilda repressed the urge to scream and instead managed a firm, quiet voice. "Why did she not accept?"

"He wouldnae take ye in the bargain."

Gilda's heart tripped as a sour taste rose in the back of her throat.

Cook settled a comforting arm about her shoulders. "Laird Macrory has always loved ye like his own. He brought tears to all our eyes the day he married yer ma and swore ye fealty as well."

Gilda nodded once, too stricken to heed Cook's words. She'd always known Ranald was not her real father. But none had ever mentioned it in her presence. She'd never felt the sting of illegitimacy from any at Scaurness. Until now.

"The Macraig wouldnae raise a bastard?" she bit out, her throat tight and clogged with tears.

Cook's gaze wavered from the woman beside her to Tavia's back. Neither offered her help answering Gilda's question. Finally she replied, "Yer ma has never said who yer real da is. But he wasnae honorable, and the laird has raised ye right."

Gilda forced a brittle smile. "Of course he has. He has never treated me as other than his own daughter."

She wiped her hands absently down the sides of her skirt and turned away. She wandered aimlessly from the bustling room to the relative peace of the kitchen garden. Seeking refuge in weeding a small patch of vegetables, Gilda tried to turn her thoughts to happier things. Facing the fact Ranald was not her father rarely occurred to her—she'd called him 'Da' as long as she could remember.

Knowing she'd been sired on her sweet mother by a man considered dishonorable sent a chilling spike through her heart.

Ryan paced the floor.

Conn waved his hand in complaint. "Leave off. Ye try the patience of a saint."

"How would ye know?" Ryan retorted, stopping to glare at his friend. "Ye are no saint."

"Och, ye think too much. Yer da accepted the invitation to the meeting at Scaurness. As his heir, ye must go."

Ryan snorted. "Invitation? 'Twas worded like a royal command."

Conn shrugged. "Mayhap it was. Pirates are a concern to the king."

"Aye. 'Tis verra important to hold the River Clyde for the king." Ryan dropped into a chair.

"A *birlinn* followed us for a couple of days but cried off as we approached the harbor. It dinnae get close enough to identify. I wonder if it was a pirate ship?"

"I dinnae see it." Conn yawned, his apparent unconcern not fooling Ryan. Conn was astute, rarely missing anything of importance or interest, though he hid it behind his languid actions and ready friendliness with the lasses.

"Ye dinnae see beyond yer bucket." Ryan flung the brusque reminder at him as he rose from his chair. "Come on."

With a half-stifled groan, Conn followed Ryan from the room. People bustled about the great hall, and tantalizing odors drifted from the kitchen.

"It smells as though they prepare a feast." Conn took an appreciative sniff.

"As long as it isnae a funeral banquet." Ryan's dour remark earned him a sharp look.

"Is forming an alliance with the Macrorys fraught with such danger?"

A tug at his sleeve turned Ryan's attention. A shock ran through him at the sight of amber eyes amid a cloud of dark hair. He had not yet become accustomed to seeing himself reflected so completely in his sister's face.

"Aye?"

Lissa's gaze slid to Conn who regarded her with a patient smile. Lissa offered him a tiny grin in return, rounding her cheeks in an endearing manner.

"I want to go with ye."

"I am sorry, Lissa, but there willnae be any lasses at this meeting. 'Tis between men."

The child's face fell into a pout. She'd obviously heard this response before.

"But there are children at Scaurness Castle, aye?"

"I am sure the laird and lady have bairns, but 'tis not a social occasion. Ye cannae go this time."

"'Tis dangerous, lass," Conn chimed in. "What if we have to fight pirates along the way?"

"Dinnae frighten her. She is a good lass and willnae argue." Ryan raised an eyebrow in question. "Truth?"

"Can I at least ride to the boundary with ye? 'Tis not far and I am tired of being cooped up in the castle."

"Nae, lass. We cannae spare the men to escort ye back. We will leave immediately after we eat and 'twill be nearly dark." His face softened to see her disappointment. "Another time I will take ye riding, aye?"

With a small sigh, she nodded. "Can I sit with ye at the table, then?" She sent Conn another wee smile. Ryan nodded, relieved she dropped the matter. She slipped one hand in his; her other caught Conn's little finger.

Startled, Ryan exchanged looks with his friend over her head. Conn allowed Lissa to take his hand, and she led them to their seats.

Torches on the wall cast dim blades of light through the gloaming. Guards bristled along the parapet and formed an impressive shield along the barbican as men rode through the metal-studded gates. Each party of clansmen was examined closely before allowed entrance to Scaurness Castle.

Gilda sat on the stone floor of the parapet, the captured heat of the sun seeping through her skirts to her bottom, forming a contrast against the increasing chill of the evening air. Mists crept up from the ground, winding ghost-like around the horses' legs. She counted the riders, twenty in this group, eighteen in another. From her vantage point there was no way to tell the individual identities of the clans who filtered into the bailey. All attention was on Finlay and the soldiers who greeted their laird's guests and none saw the laird's daughter watching them from above.

Greeted? Gilda snorted. More likely he gave them grudging permission to enter. Other riders entered the gates, but she grew bored with the endless protocol. And additional posturing would enact at dinner. The long, boring meal she must attend.

In a fit of inspiration, Gilda resolved to take special care bathing and dressing before heading downstairs to the great hall to join their guests. With any luck at all, dinner would be at least half-finished before she arrived at the table. She gathered her skirts and pushed up from the stone, brushing dust from her bottom as she strolled to the interior of the castle and to her room.

A bath awaited her, and she halted in surprise as her mother's maid, Kyla, bustled about the room.

"There ye are, lass. Yer ma wants ye to hurry. Here is a gown for ye, I'll be back to help ye lace up after ye've bathed."

With a nod of her head, Kyla was gone, Gilda staring after her with a frown. Her plan to dally in her room took a direct hit. Kyla knew Gilda needed no help dressing. The maid's assistance ensured Gilda arrived downstairs on time.

Finally dressed and coifed to Kyla's satisfaction, Gilda impatiently shifted in her chair at the table as her mother reached for the flagon of wine and poured some into Gilda's cup.

Taking advantage of her nearness, she whispered, "I know ye are bored. Try to look less inconvenienced."

Gilda released a tiny sigh and schooled her expression into one of complete neutrality.

"As soon as the meal is finished, the ladies will retire," Riona promised.

Spurred by the reminder, Gilda managed a brief smile. She picked at the food on her plate. Cook had created a banquet worthy of their guests. Gilda should know; she'd helped prepare it. But boredom and the telltale effects of filching food as she'd worked in the kitchen, now hampered her appetite.

She studied the room. Men crowded the tables, elbowing each other as they ate. Food vanished at an alarming rate. It was easy to see the fierce warrior seated nearby favored the stewed berries. Gilda watched a fresh purple stain slide from the corner of his mouth and coat his white beard. His bushy eyebrows met in the center of his face like a pair of wooly caterpillars and she forced back a sudden grin.

All the men appeared to be of an age near her father's. There were few among them to stir the slightest interest in Gilda's heart. They seemed well-versed in filling their bellies, and how to properly pay their respects to Cook for her efforts. Gilda rolled her eyes as another man pounded a rumbling belch from his belly.

Movement at the doorway pulled her attention from the braw men near her table. The noise level in the room abated as the newcomers entered the room. Loud whispers reached Gilda's ears and she leaned forward with renewed interest.

"...*Macraigs...*"

A tall, slender man with dark, graying hair approached the laird's table. His men fanned out behind him, ignoring the remnants of the feast. His features were even, perhaps good-looking, but Gilda hated him instantly. This was the man who'd refused to raise Riona's bastard daughter. Anger burned inside as she tore her gaze away. He had no right to expect help from the Macrorys. Why had her da invited him here? They could deal with the pirates without engaging the likes of the Macraigs.

Scowling, she cast a derisive glare over the men gathered with him. It was clear from their stance they were uncomfortable in their enemy's castle.

Gilda's hands balled into fists on her lap. *Serves them right. Pledging themselves to such a man.* She cut a look sideways at her ma, but Riona sat easily in her chair, giving the Macraig laird her polite attention as he and Ranald exchanged greetings.

Laird Macraig declined the offer of a meal, bowed his head in a small gesture of thanks and turned with his men to find seating in the room. Two young men standing on the laird's right side came into Gilda's view. Their gazes raked the head table, and the dark-haired man halted in surprise as their eyes met, his amber gaze wringing a jolt of recognition. Gilda looked quickly from him to the laird and back. Their build and coloring were the same.

He could be none other than Laird Macraig's son.

Chapter Six

Ryan met Gilda's stormy gray eyes. Damn, Conn was right. Why did the lass have to be the laird's daughter? It would be much more satisfying to have no care as to the consequences of their friendship. Or dalliance. Or whatever it was destined to become. And he definitely expected it to become something more than chance meetings on the beach. Despite their tempestuous start, he had been determined to meet the red-haired lass again.

Gilda slid back in her seat and Ryan knew she prepared to rise. He stepped to the table, settling his gaze on her father.

"I am Ryan Macraig, Laird Macraig's son. Would ye introduce me to yer family?"

Laird Macrory scowled. Ryan waited patiently as the man weighed the prospect of introducing Laird Macraig's son against an outright refusal. Eyebrows slanted together furiously, the Macrory laird shot Ryan an intimidating look. Ryan's expression of polite interest did not waver.

Laird Macrory visibly ground his teeth, but spoke evenly. "My lady wife, Riona, and our daughter, Gilda."

Short, to the point, no elaboration. Ryan checked a grin. No indication the laird would welcome further conversation between his family and the Macraig heir.

Ryan offered a short bow to Lady Macrory. "My lady, I am honored to make yer acquaintance."

Lady Riona inclined her head. "The pleasure is mine, sir."

"My lady." Ryan next slid his gaze to Gilda who stared straight ahead, her lips pressed into a thin line. A moment of silence passed, then Gilda jerked. Had her mother nudged her beneath the table?

Gilda's mouth barely moved. "The-pleasure-is-mine-I'm-sure."

This time Ryan couldn't stop the grin tugging at his lips at Gilda's rebellious attempt at civility. He bowed his head briefly.

"Ladies."

Lady Macrory and the laird dismissed him with a short nod. Gilda bit her lip.

Pivoting on his heel, he crossed the room to Conn's side.

"Well, did I not tell ye? And ye thought I was daft." Conn snorted in vindicated mockery. Ryan ignored him and reached for a mug sitting on a tray at the end of the table. He took a fortifying gulp of ale, pleased to find it not watered down. With a nonchalant gesture, he half-turned to view the laird's table and caught a glimpse of burnished red hair as Gilda vanished into the recesses of the back hall.

He clamped a hand on Conn's shoulder as he shoved the mug back onto its tray, paying no heed to the ale sloshing over the side. "Stay here."

"Why?"

Ryan spared his friend an impatient look. "We arrived together. If the laird looks up and sees ye, he may presume I am nearby."

"Are ye not?"

"Nae."

"Where are ye going?"

"To find Gilda."

Gilda slipped past the guards posted behind the laird's table and into the back of the hall. She mingled with those busy trundling food and empty platters to and from the kitchen. Her midnight blue gown sparkled with silver embroidery at the low, square neckline and full, belled sleeves, making it difficult for her to blend in with the servants or be of any use in the kitchen where she sought to hide.

She cast a hurried glance over her shoulder and spied a dark-haired young man pushing through the throng behind her. Her heart quickened. Ryan had seen her. Darting to her right, Gilda slipped into the kitchen where organized chaos reigned. Cook directed her perfectly ordered dinner, far too busy to pay attention to someone unable to assist.

Gilda rushed around the edge of the room, managing to make it to the door on the far side of the room before an extended arm effectively blocked her path.

Ryan's amber gaze met her furious look, but he did not flinch. Standing close, much too close, his hand on the door frame just above her head, he kept her from moving away.

"Remove yerself, sir."

"Gilda, I would talk to ye."

"I have nothing to say."

"Most lasses like talking to me."

Gilda nearly choked. "You arrogant, presumptuous…"

"Och, Gilda, ye know I only tease ye. Let us go somewhere we can talk."

"I dinnae wish to go anywhere with ye."

Ryan ducked his head close and whispered, "Ye also dinnae want to create a scene, do ye?"

Gilda peered surreptitiously around the room. Servants' gazes were beginning to turn her way.

He grasped her hand and tucked it over his arm before she knew what he was doing and led her outside into the garden. Gilda took two steps past the door with him before she snatched her hand away, fully intending on returning to the kitchen.

Ryan smoothly snagged her other hand as she whirled, using her momentum to spin her back around, drawing her close.

"Temper, temper," he chided in her ear.

Gilda stiffened at his words. "I dinnae wish to walk with ye." She raised mutinous eyes to his.

He chuckled. "Ye are marvelous, lass. Let us call a truce."

"Are we at war?"

"I believe we have been at war since we met. Come walk with me. I promise to behave."

Lifting a brow in disbelief, Gilda at last gave a brief nod. "Follow me."

Surprised at her change of heart, Ryan followed Gilda deeper into the garden where moonlight filtered through the leaves and formed intricate patterns on the ground. A thousand stars sparkled against a velvet night sky, but he had eyes only for Gilda.

Her hair, bound by a narrow silver band at her crown, spilled across her shoulders and down her back, sparking fire and gold where the filtered moonlight touched it. Heavy curls swayed like a living thing with each step and Ryan's skin tingled with the desire to run his hands through the molten strands.

Crossing to a low wooden bench encircling an ancient oak tree, Gilda at last came to a stop and faced him, her expression unreadable. Ryan wondered if she regretted the knowledge of who they were as much as he did.

"Ryan." Gilda laid a flattened palm against his chest to halt his advance. Unexplainable sparks flew between them, and she dropped her hand to press it against her skirt, casting a startled gaze at him. Ryan stifled the urge to rub the stinging sensation lingering on his skin.

Gilda cleared her throat. "Ryan. We cannae meet again. I dinnae know who ye were, but even so, 'twas wrong for us to expect to see each other again." Her forthright gaze challenged him.

"Did ye expect to see me again? It seemed to me ye had no intention of it."

Even in the moonlight, Ryan saw the deepening shade on her cheeks and knew she blushed.

She lifted her chin. "Ye ogled my legs!"

Ryan nodded his head in agreement. "Ye have verra pretty legs."

Gilda drew back with a hiss of breath. "Ye are a rogue, Ryan Macraig!"

"We have already agreed on this, aye?"

"This meeting tonight 'twas for the clansmen to decide what to do about the pirates, not for ye to seek me out in my home." Gilda crossed her arms beneath her breasts, shoving them to the squared neckline.

Ryan mumbled the first response that came to his suddenly awkward tongue. "I dinnae know ye would be here." His tone remained reasonable even as he fought the dryness in his mouth.

"Dinnae stare at me like that." Gilda dropped her hands as she spun away, and Ryan's concentration returned with a snap.

"I dinnae know how to act around ye, Gilda Macrory. I know our parents are nae likely to agree for us to meet, but I am willing to ask. To do this right."

Gilda slowly turned, lifting her gaze to his. "To do what right?"

"To talk to ye. Listen to ye laugh. Watch yer eyes change color when I vex ye."

Gilda's quick grin told him he'd scored a point and he smiled. "I am good at vexing ye, aye?"

"Aye." Her expression remained puzzled. "Do ye like to be around me? Not just to ogle my legs?"

This time Ryan laughed. "I will ogle yer legs any chance I get. I cannae lie to ye. But, aye. I like being around ye."

Gilda gave him a thoughtful look before strolling to the circular wooden bench, lifting her skirts slightly as she climbed onto its wooden seat. Offering a look from beneath her lashes, she dropped the midnight fabric over her ankles and stepped along the boards, hands outstretched for balance. At the curve of the bench, she grabbed a low limb in a practiced move and swung about.

The maneuver caught Ryan off-guard and, thinking she fell, he lunged forward only to draw to an abrupt halt as she gracefully recovered her footing, and he realized she was quite at home climbing the ancient oak.

Ryan leaned a shoulder against a slender rowan tree and crossed his arms over his chest. "Ye are naught but a well-dressed hoyden."

Gilda tossed a lofty glare over her shoulder and continued her circuit of the tree. "I am quite unlikely to fall, so ye can stop looking at me so fiercely."

He lost sight of her on the far side of the enormous tree trunk, but refused to rise to the bait. He would wait for her.

A thump and muffled cry startled him.

"Damn!"

With a start, Ryan pushed away from the rowan tree and was at Gilda's side in an instant. She half-crouched on the ground, her slippered heel caught in the hem of her gown. Shooting him a quick glance, she frowned as she gave her skirt a final tug. She straightened, smoothing her features into a serene look.

Ryan narrowed his eyes. "Did ye fall?"

Gilda lifted an eyebrow in indignation. "Certainly not. I hopped down and slipped on the damp grass."

He let out a sigh. "I believe ye vex me, too, Gilda Macrory."

"Be that as it may…"

A brisk wind tossed her hair and interrupted her words. She raised a hand to wipe the billowing strands from her face, catching at the silver band threatening to slip from her head. The wind redoubled its efforts, lifting the hem of her gown. With a gasp, Gilda shoved the fabric down.

Ryan stepped close, blocking the churning wind, and Gilda gave him a grateful look. For a moment neither spoke. Ryan leaned closer.

Dried leaves scurried across the garden, but Gilda was oblivious to their patter. She was sheltered and warm, overly warm in fact, but it was a sensation she'd only experienced near Ryan and it left her head as airy as though she'd drunk too much wine. Perhaps she should pull back, seek a way out of this Macraig man's spell, but her limbs would not obey her, and she simply smiled.

Ryan bent closer, the scar across his cheek a dark stripe in the moonlight. Gilda lightly touched its length. "Ye've no' been tilting at bears again, have ye?"

Ryan grinned. "I leave the wild animals to the red-haired Macrory lass who tames them."

As Gilda's gaze slid from the scar to Ryan's amber eyes, her hand stilled against his cheek. "Me?"

"Aye. I saw ye tame a wolf. It clenched my heart to see ye do it."

"Why did it clench yer heart?" Gilda's fingers drifted to his chest, twitching the pleats in his plaide over the spot in question.

"Ye are special, and I dinnae want to see ye hurt."

Her heart gave a lurch. "What is special about me?" Her voice slipped past her lips, scarcely above a whisper.

Ryan lowered his head. "Yer silver eyes."

His breath was warm on her face and Gilda's lashes fluttered. She felt his mouth gently touch her eyelids, one and then the other, and she drew back, startled. Her eyes widened as she met Ryan's slow smile. Her insides churned.

Ryan trailed his fingertips over her cheek. "They are verra special. They tell me what ye are thinking."

"What…what am I thinking now?"

"That ye would like me to kiss ye again."

Gilda wanted to deny it, but lying had never been her strong suit. She'd relied on charm and wit to avoid trouble most of her life, and now, when she most wanted to tell him she certainly did not want him to kiss her again, knowing she shouldn't allow it, she couldn't form the words.

His gaze lingered on hers then dropped to her mouth—and Gilda melted.

Ryan's arm slid around her waist as she sagged against him. She lifted her face, waiting for his lips to press against hers. The suspense built unbearably and her heart pounded in her chest.

And then, Ryan kissed her.

"Ye were missed," Conn hissed between clenched teeth as Ryan scooted onto the bench beside him.

Ryan leaned his elbows on his thighs, and peered past Conn. His father sat a few feet away, and though he stared straight ahead, Ryan rather suspected his father knew he was there.

"What did ye say?"

"That yer head was botherin' ye." Conn turned slightly. "'Twas the truth. Yer head has been addled since ye met the lass."

"My thanks." Ryan gave a low snort.

The Macrory laird stood before them, extolling the ravages the pirates laid to the coastline. Ryan's attention wandered. Pirates always pillaged coastal villages. The Macraigs would be glad for the alliance to help keep the pirates at bay until they were either killed or convinced to find easier game elsewhere.

"The MacEwen's nephew, Acair, has rallied the scattered clan," the Macrory stated. "He has no fear of retaliation or war. He encourages us to do battle with him."

Laird Macraig rose to his feet. "What drives Acair to be so bold?"

"He calls it revenge."

A murmur arose from the crowd. Ryan swung his gaze around, wondering what he'd just missed.

His father took a step forward and all eyes swiveled to him. "Revenge for what?"

Laird Macrory's gaze locked on the Macraig laird, and Ryan felt hostility spark between the two men. He sat up straight and his hand drifted to his empty scabbard before he remembered he'd left his sword and other weapons at the door.

"His uncle's death."

"Then it has nothing to do with us. Only ye."

"He has pillaged up and down the coast," the Macrory pointed out. "He uses his claim of revenge to bind his scattered clansmen together."

The Macraig snorted. "So, if ye were dead, his lust for revenge would be satisfied and the problem would go away for the rest of us?"

Harsh voices spilled around Ryan as he gaped in disbelief at his sire.

What the hell is he doing? Ryan cut his eyes to Conn who shrugged, frank curiosity in his expression.

"I thought ye said ye werenae at war with the Macrorys?" his friend asked.

Ryan shook his head, staring at the man he scarcely knew. Surely, his father wasn't about to decline the offer of help? Any time now the man would nod and give apology for such a brash statement. Tense moments passed as the two lairds glared at each other and speculation charged about the room.

With a feeling of doom, Ryan sighed. "We soon will be."

Chapter Seven

Wooden benches scraped across the stone and tumbled noisily to the floor as men erupted to their feet. Ryan rose swiftly to his father's side. His abrupt movement brought him directly in line with the enraged Macrory laird's sight, but it couldn't be helped. It was too late now to hope to gain the man's approval where Gilda was concerned. Ryan's best tactic was to support his father until he could somehow understand what the hell his sire was up to and perhaps minimize the damage between the clans.

Laird Macrory fought visibly to bring his anger under control. Jaw clenched, his chest rising and falling with each furious breath, he raised a hand for silence. His captain, a large, burly man who'd probably never been gainsaid since acquiring his impressive height, stepped to the laird's shoulder, lending support.

Slowly, the room retreated beneath their demanding glares. Ryan released a deep breath of relief and offered a quick prayer of thanks. Around him men righted benches and reclaimed their seats. Ryan longed to take his own seat and listen to what the Macrory laird had to say, but his father remained standing, chin jutted outward in defiance. Short of tugging his sleeve to encourage him to sit, hoping for cooperation he wasn't likely to get, Ryan had no choice but to remain at his side.

"'Tis well known ye are an outsider, Laird Macrory." Disdain colored Laird Macraig's voice. "'Twas a ruinous day a Scott laid claim to Macrory land. A man who gave up his own clan to rule another for the king."

"I have always been loyal to the crown, and the Macrory people are kin. We dinnae share a name when I arrived here, 'tis true, but I am proud to be called Macrory."

A murmur swept the crowd again. Heads nodded in approval. Then again, more than half the men in the room were Macrorys, and all apparently quite loyal to their laird. Ryan's blood quickened. Were they to bring the old feud into the open?

His father took a half-step forward. "Ye had no real claim to this land or clan."

Laird Macrory's eyes flashed. "The king sent me here at the auld laird's request."

"We would have done better without ye here. I would have married the daughter and forged a strong bond between the clans."

"The auld laird had his reasons for denying yer offer, as ye well know. And Scaurness has prospered these past years even with an *outsider* at its head."

Tension bristled around the room. Ryan's blood ran cold at the animosity between the two lairds. Murmurs rose in the room like the buzz of angry bees.

"Enough!"

Heads swiveled at the new voice. A heavy-set man with a bull-like neck climbed to his feet. Torchlight glinted from his partially bald pate above a retreating hairline, and thick tufts of red hair peeked from the neckline of his leine. With a glare from beneath bushy brows for both the Macrory and Macraig lairds, he turned to his host.

"I dinnae come here to listen to the twa' of ye fight over something long since done. The Maclellans have always profited from our alliance with the Macrorys. If the MacEwens are again raiding our shores to avenge such nonsense as young Acair speaks, then we will band with Laird Macrory to see it ended." Laird Maclellan turned a pointed look on The Macraig. "Whether ye are with us or not."

Laird Macraig did not break his stare from Ranald Macrory's face. The animosity between the two men was palpable and Ryan's throat went dry as he awaited his sire's next move.

Drawing himself up to a regal height, the Macraig spat, "We willnae be a part of an alliance with a bastard Macrory." With a swish of his plaide, he turned and left the room, men parting quickly to accommodate him.

From the corner of his eye, Ryan caught a glimpse of burnished red hair and wide grey eyes as Gilda watched him from the shelter of a wide pillar on the edge of the hall.

Gilda stared in disbelief as Ryan's gaze met hers and his step did not falter. How could he simply walk away? The plaide draped across his shoulder swayed with each stride and her skin twitched to remember the fine texture of the wool she'd pleated beneath her fingers as he'd kissed her.

The Macraigs disappeared through the double doors of the great hall and into the night. Shouts in the bailey as they called for their horses sounded loud against the stunned silence of the hall. The great doors closed.

Gilda looked over her shoulder. The Maclellan laird remained standing, arms crossed above his broad girth, feet planted wide, as though expecting further challenge. Light from the candles shone on his forbidding visage, and Gilda shivered. The menace radiating from the laird could not be mistaken. She would not like to be the man—or woman—who came against him.

Laird Maclellan faced Laird Macrory. "How do we defeat the pirates?"

Darting looks around the hall and at each other, the men returned to the business at hand. Gilda drew back into the shadows, her heart a sharp ache in her chest at Ryan's easy betrayal. Panic set in. She needed to escape, to be anywhere but in this room.

Her slippered feet flew up the stairs, a mist of tears veiling her sight, but she needed nothing more than the touch of a hand to the stone wall to guide her.

"Where are ye going, Gilda?"

She gasped and spun in the direction of the voice. She blinked as the twins' faces peered at her from behind a tapestry.

"To my room. And ye both were to be in bed an hour ago," she retorted.

"Och, dinnae fuss. We heard the *stramash*. What happened?"

"Never ye mind. Get to bed. The both of ye."

"We'll tell Ma ye were down in the great hall."

Gilda frowned. She was supposed to be confined to the upper hall while the men conducted their business. Her da did not allow unruly behavior or drunkenness in the castle, and men who approached that state were encouraged to recover their wits outside. But when a large number of men from other clans drank and feasted in the great hall, she knew her personal safety could not be ensured if she were so foolish as to wander about unescorted.

She gave the boys a narrowed look and the smallest information possible to garner their cooperation against tattling on her. "There was a disagreement."

"Was there a fight?" The twins scrambled from their hiding place and jumped up and down the corridor in mock fighting stances. "Was there blood?"

Gilda rolled her eyes and sighed. "There was neither, ye *louns*. They have better manners than ye do." She made shooing gestures with her hands. "Now off to bed with ye."

Jamie and Finn stopped their antics and turned to face her. Something in their expressions sent a warning chill up Gilda's spine.

"Who were ye talking to in the garden?" Finn asked.

Rage overruled the shiver of warning. "How dare ye spy on me? Get out of my sight!"

Jamie piped in. "We saw ye kiss him."

"Who is he, Gilda?"

"If ye get us some pastries, we won't tell Ma."

As her brothers voiced their demands, Gilda rounded on them. "Ye are both horrible! Leave me alone! I dinnae want to see ye again!"

She pushed past them and fled to her room as Jamie grumbled, "She isnae going to get us pastries, Finn."

Fighting back tears, she slammed the door, leaning against the sturdy frame. Her chest heaved, the air in the room heavy, seemingly too thick to breathe. Gilda darted to the window and pulled open the shutter. Cool, moist air rushed over her face. She tried to shove thoughts of the past hour deep inside her, but Ryan's curious, amber eyes rose firmly in her mind. Memory of the feel of the hard planes of his chest as she leaned into his kiss returned to tickle the palms of her hands, and she scrubbed them against the rock frame of the window.

Bewildered, Gilda leaned her forehead against the stone and stared blindly into the night. She knew there had not been an alliance between the Macrorys and the Macraigs in many years, but Ryan had sounded so confident he could change things.

Why did she want him to? He was an unabashed rogue. Gilda's

lips curved in a secret smile. He also made her long for him to touch her, which certainly vexed her, but the circle of his arms was an exciting place she'd never dreamed of, and his smiles made her melt. She raised a finger and touched her lower lip. It still quivered from his kiss.

A shout from a guard on the parapet caught her attention and she stared into the bailey below. The yard was empty except for two men who walked unhurriedly from the stables. The Macraigs were gone. Once again Gilda's heart grew heavy. Had Ryan played her false? Had he meant the sweet words he'd whispered?

Her eyes brimmed with tears. Why did she feel so hollow? What was happening to her?

Morning sunlight pierced the narrow window. A splash of cool water eased the tightness of her eyelids, swollen from too much crying and too little sleep. Gilda reached for the linen towel hanging from the hook near the bowl. The unexpected dampness of the cloth registered in her sleep-deprived brain as she lifted the towel to her face, then recoiled at the foul odor it contained. She drew back in alarm, noting the discolored areas on the normally white cloth. Gingerly she sniffed the towel. It reeked of rotting fish and salt.

"Finn! Jamie!" Gilda stormed from the room, the abused fabric clenched tight in her fist. "Ma!"

Snorts of barely stifled laughter echoed in the hallway, giving Gilda no indication where the twins were other than somewhere nearby. And that was entirely too close to her this day.

"Ma!"

Riona appeared in her doorway, a finger raised to her lips. "Silence! There are guests in this castle, and ye willnae cause a scene."

Gilda propped her hands on her hips, unable to soften the anger on her face. "The *louns* in the hall below are fair *puggled* after their meeting last night. I doubt the baying of hundred *cu sith* would move them."

"Gilda!" Riona gaped in shock. "What has gotten into you?"

For answer, Gilda waved the foul-smelling towel in the air. Riona ducked, her nose wrinkling in objection as the odor wafted toward her.

She lifted a hand in surrender. "Finn! Jamie!"

To Gilda's surprise, both boys darted from their hiding places and ran to their mother. Pulling at her skirt, they clamored about her feet.

"Are there *cu sith* here?"

"*I* saw their footprints outside—"

Finn rounded on Jamie. "Ye dinnae!"

"Aye!"

"Dinnae!"

Jamie shoved his brother. "And they were covered in blood!"

"Lads!"

Abashed at the sound of their father's tone, they fell silent, but did not move from Riona's side.

Ranald strode from his room, a thunderous look on his face. "What is the meaning of this *rippet*?"

The twins cut their eyes to Gilda. She clenched her teeth and glared at them.

"Tell me, Gilda."

"Da, they snuck into my room and stole my towel and steeped it in something foul and..."

Jamie peeked his head out. "We dinnae 'steep' nuthin'."

Ranald's eyebrows jerked upward, and Jamie dropped his gaze. "I doubt the lads used hot water for their prank." He wrinkled his nose at the odor. "A swipe or two across a rotten fish would be enough."

Gilda rolled her eyes. "Da, I dinnae care how they did it. They snuck into my room again!"

Ranald nodded. "Aye. And they know the punishment." He fixed a disapproving glare on his sons who hung their heads, chins bumping their chests, a picture of abject repentance. "Well?"

"We're sorry, Gilda. It willnae happen again." They offered her winsome smiles, begging to be forgiven the rest of the punishment. Gilda's dark frown answered their silent plea and their faces fell. "An' we will clean Fia's stall for a sennight."

Once, Gilda would have laughed at the sound of their sorrowful voices pitched in perfect unison. It had happened too many times. So many, in fact, their chorused response was not merely chance, but the well-worn chant they'd repeated oft before.

"Gilda?" Her da prompted her gently.

She should reply she'd forgiven them and accept their apology—and their penance. It was the expected response. To her surprise and horror, she burst into tears. Whirling, she ran back into her room, slamming the door behind her.

Ranald lifted his shoulders in query to his wife at Gilda's unprecedented behavior. Riona nodded slightly toward the lads, an indication she would discuss their daughter behind closed doors.

Ranald turned to the twins. "Ye are too old to be pestering yer sister. The next time yer punishment willnae be inside the stable, but behind it. Do ye understand me?"

Solemnly, Finn and Jamie nodded their heads. Ranald jerked his chin in assent and the boys pelted down the hallway at top speed.

He turned to Riona. "Would ye care to tell me what is bothering Gilda?"

Riona sighed and entered their rooms, Ranald following to shut the door. With a quick look to the crib, she sat in a chair and motioned for Ranald to do the same. "At least they dinnae wake the bairn," she said.

Ranald sat wearily. "Wee Sara is the only person that *stramash* dinnae waken. What has gotten into the lass?"

"Ranald, she is growing up and tired of the ceaseless pranks the lads pull."

"They are a handful, I will admit. But Gilda has never burst into tears like that before." His brow furrowed in concern.

Riona smiled softly and leaned forward, placing a hand on Ranald's knee. And repeated softly, "She is growing up."

Ranald felt the warm weight of Riona's hand through the fabric of his trews and lost his train of thought. His gaze wandered to the still-rumpled bed behind his wife and wondered how much longer wee Sara would sleep. Riona squeezed his knee, bringing his attention back. He lifted his gaze to hers and saw the question in her eyes. What had she asked him?

Riona sighed again. "Ye arenae listening to me. Gilda is likely overly emotional because she is becoming a woman. All lasses go through this." She patted his knee and settled back in her chair.

Ranald jerked as though stung. His breath left his lungs in a whoosh of sound. Belatedly he realized his mouth hung open and he closed it with a snap. Riona's look of gentle pity didn't help. He leapt to his feet and paced the floor, running a hand through his hair.

"Ranald, you realize she cannae stay a bairn forever. Being away from home of late, ye probably havenae noticed how much she has grown. She started her courses more than—"

Ranald waved a hand in the air. "I dinnae want to know."

Riona laughed. "Not knowing doesnae mean it isnae happening."

Pivoting on his heel, Ranald dropped into his chair. He scrubbed his palms over his face then stared at his wife. "Am I the only one who hasnae seen her grow up?"

"Nae, love. Ye have watched her grow and loved her through her skinned knees and pony rides. Now ye must realize she will be a grown woman soon. Indeed, many lasses her age already are married and starting families."

Riona rose and crossed to him, seating herself on the cushioned arm of his chair. She ran her slender fingers through his abused hair, smoothing the strands. "Ye have a bit more grey in yer hair today."

"I wouldnae be surprised if it all showed up this morning."

Riona kissed the top of his head. "She asked me yesterday if ye had plans for her to marry."

A chill passed through Ranald. His sweet Gilda, married? His thoughts drifted to the prior night's events and he turned his head to stare out the window.

"What is it?"

For a moment, Ranald did not answer. He remembered the Maclellan laird's words only too clearly, though he hadn't wanted to hear them. Ranald reached for one of Riona's hands and brought it to his lips for a kiss.

"Laird Maclellan proposed a betrothal between Gilda and his son last night," he murmured.

Riona was silent and Ranald tilted his head to her. She blinked rapidly, but Ranald saw the sheen of tears in her eyes. "This doesnae please ye?"

"I dinnae know what to say. The Maclellan has always been a staunch ally, though his lands scarcely border ours to the east along the River Clyde. I dinnae know his son. What sort of man is he?"

"I know little of him. He stood respectfully with his sire at the meeting. He is a summer, mayhap two, older than Gilda. It could be a good match, though I dinnae consider it last night. I thought Gilda too young…"

Riona leaned against Ranald's shoulder. He drew her into his lap, seeking her comfort against the change in their lives looming on the horizon.

Riona placed her hand against his chest. "Please dinnae make a decision until ye talk to Gilda."

Ranald did not answer. He was thinking of another young man who stood with his father, despite that one's disastrous tirade. A braw young man who had boldly asked for an introduction to Gilda, though there was a nagging suspicion in the back of Ranald's mind the lad had needed no introduction.

He frowned. The Macraig heir would bear watching. Perhaps it would be best if Gilda were safely married to the Maclellan's son. It would not do for Gilda's head to be turned by Ryan Macraig. Ranald clenched his teeth.

He'd be damned before he let his daughter marry a Macraig.

Chapter Eight

Sleepy stable lads collected the spent horses as they entered the bailey at Ard Castle. Ryan gritted his teeth and grasped his father's upper arm. Laird Macraig whirled, his face a dark mask.

Ryan held his ground. "I wish to speak with ye." Ryan's clipped, almost-civil tone deceived no one. Men hunched their shoulders and found things to do elsewhere.

The Macraig inclined his head. "In my chamber."

Guttering candles cast faint illumination around the great hall. Men and a few women lay scattered about, the sounds of their rest punctuated by the brisk thud of booted feet. Several heads lifted, but quickly lowered as the laird and Ryan passed.

The small room just off the main hall was pitch dark. No fire had been laid on the hearth in the laird's absence. Ryan stepped back to the hall and jerked a candle from a nearby sconce, using it to light the others in the room. Finished, he tossed the taper onto the hearth and the tang of smoldering peat began to fill the air.

He faced his father. The laird returned his stare with hooded eyes, his jaw clenched tight. Ryan recognized the same stubbornness he'd had occasion to regret in himself. It would be difficult to get unbiased information from his father tonight, and downright impossible to garner any concessions.

Ryan took a deep breath to steady his voice, struggling to keep censure from his tone. "Would ye care to tell me what happened at the meeting?"

Laird Macraig waved a hand dismissingly in the air and yanked his chair from beneath his desk. "The Macrory is not a friend of ours."

"Why, then, did ye even attend the meeting?"

"I wanted to hear about the pirates and to see what other *kiss-ma-luif* men hopped to do the Macrory's bidding."

Scorn for such sycophant behavior slurred the laird's voice. Ryan clenched his fists, holding tight to his temper. "If Acair MacEwen is as dangerous as Laird Macrory says, we may need their help 'ere this is over."

The Macraig slammed the palms of his hands on the desktop. An inkwell and several rolls of parchment skittered on the wooden surface. "Nae!"

Ryan's heart thudded in his chest, but he did not falter. "Ye must set aside this trouble that has brewed between ye for these past years. I am sorry the auld laird dinnae approve of a match between ye and his daughter. But she is wed and it is in the past."

The Macraig's skin blanched, his look haunted. "Ye dinnae know what ye speak. It would have been a good match and benefited both our clans."

"Da, we can still correct this. We can still forge an alliance between the Macraigs and the Macrorys. The laird's daughter, Gilda—"

"Nae!"

Ryan recoiled at the force of his sire's response. "Why—"

"Dinnae bring this up again. There will never be an alliance between us." His father sank into his chair. "Besides, ye are betrothed to Laird MacLaurey's daughter, Mairead."

Ryan's heart clutched. He was well-acquainted with Conn's sister, older by nearly a year. Mairead had never outgrown her childish resentment of feeling as if she'd lost her parent's favor to their son and heir. Very little pleased her and she'd made Ryan and Conn's lives miserable as lads. Repaying her constant carping with boyish pranks had landed them in repeated trouble.

Had his da lost his mind?

Ryan cleared his throat, alarm drying up all moisture. "Ye cannae be serious."

"Aye. The Macraigs make their own alliances."

"Da, that woman is a menace. I spent ten years around her and I willnae marry the *targe*."

"Ye will. I began negotiations with Laird MacLaurey in the packet I sent with my soldiers who escorted ye home."

"There is no love or even kindness between Mairead and me. I tell ye, I willnae do this."

His da's face contorted with rage. "Ye think to marry for love? I suppose ye have yer eye on Laird Macrory's bastard daughter?" His voice rose shrilly. "She isnae good enough for ye!"

Ryan's face blanched. "What are ye saying?"

"The Macrory isnae her da. She was four when he wed her ma, and Riona wouldnae name the sire."

Ryan's ears rang and his mind faltered at the unexpected, vicious words spewing from his father's mouth. "I would have no trouble choosing between an evil-tongued woman of certain parentage and a sweet-tempered lass without her father's name," he shot back.

"Ye have no choice. Yer betrothed will be here within the month."

Ryan slung his cloak across the room with enough force to send it skimming across the top of the chair to land in a rumpled heap at the foot of his bed.

What the hell was he going to do? Ryan glared at Conn. His friend nudged the door closed with a foot and propped his shoulders against the sturdy portal.

"What has ye more worked up? The fact the Macraigs will have to deal with the pirates on their own, or the fact ye willnae have a chance in hell of seeing the red-headed lass again?"

"Shut up, Conn." As soon as the snarl left his lips, Ryan gestured wearily. "I am sorry. I am not angry with ye. I just need to think." He shoved a hand through his hair. "I dinnae know what to do."

Conn shoved away from the wall and strode to a chair. He folded his tall frame into the seat and propped his feet on the hearth, motioning to a flask on a small nearby table. "Pour us both a drink and sit down before ye damage something."

Ryan stalked to the table and splashed whisky into a mug. He stared into the amber depths for a moment then tossed back the fiery liquid. With a grimace, he prepared a second libation for himself and one for Conn. Sketching a mocking salute with his mug, Ryan downed the contents in one gulp.

"Ye will rot yer gullet drinking like that," Conn observed, raising an eyebrow in mild rebuke.

Heat spread through Ryan as the whisky bounded through his blood. He shrugged, uncaring.

"What did yer da say that has ye so riled?" Conn wondered.

"My sire has seen fit to form an alliance between our clans by marriage."

Conn eyed him askance. "Between which clans?"

"Why, the Macraigs and the MacLaureys, of course."

Conn's eyes widened. "Whose marriage?"

Ryan bit back a curse. "Mine. To Mairead."

Conn gave a low whistle. "And ye agreed?"

"Are ye daft? There are no two people I can think of less suited for marriage." He set his mug on the table with a thud. "I refused."

Conn nodded. "A wise move, but can ye?"

"I willnae wed the *targe*." He cast an apologetic look at Conn. "Ye know how she is. I cannae think a forced marriage to me will improve her disposition."

"Nae. That one needs the firm hand of someone who doesnae know her childhood secrets. Not one of the *pliskie* lads who pulled pranks on her."

Ryan crossed to the bed and flopped face-up on the coverlet with a sigh. "I dinnae expect to talk of marriage so soon. But I offered an alliance between us and the Macrorys."

Conn chuckled. "I can imagine yer da's response to that."

Ryan remembered his da's words condemning Gilda as a bastard, but couldn't bring himself to share the information with Conn. "He wasnae interested in hearing my thoughts on the subject."

On the hearth, the peat crackled and a flame shot into the air. Red and gold lights danced across the worn stone of the hearth, conjuring the memory of Gilda's fiery hair in the moonlight. Ryan's thoughts swept back to soft, pale skin trembling beneath his touch, and trusting, silver eyes as he claimed her lips in a kiss. He groaned.

Two stubborn old men stood between him and Gilda. And to discover his da had signed a contract binding him to Mairead?

Conn rose to his feet and stretched. "Good night, then. I'll leave ye to decide if yer groans are for the thought of marriage to my sister or for the red-haired Macrory lass ye cannae have."

Gilda forced the sweetest smile she could muster, the strain pulling at her cheeks. "Ma, it has been nearly a sennight, and no pirates have been seen. May I please go outside and take Fia for a ride?"

Her mother looked up from her conversation with Cook, a frown on her lips. Gilda took a quick breath, forestalling any obvious denial. "Please, Ma. I will take auld Fergus with me and willnae go far. Just to the beach—I could even visit a bit with Tavia."

The mention of her mother's old nurse had the desired effect. Though Tavia spent a good deal of time at the castle, she insisted her home was the cottage on the beach, and had declared the pirates daft should they think to harm a seer woman. No one had seen Tavia in nearly three days.

Her ma sighed. "Yer da isnae here to decide."

"But Ma, he only said I had to tell one of ye before I left the castle, and with nothing amiss on the borders, surely he wouldnae mind if I left for a wee bit?" Gilda tried for charm, pasting what she considered a winsome smile on her face. She could sense her mother's waver.

A crash of metal and wood on the stone-flagged floor caused everyone to jump. Riona whirled about and Gilda snatched her skirts to one side as two small forms darted past.

"Ye wee *louns*!" Cook shouted, shaking her fist at the lads who chortled with glee, a pastry in each chubby hand. With practiced ease, Gilda and her mother each grabbed a twin by their collar, halting their dash for freedom.

"Lemme go!" Finn twisted in Gilda's grasp. Jamie eyed his mother and dared say nothing.

"Put those pastries…" Riona's gaze lit on the stout fingers buried in the flaky crusts and the purple juices running down the lads' bare arms. She sighed and turned to Gilda.

"Ye may go down to the beach, but ye will take the twins with ye."

Gilda's eyes widened in protest. "But, Ma! Ye cannae be serious?"

Her mother nodded firmly. "Aye. The lads are needing a bit of time away from the castle as much as ye."

What a disaster! Gilda's mind whirled. "It would hardly be fair to ask auld Fergus to mind the lads."

"Fergus willnae be minding the lads. It is up to ye to keep them out of trouble. Fergus has the job of keeping ye safe."

"Ma!"

Gilda followed her mother's attention to the lads who had stopped squirming, their interest on the conversation.

"We willnae get into trouble."

"We want to go to the beach."

Gilda shot her mother a final pleading look, to no avail.

"What pirate would approach ye with the twins nearby?" her ma reasoned, an innocent smile lighting her challenge.

Gilda's shoulders slumped in defeat. "Do I have to bring them back?"

Holding Fia to a slow jog was a supreme act of skill when both horse and rider longed to run. The twins' sturdy ponies trotted gamely behind with auld Fergus's mount bringing up the rear. They passed regular groups of sentries posted along the cliffs above the beach, and Gilda knew more scoured the woods for signs of miscreants. Though she'd been raised on the heart-quickening tales of pirates along the coast, Scaurness was amply protected and Gilda had always felt safe.

Cool breezes off the water lifted her hair and she raised her face to the gentle caress, the sound of the twins' chatter fading blissfully away. She urged Fia into a canter, relishing the cleansing rush of the wind. She leaned forward, strands of her horse's mane streaming over her hands.

"Gilda!"

Reality jerked at her and Gilda wished she could ignore the summons, but she did not want her mother to refuse her request the next time if she vexed Fergus now. With a sigh, she obediently reined Fia to a walk and glanced behind her. To her surprise, Fergus and Jamie were many lengths behind, though Finn's pony trotted hard to catch up with her. She saw Fergus bend over, his hand on Jamie's pony's leg. Had he picked up a stone or done himself a more sinister injury?

Finn pulled his fat pony to a halt. "Jamie's pony tripped."

"Tripped or stepped on a stone?"

Finn shrugged. "I dinnae see. We ran fast as the wind to catch ye."

Gilda smiled at Finn's description of his mount's stubby-legged actions. "Ye spurred him on, aye?"

Her little brother nodded vigorously and patted his pony's stout neck. "Jock is a braw lad, but I'm almost too big for him, aren't I, Gilda?" He cast a hopeful look her way. Gilda lifted an eyebrow and eyed the pair. In truth, Finn's legs no longer stuck out awkwardly over the well-sprung barrel.

"Ye might ask Da about a bigger pony when he gets back," she allowed. Finn shot her a grateful grin, and Gilda was taken aback at the sweetness of his smile.

She turned to Fergus and raised her voice. "Finn and I will look for shells." She pointed up the beach as Fergus straightened to listen. "We will be careful."

Auld Fergus hesitated then waved a hand to indicate he'd heard her. Gilda saw Jamie stomp his foot, but knew Fergus would keep the lad to attend his injured pony.

"Come on, Finn. Let us see what has washed up on shore today."

Lissa's eyes threatened to spill tears down her cheeks. "But, Ryan, ye promised."

She turned a pleading look to Conn, and he fidgeted beneath her gaze.

"Och, take the lass outside. Yer da lifted the ban yesterday, and I, for one, could use the exercise."

Ryan indicated the stairs with a jerk of his head. "Change into something ye can ride in, and be quick, mind ye. We dinnae have time to waste on pampering a lass."

Lissa's face lit with happiness and she sprang up on her toes to give each of them a quick kiss before darting to the stairs.

As she flew up the steps, Ryan turned to Conn with a frown. "Ye seem to champion her whims. Dinnae spoil her."

Conn shrugged. "'Tis easy to say 'aye' when asked so sweetly."

"She is but ten summers and has already learned to twist ye around her finger," Ryan observed dampeningly.

"At least she doesnae carp and whine."

"Aye." Ryan shuddered.

Conn clamped a hand on Ryan's shoulder. "Dinnae worry. If ye have to marry Mairead, ye can still put a few croaking *puddies* in her bed instead of climbing in there yerself."

Ryan knocked Conn's hand from his shoulder with a muttered curse. *"Haud yer wheesht.* I tell ye, I willnae marry Mairead."

"Braw words. I hope ye can keep them, my friend."

Lissa reappeared on the stairs, her boots clattering on the stone. She waved her cloak in the air. "I am coming!"

"Now, watch." Gilda took the smooth, flat stone between her fingers and with a flick of her wrist, sent the pebble skipping across the surface of the tidal pool.

Finn fisted his hands on his hips and scowled. "Why dinnae mine do that?"

"Ye have to pick a flat stone, not the round ones, and toss it sideways. Here. Let me help ye."

Gilda circled, searching for a perfect rock. Movement on the rise behind them caught her attention. Shielding her eyes, forcing her heart to a normal rhythm, she studied the three riders on the ridge. Two were men, their size and bulk unmistakable. But the third appeared small enough to be a child, and Gilda let out a sigh of relief. Surely pirates would not have a bairn with them.

A second look caused her heart to thrum. She shoved a slim rock into Finn's chubby, sand-encrusted hand.

"Go show Fergus yer new trick." Gilda took her brother's shoulders and turned him toward his pony.

Finn's head snapped around, a defiant scowl on his face. "I dinnae want…" His eyes grew round as he caught sight of the three riders coming toward them. "Look!"

Gilda bit her lip. What would she say to Ryan?

Chapter Nine

Ryan's hand tightened on his reins. He knew they crossed into Macrory territory, but he was unable to force himself to turn back. Lissa was charmed by the ride to the beach, and her wind-burned face glowed with happiness.

Conn pulled his horse to a halt. "There are others up ahead."

Ryan nodded as he urged Duer down the sloping bank. He recognized the red-haired lass. "Aye."

Lissa's voice piped up. "Where are we going?"

"To look for seashells." Ryan didn't bother looking over his shoulder. He could feel Conn's disapproving gaze burning a hole in his back. He shrugged off the sensation. Hell, he wasn't the one who'd suggested the outing.

Duer's massive hindquarters lurched side to side as he half-slid down the embankment. Ryan swayed in the saddle, echoing the horse's movements. His sister's voice rose in excitement and he knew she'd spotted people on the beach.

Gilda's thick braid glinted fiery gold as it bounced across her shoulders. She pushed at the lad beside her, but to no avail. The lad drew against her then straightened, and Ryan smiled at his attempt at bravery.

"Who are ye?" the lad demanded.

Ryan reined Duer to a stop and leaned forward, his arms crossed casually across the high pommel of the saddle. "My name is Ryan." His gaze cut to Gilda. Her eyes were round with uncertainty, and he winced. Damn two old men who couldn't see past their feud.

"Ye arenae a Macrory."

Ryan returned his attention to the wee, puffed-up lad before him and slid from his horse. "Nae. But I am a friend."

He heard a dainty snort and flashed Gilda a grin. *That's my lass. Quick-tempered and full of yer own opinion.*

Ryan leaned casually against his horse's shoulder and turned back to the lad. "What is *yer* name?"

"My name is Finn. And ye cannae be a pirate, can ye?"

Ryan heard the half-hopeful lilt in Finn's voice and sighed with exaggeration. "Nae. I am no pirate. I have a sister, Lissa, and a friend, Conn." Ryan gestured to the two behind him.

"Watch what I can do!" With the abrupt decision-making given to the very young, Finn left his defensive posture and turned excitedly to other things. Taking the rock already clutched in his hand, he flung it at the stagnant tide pool. It skipped once, then sank to the bottom.

His hands flew to his hips and he stuck out his chin. "My sister can do it better than that."

The disgust was so evident in the lad's voice, Ryan smothered a laugh and bent to find a rock of his own. "Here, lad. Choose yer rock carefully, then give it a solid toss." With honed skill, Ryan slid his rock through the incoming waves.

Finn's eyes grew wide as the rock made four complete skips before vanishing beneath the foam. "Can ye teach me that?"

Ryan took a step back, aware Conn stood just behind him, and clapped his friend on the shoulder. "Nae. This man is much better at skipping rocks than I am. He is the one ye need to ask."

With a firm, meaningful shove, Ryan forced Conn toward the lad. "Take this braw lad and Lissa and teach them to skip rocks."

Conn brushed past Ryan. "I dinnae know what ye will owe me for this, but ye *will* owe me."

Ryan didn't care. Even if it only lasted a moment, he was again alone with Gilda.

Observing how Ryan smoothly sent the others away, Gilda half-admired his confidence, half-feared he would hear her heart trying to beat out of her chest. She should be angry with him for abandoning her the other night, without explanation or word that he would try to meet with her again.

His gaze drifted over her and she weakened. Utterly boneless and too overwhelmed at seeing him again, she forgave him everything.

Ryan took a hesitant step toward her, a question in his eyes. Gilda smiled and relief washed over his face. His amber eyes danced and Gilda longed to rush into his arms, but the last bit of sanity left to her kept her feet glued to the sandy ground.

"I have missed ye." Ryan's voice pitched low, but Gilda heard every word.

"Why did yer da…?" She hesitated.

Ryan waved his hand in an abrupt gesture. "He is still consumed with anger at being denied his request to marry yer ma. We must talk fast. Do ye wish to meet me again?"

Gilda's skin tingled. "Of course, I do. But—"

"Ye must listen to me, then. Are ye allowed out of the castle without an escort?"

Gilda stole a look down the beach. Fergus stood tall, his gaze fixed on her and the newcomers. He motioned to Jamie and began to jog toward them.

She made her decision. "I can get away. Where?"

"Meet me at the blacksmith's in the village tomorrow just after noon. If ye cannae come, I will be there again the next day, but I cannae say if I can return after that."

Gilda touched his arm, feeling the warmth of him beneath her fingers. She trembled. "I will be there."

Ryan slid his hand into hers and gave it a quick squeeze before he dropped it and strolled casually to where Conn and the children tossed pebbles into the sea. Gilda released a breathless sigh and picked up her skirts to hurry after him.

Finn's voice rose over the sounds of the lapping water. "Watch this, Fergus! I can make my rock skip all the way to those fishing boats!" He threw his pebble in a sweeping, underhanded arc. It struck a partially submerged stone and bounced high in the air again, landing several feet out into the incoming tide.

"It dinnae go so far." Lissa's voice piped scornfully and Finn whirled on her.

"It did! Ye dinnae see how far it went *under* the water."

Gilda grabbed Finn's shoulder, hauling him back from the argument in time to turn a sweet smile on her protector. "'Tis not I who needs watching, Fergus, but this wee *loun* with the atrocious manners."

Lissa gave a regal shrug. "Ach, he is just a lad. I dinnae expect better."

Gilda's smile froze on her lips. 'Twas good the lass dinnae say, 'just a Macrory.'

Fergus ignored the children's banter, his eyes fixed on the two young men. "Where aboots are ye from?" His question rang with challenge, barely civil. Gilda cringed.

"We are from up the coast. 'Twas a pleasant day and my sister had been too long cooped up for fear of pirates."

Gilda flashed Ryan a grateful look for his calm answer.

Fergus' eyes narrowed. "Macraigs?"

"Aye," Ryan answered easily. "I fear we have trespassed. I beg yer forgiveness."

Fergus' gaze scanned the group. With heightened awareness, Gilda glanced around her. Surely he would see little wrong with their innocent conversation? Finally, he advised gruffly, "Be gone back to yer clan's holdings. We dinnae tolerate the likes of ye here."

Gilda's heart fell. What would Fergus say to her ma?

"He is not like his da." Gilda struggled to keep her tone light.

Her ma sighed. "It doesnae matter. He isnae welcome at Scaurness."

Gilda swallowed her dismay. Truth, she'd expected that sort of reply, but she'd hoped, oh, how she'd hoped her ma would understand.

"I dinnae meet him on the beach on purpose." But, heaven help her, she planned to meet Ryan at the blacksmith's tomorrow.

"Mayhap not. But 'tis not the point. Yer da would have a fit if he knew ye were friendly with Laird Macraig's son."

Gilda shrugged and looked away, trying for nonchalance. "Och, he showed Finn how to skip a rock, and his sister seemed nice."

"Gilda. I know ye think it would be good for the clans to end their feud. The Macraigs were offered a chance and not only dinnae take it, but were arrogant about their refusal. Dinnae push this."

Lifting her gaze, Gilda met her ma's concern. "I know why ye and Da dinnae like the Macraig laird. 'Tis because he wanted to marry ye but dinnae want me because I am a bastard."

Her ma gasped, one hand flying to her throat in an astounded gesture. "Gilda! Ye must never say such a thing!"

"Och, I know Da has never treated me as such, and I thank ye for not marrying Laird Macraig. But 'tis the truth, though it was harsh of him to demand ye give me up."

Tears glistened in her ma's eyes and Gilda ran to her. She threw her arms around her waist and gave her a fierce hug. She leaned back in the circle of her mother's embrace and peered at her.

Her ma seemed to hesitate some before she stated, "Yer da has had an offer of marriage for ye."

"Really?" Gilda tried to ignore the sudden hole that bore through her stomach. "Why dinnae he say something to me?"

"He hasnae come to grips with the young lady ye are becoming." Her ma smoothed back a curl from Gilda's face with a wistful smile. "He still thinks of ye as his wee Gilda."

"I am not a bairn anymore."

"I know. If he takes the offer seriously, he will talk to ye."

"Who was it from?" As apprehensive as she was, Gilda couldn't stop the curiosity spreading through her.

"Laird Maclellan on behalf of his son."

Gilda wrinkled her nose, her brows furrowed in distaste. "Laird Maclellan makes me feel *eerysome*."

"I agree he is a bit overbearing. But he is a powerful man and wouldnae be laird if he was soft and not respected by his enemies."

"I dinnae want to marry his son."

"Och, I should not have told ye he spoke to yer da. 'Twill only worry ye."

Gilda chewed her lip. "I love ye, Ma. I am glad ye told me. I promise I willnae worry."

"Good." Her ma pressed her cheek then released her. "Now, help me find yer brothers. I must get them washed for supper. I dinnae know how they can get into such messes in such a short amount of time."

"Aye, I will help ye. And tomorrow I need to take Fia to the village blacksmith to have a shoe checked. I think it is loose."

"Why not have the blacksmith here take a look at her?"

"I thought I would visit Anise, too."

Her ma frowned. "I dinnae know what yer da would say."

Gilda remained silent. She knew exactly what her da would say.

The noise of the busy village grated on Ryan's nerves. He was tested in raids and skirmishes with clans bordering the MacLaureys, and he recognized the fine lashes of tension racing through his veins as he awaited Gilda.

Chickens squawked noisily in their wooden crates and pigs herded down the narrow street grunted a low baritone. A high-pitched squeal jerked Ryan's attention from the blacksmith's shop. There, just within sight, was a glimpse of red hair amid the throng of villagers, and his heart leapt at the sight. His gaze followed the flaming beacon through the crowd, and he sighed with disgust as a young lad, his arms laden with a stack of fresh-cut peat, proved to be the owner of the brilliant thatch of hair.

A horse nickered behind him, much too close. Ryan whirled, tension fleeing as he encountered Gilda's sweet smile.

"Ogling boys, are ye?"

Ryan gave her an abashed grin. "I thought 'twas ye."

Her eyebrows rose in challenge. Ryan's gaze slid from her dancing eyes to the slender white column of her neck and the deep neckline of her simple, blue dress.

He shook his head slowly. "Nae. The hair may have been the color of yers, but the body could never match."

A pink flush rose from the scooped neckline and Ryan gave a nod of satisfaction.

"Ye are still a rogue, Ryan Macraig."

"'Tis why ye agreed to meet me." Ryan's eyes locked on Gilda's and they stared hungrily at one another.

Her horse snorted and stomped a foot, breaking the spell. Gilda laid a settling hand on the horse's shoulder. "Let me turn her over to the blacksmith. She may have a loose shoe, ye know."

Ryan gestured for her to lead her horse to the open stall. Heat billowed in palpable waves from the fire pit. He watched Gilda tie her black mare to the post and exchange words with the blacksmith. The burly man gave a curt nod of understanding.

A moment later, Gilda rejoined him. "I have a friend I want ye to meet."

Ryan frowned. "I dinnae come here to meet yer friends."

Gilda tugged his hand, her eyes slanting in promise. "Ye will like this one."

Ryan allowed himself to be led to a tiny cottage on the edge of the village. Gilda rapped once on the door then entered. He ducked his head to avoid hitting the low lintel and blinked against the interior gloom. Peat glowed in a fireplace against one wall, and a petite young woman stared at him with an assessing look.

Gilda gripped his hand tighter. "Anice, this is Ryan." She turned her gaze to him. "Ryan, this is my best friend. She has given us permission to stay here and talk to avoid meeting anyone from the village who might know me."

Ryan heard her subtle stress on the word *talk*, and fought the question on his tongue. Did she really think they would sit and chat like a couple of silly girls?

He dragged his attention to her friend. "'Tis my pleasure to meet ye, Anice. I am grateful ye would give us a wee bit of privacy to *talk*."

The lass didn't seem impressed. "I have known Gilda since we were bairns. I trust ye to treat her honorably."

"Of course. She has my very highest regard."

Anice turned to Gilda, her eyes flashing as she tossed a saucy look at him over her shoulder. "Ye watch yon rogue. He doesnae deceive me."

Ryan held his tongue as Anice and Gilda embraced and tried not to be concerned as they each whispered in the other's ears. Judging from the heightened color in Gilda's cheeks, she dinnae think they were here to *talk*, either.

With a last pointed nod at him, Anice collected her woolen plaide from a hook by the door and left the cottage, closing the door firmly behind her. Gilda turned to him, and he was staggered at the open adoration on her face. And the hesitation.

Spreading his arms wide, he beckoned her, and to his delight she required no further urging. She darted across the floor, trusting him to catch her as she flung herself against him. He crushed her slight body to him, savoring the slender curves that fit against him so perfectly. Her arms wound tight around his neck and he nuzzled her hair. Gilda tilted her face to him in invitation, and he met her lips with his. Her fingers tangled in the hair at his nape. Chills raced up and down his spine, fueling his passion as he deepened the kiss, splaying one hand across her buttocks as he pulled her closer.

Gilda abruptly stiffened in his arms and reality washed over him. She may have confessed to being nearly seventeen years old, but she was clearly overwhelmed by such a raw show of passion. Ryan took a deep breath and allowed her take a half-step back.

He bent his head to hers, their foreheads touching. "I have missed ye badly."

Gilda gave a shaky laugh. "I thought I missed ye more."

"Mayhap we should sit, but I confess I dinnae want the table between us." He scanned the cottage but found nothing suitable for sitting but the oversized bed in the corner of the room. Not at all proper.

"Mayhap we could sit there," she gestured with her chin.

Surprised to see her nod at the bed, he realized she was much more naïve than he thought. Ryan stifled a groan. The lass would be the death of him.

"Let us try the edge of the hearth." He lifted an eyebrow in a wry smile. Gilda gave a startled gasp, turning wide grey eyes on him as realization dawned.

Mayhap she isnae so naïve after all. Just inexperienced. Satisfaction shot through him. He liked that notion.

The hearth was swept clean, but Ryan grabbed a folded blanket from the foot of the bed to cushion the hard stone. Gilda's smile of thanks was all he required. He sat next to her, their hips and thighs touching. Heat flared instantly between them.

He picked up one of her hands and twined his fingers through hers. "I apologize for my da's behavior the other night. I had no idea he would react as he did."

Gilda shrugged. "We cannae spend our time apologizing for our parents. We would never get to anything of importance."

"What is important to ye, Gilda?"

With a gentle gesture, Gilda swept the backs of the fingers of her free hand across his cheek and leaned forward to brush her lips in their wake. "This."

Chapter Ten

$\mathcal{A}$ knock at the door signaled their time was at an end. Gilda hastily shrugged the shoulders of her gown into place, but could not bring herself to leave her half-reclining position against Ryan's side.

Anice peeked around the door before stepping inside the cottage, and Gilda waited for the censure she felt sure to see in her friend's expression. Anice's brown eyes glittered as she took in the sight of them snuggled comfortably side by side on a thick blanket on the narrow hearth, the bed untouched.

Her lips curved in a gentle smile. "I need to see to Colin's supper."

With an effort, Gilda pushed away from Ryan, uncurling her legs. She stood, tugging on his hands until he, too, rose.

He dropped a quick kiss on her nose and turned to Anice. "I return Gilda to yer keeping. She is verra precious to me and I would ask ye protect her."

Anice nodded her agreement, the need to keep silent about their meeting obvious.

Pushing aside the dismay welling at Ryan's imminent departure, Gilda faced him with a brave smile. "I will miss ye."

"And I will miss ye, Gilda."

"When can I see ye again?"

"I will try to come tomorrow. Do ye think ye can manage?"

"Aye." Gilda stepped into his embrace. The gentle noises Anice made as she prepared the evening meal faded into the background. Gilda's world became the beat of Ryan's heart, the horse and leather scent of him, and the feel of his finely woven plaide beneath her cheek. Warmth from his arms surrounded her and she would have been content to stand there forever.

"I must leave, *a stor*."

My darling.

She nodded and reluctantly drew back. "*Graim thu*."

I love you.

The ride to Scaurness Castle was a blur as Fia picked her way home without Gilda's guidance. Her thoughts were a blissful haze as she recalled the sweet heat of Ryan's kisses and the slow burn of his lips against her skin. She tingled in places she'd never considered before and had a much greater knowledge of his restraint as she wondered what it would be like for him to touch her in those forbidden places.

Her cheeks heated as she handed Fia to the stable boy, certain he could see a change in her. But he merely yawned and stumped away, obviously annoyed at being woken from his nap. Gilda slipped inside the castle, falling once more into her dream-like state as she contemplated the feel of Ryan's hands on her breasts.

"Gilda! There ye are! Ye must wash and change quickly. Supper is almost ready."

Gilda snapped back to the present. Her ma made shooing gestures at her, a frown on her face.

"I will wash and be right back down," Gilda replied, unsure what the fuss was about. Her ma didn't usually demand she change her gown for supper.

"We have visitors, Gilda. Hurry. There is a bath waiting for ye."

A bath? Warning bells went off in Gilda's head. "Who are our guests, Ma?"

Her ma gave a thin smile. "Laird Maclellan and his son are here."

The outer bailey was nearly empty, most of the familiar crowd hurrying for their supper. Shadows lengthened and the glow of torches brightened the walls of Ard Castle.

"Ye are completely out of yer mind."

Ryan whirled. Conn, directly behind him, pulled up short.

"I dinnae ask for yer opinion," Ryan growled. "Keep it behind yer teeth or I will see that ye do."

Conn shook his head. "She is a comely lass, I will grant ye that. But ye are obsessed with her. No good will come of it."

Ryan stiff-armed his friend, shoving him backward. "I told ye to keep yer opinion to yerself. I willnae tell ye again." His voice was heavy with warning.

Conn brushed Ryan's hands away with an upward sweep of his arms as he advanced. "Ye *amadan*. Yer da will kill ye, and her da will castrate ye."

"I dinnae dishonor her."

"I will bet ye came close."

Ryan slid his sword from its sheath. "Shut up, Conn."

Conn's hand went to the hilt of his own sword. "Make me."

Steel hissed against leather as Conn drew his weapon. The pair circled slowly, warily, blades black in the evening shadows.

"Ye are as testy as an auld boar. Find a willing wench and be done with it. Leave the Macrory lass alone," Conn warned.

Ryan's eyes glinted dangerously. "Why should ye care? Do ye want her for yerself?"

"Dinnae be daft. I dinnae want the lass. Ye are betrothed to my sister."

Ryan lunged at Conn. The move was expected, and Conn slipped easily to the side. They parried, the ring of steel loud in the crisp evening air. At last they fell back, breathing deeply. Conn rotated his arm in a wide circle, rubbing his shoulder. Ryan brushed a hank of hair from his forehead.

"Ye want me to marry Mairead?" he panted.

"I dinnae want a knife in yer back from Gilda's da."

"I suppose being knifed by yer sister is a better idea?"

The absurdity of Ryan's predicament struck, and Conn sheathed his sword. "I cannae kill ye. Though ye may not appreciate my kind gesture in the future. What are ye going to do?"

Ryan frowned. "I must convince two stubborn auld men to end their feud."

"How do ye plan to do that?"

"I have no idea."

"Laird Maclellan?" Gilda's voice rose in pitch. "Ye said Da would talk to me before he signed a betrothal contract!"

"Wheesht, Gilda. Yer da dinnae ask them here. I would guess a betrothal is on their minds, though it could as easily be the pirates."

Gilda forced herself to calm. "I cannae marry him."

Her ma sighed. "Gilda. No one is asking ye to marry the lad tonight. Come to supper, be pleasant, talk to the lad. Ye may like him."

Mutiny and desperation set Gilda's jaw.

Her ma flung up her hands. "Fine. Mayhap ye willnae like him. He seems over-quiet, though that may just be a natural response around his father." Her ma shooed her once again toward the stairs. "I can send Kyla up to attend ye."

Gilda understood the threat for what it was. "Nae. I can dress myself."

She hurried down the corridor, not to obey her mother's command, but because her world was crashing around her and she needed sanctuary. She managed to make it without encountering the twins, and slipped inside her room, latching the door firmly behind her. On a sudden sob, Gilda slid to the floor, tasting salt as tears ran down her face.

What was she to do? She did not want to sit at the table and smile and pretend nothing was wrong. She especially did not want to smile at the silent, *feartie* lad or his overbearing father. Gilda hiccupped on a breath at the thought of the huge man as her father-in-law. Surely, her da wouldn't marry her to a man whose father frightened her?

Her thoughts turned to Ryan. She loved everything about him. His easy smile, his quick wit—though he used it to vex her often enough. It was exciting to be in his arms, to savor his kisses. She shuddered. Never could she allow the Maclellan's son to touch her in the ways Ryan had.

Gilda swiped the back of her hand across her face, using the fabric of her sleeve to dry her tears. She would wait and see what the Maclellans intended. If they proposed a betrothal, she would simply tell her da she was not interested. Should they be here to talk of the pirates, she would have worried about nothing.

Taking a deep breath, Gilda rose and stripped away her gown, stepping into the lukewarm water of her bath. It was too late to wash and dry her hair, but the bath refreshed her and she felt confident again as she dressed in a thin woolen gown of peacock blue with a modest neckline and simple, fitted sleeves. She braided her hair and let it hang down her back, unwilling to waste time on a more elaborate style. There was no one downstairs she wished to impress.

Fergus met her at the head of the stairs as she left her room. "Yer ma is waiting for ye."

Gilda smiled at the old man, knowing he deserved her respect, not her pique at being summoned before their guests like a horse her da wished to sell.

"I am hurrying, Fergus. We dinnae want to be late for our meal."

She suited her actions to her words and lifted the hem of her skirt as she increased her pace. The sounds of mealtime in the great hall were nothing out of the ordinary, but as she entered the room, one look told her there was very little normal about this gathering.

The hall was dim as Ryan made his way to the kitchen in search of a bite to eat. His dalliance at Scaurness had meant missing his supper, but that did not bother him. There would be enough tucked away in the larder to fill his belly, and, to his surprise, he really wasn't that hungry.

His mind was full of Gilda's sweetness, and he absently tucked a wedge of cheese and a chunk of bread into a linen napkin as visions of unbound red hair and pale, glowing skin slid through his memory. Half of a small pastry sat on a platter, and Ryan added that to his haul. A corked bottle of ale completed his search, but he had to shift the pastry to his mouth to manage everything.

He turned, halting in surprise. His da stood in the doorway, a disapproving look on his face.

"Where have ye been?"

Ryan placed the bottle of ale back on the table and removed the pastry from his mouth, setting it aside. "I have been exploring."

"There is so much to explore in the hamlet ye cannae make it home in time for supper?"

"Several things occupied my time."

His da stared at him for a long, uncomfortable moment. "Lissa says ye took her riding yesterday."

"Aye."

"And ye met Macrorys on the beach."

"A lass and her brother. Aye, they were Macrorys."

"A crofter's lass doesnae have a soldier for a guard."

"I dinnae say she was a crofter."

Laird Macraig exploded. "Dinnae play games with me! Ye are betrothed to Mairead MacLaurey and ye willnae disgrace this clan by consorting with the Macrory bastard!"

Ryan dropped the linen napkin. The cheese and bread tumbled unheeded across the table. He advanced on the older man. "Ye willnae call Gilda a bastard again. Neither in my hearing nor out of it." He stopped just a step distant and pointed a finger at his sire's chest. "I willnae marry Mairead MacLaurey. She is a complaining *besom* who will make her husband's life a constant misery. And ye will treat *whomever* I marry with the utmost respect, be it Gilda Macrory or another."

His da drew back. "Ye are a disrespectful lad."

"Nae. I give ye the respect due ye as my sire and as laird of this clan. It doesnae mean I always agree with ye."

Laird Macraig snorted. "I have signed the contract."

"*I* havenae signed it. And I willnae."

Ryan waited, breathless, for his da to speak again, but the man seemed deflated, his bluster gone. Repacking his dinner, Ryan nodded. "Good night to ye."

"I hope there is a flask of whisky in that bundle."

Ryan jumped. Conn pushed away from the shadows of the hallway and strolled alongside.

"I heard yer discussion with yer da."

Ryan looked at the items in his hands. "Damn. I forgot the pastry."

"'Tis whisky ye need, not sweets."

"Ye are most likely right. But I was all set for a nice pastry."

"Will he cease harping on the Macrory lass?"

"The bigger question is, will he stop trying to foist yer sister off on me?"

Conn nodded. "Aye. That needs to be stopped. Mayhap he will send a rider before they leave home. 'Twould do no good to give her the sad news after she is already here."

Ryan stopped at his doorway, a pained expression on his face. "Do ye have any happy thoughts to impart, or do ye just want to go away now?"

Conn thought for a moment. "I will get the flask of whisky from my room and come back. Ye will need it."

The head table had been rearranged to accommodate the guests. Rarely did her da seat guests on the dais with the family. Gilda's gaze slid to her chair and the golden-haired boy seated to her right. Her chest grew tight in panic. The space left for her was too small, too close to the Maclellan heir.

Her gaze flew to Finlay, her da's captain and her own trusted confidant since she was a small child. The kind look on his face nearly undid her. Even Finlay knew why the Maclellans were here.

"Here is my daughter." Her da's voice pierced the fog surrounding her. "Come, Gilda, and take yer seat. We are nearly starved waiting on ye."

"Starved, but not parched!" Laird Maclellan's laugh boomed heartily and he raised his goblet. "'Tis a fine wine ye serve at yer table, Laird. After supper, ye will break out yer best whisky, aye?"

Gilda halted her steps. Did the man expect to toast the betrothal? Or was he just looking to indulge in her da's well-known drink?

"Come, lass. Take yer seat." The Maclellan motioned her forward and Gilda moved to her chair. Casting a wary eye on the lad next to her, she tucked her skirt close and slid her chair beneath the table.

"Should have held the chair for her, ye wee *loun!*" the Maclellan announced with an air of disapproval. The lad's cheeks flushed and he gave Gilda a sullen smirk of apology.

"My son, Boyd. A fine young man he is. Scarcely a year older than yerself, lass, and already has the lasses at home eating out of his hand." Laird Maclellan's laugh burst forth again, perhaps a bit forced.

Gilda lifted an eyebrow at the way Boyd Maclellan hunched in his seat, his gaze on his plate as he studiously avoided looking at her.

"Sit up, lad, and hand the lass some food. She needs some meat on her bones," the Maclellan snapped.

Somehow Gilda managed to make it through the meal, though the food stuck in her throat and she changed her wine for clear water to wash it down. At last the servants began to clear the dishes away. Gilda's heart pounded too quickly, the moment of truth imminent.

With an explosive, rolling belch, Laird Maclellan pushed from the table and sprawled in his chair. "Laird, I would like to continue our discussion from the other night. The pirates seem to have disappeared from the coast, and it is time to speak of more weighty matters."

"I think I told ye my daughter is not yet of an age for marriage."

"Nonsense. Why, look at her. Too thin, of course, but good hair and skin, and of a good size for breeding."

Gilda heard the collective intakes of breath around her. To her left, her ma shifted in her seat and laid a hand atop hers, grasping her fingers.

"I think the men would be more comfortable in my husband's private chamber. I will send a servant with whisky," she said.

"Good idea! Fine woman ye married, Laird. Knows just what to say." Laird Maclellan rose to his feet. "Show me the way. Business *is* private, ye know."

The room emptied except for the few servants clearing the supper remains. Gilda peered at the young man at her side. He was tall and lanky, unlike his sire, though muscles bunched and smoothed in his arms as he moved platters about on the table. A sullen look on his face caused Gilda's fervent hope her da would simply decline the Maclellan laird's betrothal suggestion.

Silence between them lengthened and Gilda fidgeted in her seat. She struggled for something to say, finally mumbling, "Ye look to be verra tall."

Boyd turned. His brown eyes bored into hers, sending a chill down Gilda's spine. "Ye are verra pretty."

Gilda flinched at the monotone voice. "Dinnae say that."

Boyd slouched in his chair. "My da told me to say it."

Gilda edged away from him. It was apparent he was no more interested in a betrothal than she. Given the conversation taking place behind closed doors between their fathers, she was not sure whether to be alarmed or relieved.

"Boyd, do ye really want to get married?"

He scowled. "Nae."

"Why not?"

"I have a lass at home. She is verra nice and treats me well." Boyd's eyes raked over her. "I like a willing lass, and one who doesnae mind if I stray a bit."

Gilda's eyebrows lifted in disbelief. "A man could wake up missing vital parts with an attitude like that."

Boyd sat straight in his chair, his face reddening. "Ye think to threaten me? My da—"

"Yer da is a bully and so are ye."

"I am not a bully."

Gilda sent him a chilling glare and leaned close so he could not mistake her words. "I think ye are, and I wouldnae marry ye if ye were the last man on earth."

"Och, so the bairns have made friends?" Laird Maclellan boomed as he entered the hall. Gilda jumped at the sound of the laird's voice and landed back in her seat.

The laird gestured with a beefy hand. "Come, lad. We will rest and take our leave in the morning."

Gilda glanced at her ma, a shadow in the doorway behind the men. Her spirits rose. Had they not reached an agreement? She frowned. Laird Maclellan was taking his disappointment, if indeed it was, too well. There was no toasting, but no disgruntlement, either.

What had her da promised?

Chapter Eleven

$\mathcal{R}$yan cast a critical look at the sky. Clouds rolling in from the sea cloaked the late afternoon sun. His ride home looked to be dark and wet.

Where was Gilda? He battled back his irritation. There was nothing he could do if she was detained at the castle. In truth, he missed her with a ferocity that amazed him. He'd clung to his temper with an iron fist this morning until he finished taking care of clan business with his da and could slip away to see her again.

Damn. There was much for him to do tomorrow. He couldn't dodge weapons practice every day, and someone was bound to become suspicious if he was unavailable for hours every afternoon. He couldn't risk coming back tomorrow. Ryan chaffed at the empty feeling stretching his insides, knotting him until he could no longer sit still.

"She is late?" Anice queried.

From his vantage point on a stone bench near her front door, he could see much of the narrow trail wending to the village, but no sign of Gilda.

He shoved at his hair in frustration. "Aye."

Anice stepped outside. "She would be here if she could."

"I know. It doesnae make the wait any easier."

"Nor the disappointment."

Ryan stared at the young woman. "Why do ye do this for us?"

Anice smiled. "Because she is my best friend, and I want her to be happy. I have seen the way ye look at her, the way she lights up when she is around ye. I believe ye could make her verra happy."

"I love her. I dinnae know how much longer I can tolerate meeting her like this."

Anice's laughter bubbled. "Ye have just met her here the once."

"Aye. And it nearly tore my heart out to leave her then."

The young woman sobered. "Will ye take her to wife?"

"Aye. 'Tis my plan."

"What will ye do about her da? He isnae likely to give permission."

"I would do nothing to estrange her from her family, but if necessary, I would marry her without her father's blessing." *She isnae likely to receive a blessing from* my *father, either.*

He searched once more down the village path and was again disappointed. With a sigh, he rose. "If she comes here, tell her I am sorry I missed her. I will send word to ye when I can return if ye think ye can get it to her."

Anice nodded. "I will see she receives yer message."

Ryan untied Duer from the post. Checking the cinch on his saddle, he led the horse past the cottage and into the cover of a grove of trees. He gathered the reins and placed one hand on the pommel, the other on the cantle as he prepared to mount.

"Ryan, wait!"

He whirled at the sound of Gilda's voice in time to catch her as she hurtled into his arms. He hugged her to him, glad he had waited as long as he had. He felt her body tremble against him, and it was several moments before he realized she was crying.

Anice handed Ryan a cup of water. He nodded his thanks and offered it to Gilda. She leaned her head against his chest, cuddled in his lap, her arms wrapped around him.

Anice walked across the room, picked up her arisaid, and draped it over her shoulders. "I will fetch more water. I think I will walk all the way down to the burn."

Closing the door softly behind her, Anice left them alone in the cottage.

Ryan set the mug on the table. "Tell me again what happened."

Gilda took a shuddering breath. "Last night Laird Maclellan brought his son to the castle to talk to Da about a betrothal between me and Boyd. When their meeting was over, the Maclellan seemed to be neither cheerful nor angry, and Da didn't say anything to me. I thought Da had put him off again."

"The Maclellan had approached yer da before?"

Gilda nodded. "The night of the clan meeting. Ma said he dinnae want to talk about a betrothal because he dinnae think I was old enough to wed."

"Something changed his mind?"

"Mayhap he realized I will be seventeen tomorrow." She shrugged. "I dinnae know what happened. But this morning Laird Maclellan insisted I take his son for a walk through the gardens before they left. And then…"

Gilda turned her face into his chest. Ryan stroked her hair, absently fingering the wayward strands poking out of her braid.

"Da took me to his office and told me he had considered the Maclellan's offer and it was a good match. He wanted to know what I thought."

"And ye told him." Ryan sighed. "Did ye not consider what his reaction would be when he discovered we had met?"

"Oh, Ryan, what will we do? He sent me to my room and I had to wait forever until he and Ma were closed in his private chamber before I could slip away. They will soon realize I am not there and come looking for me."

"Do ye think they will come here?"

Gilda nodded her head. "Aye. I have visited Anice several times in the past week."

"They will assume it was to meet me. We must decide what to do, and quickly."

"I willnae marry Boyd."

"Ye dinnae have to, *a stor*. Ye will marry me."

"Truly?" She leaned back, tilting up her face, hope in her grey eyes. "How? When?"

"As soon as I can find a priest." He crooked a finger beneath Gilda's chin, bringing her gaze to his. "Do ye trust me, Gilda?"

Her eyes widened and she nodded. "I do."

"Then come with me to Ard Castle. Marry me."

Gilda's face clouded and Ryan knew the implications sank in. "Ye will leave yer family. They willnae like this and mayhap will even be angry with ye. Can ye trust me to love ye through this and wait for yer parents to understand?"

For a breathless moment Ryan thought she would not do it. Then she relaxed and touched her hand to his cheek.

"*Graim thu*, Ryan."

He took her hand and kissed it then pressed it to his heart. "As long as I live, ye will want for nothing. This I swear to ye."

Gilda smiled and his doubts fled.

Candle flames flickered in the draft as Ranald spun about, the sweep of his plaide billowing as he paced. His footsteps pounded the floor and Riona fancied the solid rock walls shook.

"What was she thinking?" His low voice growled the much-asked question, and Riona sighed.

"She wasnae purposefully disobeying. Ye hadnae told her not to speak to the Macraig's son."

"She should know better. There is no alliance between our clans."

"Aye. But there is no feud, either."

Ranald shot her a furious look. *There is now.*

Riona left her seat and crossed the room to stand before her husband. She placed the palm of one hand gently against his chest and looked into his stormy eyes. Slowly, she fingered the length of plaide draped across his chest until she felt some of the tension leave him.

"Did ye really want Gilda to marry the Maclellan lad?"

Ranald narrowed his eyes. "His clan is powerful."

Riona raised her eyebrows, but said nothing.

"The Maclellans have been staunch allies."

This time Riona tilted her head.

"Damn it, Ree, I am new at this. I wouldnae marry her to the first man who offered for her. But it was an honorable proposal."

"But ye dinnae expect her to fancy herself in love with a young man ye consider the least suitable for her, either."

"Laird Macraig is not a good man. As overbearing as the Maclellan is, at least he is respectable." Ranald stroked the back of his hand down her cheek. Riona leaned into the caress. "Macraig insulted ye and Gilda both with his marriage proposal."

Riona nodded once. "'Twas years ago."

"The man still holds a grudge."

"'Tis apparent his son doesnae."

Ranald's hands cupped her face, tilting it to his. Eyes the color of the sea at night stared back at her. She leaned up on her toes and pressed a kiss against his lips. Tension of a different sort hummed through him now, and Riona wound her arms about his neck.

"I sent Finlay to retrieve Gilda from her room," Ranald murmured against her lips. "Mayhap we could explore this more fully later?"

The chamber door burst open behind them. Finlay's face was pale and strained.

"Gilda is gone!"

The first raindrops fell before they reached the edge of the forest. Gilda stopped and pulled the edge of her arisaid over her head. Thunder rumbled and Gilda grabbed at Ryan's outstretched hand as though she were drowning.

He urged, "Can ye make it?"

The old childhood fear clutched her as lightning flashed in the distance, but Gilda nodded bravely, her throat too dry to speak.

"We will mount up now we are out of sight of the village. 'Tis over two hours of hard riding to Ard Castle from here, and with us both on Duer's back, 'twill take longer."

Ryan's warhorse was much larger than Gilda's dainty mare, and Ryan's hand splayed against her bottom as he boosted her into the saddle. Heat slid through her, overriding her fear of the storm. Before she could remark it, Ryan was behind her, urging Duer on.

Water slid down the leaves and dripped off the edge of Gilda's arisaid. Warmth from Ryan's arms around her helped, but the cold, driving rain soon saturated her cloak and seeped through her gown. She shivered and clenched her teeth to keep them from chattering, wishing they could travel faster than the slow pace the storm demanded.

Duer reared in fright as lightning flashed with a loud crack of thunder. A nearby tree toppled, crashing through the underbrush with a great swoosh of sound. The acrid odor of smoke filled the air. Ryan's arms tightened around Gilda.

He soothed the big horse, but did not send him forward. Gilda peered into the storm-fed gloaming. A small red glow lit nearby, evidence of the lightning strike.

"The rain will put out the fire, but we need to find shelter." Though he spoke into her ear, Ryan raised his voice to be heard over the deluge. Gilda grasped her arisaid close around her and nodded. She was cold and wet and frightened. This was not how she had envisioned starting her life with Ryan.

"Where is that cave?"

Taking a moment to get her bearings, Gilda blinked through the rivulets of water streaking her face. She pointed to their right, her directions leading them to the shallow cavern they had sheltered in more than a sennight ago. Ryan swung down, lifting his arms to help her dismount.

"I will tie Duer. Get inside."

Gilda brushed aside the heavy branches covering the entrance to the cave. A musky odor assaulted her and she hesitated. Listening intently, she gave her eyes time to adjust to the darkness, but could detect nothing in the gloom save a couple of large rocks. The wind howled, driving Gilda inside. She stood just beyond the opening, hesitant to go deeper.

"Is anything wrong?"

Gilda jumped at the sound of Ryan's voice. Her hand shot out, fumbling for his. His fingers twined with hers and she felt immediate relief.

"It smells like a wild animal has been here." Ryan took a step further. "I dinnae see anything now. Sit here. I will find some dry wood for a wee bit of warmth."

The dusty rock floor was dry, but cool, and Gilda gathered her skirts and arisaid beneath her to cushion her against its chill. Sounds of the storm echoed eerily around the cave, and Gilda focused on Ryan gathering bits of bracken and limbs in the mouth of the cave, which had avoided most of the rain. He reached inside his sporran and pulled out a tiny handful of delicate tinder, then piled the smallest twigs around it on the floor near the cave's opening.

"Some of this is still a bit green and may smoke, but it will hopefully drift outside." He produced a bit of flint and steel and within moments, a small flame licked hungrily at the wood.

"I will be back in a moment." On his promise, he disappeared through the entrance. Gilda scooted close to the small fire and stretched her hands to its meager warmth. Encouraged by the heat, she shrugged out of her arisaid and unlaced her sodden gown. She stripped to her shift and spread her gown over a small boulder to one side of the cave. Hurrying back to the fire, she huddled close, carefully feeding it small, dry twigs.

She looked up as Ryan entered the cave, his arms laden with firewood. He pulled up short and Gilda smothered a smile at the startled look on his face.

"I am warmer without the wet clothes."

She thought he replied, "Me, too," but he'd turned away to stack the wood on the floor.

He indicated one of the piles. "I found some of this beneath an old, rotted log. It is fairly dry, and the rest will dry enough to burn in time."

Ryan pivoted slowly and Gilda's heart fluttered at the hunger in his eyes. He shuddered.

"Are ye cold?" she asked worriedly.

His lips twitched, but his voice was solemn. "Nae, Gilda. But I wish we had consulted a priest before we fled the village. I dinnae expect to encounter a woodland faerie on my way home."

Gilda was at a loss at what to say, unaccustomed to the banter between men and women. Yet his words warmed her better than any wood-stoked fire. Memories of the way her ma and da touched, the way their eyes lit when they entered a room to find the other there, raced through her mind.

Here was the same look on Ryan's face as he stood silent, watchful. It occurred to her he awaited her answer.

"I am not a woodland faerie, but I will soon be yer wife," she whispered.

His eyes darkened and his breathing deepened, but he made no move toward her. "I will wait 'til then, *a stor*, if it is yer wish."

Unsure of all he meant, Gilda did know if he stayed where he was, he would not be able to kiss her. She felt the absence of his arms around her like a physical ache. If he would simply hold her, kiss her...but no, there was something different, deeper, more elemental, exciting. Her skin tingled and her breasts swelled against the confines of her thin shift. She glanced down and saw her nipples clearly outlined through the damp cloth. Embarrassed, she lifted her gaze and saw Ryan eying them as well.

"Ogling me again?" she whispered.

"As often as I can." Ryan's voice was hoarse and the sound sent a shiver down her spine.

"Will ye come sit with me?"

"Gilda, *a stor*, I cannot be that close to ye and not touch ye. Ye have promised to be mine, but we havenae the vows between us."

Silence stretched as the wind tossed the storm outside to new heights.

"We could make our own vows." The words trembled on her tongue.

Ryan skirted the small fire and knelt beside her. He took one of her hands in his and brought it to his cheek.

"Gilda Macrory, *thabharfainn fuil mo chroí duit.*" *I give you the blood of my heart.*

"Ryan Macraig, t*ugaim mo chroí duit go deo.*" *I give my heart to you, forever.*

"I pledge my love to ye, Gilda, and everything that I own. I promise to honor ye above all others, and we will remain, forevermore, equals in our marriage. This is my vow to ye."

Gilda felt a moment of panic. She had nothing to offer him. The clothes drying near the fire were all she now owned. She had even left her fine mare in the stable in her haste to be away.

"I have nothing to give ye, Ryan."

"*A stor*, ye have given me everything. I am humbled ye left yer family and trusted me enough to own yer heart. Nothing I possess, now or ever, could measure greater."

Gilda leaned forward, touching her forehead to his. Tears brimmed in her eyes and tightened her throat. "I pledge my love to ye, and everything that I am. I will honor ye above all others, and it will be into yer eyes I smile each morning. I will love and cherish ye through this life and into the next."

Ryan tilted his head and she eagerly sought his kiss. His hands moved over her bare arms, igniting heat beneath her skin. Her lips parted and their tongues twined in a feverish dance that swept through her, punctuated by the thunder and lightning as the storm raging outside became a poor imitation to the one inside the cave.

She swept the wet cloak from his shoulders and tugged at the leine tucked beneath his belted plaide. Ryan sucked in a breath, allowing his leine to pull free, and Gilda slid her hands beneath the cloth. His skin was cool but warmed instantly, and she twisted her fingers through the wiry hair on his chest.

"*A stor*, ye must slow down. I dinnae want to hurt ye."

Gilda stilled her hands. "Ye wouldnae hurt me."

Ryan's laugh was rueful and he ran a hand caressingly down her shoulder and along the curve of her breast. Fire ignited again and Gilda gasped.

He kissed her cheek. "I wouldnae harm ye for the world, but this first time we go slow, aye?"

At Gilda's hesitant nod, Ryan leaned back on his heels and stared at her for a moment. "Do ye know what happens between a man and his wife?"

"I have seen, that is, horses and cattle... And my ma told me what not to let boys do."

Ryan grinned and Gilda's heart tripped. He rose, extending a hand toward her. His strong fingers curved about hers, pulling her to her feet. He leaned her against his body and she felt the same hard planes of his chest and thighs she had the day before. Even the hard ridge pressing intimately against her belly was familiar, though he had not let her explore that much of him then.

He kissed the side of her face, his lips soft, the caress fleeting. He moved down the column of her neck and Gilda arched into the caress, closed her eyes, and let him touch her, too mesmerized to move.

"Ye can touch me, too," he murmured against her skin as he slid his hands beneath the straps of her shift, moving them over her shoulders. The neckline dipped low and Gilda's eyes flew open as warmth slid across the top of her breasts. Ryan bent his head and she watched his hands brush the fabric aside, then his mouth closed over one exposed nipple. The gentle tugging nearly buckled her knees, and he slid one arm around her waist, supporting her.

Gilda's hands caught at his leine again, this time tugging impatiently until she slipped it over his head. She stared at him, her fingers splayed across his chest, reveling in the sight and feel of his body. His hands roamed over her, lifting her breasts to his hungry mouth once again. Her hands dropped to his waist and the leather belt fastened there.

With clumsy fingers, she managed to undo the clasp and pull it free. His plaide hovered a moment on his hips then slid to the floor. His cock, fully erect and straining toward her, was bared to her gaze. She couldn't keep from gaping.

Ryan pulled her against him, and the heat of him burned through her shift. "Worried, *a stor*?"

"Nae. But I dinnae know how this will work. What does it feel like?"

Ryan choked. "I will unwrap my leggings while ye slip out of yer shift. Then we will see to yer curiosity. It will work, I promise."

Chapter Twelve

Ryan's blood shot like fire through his veins. Every fiber of his being pulsed with anticipation. His trembling fingers loosed his leggings, needing no instruction from his brain. His attention focused solely on Gilda.

Her body glowed, a pale beacon in the murky cave. Firelight licked across her skin, tinting it honey and amber. Her shift slipped down, revealing more as she let it drop. Ryan's mouth went dry.

"Ye are so beautiful."

A pink blush raced across her skin.

"Dinnae be embarrassed, *a stor*." He straightened and took her in his arms, the warmth of her crackling against him. "Ye are mine and mine alone." He kissed the top of her head, then tilted her so he could see her face.

Thunder boomed and startled her.

"The storm cannae touch us. Come with me." He gave her hand a quick squeeze. "I will be embarrassed if ye think on the storm overmuch."

Ryan settled them on the ground, cushioned by their mingled cloaks. He rolled to his side, facing her, and Gilda's exploring fingers became a sweet torture. She draped a leg over his, bringing their bodies as close as possible, pressing against his cock until he thought he would expire. He rolled her gently onto her back and hovered over her, letting cool air pass between them as he battled back the hot desire raging in him.

She whimpered and stretched her hands to him.

"Ye will be the death of me, Gilda." He smiled at the look of surprise on her face. Grasping her wrists, he placed them over her head. "Leave them here for a bit."

"This is no fun." Gilda wiggled her fingers.

"Then place yer hands on my shoulders."

Her fingers curved around his upper arms as he nudged her knees aside, giving him room to kneel between them. He leaned over her and kissed one breast. His tongue swirled around her nipple and drew it into his mouth, tugging gently until she moaned. Moving to the other breast, he let his hands drift down her sides, across the prominence of her ribs and to the soft skin of her belly. She released a shuddering gasp as she shifted on the bed he'd made of their clothing.

Ryan released her breast and nuzzled her neck. "Still no fun?"

Her breath quickened, giving him the response he sought, and he smiled as he splayed his hands down her abdomen, brushing the soft hair between her legs. Her thighs clenched, but could not close with him positioned between them.

He held her gaze. "Do ye want me to stop?"

Gilda shook her head, meeting his gaze as her teeth caught her lower lip. "I want to be yer wife, *mo chroí*."

Ryan kissed her and she trembled as his fingers slid through the damp curls beneath his hand. She moved against him, meeting his demands with her own until she tensed and cried out, surprise in her voice. Ryan gently released the grip of her hands from his arms and Gilda stared at him in wonderment.

He smiled. "Ye can touch me now."

Her breathing slowed and she looked at him with renewed interest. Ryan closed his eyes as her hands found him, running over the taut lines of his body, lifting her head to tease his hard, flat nipples with her teeth.

With a groan, he lowered his body to hers.

Riona's hand flew to her throat as Ranald flung himself toward the door. "What do ye mean Gilda is gone?"

Finlay lifted an eyebrow. "Gilda isnae in her room. I have asked about the castle, but none have seen her. Her horse is still in the stable."

Ranald whirled to confront her. "Do ye know where she could be?"

Riona blinked, her thoughts jumbled, struggling to remain calm. "Gilda has spent time with Anice in the village in the past few days."

"With that bastard Macraig, no doubt!"

"Ranald!"

"She deserves better than him."

Riona placed a steadying hand on Ranald's arm. "Mayhap she has gone to Tavia's for a good cry."

Ranald glared at her then turned to Finlay. "Go to the seer's and search for her there. I will go to Anice. Dinnae raise an alarm."

Finlay clapped Ranald's shoulder in a reassuring grip. "We will find her."

Riona looked at the men's grim faces. *Yes, but before it is too late?*

Even with the small fire, it was cold in the cave, and Gilda shivered. The corner of her arisaid had slipped to the side, leaving her backside uncovered. Her front was pleasantly warm, curled against Ryan's side, his arm holding her protectively close. The evenness of his breathing told her he still slept despite the howling winds outside.

She reached behind her, careful not to disturb Ryan, and fumbled for the edge of the woolen cloth. It evaded her fingers, and she wriggled, trying to bring it within her grasp. Ryan's arm tightened and her gaze flew to his face. A smile curved his lips, the glimmer of passion stirring in his amber eyes.

"Yer arse is cold."

"Aye. I lost my covers."

Ryan's hand splayed across her bare bottom. "I know an excellent way of warming it if ye've no objection."

Gilda pressed closer, liking the way his breath hitched. "Och, none at all."

The candles guttered, the flames licking low. Riona stared at the tiny fires, scarcely heeding as one winked out. Outside, she could hear the storm raging off the sea, winds battering the stone walls, seeping into the room through the shuttered windows, lifting the tapestries in a ghostly dance. Caught in a draft, another candle went out.

She shuddered to think of Gilda out in the storm, of all of them at the mercy of the fury of gale-force winds and driving rain. She knew Ranald and Finlay would not return until they found her, and even if the storm halted their search, they would endure the weather until they could continue.

Would they reach Gilda before she arrived at Ard Castle? What would be the cost of her happiness? Long ago, Riona had offered her life for Gilda's, and she would not hesitate to do so again, but she had given her promise to trust Ranald years ago, and she must await the outcome.

She hated waiting. Riona resumed her pacing.

When Gilda next woke, Ryan leaned over her, his amber eyes alight. "The storm is dying. We must be away."

Gilda gave him a sleepy smile. "I dinnae want to leave yet."

"We must, *a stor*. If for no other reason than I am fair certain yer da is searching for ye."

Gilda sat abruptly, grabbing for her shift. If her da was to find her, she much preferred meeting him fully clothed. Ryan donned his own clothing and stamped out the last embers of their small fire. Gilda finished dressing and stepped to the cave entrance, wishing a moment of privacy. Her low shriek brought Ryan bounding to her side.

"What?"

"Look." She pointed to the disemboweled remains of two rabbits just inside the opening to the cave. "Where did they come from?"

Ryan pushed aside the bracken framing the entrance and gave a short grunt. "I believe yon is the culprit."

Gilda peered past him. Feral eyes gleamed from a shaggy face. "'Tis my wolf!"

Ryan chuckled. "Yer wolf? Aye, it seems he returns yer kindness. Do ye think this is one of his lairs?"

"'Twas probably what we smelled when we came here last night." She turned to Ryan, her eyes wide. "Duer?"

Ryan cursed and darted past her into the misty darkness, ignoring the wolf.

"Shame on ye if ye have frightened his horse again," Gilda told the animal. The wolf quirked his head at her. Gilda stared into the heavy mists after Ryan. Movement in the underbrush caught her ear.

"I thank ye for yer offering, but I cannae take time to cook this morning." With a smile, Gilda stepped past the wolf. Ryan appeared but halted some distance away, Duer at the end of his lead, his ears laid back in disagreeable temper.

"He willnae come closer."

Gilda ran to Ryan and he helped her mount. He sprang onto Duer's back behind her and pulled her close. "Tonight, *a stor*, ye sleep in a real bed."

"As long as ye are with me, it matters not where we sleep."

Ryan clucked to Duer, sending him into the dense fog.

Ranald swore loudly. The storm had erased all evidence of a trail. He knew Gilda and Ryan headed for Ard Castle, but he'd wanted to find them before they got there, hoping they'd been forced to stop and shelter along the way. Riding to the stark walls and demanding his daughter back was not his first choice.

Finlay's muffled voice drifted to his ears. "I cannae see in this fog."

"Nor I. 'Tis nearly as thick as the rain."

"Aye, but without the wind driving it."

"It matters not. I fear we spent too much time waiting the storm out."

"Dinnae *fash* yerself, Ranald. It wouldnae have helped to send the horses crashing over the edge of a cliff while we blundered about in the rain."

Ranald reined his horse to a halt at the edge of a small glen. "Here." He fingered the splintered edges of a broken branch. "They rode this way."

Finlay nodded. "'Tis not likely any others were out in this."

Ranald dismounted, handing his reins to Finlay. He eyed the dangling branch. "Mayhap he tied his horse here." Slowly, he turned, his sharp eyes missing nothing. He knelt and touched his fingers to the grass.

Finlay leaned forward. "Leaves were stripped from the branch. Do ye think something startled the horse?"

Ranald stared at the churned mud. Shredded leaves littered the ground. His horse snorted and tossed its head. Was that *something* still here? He stared into the underbrush, but the mists hung heavy in the trees, obscuring everything more than a few feet away. He stood and stepped to his right.

"Over here," he called. Leaving Finlay to see to the horses, Ranald slipped noiselessly into the bracken.

The musky odor of something wild reached his nostrils. Ranald froze. Ahead, something blacker than the pre-dawn darkness loomed. He took a cautious step forward, pushing aside the tangled brush as he entered the cave.

"Here is what likely spooked the horses." Returning to the small clearing, Ranald held up the remains of a partially-eaten rabbit, the blood dry on its pelt. His horse snorted as if in agreement.

"Supper?"

"Nae likely. Even a skilled hunter couldnae catch rabbits last night. This is too fresh." He tossed the carcass into the brush. "I would have said 'twas a wolf's lair, but I found the ashes of a fire inside."

Finlay nodded. "Mayhap they sheltered there and left before the wolf returned."

Ranald raised his gaze to his friend, a bleak expression on his face. "The ashes were scarcely warm. If Gilda and Ryan sheltered there, they are at least an hour ahead of us."

He took his reins and swung up onto his horse, wheeling it in a tight circle. "We ride to Ard Castle."

Gilda clung to Ryan, swaying with the rhythmic motion of the galloping horse as it broke the shelter of the forest. The pink light of dawn gave them confidence, but great clouds of mist boiled up from the ground, obscuring the path before them.

"Look! Ard Castle."

Ahead loomed the walls of the castle and Gilda drank in her first sight of her new home. The stone, wet from the night's rain, glimmered pink and yellow in the early morning rays. Torches, their flames blending into the growing light, winked from the heights. Men, black stalks against the pearl-hued sky, strode the ramparts.

Wind tangled loose tendrils of hair across her face, and Gilda brushed them away.

"A Macraig!" Ryan's cry whipped across the ground, alerting the guards. They clustered above the gate, and the sound of the portcullis being lifted screeched in discord.

Suddenly, Ryan stiffened and Gilda turned her head. Caught in the streaks of sunlight piercing the mist, two riders rode hard after them, stretched low against their mounts' necks.

Gilda could not see their faces, but she recognized them, nonetheless.

Her heart leapt to her throat.

Finlay and her da.

Chapter Thirteen

Gilda grabbed frantically at Duer's reins. "Stop! Stop!" Her voice sounded shrill and wild as she tore her look from the two men racing toward them to the castle guards, their bows raised and ready. "Dinnae let your men hurt them!"

Ryan reined the horse to a skidding halt and Gilda flung herself to the ground, stumbling as she landed.

"Gilda!"

She heard Ryan's voice, but did not falter as she fled headlong toward her father. Her breath hitched as she ran and she tensed for the hiss of loosed arrows from the archers on the walls of the castle. The big horse slid on his haunches as her da hurtled from his saddle. She found herself in his arms, his protective grip choking the breath from her.

"What the hell were ye thinking, lass?" His voice, gravelly and deep, betrayed his fear for her, but did not mask his anger.

Gilda tore from his grasp and swept a lock of hair from her eyes, giving him a defiant stare. "I cannae marry Boyd."

"We will speak of this later." Her da reached for her, but she took another step backward.

"I cannae go back with ye, either."

He gave her a thunderous look. "Ye can and ye will."

Gilda shook her head, her throat tight as she fought tears that threatened. "I cannae. I am wed to Ryan. My home is with him."

She felt a presence behind her and saw her da glance over her shoulder. A hand gripped her arm with firm reassurance.

Ryan's voice was steady. "We are committed to this, Laird."

"Committed? Who gave ye permission to commit yerself to my daughter? Tearing her from her home and family is no way to start a new life together."

"Da, I…" She whirled to Ryan. "I want to stay with ye." Her eyes pleaded with him even as her da's voice rose behind her.

"Gilda. Come home with me and let us discuss this."

She confronted Da, bitterness in her words. "Like we *discussed* my betrothal to Boyd?"

He winced. "I willnae ask ye to marry him."

"Will ye bless my marriage to Ryan?"

His jaw clenched and Gilda saw a dark flush of anger cross his face. "I cannae."

Gilda's chest tightened and she clung to Ryan's hand. "Then, I cannae return with ye."

"Dinnae do this, Gilda. I am taking ye home, but I would prefer ye come willingly."

Ryan pressed her hand as he drew her close. "Nae. Ye willnae take her against her will. She is my wife."

Ranald shrugged off Finlay's hand the moment the big man's grip loosened. He watched Gilda and Ryan enter the castle gates, then turned and mounted his horse. Without a word, he yanked Hearn's head around, kicking him to a run toward the forest trail. The two men rode in silence, neither sparing his mount as the wind whistled angrily and the forest swept past them.

Ranald's horse stumbled, exhausted from the punishing speed. Scaurness Castle loomed ahead and Ranald finally slowed him to a walk.

Finlay pulled alongside. "Ye would rather she watched ye die beneath their arrows?"

Ranald set his jaw and said nothing.

"Threatening the laird's son would have been all the provocation they needed," Finlay added.

A flash of anger infused Ranald's blood and heated him almost beyond endurance. He squared his shoulders and kept his hands firm on the reins, resisting the urge to smash his fist into something hard. Finlay's jaw was a tempting target.

The man would not take the hint. "Have ye thought what ye will tell yer wife?"

Ranald leveled his gaze on Finlay. "'Twould be best if ye stayed out of my sight for a bit."

Finlay lifted an eyebrow. "Aye. Mayhap I have saved yer life one too many times."

"Ye are my friend, but I dinnae like ye right now."

"Fair enough. Though I still believe Lady Riona will thank me for bringing ye home alive."

"I dinnae think so." Ranald lifted his sights to the tower beyond the castle gate where his wife waited. He felt Gilda's absence with a bleak hollowness and fear of Riona's reaction for his failure to bring her daughter home.

A shout went up from a guard at the wall. The muffled sound of well-oiled chains followed as the portcullis rose. Ranald rode into the bailey and left his lathered horse with a stable lad. Taking a deep breath, he strode into the great hall.

Riona lingered on the stair, the strain of the past hours evident in the taut lines of her body as she stared past him. Her anguished look rushed back to his face, a question silently asked and answered. Gilda was not with him. Ranald gave her a short nod and she turned and climbed the stairs with a faltering step.

He entered their bedroom behind her and closed the door. He looked around the room, seeing it in a haze of suspended reality. How could things appear so normal with Gilda gone? Everything lay in its place, the coverings smoothed across the bed, blankets folded neatly at the foot. At the window, sunlight streamed through the green glass, falling to a colorful muddle on the wooden floor. Even with the cheerful denial of the stormy night just past, a chill gripped Ranald's heart.

"She is at Ard Castle?"

Ranald turned to his wife, startled at the brittle, hopeful sound to her voice. He crossed the floor to her, cursing himself for his blunder.

"Gilda is fine." He took Riona in his arms and held her as choked sobs burst from her. Stroking her hair, he murmured reassurances in her ear.

"She and the Macraig lad sheltered in a cave. We caught up with them on the approach to the castle."

Riona sniffed and wiped her face with the apron tied about her waist. "I am sorry. When I dinnae see her with ye I was afraid... Why did she not return with ye?"

"Our Gilda is in love with the lad and he has made her his wife."

"In truth?"

"They havenae faced a priest, but she is his wife."

Riona drew away and stepped to the window. She unfastened the clasp and swung the panes open wide. Silent, she stared into the distance.

Ranald moved behind her. "I was about to force her home, but the lad showed a bit of backbone." He shook his head. "If Finlay hadnae intervened, I would have accepted the challenge."

Riona did not answer. Ranald placed his hands on her shoulders and gently turned her to face him. "I would have earned her lasting hatred and started a verra short battle and a bitter war. The archers on the wall had their bows trained on us." He hesitated, then sighed. "Finlay thinks he did the right thing, stopping me. I am not so sure."

Riona cupped his cheek in her palm, gentle love showing behind the sheen of tears. "I am."

Ryan dismounted and helped Gilda down. Her body trembled and he grew alarmed by the pallor of her skin. He wrapped an arm about her waist and led her forward. "Are ye ready, *a stor*?"

Gilda nodded but did not relax.

The door to the hall opened and Laird Macraig strode through, his boots beating an angry tattoo on the hard ground. He stared from Ryan to Gilda and came to an abrupt stop, rocking back on his heels in surprise.

Ryan stepped before him, tucking her against his side. "Da, welcome my wife, Gilda."

The laird's face paled. "What have ye done?"

At a hard glare from Ryan, his sire snapped his mouth shut and drew back. "We will discuss this in my chambers." He raked Gilda with a contemptuous stare. "Yer betrothal to Mairead will need to be addressed." With that parting shot, he pivoted and stormed into the castle.

Gilda squeezed Ryan's hand and a rush of harsh color stained her cheeks. "What did he mean, your betrothal to Mairead?"

"It means nothing, *a stor*. 'Twas the wish of a foolish auld man, not mine."

"Was there a contract between ye?"

Ryan stifled his impatience. "My da signed the contract, but I dinnae."

Gilda's eyes widened into a look of dismay. "Och, Ryan. What have we done?"

He touched her shoulder, wincing as she flinched at his touch. "Nothing matters except we are together. Dinnae worry. Everything will be fine."

He could tell by the hurt in her eyes she did not believe him.

Gilda allowed Ryan to lead her into the castle. Stares from the people they passed seemed overly curious to her tightly strung nerves. Her headlong flight into Ryan's arms on the heels of her da's furious tirade the day before had seemed so unerringly right. Now, amid strangers and the reality of leaving her family behind, her stomach churned and she could not focus on anything more than placing one foot before the other.

"Gilda."

Ryan's voice echoed fuzzily in her head. She peered at him and realized she stopped at the foot of the stair.

He gave her a reassuring smile and cocked his head. "Our room is up two levels. Will ye walk with me?"

She stared at the stone staircase, the handrail a heavy rope clinging to the wall on her right, the left side open. It was nothing like the airy, carved wooden stairwell at Scaurness, with the upper stories open to the great hall below. Ard castle was built solely for protection and defense, its starkness cold and unwelcoming. She placed a foot on the first riser and nodded.

At the curve in the stair, the walls of the castle enclosed the stairwell and a shudder ran through her. Here, no light other than torch flame lit the way. Sinister shadows danced on the walls as she and Ryan passed each flickering blaze. Four doors faced the hall and Ryan led her to the second one.

"This is our room. That one is Da's. My sister claims the one on the end, and Conn has this first one."

"There are only four bedrooms?"

"Nae. There are chambers for guests in the south tower, but they are little used. Castle workers either sleep on pallets on the floor in the great hall or have a cottage nearby."

"'Tis a very old castle, then."

"Aye. 'Tis more of a fortress, but there are plans to have an addition built soon." He opened the door. "We will be comfortable enough until then."

Gilda stepped across the threshold and glanced about the room. Tapestries hung on the walls as they did at Scaurness, lending the room color and warmth. Two narrow windows along the far wall admitted little light, their function defense. But a wider window was glazed with green glass and sunlight forced its way past the thick panes. Gilda crossed the room and released the catch to open the window. Sunshine broke free to warm her face and she stared out to the bailey below. People moved about much as they did at Scaurness and she was comforted.

Turning to the room, she warmed further at the sight of the large bed against an inner wall, its curtains drawn aside to reveal the soft, inviting pile of furs and woven coverings. She bit her lip and shifted her gaze to the other items in the spacious room, the large chest at the foot of the bed, the two comfortable chairs flanking the hearth, and the low table nearby.

"I will have another chest brought to hold yer clothing and such. 'Twill be no problem to have dresses made for ye. My sister, Lissa, will be happy to help ye."

"How do ye know she will like me? Yer da doesnae."

"Lissa is a sweet child who will be glad to have a sister to talk to, though she is enough to try the patience of a saint."

Gilda twisted the fabric of her skirt between her fingers. "But yer da doesnae like me."

Ryan sighed. "He still harbors a grudge against the Macrorys. Ye must nae let him worry ye."

Gilda's eyes burned with tears and she blinked furiously to hold them back.

Ryan rushed to her and folded her in his arms. "Och, Gilda. Ye dinnae think it would be this way."

"I dinnae know how much it would hurt to refuse to go home with Da. I am so confused."

"It will take time. 'Tis my hope ye will feel free to visit and talk to yer parents soon."

His words, meant to comfort, tore at Gilda's heart. *I miss my ma and my da.* She clenched her teeth to avoid saying the words aloud. She wanted to be Ryan's wife more than anything in the world. But the price was tearing her apart.

Ryan found Conn in a corner of the great hall, nursing a hunk of bread, a cup of water at his elbow.

Conn waved him to a chair. "Have a seat. I am afraid this is all that is left."

"Nae. I cannae linger. Da is waiting for me."

"Ye have a lot to account for."

"It will work itself out. She is my wife and nothing can change that."

Conn frowned. "She dinnae look well."

"She and her da had words, and she is remembering she is his daughter."

Even with Gilda's protestation she wanted to be with him, would she change her mind and want to return to her family? Emptiness clenched his gut at the thought. "We will make the marriage binding with witnesses as soon as possible."

"Ye havenae already seen a priest?"

Ryan glared at his friend. "Nae. The storm caught us and we were forced to shelter in a cave. We pledged to each other then."

Conn snorted. "I told ye 'twas a bad idea the first time ye went to the cave with her. Now ye are marrit, yer da is angry, as is her da, I have nae doubt. My sister will be unhappy, even if she had no intention of going through with the wedding, and yer wife doesnae appear too pleased with her decision, either." He rose to his feet and shrugged. "Nae. Ye should have left the Macrory lass alone."

"Cease yer harping about Gilda. She is my wife and I willnae hear a word against her."

Conn's eyes widened in surprise. "I think ye foolish to have married the lass, but I mean no disrespect to her. I knew she would bring trouble from the first time I met her, but I hoped ye would keep things in check. I meant nothing more by it."

Ryan bit back his retort, aware his warning to Conn was groundless. His friend would be civil to Gilda, perhaps befriend her when he got to know her. "I am sorry. I am overprotective," he admitted.

Conn nodded. "Accepted. Ye best go placate yer da. I believe I see smoke seeping beneath yon door."

Ryan glanced at the closed door of the laird's private chamber. "Aye. It willnae be to his liking, but 'twill be the last time he speaks to me of a betrothal to Mairead."

A gentle knock sounded at the door. Gilda crossed the room and cracked open the portal. A sweet face with amber eyes and long black hair stared back at her, and Gilda recognized Ryan's sister.

Gilda opened the door wider. "Come in."

Lissa came inside, a young woman in her wake, a stack of clothes in her arms. Lissa perched on the edge of one of the chairs, her head cocked to the side as she studied Gilda.

"This is Keita." She gestured to her companion. "She will be yer maid."

Gilda stared at the dour-faced woman. "I have no need for a maid. I can care for myself."

Keita's chin lifted. "Ye are Lady Macraig. I will tend yer needs as bid." She placed her stack of clothing on the bed and rummaged through it before holding up a gray gown, eyeing first Gilda then the gown, as though to determine its suitability.

As Gilda pondered the need for a surly maid, Lissa's voice piped in. "Ye are the lass from the beach. I knew Ryan liked ye."

Gilda lifted an eyebrow at the girl's matter-of-fact statement. "How could ye tell?"

Lissa waved her hand dismissingly. "Och, he has worn a *soor* face the past few days and 'twas easy to tell something was wrong. He lit right up when he saw ye and made Conn take me down the beach with yer little brother. He wanted us out of the way, ye know."

Keita thrust the gray gown beneath Gilda's chin, tsked her disapproval and returned to her task. Gilda gave a wan smile and sighed.

Lissa sat back in her chair, an earnest look on her face. "Do ye not like being marrit to my brother?"

Gilda peered at the girl. "Och, I like yer brother verra much, and I like being marrit to him, but I miss my family."

"Ye did marry quickly," Lissa agreed solemnly.

"My father is verra angry with me. He wanted me to marry to benefit the clan. But I couldnae marry someone I dinnae love. Not after I met Ryan."

The girl nodded slowly. "I think 'twould be difficult to love someone and be marrit to somebody else."

Gilda felt a sharp pain stab her chest and she forced a light laugh. "Och, Lissa! Ye are much too young to be worried about such. I am sure yer da will marry ye to a fine man."

"Mayhap. A laird's daughter doesnae often get to plead her case."

"Ye are verra wise for yer age."

"Will ye stay here and be my sister?"

Gilda started at the change in subject. "Ye think I will leave?"

"Well, ye seem verra sad. If ye miss yer family enough, would ye go home?"

Gilda bit her lip to forestall the tears. "I dinnae think I can go home, now."

Chapter Fourteen

Ryan raised his fist to knock on the door to his father's chamber but hesitated. *This cannae go well.* With a scowl, he rapped his knuckles on the portal, the heavy thud echoing in the hollowness of his gut.

"Enter."

He released the latch and opened the door. The room was bathed in the light of too many candles, he recognized at once as their cloying scent reached his nostrils. His gaze moved to the single slitted window on the far side of the room and noted the tapestry partly blocking the opening.

"Sit."

Ruffled by the terse single-word command, Ryan pulled his attention to his father and sat as bid. The scrape of the chair's legs on the stone floor echoed in the silence. His father's steely gaze flared across the table. With conscious effort, Ryan held his tongue.

"Ye couldnae keep yer hands off the Macrory's daughter, could ye?"

Ryan gritted his teeth, hating being on the defensive. "'Twas not like that."

His father rose to his feet, his hands flat on the table. "How was it, then, lad? D'ye not know ye dinnae have to marry every lass who lifts her skirt for ye?"

Ryan bolted to his feet. "Ye willnae talk about her like that!"

"And what, me lad, do ye think will happen when Laird MacLaurey discovers ye have broken the betrothal with Mairead?"

"I dinnae want a betrothal to the *besom*!"

"I willnae have that pirate's bastard in my castle!" the laird thundered.

Ryan's breath expelled in a whoosh of disbelief. "How can ye hold this over her head? None of it was her fault."

For a lingering moment, Laird Macraig glared at Ryan across the table. His eyes bulged, distorted with his rage.

Ryan feared his da had gone quite mad.

Gilda rounded the final turn in the stairwell and stopped, her fingers clenched about the rope railing. A shout of laughter and answering response punctuated the murmur of voices in the hall. On the far side of the room, the double doors were open wide, and midday light streamed within.

At her side, Lissa tugged her hand. "Come. Ryan will be waiting for ye."

"I wish I had not agreed to come down for dinner."

"Och, ye will be fine. Ye look grand in that gown. Ryan willnae be able to take his eyes from ye."

Gilda turned her attention to the pert girl at her side. "Ye are entirely too young to be saying such things."

"Ye must come down or Ryan will come looking for ye."

"Then, let us go." She touched a hand lightly to her hair, resigned to the wisps of curls already escaping from the tight braid. She and Lissa entered the hall and conversation ground to a halt as heads turned in their direction. Her gaze went unerringly to Ryan, who leapt to his feet and hurried to her side.

He took her free hand and raised it to his lips, his eyes questioning. "Are ye well?" His voice was pitched low.

Lissa squeezed her other hand before she slipped away to her seat. Gilda scarcely noticed her absence. Ryan's attentions filled her with warmth and her cheeks heated. "I am always fine when I am with ye."

Ryan took a step toward the head table, keeping her hand firmly in his. "Come. I will introduce ye."

Her warmth fled. These were people foreign to her, a clan at odds with her own, and unprepared for the fact their laird's son had married against his father's wishes. Gilda's heart pounded and her bravery slipped a notch. Within moments, she was the center of uncertain attention.

Ryan faced the room. She refrained from leaning into him, certain it would appear she feared their scrutiny. It would not do to be seen a coward. If she truly wanted to be Ryan's wife, she would take the title as Lady of Ard Castle and all else her new life entailed. She fancied Tavia's voice in her head. *'Tis an ill bird that fyles its ain nest.* She lifted her chin and hid the turmoil inside.

No, she would not start her marriage with cowardice in the eyes of her new clan.

The bedroom was dim, lit only by several candles, their wicks burned low. Gilda gasped and stuck her finger in her mouth. Her eyes watered and she quivered between exhaustion and anger. She hated sewing, hated her needle-pricked finger, hated the uneven stitches even she could tell needed to be pulled out and redone.

Wed less than a day, she felt abandoned by her new husband.

She pulled her finger from her mouth and examined it with a critical eye in the light of the candle on the table at her elbow. A tiny dark spot marked the needle's entrance, but the injury was, in reality, slight. She set her sewing aside and climbed wearily to her feet. The clanging sounds from the practice field had ceased hours ago as the men hurried inside for their supper. Then, just as quickly, they were gone as news of the pirates interrupted the meal.

The usual nighttime noises drifted from the bailey below, none bringing news of the soldiers' return, and Gilda did not know if she would see Ryan this night or not. Was he safe? Would he return to her?

The door latch rattled softly and she whirled.

Ryan stood in the doorway, a surprised look on his face. "I expected ye to be asleep." He tossed his plaide to a chair and opened his arms.

Gilda rushed to him, wrapping her arms about his waist as she buried her face against his chest. His embrace tightened and her fears fled. His kisses rained on the top of her head and she tilted her face to receive them properly. He was as hungry for her as she was for him, and within moments she was naked beneath him, the soft furs on the bed sleek against her back.

She clung to him, demanding he claim her, wanting to know, in the deepest part of her, if his need was as great as hers. His splayed hands warmed her, set fire beneath his touch. His name escaped her throat on a harsh cry and her nails dug into his flesh as passion swept through her.

Ryan shuddered over her, his breath a groan torn from his chest.

His breathing slowed and he lowered his head. Gilda tasted ale on his tongue as it played lazily with hers and she twined her trembling arms about his neck.

He turned his attention to the curve of her ear. "I wish I could have been with ye all evening." He pushed his hips against hers, sparking another tiny jolt of passion through her. Gilda gasped and wriggled. Ryan chuckled. "But this wasnae a bad welcome, at that."

She considered a swat to the side of his head for his impertinence, but hesitated, amazed at how boneless she felt. Perhaps he didn't deserve the swipe after all. She ran her fingers through his hair instead. "Yer hair is damp."

"Ye would have noticed earlier if ye hadnae been so eager to get me into yer bed." Ryan's teasing voice made her smile.

She tugged gently at a dark lock in reprimand. "And ye stopped to eat."

"Nae. I grabbed a draught on my way through the hall. My only appetite was for ye." Ryan moved against her and she felt him grow hard again.

His rhythm increased and she gave herself up to the sensations building inside. He took his time, nibbling along her sensitive skin, taking her to the brink of pleasure before changing direction, leaving her clinging to him in breathless anticipation. At last he joined her, pushing her over the edge of passion.

Ryan rolled onto his back and slid an arm beneath her shoulders. "Put yer head on my chest, *a stor*."

Gilda nestled against him, the thud of his heartbeat loud in her ear. With a sigh of contentment, she closed her eyes and drifted off to sleep as his fingers moved soothingly up and down her back.

Gilda's hand spread across the pillow beside her, startled to find it empty. She sat up, no longer sleepy, and peered about the room. Sunlight spilled pale through the window, illuminating dust motes dancing midair. The peat fire lay banked on the hearth, glowing embers marking where it smoldered. Ryan was long since gone.

She pushed the blankets back and swung her feet over the edge of the bed. Bracing against the impact of the cold floor, she darted to the hearth, snatching her shift from the back of a chair to slip it over her head. Shivering, she perched on the warm stones next to the fire, her feet tucked beneath the hem of her shift, and stirred the embers to life. The growing flames warmed her and she basked for a moment as the morning chill became a fleeting memory.

Yesterday seemed very far away. Though Ryan was again gone— she was foolish to think he could spend every waking moment with her—she did not feel the ravages of leaving her family as much this morning, not after the night she'd spent in Ryan's arms.

She bit the inside of her lip as a wave of longing passed through her. Would her life be like this forever? Nights of passion followed by long hours of waiting for Ryan's return? She sighed. There had to be something she could do to keep busy. Anything that would take her mind off her husband's absence even for a little while.

Well, anything except sewing.

The pattern of sunlight shifted to the floor and Gilda surfaced from her reverie. A soft knock sounded on the door and she slipped across the room to answer the gentle summons.

Lissa's smiling face met hers. "Are ye awake, then?"

A disapproving voice drifted from behind Lissa. "M'lord said ye werenae to be disturbed, but this one said ye might like a bath."

Gilda looked past Lissa to the frown on Keita's face. She smiled through her pique at the dour woman. "That would be lovely."

She opened the door wider to admit Lissa and Keita and two lads laden with pails of steaming water. Behind them, two more lads hefted a small wooden tub.

"Most bathe in a room behind the kitchen…" Censure sounded in Keita's voice.

"'Tis no problem for ye to bathe in private, Gilda." Lissa's firm voice cut through Keita's sullen announcement.

Gilda shook her head. "I can bathe same as the others."

"I am sure 'tis only right ye bathe in privacy." Keita sniffed. She turned and planted her hands on her hips as the lads upended the buckets, splashing water on the floor. "Ye wee *louns*! Dinnae make such a mess. Practice is what ye are needing. Go fetch another round of hot water."

Gilda stared at Keita. The woman might not like her, but she was certainly used to her orders being followed. Could she change her hostility into, if not friendship, at least a truce?

"I thank ye for a chance to bathe this morning. I am afraid I slept later than I am accustomed to. 'Twas a busy day for me yesterday." Gilda saw the other woman's lips twitch.

Could Keita be tempted to smile? Perhaps it was too much to expect so soon.

The lads returned in haste with their buckets of hot water. Keita watched critically as they emptied them into the tub. With a curt nod she dismissed them and latched the door. "Into the tub with ye, m'lady. We havenae got all day."

Gilda slipped out of her shift and slid into the water. She closed her eyes as the heat ebbed through to her bones.

Lissa handed her a square of fabric. "Here is a cloth and some soap I brought with me. Ryan bathes either downstairs or at the barracks."

Gilda mused over that bit of information. She wiggled her toes, dismayed to realize the tub was too small to consider adding Ryan. Heat licked her ears and cheeks. Perhaps that line of thought should be aside for a bit—especially with Ryan's little sister near.

Instead she queried, "What are the men about this morning, Lissa?"

The girl perched herself on the edge of a chair by the hearth. "Ryan is out on a patrol. The pirates were pushed back to the water yesterday, and havenae been seen since. Da insisted they double all patrols on the beach."

Gilda nodded. "A wise move. My da…" She stopped a wave of longing sweeping unexpectedly through her, firmly tamping it down. "My da will likely be doing the same."

She quickly finished her bath, though she would have enjoyed a quiet soak. It was clear she had let enough of the day pass her by.

Toweling dry, she slipped into her shift and a gown Keita held out for her. "Thank you for helping me with clothing, Keita."

"We will visit the storerooms today and pick out some fabric. Would you like that?"

Lissa's eager look warmed Gilda's heart and she smiled. "Of course!"

As Keita and Lissa gathered the linens, the door opened and Ryan strode in, his smile turning to a look of surprise as he took in the activity in his room.

"'Tis good to see ye so well cared for, *a stor.*" He dropped a kiss on Gilda's cheek as he tossed his cloak to the chest at the foot of the bed.

"They have been verra kind." Her smile of thanks faded to concern as she turned to her husband. "Have ye seen any more of the pirates?"

"Come downstairs and sit at the table with me and I will tell you what I know. I am starved and the tables were being set as I came up."

Gilda's heart tripped with anticipation. She knew she would just die if they were confined to the castle again. The sea called to her and her lungs ached for the clear air above the firth.

She grasped Ryan's hand, fairly skipping down the stairs.

Chapter Fifteen

$\mathcal{E}$xcitement swept the castle several days later, even as turmoil rushed through Gilda. Word had reached them that visitors approached and would likely arrive in the next day or two. Ryan's patrol had been absent for the past three days and Gilda's tension was already high.

The expression on Lissa's face as she shared the news of their visitors set off new anxieties for Gilda. She'd discovered the visitors were none other than Laird MacLaurey and his daughter, Mairead, the woman for whom Ryan's da had signed a betrothal contract.

Servants bustled about, preparing the tower rooms, and Cook kept a close watch on the kitchen staff as food was prepared. Gilda and Lissa oversaw their actions, though very little help was needed. Keita, acting chatelaine since Lissa's mother died three years earlier, had things well in hand.

"Is there anything ye would do different, Gilda?" Lissa asked. "Ye must have many visitors at Scaurness. I've been told 'tis a wondrously large castle."

Gilda blanched at the thought of suggesting Keita change how she ran Ard Castle. Taking Lissa by the hand, she found an alcove beside the hearth where they could be out of the way.

With a sigh, she sank into one of the chairs. "I think everything is fine," she confided to the girl. "Yes, Scaurness is a larger castle, and not as old. My da has visitors frequently, and my ma handles things much as Keita does here." She gave Lissa a rueful smile. "In short, she works us half to death cleaning and preparing food, but on a grander scale."

Lissa nodded, apparently satisfied with Gilda's answer. "Would ye like something to drink?" She shot a quick look over her shoulder. "We could take a wee break as long as Keita doesnae suspect."

Gilda swept the area with a look. "Nae. What I would like is whatever ye can tell me about Mairead."

Lissa gave her a startled look. "She is Conn's sister. Why?"

Gilda chewed her lip. "Oh, I suppose I just wondered about our visitors."

Lissa leaned close. "I dinnae think Ryan or Conn are particularly happy they are coming."

"Why not?"

The girl shrugged. "Just a feeling I have. They both are quiet and grim whenever her name is mentioned."

Gilda sighed. "Well, I suppose we should get back to work. I thank ye for stopping to talk with me."

Lissa smiled as she rose. "Dinnae fash about Mairead. She likely willnae stay long."

Worry clutched Gilda again. If only she felt as confident as Lissa sounded.

Riona blew softly on the parchment, the shine of wet ink dulling as it dried. She touched the words she had written with gentle fingers, as to infuse them with her feelings of love for her daughter.

"Are ye ready?" Ranald approached, his hand out to receive the message she had written to Gilda. Folding the parchment in thirds, she sealed it with wax from the candle on her desk. Giving it a moment to dry, she held it out hesitantly to Ranald.

She sighed. "I wish I was taking it to her."

Ranald took the missive and lifted Riona's fingers to his lips for a quick kiss. "I know ye do, but 'tis still too dangerous for ye to travel. 'Twill be enough for her to know ye are thinking about her. I swear I will take ye for a visit as soon as the pirates are gone." He echoed her sigh. "Or at least chased back. If we could find their camp, 'twould be a simple thing to erase their threat."

Riona's eyes rounded with concern. "'Tis no simple thing to battle pirates, *mo chroí*. Nor any man bent on destruction."

"Ree, I would have all threat to ye and our family eliminated. 'Tis my job as laird and yer husband to see ye safe."

She smoothed slow fingers across his jaw, turning them to cup his cheek. "Promise me ye will be safe taking this to Gilda."

Ranald grinned at her. "I will go armed and guarded as always, dearling. Dinnae fash about it."

"I will worry until ye return, ye know."

Noise clashed in the hallway as shrieks rent the air. Ranald hurtled across the room, his hand on the hilt of his sword. He threw open the door, one aggressive stride landing him in the corridor. Something small and hard hit his legs, buckling his knees. Riona was a step behind him and paused when she saw the source of the commotion.

"Ye are a pirate, Jamie!"

Ranald righted himself and caught the blond-thatched imp grabbing at his trews, sliding around his legs. A wooden sword waved in the air, and Ranald twisted neatly out of its path.

"I dinnae want to be a pirate, Finn. I want to be a warrior."

"One of us has to be a pirate," Finn pointed out as he came to a stop on the other side of his da. "'Tis a fight to the death and ye always lose."

"I dinnae!" Jamie shouted his outrage and dove at his brother, his hands balled into tight fists, wooden sword ringing on the floor as he discarded it for hand-to-hand combat.

Ranald grabbed each boy by the scruff of the neck, pulling them apart. He released them, his body firmly between the dueling pair. "Wheesht, the both of ye! 'Tis no way for brothers to act."

"Fergus says brothers always fight," Finn replied, his voice matter-of-fact.

"'Tis only because he see the two of ye." Ranald grunted. Riona made a mental reminder to speak to Fergus about the weans having big ears.

"Finn willnae let me be a warrior," his brother complained.

Ranald surveyed the lads. "Take turns, the both of ye. Or I will put yer energy to better use."

With the threat implied, both ducked their heads, not willing to test their da's temper further. Riona relaxed against the door frame, arms folded across her chest, teeth firmly clenched to hide her mirth.

"Off with ye, now." With a shooing motion, Ranald sent the twins on their way, their feet scudding on the floor as they beat a hasty retreat.

"Will ye engage a tutor for them as ye did Niall?" Riona let the corners of her mouth tug upward, unable to resist teasing her husband. His harried look broke her self-control.

He shoved a hand through his hair. "They need bailiffs, not a tutor." He shrugged. "Mayhap they should be fostered separately."

Riona frowned at the thought of sending the lads away. "I think that would be best, though not for another year or two."

Ranald grinned. "Ye are willing to keep them around that long? Ye are indeed a saint."

This time Riona laughed. "Just a worried mother, and afraid of losing friends willing to foster lads from Scaurness."

"Aye. I am afraid their reputation will precede them. It may not be so easy to foster them."

Riona regarded him solemnly. "Mayhap ye should start negotiations now."

A single horn blast sounded, startling Gilda. Her stomach clenched. Could the MacLaureys be here already? She scrubbed her damp palms down the sides of her skirt and hurried to the hall door.

The Macraig captain, Breac, approached her. "M'lady." He gave a nod.

Gilda turned her anxious gaze on him. "Aye?"

"Riders approaching from the south."

"From the south?" Her eyes narrowed in puzzlement. "I thought the MacLaureys would arrive from the east."

"Aye. I believe they are from Scaurness."

Gilda's jaw dropped open and she closed it with a snap. Her heart raced and she struggled to regain her wits. Hurrying footsteps sounded behind her and she peered over her shoulder.

Laird Macraig blustered past her, not sparing her a look. "Who approaches?"

Breac ducked his head in deference. "Riders from Scaurness, Laird."

Red splotches of anger stained the older man's face. "Dinnae let them in. Warn them away."

"Nae!" Gilda darted past the men. The iron-studded gates stood open, though the portcullis barred the way. She waved at the guards. "Let them in!"

Gazes flickered from her to the two men behind her.

Damn! Stubborn old fools! The guards would never obey her orders over the laird's. She whirled, her gaze seeking the narrow gate in the wall well away from the main entrance. She lifted her skirt with her hands, yanking the cloth out of her way as she rushed to the slender portal.

With a fierce look daring them to stop her, she startled the posted guard into inaction as she gave the latch a solid yank. Pulling the gate open, she ran through the door and straight into the path of the approaching horsemen.

Her eyes misted; whether from the emotions swirling inside her or the cold wind in her face, she wasn't sure. Her heart pounded in her chest and in a move she'd long perfected, she lifted her arms to her da's embrace.

He swung her up to his horse's back, reining him to a halt as he tightened his grip on her. "Are ye wanting to go home, lass?"

His rough voice filled her with the sense of security she missed, his willingness to champion her evident. Realizing how her actions must seem, Gilda shook her head, speechless as tears clogged her throat. They sat for a moment, wrapped tight together as she steadied herself.

She dragged the back of a hand across her eyes. "Nae. I am just glad to see ye. I dinnae expect…"

Her da cupped her chin in his hand, tilting her face up. "Dinnae expect what, dearling?"

Gilda swallowed and tried to still her trembling smile. "I dinnae expect to see you again. Not so soon."

"I still love ye, *mo chroí*. Ye will always be my sweet Gilda." He peered at the archers posed on the parapet above them. "Do I sense a less-than-cordial welcome from yer father-by-marriage?"

She followed his gaze and nodded. "Aye. He dinnae want ye allowed inside." She laid a hand on his arm as her gaze traveled over the twenty men with Da; stout, armed and ready for battle. "I am not sure if he would honor my request to see ye welcomed and fed."

Her da snorted his opinion. "I have no doubt of our welcome." He shifted in his saddle and reached inside his sporran. Pulling out a piece of parchment, he handed it to her. "Yer ma sent this to ye. She wanted to bring it, but 'tis still too dangerous."

Gilda gave him a startled look. "But ye came."

He smiled at her. "I dinnae think the pirates will bother the lads and me. And I brought ye Fia."

Beaming with delight, Gilda spotted her mare tethered to a soldier's saddle.

Her da touched her hand. "I dinnae know what the letter says, though I can guess. Mayhap ye would like to read it when ye are alone." His face held a gentle, loving expression.

Why had she doubted Da had her good at heart? Not that she believed he would have allowed her to marry Ryan, but she should never have wondered if he loved her. Tears filled her eyes and she leaned against his chest.

His arms settled around her and held her close. "Yer ma and I would like to visit when things settle down. Ye are always welcome at Scaurness, Gilda. No matter what."

She nodded and sniffed as she straightened. "I would like to visit. How are the twins?" She laughed at her da's pained look. "And my wee sister?"

"She grows every day." He brushed a strand of hair from her face. "She will be a beauty like ye."

Gilda's breath hitched. "I miss ye. Mayhap even the twins. But I love Ryan." She took note of the men who stood at attention on the walls. "I should go." She clutched her ma's letter to her chest. "Tell Ma I love her."

Da's eyes clouded, but he nodded his assent. "I will."

Gilda slipped to the ground, accepting Fia's lead. She placed a restraining hand on his leg and looked up at him. "I love ye, too, Da."

Ryan's eyes narrowed as he peered across the water. Behind him, horses snorted and pawed the ground. Bits jingled and leather creaked. One of the men coughed.

"Still no sign of them?" Conn asked.

Ryan shook his head. "I dinnae know how they disappear so quickly." He turned his unwilling gaze to the still-smoking ruins of the tiny sea-village. Faces blackened with soot stared hopelessly at him, their lives in shambles, their numbers decimated.

He gestured toward the destruction. "Where am I to get the men to replace those lost? How will I house them soundly before winter?"

Conn edged his horse closer. "Leave a few of your men here to do the work. Have them build a few large cottages instead of one for each family. The labor will be less, and house them quicker."

"Aye. And a few fighting men may tip the odds in their favor should the pirates return." Ryan reined Duer in and faced his soldiers. "We must rebuild. If any of ye are without family and can stay to help, I ask it of ye. We will not let our clan's people starve this winter."

To his surprise and pleasure, six men rode forward. With grim expressions boding ill for returning pirates, they headed toward the village with the promise of supplies to come. Ryan motioned for the rest to follow him. Tired though they were, no one complained.

He shifted in the saddle. "My arms are sore from hauling water to put out the fires. My butt is sore from days in the saddle chasing down pirates who refuse to be caught. My lungs are tight from breathing the foul smoke of burning cottages." He crooked his head to first one side then the other, stretching sore muscles, the bones of his neck shifting with a crack.

Conn sighed. "Thank goodness we are headed home. I am ready for peace."

Gilda set the letter gently on the coverlet, her lingering touch not wanting to release the connection, however tenuous, with her ma. Her heart grew heavy and silent tears streamed slowly down her cheeks. How could her ma have known the words to give her the encouragement she needed? Why had she convinced herself she was no longer welcome at Scaurness?

She slid from the bed, feelings of peace nibbling away at the invisible wall she'd set against the rejection she'd feared. Leaning against the narrow window aperture, cool air dried the tears as she lifted her face to the waning sun. She looked to the horizon, willing Ryan to return, wanting to feel his arms around her, to hear his voice whisper all would be well. A week ago she had no words to describe the incredible sensations of giving herself fully to the care of another, releasing herself to the wonder of passion, to the joy of caring for another and of being loved in return.

Wrapping her arms tight around her waist, she closed her eyes and imagined his footstep in the hall, his voice in the bailey as he called for a stable lad.

A shout startled her from her reverie, and she jerked upright, pressing herself against the aperture, seeking the reason for the guard's alert. Her heart tripped, hammered in her chest. From her narrow vantage point she spied the edge of a cluster of armed men. On the parapet guards faced the land outside the castle walls. Beyond, riders approached, a banner flapping in the wind. The party stretched forty or fifty strong, and she knew it was not Ryan and his patrol.

"Gilda!"

She pushed away from the window. Crossing the room, she opened the door. Lissa's face, excited but pale, met hers.

"Come, Gilda! We must see to our guests!"

Dread settled cold in her stomach as she forced a smile to her lips. "I was hoping Ryan would make it back before the MacLaureys arrived."

"I know, but ye must come. As Ryan's wife, ye are now Lady Macraig."

Gilda patted her hair, wishing she had time to comb and rebraid the rebellious curls. At least her gown was clean and freshly donned that morning. As though granting a silent wish, Keita appeared in the doorway, an overdress draped across her arms.

"Here, m'lady. Put this on." She settled the fabric over Gilda's head and arms, smoothing the gold trimmed, costly velvet over her gown. Sleeves, split from the shoulder, fell with regal splendor past her wrists where they fastened with elaborate gold braid.

"I thank ye, Keita. I feel like Lady Macraig, now."

Keita narrowed her eyes, her lips pursed as she waved away Gilda's praise. "Ye willnae face guests in anything less than proper attire." She cast a critical look over Gilda. "Yer hair could use a comb, but the curls are becoming. Ye may go down."

Mirth threatened as Gilda considered the maid's words. She turned conspiratorially to Lissa, leaning close as they headed down the hall. "I believe I have just been given Keita's approval. Surely I can face anything now!"

Chapter Sixteen

Piercingly dark eyes met Gilda's questioning gaze. She brushed her skirt with work-roughened hands and wished she'd taken time to brush her hair as she took in Mairead's appearance. After a long, tiresome journey, the other young woman's night-dark hair was smoothed in a tight, flawless braid, her cloak fresh and untainted by the dust of travel. Gilda decided to hate her on the spot.

She sighed. Perfection was no reason to dislike anyone, even if this particular annoyingly effortless piece of flawlessness believed herself betrothed to Ryan. She watched as Mairead was handed down from the wagon, her descent stately and unhurried. Gilda quelled the impatient tapping of her foot and stretched her lips into a tight smile.

Laird Macraig strode forward, his head high as he passed her without acknowledgement. Arms spread in welcome, he greeted the burly man standing at Mairead's side.

"Welcome to Ard Castle. I trust yer journey was pleasant?"

The man gave a curt nod. "Me name is Sim and I have the charge of m'lady, here. The laird bids ye pardon his absence, as there was a matter he had need to settle." He watched his charge step daintily to the ground and give her skirts a quick shake.

Sim turned to Laird Macraig. "The journey was long enough, though ye could have sent an advance party to warn us of the trouble ye've had with pirates. We saw a spiral of dark smoke from the coast and sent a scout to check it. My man reported an entire village all but wiped out."

Cold tendrils of fear clenched Gilda's heart. Mairead forgotten, she approached the MacLaurey's man.

"Please, tell me what ye found."

"Milady, pirates hit the village early this morning, destroying most of the buildings and killing many of its people. He said Macraig soldiers came, but they were too late to do much beyond try to save as much of the crofts as possible."

"There was no fight?"

"He said the pirates disappeared when the soldiers approached."

Just then, Mairead cleared her throat with a small, kitten-like noise.

Sim took a step back and offered a short bow. "M'laird, this is Lady Mairead, daughter of Laird MacLaurey, betrothed to yer son, Ryan."

Mairead smiled thinly and nodded to the laird. Pausing a moment, she turned her questioning gaze to Gilda. "And, who are ye?"

Gilda met her look evenly. "I am Lady Gilda Macraig. Ryan's wife."

Gilda and Lissa huddled together in their chairs at the middle of the head table, trying hard to pretend nothing was wrong as they stabbed haphazardly at the food on their platters. On the other side of the laird's chair, Mairead sat arrow-straight as she picked at her own meal with a noticeable lack of appetite. Servants busied themselves around them, but the three places between the women were glaringly empty. Ryan, just in from patrol, his father, and Sim were still closeted in the laird's chamber.

"Was Ryan really supposed to marry her?" Lissa whispered in Gilda's ear.

Gilda nodded and tried to swallow the piece of venison she'd been chewing on for the past several minutes.

Lissa pushed a piece of bread around on her platter then leaned around Gilda to peer at Mairead again. "She doesnae look verra friendly, does she?"

Gilda turned her head and looked at the girl three empty chairs away. Her cheeks flamed pink as she dropped her hands to her lap and Gilda felt a surge of pity for her.

She rose, pushing back her chair, and gave Lissa a stern look. "Friendly or not, she is our guest."

She stepped to Mairead's chair and laid a hand on the armrest. The young woman's lips drew back in a pained grimace. Gilda took a deep breath and forced a reasonable tone to her voice. "Would ye rather have a tray brought to yer room? I would imagine ye are tired after yer travels."

"That would at least get me out of yer sight, aye?"

"Wheesht! Ye shouldnae worry. Ryan told me his father spoke of a betrothal between ye. However, 'twas after he and I wed. I am simply sorry ye made this journey and offer ye a chance to recover without all the prying eyes ye see here."

Mairead's lips pulled into a frown. "I would prefer not to be the subject of speculation."

Gilda laughed. "My lady, ye and I are the most fascinating objects of speculation here whether ye wish it or not. Come. Let us take ye to yer room. The men are likely to be in discussion for a while yet."

She reined in her irritation as Mairead rose stiffly from her chair, pulling her skirts back as though reluctant to come in contact with her rival. Signaling for a serving girl to bring a tray of food, Gilda motioned toward the stone staircase.

Mairead looked at the ancient stone fortification and squared her shoulders. Head high, she glided across the floor and to the room she'd been assigned earlier.

Gilda and Lissa followed, the serving girl in tow. Mairead entered her room and, without pausing, closed the door behind her. The trio drew up short, trading startled looks. With a shrug, Gilda turned the latch and entered the room.

Mairead glared at them, hands fisted on her hips. "Is there no lock for this door?"

The servant girl deposited the tray on a low table near the window and scurried away. Gilda felt a tug of envy as the girl left, but held her ground. "Ye may throw the bolt if ye wish. But there are only four rooms on this floor and easy enough to keep secure."

"If those stairs are the only way to get up here, then ye are right." Mairead's tone was derisive.

Gilda bristled, raking Mairead's elaborate clothing with a glare. "Those sturdy stairs were built to withstand a direct attack, and ye best appreciate the fact. After yer fancy men are bloody on the ground, my braw soldiers could hold back a horde bent on taking the castle."

"Yer soldiers?" Mairead scoffed.

"Aye. Any Macraig soldier is worth at least three MacLaureys."

"Mayhap our guest would like to eat her dinner before 'tis cold." Lissa's voice piped through their hostility.

Gilda settled, guiltily reminded of her resolution to behave as lady of the castle and not the laird's son's young, untried bride.

"My apologies, my lady. It has been a long day for everyone and we all need food and rest. Mayhap we could meet again in the morning with clearer heads."

Mairead sent her an appraising stare. Without another word, Gilda and Lissa left, each seeking her own room and solace.

Ryan found his wife curled beneath a blanket on their bed some time later. He watched the rise and fall of her breast as she slept. With an impatient tug, he loosened his garments and let them fall to the floor, heedless of the jumble as he sought his young wife's passionate welcome. Heart-sore after the long hours closeted with his da and Laird MacLaurey's captain, he was at last able to recognize the untenable position he'd put Mairead in.

Though he would not trade his impetuous marriage with Gilda for anything.

Flaming curls tumbled across the pillow, and with a groan, he reached for her. He wanted absolution in her arms. His weight dipped the mattress and Gilda stirred, rolling sleepily to face him. The edge of the blanket fell from her shoulders and he realized she wore nothing but a thin shift.

Shadows beneath the sheer cloth beckoned him, more alluring than any faerie light and he slid beneath the covers and into her welcoming embrace.

Their loving was hard and fierce, demanding commitment, taking them quickly to the edge of passion. Her arms closed tight around his body as she shuddered beneath him and he rained kisses across her face, tasting salt on her cheeks. His world exploded and he shouted her name, tremors wracking his body.

Spent, he slipped carefully to the side and gathered her in his arms. His breathing slowed, and he touched the pad of his thumb to Gilda's damp cheek. "What is wrong, *a stor*?"

Wordless, Gilda tightened her grip and buried her face against his shoulder. He stroked his hand over her hair. "I am sorry for what this day has cost ye. I never would bring hurt or shame to you willingly."

Gilda nodded and sighed. She sat up and pulled the crumpled shift over her head, and Ryan lost his line of thought as she settled her hair about her shoulders with a toss of her head. She slid back beneath the blanket, tucking herself close against him and he swallowed a moan as her soft flesh pressed against his.

"What will happen now?" she asked.

Ryan blinked, shifting his focus to her question. "Mairead and her escort will stay here a few days to rest. Also, the pirates are actively plundering the coastline. Sim will take her home soon, but not until the danger is gone."

Gilda slid a hand down his chest, and his skin tightened. "Not soon enough, *a stor*," she whispered. "Not soon enough."

Morning's sun found Ryan on the parapet, his body relaxed against the damp, cold stone, his mind running over and over Mairead's arrival.

How could I have handled things differently or better? He stared across the misted grass, seeing no answer in the muted sparkle. A gull languished on the drafts of the early morning wind, suspended in the air, moving neither forward nor back.

He felt the same. He couldn't take back his marriage to Gilda. Nor did he want to. Yet until this was resolved with Mairead, he couldn't move forward. He slammed his fist backward into the stone. *How was I to know she would arrive so soon?*

Footsteps slapped on the walkway behind him, pulling his attention from the bird above. Conn reached a spot near him and slouched his frame over the rock wall, between the crenellated stones.

"Ye look *fashed*." Ryan noted the slump to his friend's shoulders, his head dangling near his chest.

Conn waved him off but did not look up. "My head is pounding."

"Nae surprise, as fast as ye were tossing back whisky last night."

"I was *fashed* then. I am hung-over now."

Straightening, Ryan pushed away from the wall. "I dinnae mean to cause yer sister ill."

Conn spun about, fury glinting from his narrowed eyes. "My sister is in yer home being treated as yer discarded leman—"

"I never touched her!" Ryan roared, shock at his friend's words sparking more anger.

"She is too good for the likes of ye!" Conn advanced, chin jutting out, shoulders hunched forward.

Ryan's eyebrows jerked upward in amazement at Conn's sudden defense of Mairead. "I dinnae like yer sister!"

"And now everyone knows it! How do ye think she feels to be promised to ye in marriage, to have traveled all this way to form an alliance with someone she doesnae have a fondness for, and to be cast aside without a care. Without the least pity or concern."

The pair met eye to eye, fists clenched, each man's breathing deep and labored. Ryan broke the silence. "Ye know I dinnae like her. I dinnae bring her here. I would have stopped her if I could. Why are ye against me?"

Conn relaxed his shoulders, his outrage stepping down slightly. "I agree she is a wee bit difficult-"

With a snort, Ryan indicated his opinion of Conn's allowance. Conn glared, anger lighting anew. "She isnae just any man's woman. But I am her brother and supposed to protect her. At home, I never had to. Here, seeing her upset, slighted—it bothers me, Ryan. I cannae help it. She shouldnae be so shamed."

"At least ye dinnae blame Gilda," Ryan stated. Conn continued to stare at him, offering no word of agreement. Ryan scowled. "Ye cannae blame her. She knew nothing of what my da had done."

"Ye knew. Ye knew and still ye married her before ye could make amends with Mairead."

"Again, that isnae Gilda's fault." Ryan's voice grew harsh as he defended his bride.

"Nae, but having her here is a slur against Mairead's honor."

Ryan threw his hands in the air. "Where do ye want me to keep my wife? She belongs here!"

The stubborn line to Conn's chin told Ryan he had no answer to that, and no thought beyond his sister's hurt.

"Mayhap ye should see yer sister home," Ryan offered quietly.

"As soon as 'tis safe to do so," Conn replied, a hard, bitter line to his mouth, "I will."

Movement behind Connor caught Ryan's attention as sunlight glinted off Gilda's burnished hair. She stepped through the parapet door, pausing as surprise lit her face. "Ryan?"

Conn shoved past them and stomped away. Ryan took a deep breath and forced his lips into a smile. Clearing his throat, he managed to greet his wife pleasantly. "Good morning, *a stor*," he said, lifting a hand in welcome, inviting her close.

Gilda approached, leaning into his embrace as she peered around him. "Is Conn upset about something?"

Ryan struggled to keep the hurt from his voice, but his friend's words wounded him deeply. "Mairead's arrival has left him a bit *nippet*."

"Bad-tempered? He wasnae *for* the match, was he?" Gilda stepped back in surprise. "Ye told me how she tormented the both of ye as lads."

Running a hand through his hair, Ryan sighed. "Nae. He knows what a *targe* she can be. Hell, we spent plenty of time over the years avoiding her and her demanding ways." Ryan shook his head in light remorse. "Mayhap too much time."

He felt a light pressure on his forearm, Gilda's slender hand laid against his sleeve. Her clear gray eyes stared at him, their corners rounded in concern. "Does he blame me for this?"

Ryan glowered at the anxiousness in Gilda's voice and tried to dismiss her worry with a laugh. But her skin paled and he knew he missed the mark. "Ye willnae fash over it, *a stor*. 'Tis not important what he thinks."

"I dinnae care what he thinks of me. Except..." Gilda bit her lip and looked down. Ryan caught her hands and drew her toward him. She resisted briefly then took a stumbling step forward.

"Except what?" he urged.

Her eyes full of anguish, Gilda tilted her face to him. "Except he is your friend and I dinnae wish to cause a rift."

Wrapping her in his arms, Ryan tucked her beneath his chin as he stroked the satin of her hair. She needed all the comfort he could provide her, and he did not want her to see his face when he lied to her. "Ye cannae ruin our friendship, Gilda. We have been like brothers for more than ten years. This is a disagreement, nothing more. Conn and I will be fine. Dinnae *fash*."

But their heated conversation played over and over in his head as he stared beyond the castle walls where a darkening cloud stained the horizon. In his heart he wondered if Conn would ever forgive him.

Chapter Seventeen

*G*ilda absently twirled a strand of her hair around one finger as she stared into the distance. From her high perch along the parapet, she could see the treetops of the forest, already exposed to the morning sun's piercing rays as mist fled before the radiant onslaught. It promised to be a beautiful day.

I cannae abide sitting here any longer. Her insides quailed at the thought of spending yet another day cooped inside the castle. Tensions were running high and heated tempers simmered just below a façade of brittle politeness. Conn and Ryan had reached a grudging truce, but Mairead couched numerous complaints and demands in a longsuffering, yet apologetic way that was slowly driving Gilda and all around her to impending madness.

"How are ye this fine morn, my bonnie bride?"

Gilda whirled at the sound of Ryan's voice and, to her dismay, burst into tears. His arms enveloped her and his cheek brushed against her hair as she gulped back her sobs.

"Here now, *a stor*. Why are ye *greetin* so?"

Wiping away the unexpected tears, Gilda snuffled. "I dinnae mean to do that. I am just so tired of being cooped up in the castle. Mairead has been here less than a week but it seems like months!" She grasped the front of his shirt. "Could we please take a walk outside today? There have been no signs of pirates, the weather is clear, and I will *die* if I have to listen to that woman's complaints even one more day!"

Not giving Ryan a moment to reply, she pushed away from his embrace and began to pace the stone, bitter words tumbling from her mouth, her tone pitched high to mimic Mairead's voice. "'I know ye are busy, but the candles in my room have burned down almost halfway and I require new ones. And there is no way ye should know, but the smell of burning tallow makes my head ache. I dinnae suppose Ard castle has even a few beeswax candles...'"

She raised a hand dramatically to her brow. "'Nae, dinnae trouble yerself on my account. If there are no beeswax candles to be had, I am sure I will simply endure until I return home.'"

Gilda halted on a quivering, half-wailing note, glaring at Ryan, fisting her hands on her hips. He said nothing, and for a moment, she was sure he would chastise her for mimicking Mairead in such a manner. But instead, he shook his head and reached for her.

Reluctantly, she allowed him to pull her close, and he cupped her face in his hands. "I believe Cook may need some berries for pastries. Do ye think there are any left on the bushes?"

Hope rose in her. "The season is not yet over."

"Ye are the best berry-picker I know." Ryan's mouth curved into a smile.

Gilda beamed with happiness. She twined her arms around his neck and kissed him soundly, then flung herself away, twirling with excitement. "Can we leave now? Before the others are up?"

Lissa's voice piped from the doorway. "Leave? Where are you going?"

Gilda chewed her lip impatiently as the riders mounted. A small wagon had been brought when Mairead announced she did not like riding. Gilda had felt a wee hope at the news, that perhaps Mairead would not join their outing. But the woman continued to pout and at last declared she was simply desperate for an outing away from the castle.

Gilda had bristled at the way Mairead accented the word 'castle' to mean 'ancient heap of rocks.' And she'd suffered anger when the laird ordered a wagon brought forth for Mairead's use.

Sim settled his charge onto her seat and she carefully arranged her skirts around her. With a regal inclination of her head, Mairead accepted a blanket to lay across her lap to protect her dress from the detritus of the road.

"We will never get to go if we have to wait on her." Lissa's petulant tone rose.

"Wheesht! Lower yer voice. We dinnae need to give her another cause for resentment." Gilda leaned forward to stroke her mare's silken neck. "We can risk a canter once we are free of the castle."

Lissa's golden eyes gleamed. "I will race ye to the trees!"

"That will get us sent back to the castle," Gilda scolded. "We cannae leave our guard so far behind."

"'Tis not dangerous," Lissa scoffed. "The pirates are gone. Our soldiers will keep us safe."

Gilda frowned. "Dinnae talk like a child. We must be careful."

Shoulders slumped at the chastisement, Lissa reined her pony toward the castle gate as the guard filed out. Gilda urged Fia forward and leaned toward her friend. "Dinnae fash. Mairead willnae want to walk through the brambles and gather berries. We will have the entire morning to ourselves."

"Mayhap. But she asked for one of yer auld dresses to wear. So she wouldn't tear any of her pretty ones."

Startled, Gilda's eyebrows twitched. "She would wear one of my dresses to keep from dirtying her own? The *besom!*"

"Keita says that is a bad word!" Lissa hissed.

Both girls nodded and smiled at the guards as they passed through the gate. Riders paced before them and Mairead's wagon and guard brought up the rear, Ryan and Conn riding midway down the line. The squeak of wooden wheels groaned loudly in the din of movement. Metal bits chimed against the horses' teeth, mingling with the slap of leather.

Lissa and Gilda rode side by side, their mounts prancing with excitement. "Aye, 'tis a bad word, and I am sorry I said it," Gilda apologized once they were clear of the castle and listening ears.

Lissa giggled. "I am not. Her tongue is *clippie* and she has not been very nice, especially to you."

"She has had a rough time of it, Lissa." Gilda looked back toward Mairead. The woman sat stiffly upright on the hard wooden seat, hands folded on her lap. "Ryan says she tormented them when they were lads. I wonder if she has any friends."

"I dinnae want to be her friend," Lissa declared. "I dinnae trust her."

Gilda pursed her lips thoughtfully. "Nae. I dinnae trust her, either. Do ye think she is this unhappy at her own home?"

"I dinnae think she likes anything." Lissa settled back in her saddle. "Or anyone."

With a toss of her head, Gilda shook off the seriousness. "Let's pick up the pace a bit, aye? Just enough to feel the wind," she cautioned her young friend.

Grinning, Lissa leaned forward, shortening her reins as she urged her pony into a canter. Fia exploded beside her, scarcely needing the prompting of Gilda's heels. They flew past the guards at the head of the column, laughing at the startled looks on their faces. Several lengths later, the girls wheeled their mounts and raced back to their place in line, Ryan in place and awaiting them.

"If the day passes without sighting pirates, I will suggest Mairead and I leave the day after tomorrow," Conn said.

Pain sliced cleanly through Ryan at his friend's words. Their friendship had been patched, but the easy camaraderie was gone, and he felt its loss acutely. "Ye dinnae have to leave with her. I was angry—"

"I know. We have said this a hundred times. But it is right I accompany her home. She needs the added protection."

Ryan perused the line of soldiers he'd ordered out to protect three women on a morning outing and could not argue the truth. The roads were dangerous and if Mairead was attacked by ruffians or pirates, Conn's fighting ability would likely turn the balance.

"Look!" Conn jerked his chin toward the front of the line. Anger burst white-hot as Ryan watched his wife and sister break past the guard, their horses flying.

"Shite!" he snarled, yanking Duer around and sending him into a gallop. Moments later the girls wheeled their mounts and Ryan pulled his horse back to a walk. They reined neatly back to their place in line and met him with flushed faces and sweet smiles.

He saw Gilda flinch and her smile vanished, but she squared her shoulders and did not look away. Unable to bring himself to spout the blistering reprimand on the tip of his tongue, Ryan struggled to hold his peace.

"The gallop felt wonderful," Gilda offered. Lissa opened her mouth, but closed it as Gilda's mare collided with hers. As much as Ryan wanted to hear what Lissa had to say for herself, he had to admit it was probably best she kept silent just now.

"I dinnae want ye haring off on yer own again," he managed in a stern voice.

"I wouldnae dream of putting us in danger," Gilda replied breezily. "We but galloped a few lengths and returned."

"All the same, it wasnae a good idea."

To his surprise, neither Gilda nor Lissa protested. They rode a bit further in silence. As they approached the forest, the soldiers tensed visibly. Apprehension sizzled along Ryan's spine, racing through him, sharpening his senses. The devastation of the seaside village loomed, still stark in his memory. Overhead, tree limbs swayed gently in the breeze, causing the shadows on the forest floor to shift beneath the horses's hooves. Birds called overhead, but their song didn't seem distressed at the line of horsemen traveling the paths below. Still, Ryan tensed.

They emerged from the shadows of the trees above the beach. The air was fresher, tart with the tang of seawater. Waves crashed on the rocks far below. The only way to the sea was a narrow trail that wound through sea grasses and outcroppings of weathered rock.

Ryan raised his arm and the party halted. "Ye ladies may spread yer blankets for lunch here. Gilda, there are berry bushes deeper in the forest, but I'd ask ye only go with guards. Aye?"

Gilda slipped lightly to the ground and handed him her mare's reins. "Aye. We will get started now!" she sang out happily. Lissa landed beside her and untied the basket laced to the back of her saddle. They clasped hands and ran across the grass, skirts and hair flying behind them, woven cubbies bouncing at their sides.

Ryan shook his head ruefully. For all that Gilda was now a married woman, she scarce seemed older than his sister. With a tilt of his head, he sent four soldiers after the two women.

A prim cough from Mairead interrupted his thoughts. "I dinnae want to sit here unsheltered. 'Tis unfair to ask it of me. My skin will burn in this wind and sun."

Then why, by St. Andrew's teeth, did ye come? Ryan grumbled to himself as he prepared to meet Mairead's complaint.

"Look! They are setting up a shelter for Mairead!" Lissa pointed to the white canvas fluttering from four rough-cut timbers. The slender poles swayed gently and Gilda gritted her teeth, damping down the image of the entire structure caving down upon Mairead and her ceaseless harping.

"Wheesht, and it will be nice to eat our lunch in a bit of shade, won't it?" Lissa's unladylike snort answered Gilda's question. She patted her partially-filled cubbie. "I am getting hungry. Let us settle and eat our lunch. We will then have time to finish filling our baskets before returning to the castle."

"I wish we could stay out longer," Lissa whined. "I havenae seen a pirate or anything dangerous all morning."

"I am sure yer brother has better things to do than nursemaid us," Gilda answered tartly, ignoring the longing in her own heart to bask in the open air and freedom. She grasped Lissa's hand and tugged her along. "We must not put the men in danger by staying out past gloaming."

They reached the rigged shelter and sank down on the blanket spread beneath, dropping their baskets beside them.

Curled on a large blanket, Mairead leaned forward and peered at the berries. "Were there no more than that?" Her question was little more than a plaintive sigh. "That willnae make many pastries at all. Hardly worth the time and effort."

"At least ye dinnae get yer gown soiled," Gilda replied as she popped a juicy berry in her mouth. She heard Lissa's small gasp and a pang of guilt went through her at baiting Mairead so. Especially at Mairead's look of horror which sent a warring feeling of smug satisfaction through her middle.

"'Tis not *my* gown," Mairead said with a tiny shudder. Her long, delicate fingers plucked at the coarse linen. "I asked for a rag to wear so my clothing wouldnae be soiled or torn. I dinnae have such an item in my chests, but I felt sure one could be garnered." She turned her dark gaze directly on Gilda. "From ye."

Heat traveled up Gilda's neck and along her arms, prickly as a rash. Her hands trembled but she forced her fingers to pluck another berry from the basket.

"I wouldnae ask ye for a thing, Lady MacLaurey." Gilda ate the berry in her hand and flashed Mairead a mirthless smile. "Ye have nothing I need, and everyone knows ye cannae gather berries off a *whinbuss*."

Ryan's knife thudded onto the blanket and she knew she'd shocked him with her two-sided proverb.

I dinnae care. She is an ill-tempered besom and I wouldnae ask a favor of her if my life depended on it. Gilda smoothed her hands on her skirts and rose to her feet. "Lissa and I have baskets to fill. If ye would excuse us, please."

There was a murmured chorus of eager assent from the nearby soldiers. "Aye, lass, and I look forward to the pastries tonight—"

"They are my favorite, they are—"

"Ye are kind, Lady Gilda—"

With a flurry of movement, Mairead stood. "I will help ye, Gilda."

Lissa tugged at Gilda's sleeve. "What is she about? She doesnae know how to pick berries."

"She dinnae like us getting all the thanks," Gilda whispered as she bent to pick up her basket. "Bothersome *besom*."

No longer shocked at Gilda's words, Lissa snickered. They filed from under the shelter and toward the berry patch.

"Race ye to the berries!" Lissa shouted. Gilda hiked her skirts above her boots as she took up Lissa's challenge.

"Wait!" Mairead demanded as she stumbled on the rocky ground. "I cannae leap about like a wee *cutty*. Ye are disobedient and mischievous and 'tis a wonder the men of this clan dinnae stripe the both of ye."

Without remorse, Gilda and Lissa faded into the shadows of the edge of the forest. Gilda watched as soldiers fanned out around Mairead, far enough from her to dampen the sound of her complaints, close enough they would still be seen to guard her. Faith, but she could not summon the decency to feel sorry for the woman.

As Mairead fisted her hands on her hips, Gilda stepped into her line of vision. "The best berries are deeper. Where 'tis harder to reach. The others have either been picked already or are smaller and less plump." With that bit of information, Gilda slipped among the bushes and began to fill her basket.

"I am glad I am not wearing one of my good gowns," Mairead grumbled as she tugged her skirt free of the brambles.

"I am, too," Gilda admitted, "but 'twas not nice of ye to insist on one of mine."

"Mayhap not, but what else have ye offered me other than cold hospitality?"

"Cold hospitality?" Gilda sputtered. "Are ye never satisfied? 'Tis a sorry day to find yer betrothed marrit to someone else, but ye arenae making things easy, either."

"I dinnae have to make things easy for ye. Ye stole my husband!"

"And I would have to say he is glad I did!" Gilda glared at Mairead then whirled away, grasping the basket handle tight enough to throttle it had it been the other woman's neck. She stomped deeper into the thicket, yanking berries from the slender branches, flinching as she pricked her finger on a bramble.

Mairead followed close on her heels. "Ye insufferable child! Ye will never be the lady of Ard Castle!"

"Well, I am Ryan's wife, so we shall have to see, aye?" Gilda retorted.

"I am so thankful to be leaving! I hope it is tomorrow!"

"Ye couldnae pack yer bags fast enough to suit me." Gilda slid effortlessly through the thicket and out the other side. She didn't bother to stifle a grin when she heard Mairead's startled yelp. Plucking more berries, she waited for the woman's next grievance. There was only silence. Curious, Gilda stole back into the thicket.

Mairead stood rigid, fear etched into every line of her body. Coldness washed over Gilda as she peered into the thicket and the fey eyes that stared back at her.

Chapter Eighteen

Gilda's heart skipped. The amber eyes glowed unwaveringly from the darkness of the thicket. Black-tipped gray fur cloaked the young wolf's lithe body. Gilda stared at the motionless beast, unsure its intent, unable to make the first move. Something about the animal seemed familiar, however, and Gilda's gaze fell to the wolf's front paw, resting lightly on the ground. The initial jolt of fear lifted as she recognized the wolf as the one she'd set free from a trap only a few weeks earlier.

"Step behind me, Mairead," she called in a low voice, praying the woman would do as she was told without questioning. Mairead appeared to be frozen to the spot and didn't so much as bat an eyelash.

"He willnae hurt ye if ye move slow." Gilda held out a hand, palm up, motioning for Mairead to come to her.

Her movements dreamlike, not tearing her gaze from the ferocious-looking beast, Mairead reached for Gilda. She stumbled and the wolf let out an anxious whine.

"Gilda!" Mairead's plaintive voice sliced through the still air and Gilda grimaced at the sound.

"Dinnae *fash*, Mairead. I know this wolf. He is a good lad." *Please let it be so*, she added under her breath. *Let him remember me.*

With measured tread, Gilda edged toward Mairead, meeting her several feet from the wolf, still caught in his unwavering gaze. Mairead grasped Gilda's arm, her fingernails digging into the flesh.

Gilda winced at the pain. Willing to believe the forceful grip unintentional, Gilda patted Mairead's shoulder gently to get her attention.

"Ye are shaking, Mairead," she chided. "And ye will draw blood if ye dinnae loosen yer fingers."

"I…ye…'tis a *wolf*!" the other woman hissed. Rather than release Gilda's arm, Mairead pulled her closer.

Gilda forced a smile and managed to work her arm free. "Wheesht, he's no' but a wee wolf. It would take him several bites to eat ye." She bit her lip as Mairead's skin blanched white. It really was bad of her to tease so. "Come. Let us get back to the others. I am sure there are other woodland creatures the wolf would find better sport than a girl like ye who cannae run verra fast."

"Ye are mad!" Mairead sputtered, her eyes wild, her tongue suddenly loosed in panic. "I am glad ye married Ryan Macraig! Glad, do ye hear me? 'Tis a horrid, damp, ruin of a castle, full of pirates and wolves…" Her voice hitched and she glared at Gilda through red-rimmed eyes. "I willnae stay here a day longer! I want to go home!"

Grimacing at her tone, Gilda relented. "Ye are in no danger. Come along. I will take ye back to the wagon." She caught Mairead's sleeve and tugged, urging her to follow.

With a screech, Mairead jerked away. "Dinnae touch me, you wretched girl!" Her demand ended on a sob and she whirled, plunging through the thicket, heedless of the brambles that tore at her skirts and snagged her hair.

"St. Columba's bones, but she is a right *girn*, so she is! I can truly say I am glad I rescued Ryan from her peevish complaining." Gilda fisted her hands on her hips. "And she has no regard for a perfectly good dress."

A rustle of leaves interrupted her indignant recital and she spied Lissa peering through the branches.

"Gilda?" The girl's voice was a frightened squeak.

"Och, dinnae tell me ye are afeared of this poor beastie, too." Gilda harrumphed.

"'Tis a wolf!" Lissa's eyes widened and her jaw dropped.

"I am not so daft as to walk over there and pet it like a dog." Gilda tossed her head. "But I released it from a trap a couple of weeks ago and fed him a wee bit. I have seen him since, and he has never threatened me."

Lissa peeked at the animal dubiously. The wolf's gaze slid from one girl to the next before he settled and began licking his paw.

"See? The swelling in his foot is almost gone. Poor lad. I suppose one or more of the bones were broken as well as the skin. But he appears to be healing well."

Shaking her head, Lissa smiled. "Ye are brave, Gilda. I would have been too terrified to try to help him."

Deciding to keep a generous distance between herself and the wolf despite a slight feeling of friendship, Gilda began plucking berries from the bushes, keeping one eye on the beast as she worked. "Let us hurry. 'Twill be getting dark soon, and the men will want to leave. I dinnae want them to find the wolf. They may think him dangerous."

"If Mairead has anything to say about it, they will be here quickly."

Suddenly there was a crashing sound in the brambles. With a horrified gasp, Mairead plunged through the thicket, landing with a sprawl at Gilda's feet. From behind her, a man leaped into the little clearing, his eyes gleaming, a dirk clenched between his teeth. The tang of sweat and salt assaulted Gilda's nose even as she noted his stained clothing and the band of cloth wrapped about his forehead.

She released a soundless gasp.

Pirate!

Ryan surveyed the open area above the sea cliffs. No suspicious *birlinns* or other sailing vessels had been sighted in several days along the coast, but he was not foolish enough to assume Acair MacEwen and his men had merely drifted away. Reason told him they would plunder up and down the shoreline for supplies before returning to Macrory land. His gut demanded they would not be gone long and Macraig land abutted that of the Macrory clan. Something needed to be done, and soon.

Around him, soldiers leaned or reclined casually, the quiet talk among them carried away by the breeze sweeping the rocky plateau. Ryan peered at the sky, his attention on the clouds building in the west. A possible storm was brewing, but that was not uncommon. A day without rain, such as this one, was much less common. The warm day pleased him, as though he were able to gift his wife with one last beautiful autumn day before winter arrived with winds crying off the firth, bringing ice and frigid temperatures to permeate the ancient Macraig castle.

This winter, however, he would have a willing wife to warm his bed and heat their nights. The thought cast a broad smile to his face. He settled on the ground, his back against a boulder shedding warmth from the rays of the sun. *'Tis a* ferlie *thing to be marrit. Truly a marvel and a wonder.*

His gaze roamed the little shelter where the women had rested as they ate. A frown of distaste tugged at his lips as he marked the spot where Mairead had sat. *But only when marrit to the right woman.* Sending up a short prayer of thanks for deliverance from the bossy MacLaurey woman, Ryan closed his eyes and indulged himself with thoughts of a slender Macrory lass with fiery curls.

I need to start breaking camp. The words formed somewhere in the back of his mind, but Gilda's saucy image danced before him, and he shifted his shoulders, seeking a more comfortable position. *In a moment*, he allowed as the warmth building within him began to vie with the heated rock he leaned against. In the distance the cry of gulls could be heard, blending with the sound of crashing waves below the edge of the cliffs.

A feminine shriek split the air.

Ryan leapt to his feet, sword in his hand. Around him, Macraig soldiers took up battle stance, forming a shield of drawn swords around the perimeter of the area.

"Where are the women?" Conn shouted, racing toward him from across the field.

"Four men are with them at the edge of the woods." Ryan's reassurance rang flat as the sound of the shriek rang through his head. Together he and Conn sped toward the trees. Hoarse shouts from behind them spun Ryan around.

Unknown men swarmed over the edge of the cliffs, weapons in hand, their war cries sending a frisson of dread down Ryan's spine as they engaged the Macraig soldiers. Steel clanged as grunts and curses filled the air.

He caught Conn's arm in an iron grip.

"Find the women. Do whatever ye have to, but get them safe to the castle."

Conn faced him with a look of surprise. "Those are pirates, Ryan! I could—"

Ryan squared his jaw. "I know. Save the lasses. Dinnae *fash* about me." He sensed Conn's indecision and he released his friend's arm with a forced laugh. "Ye will have the bigger fight on yer hands dealing with the lasses."

With a scowl that told Ryan their long friendship had just been seamlessly repaired, Conn nodded briskly and pelted up the slope to the forest, leaving Ryan and the remaining six men to battle the pirates.

Gilda stared at the man, her limbs frozen. *Run!* She thought wildly, but the words would not pass her lips.

The man wiped the dirk on his kilt as his gaze roamed over the three girls. "What have we here? Lovely lasses picking berries, aye? And no one to run to or call for help."

"Our guard..." Gilda managed to utter the words, her throat tight with fear. At her feet, Mairead choked on a sob. Gilda jerked her gaze to the woman and saw tears streaking her face. Denial ripped through her as she looked back to the man. His grin taunted her knowingly.

"There *were* Macraig soldiers, lass. The only men left now are mine."

"That...that isnae possible," Gilda stammered. "There were—"

"Four," the man interrupted. "Four men in the woods, eight more on the cliff. But dinnae *fash*. My men will have dealt with them in a moment." His manner became serious. "The three of ye come with me, now."

Hands clutched Gilda from behind. "Dinnae let him take us, Gilda," Lissa whimpered.

The man quirked an eyebrow. "Ye are Gilda, aye?" His eyes roamed over her assessingly. "Laird Macrory's daughter?"

"I am Ryan Macraig's wife."

Shaking his head, the man grinned. "Ye willnae claim the Macrory as yer da, then. Mayhap because it is known the MacEwen sired ye?

Dizziness swept through Gilda. Mairead stumbled to her feet, clutching Gilda's arm. Lissa clung to her other side. Gilda swayed. Her vision darkened, narrowed to the evil leer of the man before her.

"Who are ye?" The words slipped from her, scarcely heard even in the suddenly silent glen.

"I am Acair MacEwen. Yer half-brother."

Chapter Nineteen

𝒢ilda's thoughts flew back to the clan gathering at Scaurness castle only a few weeks earlier to discuss an alliance against the marauding pirates. Acair MacEwen, the pirate, was her half-brother? The man who had sworn vengeance against Ranald Macrory? Her breath caught.

His father is my father. Is that why Da killed him?

"Gilda?" Lissa leaned into her shoulder.

Sensing the girl needed reassurance, Gilda patted Lissa's cold hand. With all the disdain she could muster, she pulled herself together. "This man is nothing but a pirate. He doesnae like my *father*," she added, deliberately stressing the word, daring the man to contradict her. "But he willnae take us with him."

"Think ye no?" His face turned thunderous as he advanced on them. Gilda's courage faltered as the other girls shrank against her.

"Ye will be my hostage and I will beggar yer *da* before I am finished with him," Acair MacEwen boasted. "He will live long enough to see his children starve, his woman reduced to selling herself to the meanest bilge rat to put bread on the table."

Gilda's breath caught in her throat as hatred transformed the man before her. His mocking attitude gone, he was suddenly a darker evil than she had ever envisioned, his face twisted with a venom that appeared to eat him from within. His lips snarled as he spoke and spittle beaded in the mustache that drooped to frame his mouth. The greasy, unkempt braids on either side of his face swung against his shoulders as he advanced, his sheer malevolence frightening. Looming over them, he blocked the sunlight filtering through the trees.

Gilda began to shake.

A low growl sounded. Acair paused as the sound strengthened. The pirate shifted the dirk in his hand. Gilda's gaze flew to the thicket where the wolf had lain. Beside her, Lissa gasped and Mairead sobbed behind trembling hands.

"Silence!" Acair gestured with a slicing movement of the dirk.

Gilda grabbed Lissa and Mairead and stepped backward, pulling them with her. "We willnae be yer prisoners."

"Dinnae move again." His voice threatened, but he spun as the growl in the thicket rumbled once more. He flexed his hand and the steel winked in the mottled light.

"No!" Gilda tore free of the other girls' grasps as she plunged forward to stop his throw.

With lightning speed, Acair flipped the blade in his hand, grasping it by the tip. An instant's pause for aim as he drew his arm back, he sent the long knife singing into the shadowy brambles—and missed.

Leaves and twigs exploded as the wolf launched himself at the pirate. Acair took the weight of the wolf's body directly in the chest and stumbled back, falling almost to only to leap at his throat again, fangs flashing white in the gloom. His snarls filled the air, raging amid Acair's shouts. Rooted to the spot, Gilda watched in rising panic.

The wolf's teeth drew blood yet again. His grizzled coat a blur in the dappled light of the glen as he struck, Gilda could scarce keep up with his lightning moves. The pirate grappled with the ferocious beast, shielding himself with one ripped the ground. One arm came up instinctively to protect his face and neck, and the wolf's teeth sank deep into his flesh. Blood spurted from the wounds and Acair cried out. He snatched another blade from his boot and tried to push to his feet, but the wolf released his arm

and bloody arm, the other seeking a target with his knife amid the animal's determined onslaught.

The wolf slashed at him again, his teeth missing their mark this time, and the beast danced out of reach, preparing for another attack. In the instant's respite, Acair lunged to his feet, bringing his blade to bear as the wolf sprang again. Acair's arm swung, and the wolf gave a yelp of pain.

Goaded into action, Gilda flew at Acair, grabbing his arm and holding onto it with terror-driven tenacity.

The pirate struck her with his bloody arm, breaking her grip and sending her to her knees several feet away. Dazed, Gilda lifted a trembling hand to her head, watching in shock as Acair turned to the wounded wolf.

"Ye damned beast!" he spat, crouching to counter another attack. His hands splayed wide, the bloody knife a deadly extension of himself. The wolf stood before him, head down, yellow gaze on his foe. A growl rolled from his heaving chest. One front foot dangled just above the ground. Gilda could not look away.

"Come eat my blade," Acair taunted, waving the short knife in the air.

"Pick someone yer own size," an unexpected voice commanded. The deadly tableau broken, all four whirled to the newcomer.

Mairead was the first to recover. "Conn!"

"Ye know this sniveling wench?" Acair grinned and pointed to Gilda with the tip of his knife. "She isnae such a beauty as yon lass, but ye can have yer pick when I am finished."

"Ye willnae prey on the helpless again," Conn replied as he advanced. "Draw yer sword and fight me."

"No!" Mairead cried, reaching toward the two men. Gilda lunged to her feet and grabbed the other woman.

"Dinnae distract him," she hissed in warning.

"He is my brother," Mairead sobbed, but she turned her face into Gilda's shoulder and muffled her words.

Blinking back tears and the effects of Acair's stunning blow, Gilda pushed Lissa and Mairead into the thicket, leaving the clearing to the men.

Conn spared the women a quick look, his sister sobbing into Gilda's shoulder as Gilda swayed on her feet. Lissa's sharp gasp shook him out of his inattention and he swung about, narrowly missing the blade that thudded into the trunk of the tree behind him. With a roar, he charged his opponent. Grunting, the pirate reached for his sword with his injured arm. A grimace crossed his face and he shifted the weapon to his other hand. Conn registered the bloody, tattered mess of the brigand's mangled arm.

There was scant room in the tiny glen for two fighting men to engage their swords. Conn crashed into his foe, slamming him against a tree. The pirate's breath left him in a low groan, but Conn didn't have time to follow up the slight edge as the outlaw shoved him away. Ducking, Conn dodged the downward slash of steel, pivoted and brought his sword up to block the vicious blow.

Using the force of his spin, Conn lashed out with one foot. Making solid contact with the side of the pirate's knee, he sent him crashing to the ground. With a bellow, the pirate rolled to the side, swinging his sword. Conn narrowly avoided the deadly arc, but lost his footing as he slid on the leaves on the forest floor. Arms waving, he caught his balance just before he sprawled atop the pirate, but the man was already on one knee, bringing his weapon to bear. Conn heard the whoosh of the sword as it sliced through the air a split second before it bit deep in his shoulder. Bright shards exploded in his head at the pain.

One of the girls screamed. He braced himself, stumbling to his feet as his vision cleared. A shadowed form burst past him with a rumbling growl and Conn drew back in surprise. The wolf crashed into the pirate, knocking him to the ground. He snarled atop the downed man, and the pirate's sword, hilt slippery with blood, scuttled from his hand, landing amid the bracken.

Conn staggered to the ravaging beast and grasped it by the ruff. With an effort he heaved the wolf aside and it vanished into the thicket.

Wiping sweat from his brow, Conn stared at the wounded man at his feet. Twisted on the ground, the pirate's breath whistled from his savaged throat as his life's blood pumped rhythmically into the fallen leaves. The men's eyes locked, and in an act of mercy, Conn plunged his sword deep into the pirate's chest.

For several long moments Conn stood over the dead man. The sound of faint sobbing reached his ears and he staggered to the girls. He saw the looks of horror as they stared at the dead pirate. "Dinnae dare faint on me," he rasped.

Mairead stared at him. "Ye killed him!"

"He would have killed me, and ye included, had I not."

"The wolf—" Lissa whimpered.

"Dinnae *fash* about the wolf. Hie back to the castle. Now!"

The two girls started at his voice, but Gilda's mutinous look gave him pause.

"Where is Ryan?" she asked.

"He is busy. I am taking ye home."

"I willnae—"

"*Dinnae distract him*," Conn mocked without humor, flinging her own words back at her. "Leave, before more pirates come."

He saw her pause. "I promised him I would see ye safe. I will come back for him as soon as ye are at the castle."

Gilda opened her mouth, then pressed her lips in a stubborn line. He bent to wipe his blade in the leaves, but the movement wrenched the gash in his shoulder. With a cry of pain, he grasped the wound and fell to his knees as fresh blood poured warm across his hand.

"Yer arm!" Gilda exclaimed and hurried to his side. Her fingers gently probed his shoulder and he bit back a moan. She tore a strip from the hem of her gown. "Lissa! I will need another piece for bandaging. Mairead, come hold yer brother's wound together."

He wanted to tell them to hurry, but his teeth ground against the pain as Mairead, her head averted, used both hands to push the edges of the gash together. With deft movements, Gilda wrapped the bandages around his arm, stemming the rush of blood.

Gilda cupped his cheek in her palm. "Conn, we cannae take the time to go through the forest. We must go back for the horses."

"'Tis safer through the trees."

"Ye willnae make it on foot."

Her observation gave him pause. His body trembled and he was not sure he could rise, much less walk all the way back to the castle. But there was no guarantee Ryan had held back the pirates. Dare he risk leading the girls back to the clearing above the beach?

Gilda saw the grimace on Conn's face. "Come. We will be careful."

Shouts and the sound of a horn suddenly echoed through the trees. Tremors ran through Gilda and Conn's hesitation told her he warred with his decision.

"Something is happening. Ye must go," she pleaded.

At his reluctant nod, they skirted the edge of the glen, pressing into the safety of the trees. Winding amid the trunks, Gilda clutched Lissa's hand, Mairead bringing up the rear while Conn struggled to keep the lead. Gilda's heart beat faster as they approached the edge of the forest. Voices rose in the air, but there were no sounds of fighting, no clash of steel or battle cries. She swallowed against the acrid rise of fear.

Conn halted, lifting his arm in command. "Stay here."

"But—"

He shook his head. "Ye three must stay together. I will bring the horses back. And Ryan, too."

Unsaid words of uncertainty hung between them, adding to Gilda's worry.

She saw Conn waver and he would not meet her gaze. She wanted to argue, but Lissa and Mairead pressed against her and she knew they were too frightened to be of help. "Aye," she agreed. Blinking back the sudden sting of tears, she added. "Find Ryan."

Without answering, Conn slipped through the trees and was gone. Gilda waited in silence, straining to hear anything that would tell her news of the Macraig soldiers and her husband. The forest remained eerily quiet.

"I cannae stand this," she whispered to the others. "I must at least see what has happened."

Mairead grabbed her arm. "Nae! Ye could be seen!"

Lissa's eyes, red and swollen, cast a silent plea against such risk.

"Yer brothers and my husband are out there. I must know what is going on."

"Conn will be back soon," Mairead urged. "Please dinnae leave us."

"I willnae leave ye. Ye will follow me to the edge of the trees. No further."

Lissa gulped audibly. Mairead squared her shoulders and nodded once. "Aye."

Cautiously, Gilda led the two girls through the bracken, their footsteps dulled in the thick layer of dead leaves. Moments later, they stooped behind a large bush, peering through its branches at the clearing ahead.

Lissa gasped and buried her head in Gilda's side.

Bodies lay scattered everywhere. Many more men than had ridden out with them crowded the field, their horses reassuring Gilda they were not pirates but soldiers from the castle who had ridden to their aid. Two men placed a body in the wagon, pulling the edge of his kilt forward to cover his head.

Quickly, Gilda scanned the area. Her heart plummeted when she did not see Ryan among the men. For several agonizing minutes, she watched the scene below as it repeated itself over and over. Finally, Gilda counted eight riderless horses as men roped them together for the trip back to the castle.

"Look! Here he comes," Mairead hissed in her ear. Gilda's gaze followed Mairead's pointing finger to the edge of the plateau and saw Conn, three horses in tow, riding toward them.

Alone.

Chapter Twenty

$\mathscr{G}$ilda buried her face deep in her pillow and screamed. She pounded the feathered softness with clenched fists, but the pain inside did not lessen. Bitterness ate at her, taunted her, consumed her. On the bed next to her, Lissa whimpered softly. Gilda envied the girl her sleep, drugged though it was, and craved the oblivion of numbing rest for herself. But she also feared the nightmares that would come with it, reminding her of what she had lost. She curled into herself. Deep inside, a hole burned ever larger, deeper, hollow, cold. A fierce pain that might never go away.

Over and over the voices swept through her mind, reliving the hours after she and the others had regained the castle after the pirate attack. Without Ryan. Hours during which the laird had questioned them until Gilda thought she would go quite mad. A mirthless laugh swept through her. Perhaps she was. She clutched her pillow tightly and bit her lip.

"We had no warning, laird. The Macraig soldiers fought hard, yer son hardest of all."

"Without the help from the castle, we would have all perished."

"I saw yer son fighting near the edge of the cliff. When I looked again, he was gone."

"His sword was retrieved on the rocks of the shore below. There was no sign of his body."

Nameless faces whose words she had tried desperately to shut out. How could Ryan be gone? Death was ever a reality, but not now, not when their love was so young. They had years ahead of them, aye? She and Ryan had only been married a little over a fortnight. It wasn't possible he was gone.

The love in her heart said he still lived.

The burn constricting her chest told her she would never see him again.

Gilda rubbed her swollen, gritty eyes and rolled to her back, pulling the blanket close around her. As if to mock the previously beautiful day, the weather had turned bitter, winds whistling about the castle, bringing a storm in from the sea. She shivered as lightning streaks lit the moonless sky.

She remembered Conn's defeated stance as he rode toward them. He had refused to talk to her as they mounted their horses for the ride back to Ard Castle. His averted gaze spoke volumes to her even as she begged him to tell her what had happened to Ryan and the others. Hunched over his saddle, he had led them home, his silence destroying her hopes.

Restless, her eyes refused to close, and she slipped from the bed, pulling a heavy arisaid over her shoulders against the cold. Gently turning the latch, she left Lissa to her uneasy dreams.

Below, a murmur of voices rose and the warm glow from the huge fireplace in the great hall painted the stone pale gold with its light. Gilda shivered. She longed for the warmth of the fire, but did not wish to face the pitying looks of the people still gathered. Had Lissa not cried and pleaded with her to stay, she would have gone back to Scaurness Castle hours ago, before the storm arrived.

Laird Macraig's grudging words for her to 'do as ye please' scarcely hid his hatred of her. It was clear he blamed her for Ryan's death. Had she not insisted on the outing, he would have been well-protected at the castle when the pirates struck. Gilda swallowed another scream. She blamed herself as well.

The fire's warm promise drew her downward and she clung to the shadowed edges of the room. Finally close enough for the heat of the flames to seep through the wool of her gown, Gilda sank onto a chair. She tucked the edges of her arisaid about her and closed her eyes. Voices faded in and out as she tried to erase from her mind the events of the day.

Conn saw how Gilda folded herself gingerly into a chair near the hearth. Shadows all but obscured her features, but he knew her well. Her form, her very presence burned deep in his soul. He fingered the mug of ale on the table beside him, longing for whisky to dull the ache within him.

Damn her! Why could she not have been content to stay safe within the castle walls? Why could she not have left well enough alone? Conn jerked the mug to his lips and took a deep drink. *Ryan never could nae-say the red-haired wench. Bluidy little temptress almost got all of us killed.*

He set the mug down with a thump and a glower. Gilda had not been the only one eager for a day out of the castle. The others had been impatient, too. But it *had* been Gilda who had stood firm against the pirate, Gilda who bound his arm and stopped the bleeding. He surveyed her huddled form. And it was Gilda who had lost her husband, even as Conn lost his closest friend. Hell, it was Gilda's wolf that held the pirate at bay until Conn arrived.

Unsure if it was a good idea or not, Conn rose to his feet and shuffled to Gilda's side, feeling at least a hundred years old. With a soft groan, he lowered himself to the chair next to hers. She glanced at him, pain pooling deep within her eyes. He handed her his mug.

"It willnae make the pain go away, but mayhap 'twill help ye sleep."

Without a word, she accepted the drink, downing it in a gulp. "It willnae bring him back, either, will it?" she whispered, wiping her mouth with the back of her hand.

Conn clenched his teeth. "Nae, lass. Ryan isnae coming back. 'Tis something I will live with all my life."

Gilda tilted her head in curiosity. "Why? Ye did everything ye could to help."

"I wasnae there when he needed me."

He felt her touch on his knee and saw her earnest look. "Ye did what he asked. Ye saved Mairead and Lissa." She frowned. "And me."

"I could have sent someone else. It dinnae have to be me."

Gilda pulled her hand back, tucking it beneath the edge of her arisaid. "Nae. It dinnae have to be ye. But it was. And ye killed the pirate, Acair, who would have kidnapped us. Another man might not have."

"Ye are sure it was Acair MacEwen?"

"I heard it from his own lips. He was the one who promised revenge on my father."

Silence lengthened between them. Conn remembered the clan meeting at Scaurness Castle and the night Laird Macrory asked for help against the pirates. Laird Macraig had said 'nae.' What good his prideful scorn now?

The noise around them faded as people sought their rest. Gilda and Conn sat unmoving in their chairs.

"Will ye stay here?" he finally asked.

"Um?" Gilda bestirred herself, shifting in her seat. "I will stay for a bit. Lissa seems to need me. But I will return to Scaurness as soon as possible." She picked at the hem of her gown. "Laird Macraig has no use for me."

Conn had seen the hatred for Gilda on the old laird's face, and wondered if she shouldn't leave immediately.

"Is Ard Castle not yer home, now?"

Gilda flinched. "Nae. And I dinnae want it to be." Her voice broke on a sob and Conn had to lean forward to hear her next words. "I want my ma."

He stared at her, truly seeing her for the first time since they'd returned to the castle. The temptress who had stolen Ryan's heart was gone. As was the brave young woman who had stood up to the menacing pirate. The girl who sat next to him was heartbroken and vulnerable. She needed her ma.

But it was not his concern, and he had other matters to consider.

"Mairead and I will leave on the morrow. The storm should be past by then. I believe we are no longer welcome here."

Gilda lifted her gaze to his, bleakness darkening her eyes. "Nor am I."

Lissa sobbed as Gilda mounted her mare for the ride home. "I cannae stay here, dearling," she told the girl. "I need to be with my family now."

"But am I not yer family, too?" Lissa queried, her voice thick with tears.

Gilda leaned forward and cupped the lass' cheek in her palm. "Of course ye are. And welcome at Scaurness any time. And I will visit ye sometime." She darted a look at the laird, daring him to gainsay her. In her father's presence, however, Laird Macraig said nothing.

Her da spoke. "Let us be away, Gilda. Yer ma is expecting us."

Tears prickled Gilda's eyes at her da's soft words, but she refused to shed them. For just a little longer she would be strong, give Lissa the smile of encouragement she so desperately needed, hide the brittleness deep inside.

"Let the wench go, Lissa," Laird Macraig grumbled. "Her home is with her people."

Lissa whirled on him. "Da! She was Ryan's wife! How can ye turn her away?"

His face darkened. "So *she* says. No priest married them."

"He loved her." Lissa's voice broke. "*I* love her."

Beside her, Ranald stiffened and Gilda quickly reined her mare away. "Da, let us go. Ma is waiting on us."

The group of Macrory soldiers surrounded Gilda and her da, riding through the castle gate as Conn and Mairead and their men had only an hour earlier. The path leading from Ard Castle was churned to mud by the passage of many horses and Mairead's wagon, but the Macrorys soon veered south to the forest that divided the Macrory and Macraig lands.

Huddled deep in her arisaid, Gilda took little notice of her surroundings, trusting her da to get her home. As they entered the forest, the trees formed a barrier against the worst of the wind, though she could still hear it swaying through the tallest branches.

Ryan. Ryan. The wind sighed his name. Gilda flinched and urged Fia faster. After a moment the mare broke into a trot and without comment, the rest of the Macrorys kept pace.

A single rider reined his horse next to her da and leaned close. "There is a wolf on the trail following us."

Ranald shrugged. "There are too many of us for him to be a threat. Make sure none lag behind."

The soldier pulled his horse back and regained his position at the rear of the column. Gilda swiveled around in her saddle.

"Da? 'Tis my wolf."

"*Yer* wolf?"

"Aye. I freed him from a trap a few weeks ago and he attacked and killed the pirate when I was threatened. But he was injured. I want to help him. Please, Da. He needs my help."

Her da stared at her. At best he would think her daft. At worst?

Gilda wasn't sure it could get much worse.

Chapter Twenty-one

Gilda woke to the scent of berries. Something tickled her nose and she blearily opened her eyes. Sticky jam plastered the tousled blond locks of the small head next to her. For a moment, she stared at the strange sight, then memory dawned. Finn and Jamie curled against her, one on either side despite their ma's dire warnings should they bother Gilda during the night.

They had clung to her when she entered Scaurness the night before. They had bracketed her like bookends, their fiercely protective glares keeping all but her ma and Tavia at bay. For which she had been grateful. Exhausted and brokenhearted, she'd not wanted to hear the condolences and sad welcomes home. Ever the bolder of the pair, Finn had announced he and Jamie would be spending the night in her room and she had been touched, though a little leery of their loyalty. After only one instance of boyish bickering as she nodded off to sleep, Gilda was surprised to find she'd slept rather well after all.

She eyed the broken lines of sunlight spilling through the thick panes of glass in the window. From where the yellow rays pooled on the floor, she guessed it late morning. Spying the partially eaten platter of food on the small table against the wall, she decided the twins had helped themselves to her meal before settling back in for a nap. Well, it was too soon to think of the lads as perfect.

"She is awake," Finn hissed loudly.

Gilda ruffled his hair, the side without the smeared jam. "And ye have been into my repast, ye imp."

He sat with a jolt and drew himself up indignantly. "I dinnae! Ma would skelp my hide if I ate yer food."

On the other side, Jamie leaned across Gilda and pounded his brother's shoulder. "Ye have jam in yer hair, ye *bampot*."

"Dinnae call *me* an idiot, ye *clype*!"

"I dinnae tattle! She already knew!"

Rolling her eyes in exasperation, Gilda shoved both boys toward the edge of the bed. "Away with ye both, ye wee *louns*. I dinnae want to listen to ye *haver* while I dress."

The twins scurried off the bed and across the floor, filching toast from the tray as they passed.

"Have Cook send up a fresh meal!" she called after them. "And then wash yer hair!"

The door slammed behind the boys and Gilda sighed. She was home.

"Did the wolf really eat the bad pirate?" Jamie's eyes grew round. Both boys crept closer and Gilda felt a small hand snuggle inside one of hers. With a smile, she gently squeezed the chubby fingers and Finn scooted against her hip. Those seated closest to her at the table feigned disinterest, but the story was too fresh, too tempting to be ignored.

"Wheesht, ye bloodthirsty lad," Gilda chided. "The wolf dinnae eat the pirate. Though he did attack him."

"What happened to the wolf?" Finn asked.

"The pirate stabbed him."

"But ye found him and fixed him, aye?" Jamie chimed in, not to be outdone. They'd heard the story enough times by now to know its entirety, but they eagerly awaited every word.

Gilda obliged them with the tale. "He followed me on my way here. The wound the pirate gave him was deep and he needed my help."

"Where had the pirate stabbed him?" Both boys' eyes grew round with anticipation.

"The knife bit deep in his chest. I bound it as best I could and brought him home with me."

"The horses dinnae like that!" Finn snorted and reared back, waving his hands in the air, mimicking pawing hooves.

Gilda ruffled his hair with one hand. "Nae. They werenae pleased at all. But he followed me quietly as I led him the rest of the way home. He was verra ill for several days before he was strong enough to leave the little shed in the bailey. But he is likely hunting rabbits in the woods again, doing things wolves do in the forest."

"Ye had helped him afore, aye?"

Gilda cupped Finn's cheek fondly. Amazing how much the twins had changed in the past few weeks. "Aye. Once before, I had saved him from being caught in a trap."

"He remembered!" Jamie crowed.

"He saved her life!" Finn announced.

"After she saved his!"

Gilda took a deep breath. A tussle was brewing. As she'd thought before, perhaps it was a bit early to claim the two had changed much.

"Finn! Jamie!"

Ma's voice settled the lads. "Away with ye, now. Let yer sister finish her meal." She surveyed Finn's hair. "And give yer hair a wash. Ye have jam in it."

"Again?" With a huff of martyrdom, Finn slid from his chair. "I washed it yesterday."

"That was several days ago and ye had jam in it then, too." Ma gave him a stern look. "Dinnae come back to the table with sticky hair."

The boys slunk from the room, Jamie keeping to the far side of his brother and out of Ma's direct view.

Riona slipped into the chair beside Gilda. "Ye are sweet to entertain them, but ye need to eat."

Gilda eyed her plate, the cheese an unappetizing lump atop the bread rapidly going stale. Her mug of hot tea had long since grown cold. "I cannae even try it this morning, Ma."

Riona touched the back of her hand to Gilda's forehead. "Ye dinnae have a fever," she murmured. "Is it yer stomach, then?"

Gilda nodded. "Aye. I cannae seem to abide food so early in the day." She offered a bright smile. "I will be fine by midday. I am not sick."

With a frown, her ma rose. "'Tis why ye havenae broken yer fast in the past week and why ye settle in for a nap in the afternoon. Come with me. I will have Tavia fix ye something to settle yer stomach. This has gone on long enough."

Ranald was glad he was sitting down. He wasn't sure he could have handled the news standing up. As it was, his knees felt rubbery and his legs quivered. He eyed his wife with concern. "Are ye sure?"

Riona sank into a chair with a whoosh of skirts. Apparently her legs weren't up to the job, either.

She traced the design on the fabric adorning the arm of the chair with a fingertip before answering, "Aye. Gilda is with child. The bairn should be here mid-summer."

Ranald leaned back and rubbed his jaw. "How is she?"

His wife's grey eyes were dark, her expression worried. "I cannae say. Right now I believe she is shocked."

"I believe I am a wee bit *fashed* myself." He grimaced. "Married just over a fortnight, her husband dead these past weeks, and the lass is expecting. Sweet Jesu, but this is unexpected."

"She asked me to break the news. Ye dinnae have to pretend ye dinnae know."

Ranald shook his head. "I willnae treat the lass any different. She is my little Gilda, even if now a woman grown and about to make me a grandda."

Riona leaned forward and eyed him intently. "Then what worries ye so?"

"If she births a lad, he will be the Macraig heir. That changes everything."

"I dinnae like being *mid-bearne*, Tavia." Gilda stripped the gown over her head and tossed it across a chair. "None of my gowns fit."

"Wheesht, lass. 'Twill be only a wee bit longer. The lad is growing every day."

"How do ye know 'tis a lad? I would like a lass just as well." Gilda's voice muffled through layers of cloth as she pulled on another gown.

Tavia settled the fabric around Gilda's belly. "This high-waisted gown fits ye best right now." She pointed to the bulge. "See how low the babe rides? If the babe were a lass, it would sit much higher, and ye would havenae been able to wear yer old gowns so long. And ye tend to sleep on yer left side. That always means ye are having a lad."

"If I slept on my right side would the babe be a lass?"

"Six months gone is a wee bit late to change the sex of the babe. Ye were queasy at first, but not truly sick. That means a lad as well."

Gilda sighed. "That is why Laird Macraig is here today, isn't it?"

Lissa flung herself into Gilda's arms with a shriek of happiness. She bounced against Gilda's belly and backed up a pace, eyes wide with surprise.

Gilda laughed. "Do ye not know where bairns come from, then?"

Lissa's cheeks colored. "Of course I do. Ye look different, 'tis all."

"Different? Fat?"

"Och, no, Gilda! Ye look wonderful!"

"Wonderful, is it? With my belly popped out?"

Laird Macraig cleared his throat and the girls stopped their banter. Gilda recalled her manners and motioned to a chair.

"Please make yerself comfortable, Laird. I will have refreshments brought."

Laird Macraig shifted his feet and looked decidedly *un*comfortable. "My daughter wished to see ye."

"And bring her home, too!" Lissa reminded him with a pointed look.

"Pardon? What do ye mean, 'bring her home?'" Gilda felt the blood rush from her head. A faint dizziness swept over her.

Laird Macraig's face darkened and he waved his hand in the air impatiently. "Surely ye understand. Ye cannae stay here. Ard Castle is yer home."

Gilda raised an eyebrow, her ire rising. "Since when?"

From the corner of her eye, she saw her da move toward them. "Ye cannae force the lass to return with ye."

Gilda blessed his timely intervention.

Laird Macraig folded his arms across his chest, a belligerent stamp on his face. "She carries the Macraig heir. She belongs at Ard."

"We dinnae know if the babe is a lad or lass. We will let ye know when it arrives."

"She can deliver the babe at Ard." The laird flicked his gaze back to Gilda. "Where she belongs."

"I willnae go anywhere with ye, ye old goat!" The words were out of Gilda's mouth before she could stop them. She slapped a hand across her mouth, eyes wide.

Her ma grasped her other arm. "Wheesht, Gilda. We will settle things with the laird with kinder words, aye?" Ma's voice floated soft enough so only Gilda could hear.

Gilda inclined her head, returning the faint whisper. "Ma, he hates me. I am the reason his son is dead."

"Men die in battle, Gilda. 'Twas not yer fault. There are long-standing reasons he doesnae like the Macrory clan. Let yer da handle this. Dinnae *fash*."

Ranald was firm. "My daughter makes her own decisions, Macraig. We willnae force her."

Stubbornness carved deep lines in the Macraig's face. "She married my son."

"Ye never acknowledged it before." Gilda was just as stubborn.

"The bairn is my heir."

"*If* it is a lad."

"Oh, Gilda, do ye not see?" Lissa clutched Gilda's free hand, her eyes brimming with tears. "This babe is our very last link to Ryan. Ye couldnae be so cruel as to keep him from us."

Chapter Twenty-two

Chains clanked as the man braced himself against the storm. Being a prisoner and not trusted to have the ship and its crew's best interests at heart, he had been shackled and shoved below decks as the waves flung themselves at the cog ship. All hands stayed busy topside keeping the ungainly thing afloat. It was a common enough occurrence. Winter and spring were harsh months to be at sea. But during calmer weather, they worked him mercilessly and he welcomed the respite even in this tiny, dark, airless room.

The boat pitched unexpectedly and he struck the back of his head against the rough hull of the ship.

"Shite!" The shackles kept him from protecting himself against every roll of the vessel. From past experience, he knew his wrists would be scuffed and sore from his instinctive reactions to save himself a few bumps and bruises.

A very human moan slid through the creak of twisting wood and the buffeting sounds of the sea. Startled, he cast his gaze about the room, the darkness defeating his search for the source of the noise. The sound did not repeat itself, and he waited, alert and patient, for another clue.

The ship's roll eventually slowed to the rhythmic sway of open ocean and calmer seas. Daylight seeped through tiny cracks between the planks around him. Soon, enough light leaked into the room for him to discern the lower portion of a leg protruding from behind a wooden cask. Tattered cloth drooped from the bony appendage, the booted foot twisted to one side.

Poor beggar. So that's what happened to him. He recalled the man the ship's crew had pulled from the sea the day before. Ragged and thin to the point of emaciation, the man had regaled them of the storm that had destroyed his small boat's single sail several days earlier, and left him the sole survivor. With barely enough water to keep him alive and unable to direct his course, he had drifted aimlessly across the water in the remains of his vessel, praying for rescue.

The poor bastard should have prayed for death. He would get no sympathy from these pirates.

The moan sounded again. *May as well see to him. 'Twill be a small mercy to sit with him if he is dying, and a bit of diversion if he lives.*

Another hand on this ship of death wouldn't come amiss, though he might not survive long in his condition.

The man stood, knees slightly bent to absorb the gentle roll of the ship as she tacked through the waves. The storm over, it was only a matter of time before the crew, likely exhausted from their labors, remembered him and demanded he take his place amid the rigging. Moving quickly, he rounded the edge of the barrel, careful not to bark his bare toes against the wooden staves. He stared for a moment at the ragged castaway, then sank to the floor beside him.

"How fare ye?" he asked.

For several moments he received no answer, then a rattling sigh drifted from the prone man's chest.

"Water?"

"I am sorry, but I have none to give ye." He waved his hands in the direction of the barrel. "Likely this cask contains a bit of sherry from whatever port we sailed into a week ago, but I have no way of tapping it."

"The pirates…" The castaway's voice faded away.

"Dinnae care if ye live or die. Ye can recover despite their lack of care, work hard, maybe earn a bit of bread and water, or ye can cock yer toes up and take yer last rest on the waves. Doesnae matter to them."

With an effort, the battered man roused to his elbows. "Ye are a prisoner, too?"

"Aye. These past six months."

"What is yer name?"

"That is an interesting question. Ye see, I dinnae know my true name. The pirates dragged me aboard, so they say, with a wound that nearly cleaved my head in two. I wasnae a pretty sight for a long time, and still have this scar to remind me." He tilted his head to the side and ran a finger down the length of the knotted skin.

"'Tis a miracle ye lived."

"The pirates thought so, too. 'Tis why they call me *Ferlie*." He rattled the chains on his wrists. "'Tis my thought they are a wee bit afraid to chuck me overboard. Being a superstitious lot, they dinnae know what to do with a man who is so lucky to be alive." He grimaced. "I worry one day my luck will run out."

The pirates did not question Ferlie as he went about his work mending the storm-torn rigging. Nor did they interfere as he nursed the castaway back to health. Within a week, the man, Greum, tottered onto the deck.

"Och. I never thought to see the sunlight again." Greum gripped the railing as he breathed the fresh sea air. "Do ye know where we are?"

Ferlie sat on a nearby wooden chest, fingers splicing together a torn piece of rigging. "They dinnae share their precious store of knowledge, but if I am not mistaken, we are near the coast of France."

"So far from home? What do they trade for there?"

Ferlie glanced up, lifting a hand against the bright glare of the sun. "The bilge rats dinnae trade. They will salvage any wrack and wraith they find. A ship that founders on the sea is God-sent as far as they are concerned. Take the bounty, leave the poor souls behind. France? My guess 'tis sherry and brandy they are after."

Greum gasped. Ferlie shrugged. "'Tis nothing I can do."

"Nae, I understand ye are one shackled man against thieving pirates. I wish to look at ye again. In the light." Greum motioned for him to draw closer.

Ferlie sent a wary look over his shoulder. "We cannae seem to be in deep conversation. They will assume we are plotting mischief."

Greum stared at him, his lips an 'O' of surprise. "Lad, ye must know who ye are."

Ferlie gave the older man a sharp look. "Do ye know me?"

"Nae, lad. I dinnae know ye. But yer eyes—they are the mark of the Macraig."

Pain flashed through Ferlie's head, pulling sharply at his memory. "What do ye mean?"

"'Tis the first I have seen them—in the light, I mean. They are an unusual golden color. Laird Macraig, and generations before him, stamp each of their bairns so."

One of the pirates shouted across the deck. "Get back to work, ye *scunners*! Afore we feed yer carcasses to the fish."

Ferlie handed Greum his mending. "Here. 'Tis not such strenuous labor. I will find else to do." He rose abruptly and shuffled away.

"I am so glad ye are here, Gilda," Lissa sighed. "Da and I are both glad."

Gilda caught Lissa's furtive glance in her direction. "Yer da has ignored me. He doesnae truly want me here." She raised a finger to stem Lissa's protest. "I am just visiting. I will go home to have the baby."

"But, Gilda. Ard is your home."

"Please, let us not argue, Lissa. I want to be with my ma and Tavia then."

The dark-haired girl pouted. "Aye. I understand that. But the heir should be born here."

Gilda held her tongue. She knew Lissa did not see her da's scowls and dark looks of disapproval each time he encountered Gilda. As much as he disliked the Macrorys, and her in particular, she could not fathom the reason he had allowed Lissa to invite her here.

She perused the young girl, now busily chatting with Keita as they plied their needles. Though their efforts produced charming clothing for the babe, Gilda grew weary of the endless days of sewing and embroidery. She did not feel her activity should be restricted in the least, but the laird refused to allow them to leave the castle. Of course, sitting in the solar with the women was a good way to avoid the dour man, but enough was enough. Vexed with the long days, she wanted answers to her questions, and planned to seek them out today.

Placing her sewing in the basket at her side, she smiled briefly at the other ladies and strolled through the door. Seeing a guard posted at the door to the laird's private chamber off the great hall told her instantly he was there, likely going over papers or accounts. With a gracious nod, she halted at the closed door. In a murmur sounding much more serene than she felt, she addressed the guard.

"Please announce me to the laird."

The guard was gone only a moment, though it seemed far longer to Gilda's tightly strung nerves. Without a word, he held the door open for her. She picked up her courage and her skirts as she entered the room.

She shuddered at the chill of the room. Warmth emanated from the fire on the hearth, but could not dispel the late spring cold penetrating the stone walls. Laird Macraig did not acknowledge her presence and she halted before his desk, glancing around the room as she waited.

Moments dragged by, punctuated only by the rasp of a quill as the laird moved a hand, spotted with age, across the parchment on his desk. It soon became clear he had no intention of indulging her with any of the respect or courtesies she was accustomed to. Hiding her annoyance, she swallowed to clear her throat before speaking.

"I want to know why ye summoned me to Ard Castle." She lifted her chin. "The truth, please."

Laird Macraig finally lifted his gaze from the parchments before him to stare at her, but she could read nothing of his thoughts. Beneath heavy brows, his peculiar amber eyes remained shuttered.

Shifting uncomfortably under his silent scrutiny, she took a deep breath and pursued her question. "I came here because Lissa is still heartbroken over her brother's death and talk of the babe cheers her up. She truly wants me here. I want to know why you sanctioned her request."

Shrugging, he at last replied, "If Lissa is happy, 'tis one less thing I am vexed with."

"I am not here to solve yer vexing problems."

Laird Macraig grunted. "Seems as though ye are."

Frustrated with his unflinching coldness, she spun about, her skirts swirling heavily about her ankles. Pale sunlight from the single window in the room bled a path across the floor, illuminating a sword and battered targe angled in a corner of the hearth. Ryan's weapons.

She whirled back to the laird's desk. "Ye dinnae like me and dinnae acknowledge the vows Ryan and I pledged to each other before he died. Yet ye have to believe we married for ye to see this child as yer heir."

Shifting his attention back to the sheets of vellum on his desk, Laird Macraig waved her away with a motion of his hand. "If ye carry Ryan's bairn, ye belong here."

"*If!*" Gilda all but screeched. Indignation rose in her, stifling her frustration, fueling her temper. She leaned forward and grasped the edge of the desk in a white-knuckled grip, forcing the man to look at her. "Ye are a bastard, Laird Macraig! How dare ye question the babe's father?"

He smirked, tapping his quill against his fingers. "Care to discuss who the real bastard is in this room, *Lady* Gilda?"

Her chest tightened and she fought for control. "Ye are an evil man! Ye offered for my ma when I was but a bairn, yet refused to give yer name or home to me. How dare ye? Ye felt slighted when she and her da refused yer offer, and started a feud that benefits no one. Now that I have something ye want, ye think ye can order my life? Ye are the bastard here, m'laird, make no mistake. I willnae raise my bairn in yer poisonous home."

Laird Macraig's face darkened with a thunderous look. "The bairn's heritage is here!"

"My bairn's heritage will be one of love and acceptance. I willnae raise him among auld fears and regrets."

"Ye cannae leave here. I forbid it."

"Forbid all ye want, auld man. I am going home!" Gilda pushed away from the desk, her head spinning with emotion.

Laird Macraig surged to his feet. "Guard!"

The door burst open and an armed man appeared in the opening. Gilda scarcely slowed her step. Casting him a furious look, she spat her angry words. "Touch me and I will draw blood."

With a startled glance at his laird, the man edged to the side, allowing Gilda to pass.

"Ye amadan! Dinnae let her leave!" The laird snarled his anger, and the guard took a hesitant step toward Gilda, but did not reach for her. The door between them closed.

Gilda's pace quickened. She could not, would not stay a moment longer. It took effort to control the building panic within her.

Hurrying down the hallway, Lissa caught up with her. "What is wrong, Gilda? Ye are all but running!"

Biting her lip against angry words, she huffed. "Yer da is a fool!"

"I dinnae understand."

"He wants to use my babe to continue the feud between the Macraigs and Macrorys."

"Why?" The pair rushed past startled servants who quickly stepped out of their way. Gilda gripped her skirts in both hands, lifting them away from her feet to keep from tripping over them.

"Ye are too young to understand, Lissa. Yer da is full of hate, not love. I am going home."

Lissa caught Gilda's hand, effectively halting her steps. "Oh, Gilda! Ye are my sister now, and I couldnae bear to see ye leave. Please say ye will stay with me."

Gilda's heart broke to hear Lissa's pleading, but she wasn't about to stay under the same roof as Laird Macraig a moment longer than she had to. "Come with me," she urged the young girl. "Ye would be such a help to me." *And spending time away from yer da could only help ye.*

Lissa's brow puckered, clearly unsure what to say or do. When she met Gilda's gaze again, her eyes were round with building excitement.

"Do ye think I should?"

Gilda hugged the girl's slender shoulders. "Of course! I will send a message to my da today. We will need an escort, and I doubt Laird Macraig will be willing."

Laird Macraig's cloak billowed behind him, catching the cold morning wind. Even across the bailey, Gilda felt the weight of his disapproval. She was grateful her da had responded so quickly, for she feared the lengths the auld laird would take to keep her at Ard Castle.

"How fare ye, Lissa?" She leaned close to whisper to the younger girl. To her surprise, Lissa met her question with a broad smile, her face beaming with happiness.

"I have never been anywhere but Ard Castle. This is verra exciting!"

"Good. Ye will have a grand visit. Ye know ye can come home whenever ye like."

Lissa burrowed deep within the hood of her arisaid. "I know. But I wish we were there already. 'Tis verra cold!"

Gilda shivered as a cold blast from the firth bit deep. "Most of the ride will be in the forest. The wind shouldnae be so fierce there." Accepting help from her father's captain, she climbed into the wagon, her advancing pregnancy denying her Fia's saddle. The team ducked their heads away from the wind as they exited the castle gates.

Wind whistled off the water, numbing Gilda's fingers and bringing tears to her eyes. Today was a day for staying close to the hearth. She thought longingly of the warm bed she and Ryan had once shared. Bracing against the icy rain spitting from leaden clouds, she turned her back on Macraig land.

Today was a day for going home.

Chapter Twenty-three

$\mathcal{T}$ime weighed heavily on Gilda. Her belly swollen and her mood sometimes testy, she longed for the babe's arrival. In the woods the flowers bloomed and berry blossoms turned to the promise of harvest, but her steps were measured and jaunts through the forest a thing of the past. Once or twice she'd caught a glimpse of grizzled fur lightening the shadows at the edge of the forest. She fancied the wolf watched over her and was comforted.

From her window, Gilda could see the village. Tiny people bustled about on their errands. Below, in the bailey, men shouted, weapons clanged, and smoke rose from the blacksmith's forge. Beside her, Lissa chatted gaily.

It was her second visit to Scaurness since she and Gilda returned months earlier, and normally Gilda was glad for her distractions. Today Lissa's animated prattle only reminded Gilda how confined she was.

Not wanting to stifle the girl and leave hurt feelings on both sides, Gilda stood. "I think I will go for a walk."

Lissa gasped. "Och, nae! Ye cannae go strolling around in yer condition."

With a wave of her hand, Gilda strode from the room. "I just need some fresh air. I will walk in the bailey."

Thankful Lissa did not offer to follow, Gilda stopped beyond the door and stretched her back, her palms pushing against the strain. The babe kicked, in protest or approval she didn't know. But the vigorous activity brought a smile to her lips. Covering the abused spot with her palm, she spoke softly. "'Tis good ye are so active. But have a care for yer ma's insides. They are a bit tender today."

With concern for her increasingly awkward state, she edged down the stairs, gripping the carved railing for balance. People in the hall halted their duties long enough to greet her with respectful nods which Gilda returned cheerfully.

The doors to the bailey flared open, sunlight warming the floor. Filling her lungs with soft morning air, she sought a nearby bench. It was in full sun, but Gilda did not care. The tenuous heat soaked through her dress and into her skin, right to her bones. Her toes curled in contentment as she leaned her head against the wall and closed her eyes.

Horses nickered and stamped, men called to each other in greeting. Around her, life went on as usual. The babe stirred, a shifting of position, and Gilda laid a lazy hand across the growing mound of her belly in a comforting gesture.

"So, 'tis true, then."

Gilda cracked an eye at the voice. Conn stood before her, his face shadowed, the sun to his back. He motioned to her stomach with a jerk of his head. "Ye carry Ryan's bairn."

Her heart stopped and her stomach heaved, for in that instant the sound of Conn's voice recalled the horrible desolation of the day of the pirate attack. Without warning, she burst into tears.

Hands patted her shoulder, awkwardly, gently at first, then, as she cried harder, Conn sat beside her and pulled her into his embrace. Gilda jammed a fist against her mouth, trying to contain her unexpected reaction, and after a few harrowing moments, her sobbing eased. As she gulped back the last of the tears, Conn loosened his grip and she pulled away.

"I am sorry. I dinnae mean to do that." She swiped at her cheeks with the backs of her hands. "I just…" She gave a helpless shrug.

"I am sorry I startled ye. I heard there was a bairn waiting to be born, and I wanted to see for myself."

Gilda managed a half-smile. With an effort, she turned the conversation to him. "Ye look well. Has yer arm healed properly?"

"Aye, thanks to ye. It mended well and I have since trained the soreness from it. How are ye?"

"Growing." Gilda felt the heat rise in her cheeks. "I am glad ye came. Things have been quiet around here."

"Quiet? Ye have turned the place on its wee head." Conn gestured toward the hall. "I looked for ye at Ard, but was told ye returned to Scaurness." With a snort, Conn expressed his disbelief. "I expected the babe born at Ard."

Fingering the fabric of her skirt, Gilda took her time answering. "Without Ryan there, it isnae the same."

"Think of his son, playing in the bailey. Exploring the same forests, hearing the same sounds his da did as a wean." He placed a hand on her arm in an earnest gesture. "Ye carry a great gift. The gift of Ryan's child. Even if it is a lass, she is a Macraig."

Warm earth scented the air as Gilda strolled through the garden the next morning. "Tend them well, Lissa. We need enough herbs to dry for winter, not only to cook with this summer and fall."

Lissa drew the back of a soiled hand across her brow, lifting a lock of hair from her face. "I like helping in the garden. I never knew there were so many different herbs."

"My ma and Tavia taught me much about herb lore. 'Tis a useful thing to know."

A male voice interrupted. "Might I have a word with ye, Gilda?"

She looked up, surprised to see Conn in the kitchen garden. "Could we sit on yon bench? My back and feet are a bit sore today."

"Of course, lass. I only wish to discuss a matter with ye."

Gilda eyed him with mild curiosity. "Whatever it is, ye'd best take it up with my da. I cannae imagine needing my advice on anything."

"Och, I dinnae think this is something I need to talk to him about. Not yet. This requires yer approval before I approach Laird Macrory. Ye arenae a young maid anymore."

Gilda stopped in her tracks. "What are ye dithering about, Conn?"

He laughed and motioned for her to take a seat on the wooden bench beneath a sprawling tree. With a skeptical frown, Gilda accepted the offer.

"Weel, what is it? What is on yer mind?"

To her surprise, his smile disappeared and he hunkered on his heels at her feet. Anticipation warred with suspicion inside her as he seemed to gather his thoughts. Finally, he lifted his gaze to her.

"Gilda, I want ye to marry me."

Ferlie fingered the thick, ropy scar that curved along the side of his head. Partly hidden beneath his hair, it still ached from time to time, serving as a reminder of a past he could not recollect. His knowledge began and ended with the wound, long since healed, but setting him apart from the men around him.

What did Greum mean, I am stamped with the eyes of the Macraig? Am I part of the Macraig clan? He thumped his thighs with fists clenched in frustration. Why could he not remember?

He closed his eyes, pushing to recall the day he woke aboard the pirates' ship. Pain exploded behind his lids, but he gritted his teeth and pushed harder. A flash of sunshine, the trill of feminine laughter, all gone in an instant.

Red. Why do I remember the color red? Why is this important to me? He released his breath in a whoosh of frustration. Sweet laughter. Quicksilver eyes. Then nothing. He opened his eyes and rubbed his brow against the throbbing at his temples.

"Have ye remembered anything, lad?" Greum whispered in his ear as he collapsed onto the worn wooden chest next to him with a weary sigh.

Ferlie stared straight ahead, fixed on a point he could not see past. "Red, laughter, pain. Though usually I only remember the pain and go no further."

Greum nodded. "Aye. Yer body isnae ready to remember what happened. 'Twas a fierce wound ye suffered. Ye nearly lost yer life."

"I feel I lost something more precious than my life, Greum." He braced against the pressure building in his chest, the dark cloud of dismay swelling to the point of unbearable pain. "I want to know what it was."

"Ye want me to marry ye?" Gilda's jaw dropped and she hastily shut it. "Why? Ye dinnae like me."

"I dinnae like the changes in Ryan's life. 'Twas difficult to adjust a ten-year friendship on the whims of a lass I dinnae know."

"Ye blamed me for Ryan's death."

Conn's eyes clouded. "Aye. 'Twas easier to share the blame than to shoulder it. It has taken a long time to realize 'twas neither my fault nor yers. We both did what we had to at the time."

"I thank ye for that. But that doesnae mean we should marry."

Rising to scoot onto the seat beside Gilda, Conn leaned forward. "Think of it, Gilda. Ye know I would raise Ryan's bairn as my own. And the marriage would ally not two, but three clans."

"And ye would still have a piece of Ryan," Gilda whispered. His excitement alarmed her.

"Aye! The bairn needs a da in his life. 'Tis the perfect solution."

His eager face made something twist inside her and she hated telling him no. She took a deep breath and stiffened her resolve.

"'Tis not the perfect solution for me."

Conn started to speak, but she lifted a hand to stay his protest. "I dinnae need to marry just to give my bairn a da. If a lad, there are plenty of braw men here and at Scaurness to teach him. And I am not a pawn to link these three clans. They are already allied."

"Gilda, it would give the bairn a family. A ma and a da who love him, care for him. Or her."

With sorrow in her heart, Gilda shook her head. "Please dinnae be angry with me, Conn. Yer offer is verra kind—"

"Kind?" Conn bolted to his feet, a curl to his lip. "Ye think I would offer marriage to just any lass who claimed to carry Ryan's bairn? He wasnae celibate before he met ye, Gilda. Ye cannae be that naïve!"

Gilda's breath caught and ice washed through her veins. "Nae, I am not that naïve. But I dinnae think ye would say such a thing to me."

Conn slumped onto the bench again, his head drooped low. "I beg ye to forgive me, Gilda. I know better than that. Ryan dinnae chase the lasses, though they found him from time to time. He was verra much in love with ye, and whatever happened before he met ye has no part in this."

"Thank ye." Shaken, his reaction only reinforced her decision to decline his offer.

"I said that because I was hurt. I have thought this through, and I am certain we could fare well together." He met her eyes earnestly. "I wouldnae bring ye into a loveless marriage. My heart has changed. I see the sweet lass Ryan loved, and I wouldnae dishonor him by hurting ye."

She laid a hand gently on his forearm. "Conn, I was desperately in love with Ryan. Ye deserve such in yer life, and I dinnae think I can give it. Truly, I am afraid to love like that again." Tears swelled her throat. "It hurts too much."

Conn stared at the ground at his feet. Overwhelmed by her emotions, Gilda sat beside him, pleating the fabric of her dress in dismay.

Finally, Conn rose. "I dinnae want to stay away. May I still visit? Ye and the bairn."

Gilda mustered a smile. "Of course ye may. The bairn needs a braw uncle such as yerself."

Conn cut his gaze to her. "An uncle? 'Tis all I can hope for?"

"Ye arenae in love with me, Conn MacLaurey. Ye are in love with the bairn."

"I believe ye are wrong, Gilda Macraig. Verra wrong."

Darkness was the pirate's ally. The gloaming just before the moon rose, when starlight played tricks on men's eyes and trust was a fragile commodity.

"They sighted the foundered ship a couple of hours ago." Ferlie cast his voice low as Greum hobbled to the rail next to him. "'Tis just beyond the horizon. If no other ships approach, they will scuttle it tonight."

"There is naught we can do?"

Ferlie shook his head. "I am always locked away below deck until time to bring the spoils aboard. But I cannae do this again. 'Tis not right."

Greum tilted his head. "What do ye propose we do? They willnae trust either of us with weapons."

"There are two of us this time." Ferlie turned to the older man, determination on his face. "I have a plan."

His shoulder hurt like hell, but it was just a bruise and worth the effort. The scuffle between himself and the first mate had convinced the pirate's leader he'd make a fine asset on the night's raid. Ferlie rolled his shoulder to ease the tension, then put the slight injury behind him. There was a more important task ahead.

Greum sidled over, a dirk in his hand. "Do ye think it will work?"

"The pirates arenae well organized. They are vultures, feasting on the carcasses of dying ships. Like vultures, they are also cowardly. If the crew of the other vessel shows enough resistance, I believe the pirates will retreat. They value their disreputable hides more than whatever treasure they may find aboard."

"I am to release the grappling hooks, aye?"

Ferlie jerked his chin to the ship that showed as a dark stain on the lowering horizon. "It lists badly to port. We must swap ships."

"Leaving this scurvy scum on yon sinking ship?"

"I expect a bit of resistance from both sides, but aye, that is the plan."

Greum squared his thin shoulders. "Let us be at it, then."

Slowly, they approached the foundered ship. It wobbled about like a child's ill-formed toy atop the cresting waves. Three pirates showed themselves above the *Draigled Sparra's* railing, light from swaying torches casting contorted shadows against the wooden hull. Across the water, dark forms moved about, illuminated from time to time by lanterns lashed bow and stern. At this distance it was difficult to tell how well-armed the ship was, but Ferlie knew those on board had to be frightened as they anticipated the eventual slide into the watery abyss even as much as they feared rescue by unscrupulous, mercenary pirates. No, his job would not be easy.

"Ahoy, the ship!" Eager for plunder, the pirate leader called out. Silence from the other ship lasted a few moments.

"*Ohé du navire! Parlez-vous française?*"

"'Tis a Frenchie ship, lads!"

Excited murmurs rose from the pirates huddled on the deck. Their leader braced his hands on the edge of the hull and bellowed across the distance. "Nae! Scots!"

"*Oui, monsieur l'capitaine.* We will converse in English."

A ship's length separated them now and Ferlie could see the faces of the men across from him, their skin muddy red in the lantern light and deeply slashed with shadows. Beside him, a pirate firmed the grip on his sword, the metal winking dully, pitted with hard use and little care. The odor of their unwashed bodies threatened to overpower as they huddled close together, mingling with the tang of salt water and fear.

His fingers choked the handle of his own weapon.

Suddenly, the words between the two men changed. Shouts rang out. Pirates bolted to their feet, grabbing metal hooks attached to ropes as they swarmed across the deck to the foundering ship. Swords held high, their battle cries filled the air. Hooks were flung across the dividing waters, hitting the other ship's hull with deafening thuds like the clamor of pickaxes breaking ground for the soon-to-be-dead.

Poised on their ship's railing, pirates ranged in eager anticipation. Across from them, swords slipped from scabbards, promising no easy prey.

Ferlie's gaze slid from man to man, picking out their captain. His eyes lit on a burly shape near the base of the forecastle. Set apart by his clothing and the deference of his sailors, he radiated authority. The French ship collided with the *Draigled Sparra* as the grappling hooks did their work. The captain braced himself with a hand to the elevated deck and shrugged away any who would push him up the steps to safety. He unsheathed his sword with a steady hand and faced the devils invading his ship.

Ferlie gripped his sword, flexing his fingers around the worn grip. He did not question the seamless way the blade had become an extension of his arm or the ease with which he wielded the weapon. It made him feel alive, powerful. Battle lust still coursed through his veins as his heart pounded in his chest. Blood from several shallow cuts crusted as it dried. His muscles ached and his chest heaved, but he was alive and fiercely glad for it.

As the pirates boiled over the side of the foundered ship like scum from an unwatched pot, he had located the ship's captain. Convincing him he was there to help had taken well-placed words and more than a bit of skilled swordplay before the harried captain had accepted the plan. And the work of the better part of a bloody hour to finally turn the tables and subdue the pirates.

'Twas a good thing, Ferlie mused, for after his part in the mutiny, his life wouldn't have been worth a burnt bannock to the pirates.

He narrowed his eyes and surveyed the small group of passengers and crew now aboard the pirate ship. The captain strode slowly among them, offering a soft word or clasping a shoulder as he spoke to each one. His wife and two daughters were on the ship, sailing back to France from visiting family in Edinburgh, and mercifully unharmed. For that alone, Ferlie knew he could enlist the man's help in anything. But what to ask?

Elsewhere, men hurried to get the ship under way. Cries from the pirates now aboard the listing ship drifted across the water. Ferlie wasted no sympathy on them. He sniffed the breeze, sensing a change in the weather. Stars sparked overhead, but wisps of clouds sped across the midnight sky.

Suddenly, his eyes snapped to one of the three women still standing amidships. Wrapped in their cloaks, they had been anonymous shapes, recognizable as women, though he had paid scant attention to them. With the stiffening breeze, one woman's shawl slid free to her shoulders, spilling her hair about her. Caught in the flickering torchlight, it glinted of gold and fire. Red.

His breath caught. Flashes of memory crackled through his mind. His free hand flew to the side of his head in an attempt to slow the assault. A face, sweetly feminine, lips curved in laughter, the sun bright on her skin. Her form appeared, twirling about, her arisaid caught lightly at her elbows, her molten red curls fanned out around her.

Who is she?

Lissa bounded to Gilda's side, full of youthful energy. "Who are ye looking for?" She stretched up on her toes and leaned over the edge of the parapet.

Gilda's face heated. "No one special. 'Tis a beautiful day, aye?"

Her hands grasping the worn stone, Lissa extended her arms and swung gently back and forth. "Is it time for Conn to pay a call on ye?" she asked, her tone light and overly innocent.

Gilda swatted the girl's arm. "How should I know what the MacLaurey man does? 'Tis none of my concern."

Her bluff did not convince Lissa, who spun about, her back against the wall. "He has come to visit twice in the past month and a half. He doesnae come for yer da's whisky, and he doesnae come to spend time with me." She raised her eyebrows for emphasis. "He visits ye."

"'Tis not me he wishes to see, but the bairn."

"And the bairn willnae be here for another two weeks or more. Gilda, he visits ye."

Gilda looked out over the fields surrounding the castle. To the north lay Ard, and to the west the vastness of the ocean. To the northeast was a man she'd never expected to see again after that disastrous day last autumn. Looking forward to his visit would not have crossed her mind two months ago. But she did.

"If he doesnae come soon, then it *will* be the bairn he visits."

Lissa's face dropped its teasing mien. "Oh, Gilda! Do ye have pains?"

Shaking her head, Gilda replied, "Nae. Dinnae *fash*. 'Tis that I am so big and awkward I cannae think the babe will wait much longer."

Light flashed at the edge of the trees and a shout went up from a guard. Both girls swirled about and Gilda clutched Lissa's hand.

The girl gave voice to the words in Gilda's heart.

"He is here!"

They wended their way down the staircase, making allowance for Gilda's ponderous gait. By the time they reached the bailey, Conn and his soldiers had arrived and Gilda was out of breath. Sweat prickled between her heavy breasts, and her heart pounded. She managed a smile of welcome as she put one hand to her back to soothe a sudden pain.

"Gilda? Ye are white. Come sit down." Conn took her arm and helped her to a nearby bench as the other riders led the horses away.

"'Tis nothing," she assured him with a wave of her hand. "I shouldnae have hurried down the stairs like I did."

Conn frowned. "Ye should take better care." He glared at Lissa.

"She dinnae hurry." Lissa shrugged. "She *cannae* hurry."

Gilda grimaced. Lissa and Conn's words swirled about her. Pain cut deep in her back and flared around her belly. Warmth flooded between her legs. She gripped Conn's hand.

"I want my ma!"

Chapter Twenty-four

Restlessness pulled at him, eroding his waking and sleeping thoughts like waves pulling at a sandy shore. Held captive by the pirates, Ferlie's first concern had been healing, then escape. But with Greum's hint at a heritage—a family, a place of belonging—his scrutiny turned to remembering who he was, how he'd come to awaken on the *Draigled Sparra* with a fiercely pounding, bloody head and no memory. With an effort, he tightened his focus on his host's thickly accented words.

"*Mon ami*, there is no way I could have brought this ship in without your help. Between the storm and the pirate attack, I had too many men killed or wounded to sail." He had the grace to look abashed. "As their prisoner, I am sure you would rather be on your way home than seeing the sights of France, such as they are. Again, I thank you for your kind assistance."

Ferlie forced a brief smile. "I cannae see our help as anything but mutual. Greum and I couldnae have managed alone, either. And I dinnae know exactly where home is."

Gulls screamed overhead as they banked into the stiff breeze blowing along the wharf. Men shouted and ropes creaked as ships around them unloaded their cargos. The wind brought the scent of the sea, pushing back the odors of garbage and less savory things littering the port, and for that, Ferlie was grateful.

Thumping his thick chest dramatically with meaty fingers, the captain declared, "You shall come to my home tonight. There will be decent food, clean clothing, and a soft bed. For both you and your man."

"I thank ye—"

"No thanks needed. It is you I should be thanking. My wife will have my head and my daughters be sorely disappointed if I do not bring you home tonight."

"But Captain, I wish—"

Again, the man waved aside Ferlie's protests. "Tomorrow is soon enough for wishes. You cannot sail this vessel tonight. It is not seaworthy and ye have no crew. It will take time to get you aboard another." He cocked his head. "Assuming you know where you want to go."

Ferlie shook his head. "Nae. I only know I must sail back to Scotland."

"Then it is settled. You will stay with us until such arrangements can be made. And I will be honored to pay for your voyage, *mon ami*. Very honored."

Ferlie cast his gaze to the evening sky as night rushed in. The sturdy feel of the wharf's boards beneath his feet was reassuring, the desire to leave the *Draigled Sparra* and her rotting timbers behind, strong. Somewhere behind him, past the far horizon, was his home. But where?

Does anyone know I am alive? Am I mourned? What, if anything, do I have to go back to?

The pang of a partial memory jolted through him. Red hair. A teasing smile. His loins tightened, but the full recollection remained out of reach. Pushing past his frustration, he nodded acquiescence.

"I am verra grateful to take yer offer, *mon capitaine*. After these long months at sea, what harm could there be in a few days ashore?"

Gilda rolled her head on her pillow as Tavia approached. Her ma's cool fingers stroked her sweat-damp forehead. Even exhausted, an exultant thrill ran through her. Beaming encouragingly, Tavia placed the small bundle in her arms.

"He is a braw lad, *a stor*. Strong like his ma." Tavia adjusted the bairn's head in the crook of Gilda's elbow. "There! Look at that mouth working. He will be howling to be fed soon."

"He is a beautiful bairn, Gilda. I am so proud of you." Riona kissed her cheek as she lightly touched the babe's rounded cheeks, framed by soft layers of cloth.

Gilda's heart filled and she didn't know whether to laugh or cry. Her baby opened his eyes and peered at her searchingly, blinking owlishly. Gilda burst into tears. Hands reached for the babe, but she pulled him close, rocking him against her breast.

"Wheesht, Gilda! Ye will frighten the bairn if ye greet so." Tavia clucked her tongue and patted Gilda's shoulder.

"Gilda, lass, what is wrong?" Soothing words slowed her sobs and she leaned against her ma's shoulder. Her chest eased as her ma's arms surrounded her.

"I am tired." Hiccupping, she stemmed her tears. "He is so tiny and perfect." She gently touched a finger to his satiny cheek. "And Ryan will never know him." Fresh grief poured down her face.

Ma pulled her closer, her cheek against her hair. "Ryan would be so proud of ye, Gilda. I know ye miss him and will be reminded of him often in the coming days. But ye have many people ready to love and care for yer wee man. He is a verra special bairn, ye know."

"I know. My heart *aches* to see Ryan. Especially now." At Gilda's touch, the bairn turned toward her finger. His lips puckered and his face wrinkled in a decidedly unhappy frown.

"Best feed the lad before he brings these walls down," Tavia advised.

Gilda's fingers fumbled with the neckline of her gown. Apparently deciding his ma wasn't hurrying properly, the babe released a mighty howl. Laughing nervously, Gilda pulled the fabric aside and cuddled her babe against her. His cries dwindled to a muffled sniff as he latched hungrily onto her breast. Surprised wonder filled Gilda as she watched him nurse. Soon he drifted off to sleep, milk beading along the edge of his lips.

"I will put him in his cradle so ye can get some rest as well." Ma lifted the babe from Gilda's tired arms. "Yer da and Lissa can take a peek at him, then ye must sleep."

Gilda sighed drowsily as she drifted on the edge of exhaustion. Tavia tied the lace at the neck of her gown and pulled a blanket over her, then tiptoed to the window and closed the shutters, dimming the room. Gilda heard the soft creak of the door and the muffled whispers of her ma and da as he entered the room.

Lissa's feet pattered across the floor as she darted to the cradle beside the bed. "How tiny he is!" she exclaimed.

"A braw lad," Da proclaimed with curious muffled quality to his voice that made Gilda smile.

"Wheesht, now, the bairn and his ma need their rest," her ma scolded in a whisper.

"Does he have a name, yet, lass?"

Gilda opened her eyes. "Aye. His name is William."

"'Tis a strong name." He nodded in approval.

"Oh, look!"

Gilda shifted her gaze at Lissa's soft cry. Snuggled within his bunting, William stared at his aunt.

Lissa pointed to him. "His eyes. They have golden rims." She bent closer to the babe. "They're going to look just like mine."

Candlelight glinted off the rich appointments in the long hallway outside the manor's ballroom, imparting a satin sheen to the highly polished furniture. The scent of freshly cut flowers permeated the room, their bright colors highlighting tables in enormous bouquets throughout. Ferlie dodged the overhanging blooms in a particularly large vase as he approached the doors to the room. After nearly a week at the captain's house, he knew his way around the impressive manor's corridors and doorways, though he could not say he felt at home.

As he endured the time it took to obtain passage back to Scotland, the tug to leave refused to ease. Fruitless days and nights of running the name 'Macraig' through his mind brought him no closer to knowledge of his identity. Fractured memories failed to form any recognizable picture, and he felt the lack sorely. Were it not for his host's generosity and the friendly attentions of his youngest daughter, he feared he would have lost his patience and his mind days earlier.

This was his last night at his host's house, and the captain's wife insisted on a dinner party. He and Greum would take their leave on the morrow and 'twas her way to show her gratitude once more. Ferlie fingered his waistline. Another week of their excellent cook's food would see him well recovered from the starvation diet he'd faced during his time with the pirates.

Too many people. He stared into the room from the shadows of the doorway. Though appreciative of his hosts' thoughtfulness, being on display before their friends made his stomach clench. *At least I can claim an early rising and leave the gathering without waiting for the last guest to depart.*

"I would rather drink poison than join that crowd." Greum's muttered words shook Ferlie from his thoughts. He noted the smaller man's disapproving stance. Hands fisted on his hips, face pressed into a disapproving frown, Greum echoed Ferlie's own reticence.

Ferlie clapped the man on his shoulder. "Be thankful ye are alive to make the point," he declared, more to himself than to Greum.

His friend tossed him a look of disgust and motioned to the room with one gnarled hand. "Ye first."

With a chuckle, Ferlie stepped amid the glitter and pomp.

"Here he is! *Bienvenue, mon ami!*" Speaking loudly enough all could hear, Captain Rousseau gestured grandly to the doorway. Ferlie gritted his teeth, hiding his cringe as he forced his lips upward into a more pleasing mien.

He met the captain mid-room and gripped his arm in greeting. Turning to the crowd, he motioned to his host. "This man is responsible for saving many lives. Greum and I wouldnae be here today were it not for him."

Spots of high color stained the jolly captain's round cheeks. "You are the one who saved us, *mon ami*. We needed a friend on that cursed pirate ship, and, *Dieu merci*, He sent you."

"Bravo!"

"Tout me félicitations!"

Shouts and cheers erupted around the room, glasses raised high in salute. Someone shoved a slender glass into Ferlie's hand and he lifted it in acknowledgment. He tilted the pale golden contents to his lips, twitching his nose at the subtle bouquet. Men crowded around, buffeting him with their hearty congratulations. Women on the edge of the crowd tittered amongst themselves, eyes slanting at him with interest.

Ferlie grew weary of the crush and slowly made his way to the edge of the room where tall doors opened onto the first floor gallery. Cool evening air fanned his face and he breathed deeply.

"Good evening, *monsieur*. It is quite overwhelming, *no?*"

Ferlie smiled at the young woman at his side. Her red hair swirled in glistening waves of molten fire at the back of her head. Tiny diamonds winked at him from the fine *crespine* of delicate metal mesh holding the coppery curls in place. Thick golden embroidery accented the neckline of her green silk gown, casting a glow against her creamy skin. Ferlie dragged his gaze to her face where her blue eyes twinkled with amusement.

"After months at sea, there are many sights which overwhelm. A room full of cheering people is one."

"And what of the other sights, *monsieur*? Do they overwhelm as well?"

The grin on Ferlie's face was genuine. "*Mademoiselle*, yer ma would do well to keep an eye on ye. Ye will break many a poor man's heart."

She tapped his arm lightly with her fingers in mild reproach. "Och, I have given ye leave to use my given name, monsieur. Must we blame the salt and sun for that as well?"

"Careful, Murielle. Yer Scots is showing. Though why ye insisted on practicing yer English words on a poor Scotsman, I couldnae guess."

"I am proficient in several languages. I wished to learn another."

Ferlie interpreted the insinuation that he was the experience she craved. Something inside him stirred and he cast a quick glance around them, seeking listening ears. He spied her mother's sharp look from a nearby group of women, and he gave Murielle a short bow.

"As always, m'lady, I am yer servant. But ye must cast yer hooks, lovely though they are, in someone else."

Murielle tossed her head and the diamonds twinkled in her hair. "*Maman* is watchful, but owes ye much. And I am but her youngest daughter."

"And I dinnae know who I am. She wouldnae welcome me as her son, no matter her gratitude."

"I think ye are wrong, but no matter. I am part Scots on *ma mère's* side, ye see. It would not be such a blow to her." She clasped her hands before her, her words turned serious. "I wish there was some way of helping ye further."

Relieved to hear the simple emotion unclouded by her earlier flirtation, Ferlie softened. "Ye have helped tremendously, lass. From my first day here ye have befriended me. Ye remind me of someone…" His gaze slipped to a spot beyond Murielle's shoulder.

"*Vraiment?*" Her voice, breathless with excitement, pulled his attention back.

"Aye, truth. Yer sweet disposition is of a younger sister, if I have one…" He laughed at her moue of disappointment. "And yer hair reminds me of…"

"Of whom, *monsieur?*"

Slowly, Ferlie shook his head. "I dinnae know, lass. I dinnae know."

Chapter Twenty-five

$\mathcal{G}$ilda laughed as William gurgled and churned his chubby legs. "I think he smiled at ye."

Conn shot her a questioning look full of surprised pleasure before turning back to the bairn. "I believe he did."

Tavia bustled about the room, straightening cloths on the wash stand, fluffing pillows on the bed. "Och, the bairn isnae old enough to smile at ye, lad. 'Tis likely a wee stomach ailment passing or a faerie wind tickling his bum."

Conn roared with laughter. "I prefer to believe the lad is happy to meet me at long last." He lifted an eyebrow at the old woman in a mock scowl. "Ye have been telling him about me, aye?"

Tilting her nose in the air, Tavia scoffed. "Any stories told him about ye are likely to be tainted with the truth of yer *paukie* ways."

Conn clasped his heart in a dramatic gesture. "Did ye hear yon *cailleach* call me roguish and wily?"

Tavia snorted, forestalling Gilda's answer. "Obviously this *auld woman* knows what she is talking about!"

William's arms and legs flailed and his face puckered, capturing everyone's attention with a cry. Gilda settled his blanket about him as she lifted him into her arms. His face turned eagerly against her bosom and she felt her cheeks heat.

Tavia tugged at Conn's arm and steered him to the door. "Yon bairn needs his ma now. Ye can visit with her anon." With a light shove, she pushed the young man through the doorway and closed the portal between them. She wiped her hands on her apron and turned to Gilda.

"Now, lass, ye can feed young William before the fisher fleet on the coast hear him."

With a dexterity born of a sennight's practice, Gilda unlaced her gown with one hand, jostling an increasingly distressed bairn in the other. Cradling him gently, she nestled him against her. With a snuffle and a sigh, William began to suckle.

Tavia gave a grunt of satisfaction. "Ye are a good ma to the wee lad, Gilda."

Warm reassurance rose in Gilda, but Tavia's next words caught her off guard.

"What do ye want with young MacLaurey?"

The room throbbed with the heat of a thousand candles and more than a score of overdressed bodies. Chattering voices rose to a crescendo above the merry clash of musicians, and Ferlie winced.

Murielle tapped his arm.

"*Regardez! Mon frère,* Bray, has arrived!"

Ferlie followed the line of her arm pointing to a tall young man entering the room. She bounced excitedly on her toes, instantly transformed from flirtatious young woman to the red-haired lass who'd befriended him a week ago. He smiled, agreeable to the change.

"Yer brother made it back from the horse trader's, then?"

"Not just any horse trader. The man raises fine Iberian horses. *Mon père* sent him over a month ago to choose and collect several mares."

"'Tis why he wasnae with ye on the ship," Ferlie murmured, though he knew the story well by now. "So, the impatient stallion in yer stable is to receive his mates?"

"Don't be *impertinente*, Ferlie." Murielle's soft chiding was distant, her attention clearly on her brother. "*Suivez-moi!* Let me introduce you."

Ferlie allowed himself to be led across the room. With a nod to well-wishers and a clout to the shoulders of the more boisterous among them, he followed the gentle sway of Murielle's skirts as she wove her way through the guests to her brother's side.

The slender Frenchman swept to attention as Ferlie and Murielle approached.

"*Voilà ma petite sœur*! As pretty as ever." Catching her hands, he dangled her before him. "*Juste ciel*! How you have grown, *ma petite*! I can scarce believe the beauty you have become."

Deep color suffused Murielle's cheeks as she laughed and fluttered her lashes at the brotherly flattery. She edged closer and kissed his cheeks. Grasping his upper arm, she turned him to face Ferlie.

"*Mon frère*, I would like to introduce you to Ferlie. Ferlie, this is my brother, Bray Rousseau."

Keen brown eyes swept over him, and Ferlie felt a twinge of recognition. A jovial manner hiding a canny awareness... But the vision was gone in an instant, leaving an unexpected emptiness inside, as though he'd lost more than his place in the conversation.

"*C'est un véritable héros! Mon ami*, you have my deepest gratitude for bringing my family home safe and sound."

Bray's eyes narrowed slightly, questioning, and Ferlie felt heat rise in his cheeks. What had he missed?

Hurriedly, he replied, "Och, 'twas my good fortune yer da decided to take my word I would fight on his side."

"'Tis an amazing stroke of luck, indeed, for I have rarely known *mon père* to make a hasty decision."

Laughter erupted around them and the tension coiled inside Ferlie began to ease. "'Tis good to meet ye, *Monsieur*." He accepted Bray's outstretched hand and they clasped the other's upper arm—like brothers. Again, a flash of vision swept through Ferlie, a feeling of brotherhood so strong he struggled to contain the gasp of surprise.

"*S'il vous plaît Monsieur*, my name is Bray."

Ferlie grinned. "I am called simply, Ferlie. 'Tis Scottish for 'luck,' and I am verra lucky to be alive."

"*Voilà mon héros*!" Captain Rousseau breasted the crowd like a cog ship in heavy water. His beaming gaze encompassed Ferlie and Bray. "And you have met *mon fils*. Bray, how was your trip? Was it successful?"

"*Oui, Monsieur*. I have four of the loveliest mares one could ask for in the stable as we speak."

"It is more important they are just what the stallion asks for, *c'est ça*?"

"Mayhap you would care to see them after dinner?"

Captain Rousseau swept a hand toward Ferlie. "The two of you should inspect them. Scotsmen are known to have an eye for horseflesh. Though I doubt such as these has been seen in the Highlands." He ducked his head. "No offense, Ferlie, but these are not as your Highland ponies."

"No offense taken, *Monsieur.* I would very much like to see them."

"Then it is settled. Ah! *Suivez-moi!* It appears dinner is served."

The crowd turned to follow their host to the tables where gleaming white tablecloths boasted platters of food and flagons of drink, and each seat offered the diner his own bejeweled knife. Ferlie took a deep breath. *An hour past. I can surely make it through a couple more.*

Gilda's startled glance as she responded to Tavia's direct question betrayed her. Her concern with Conn MacLaurey was new even to herself, and she could not stop the heat stealing beneath her skin. She fussed with William's wrapping, murmuring soft, encouraging noises to the suckling babe as she struggled to make sense of her thoughts.

"He is verra interested in Ryan's son." Her words were weak and unconvincing—the first thing she could voice.

"Och, the lad has eyes for his friend's babe, and bigger eyes for ye, lass."

"Aye. I know."

"He has been here often. What has he said? Has he promised ye anything?"

Gilda drew a deep breath. William's soft scent enveloped her, tightening her insides with love and regret. "'Tis true he has a fondness for William because he is Ryan's son. The bairn helps keep Ryan's memory alive, and that is a bond between the two of us as well."

The old woman waggled her head sagely. "Aye. But I am nae so old I cannae see he has eyes for more than Ryan's memory."

Conn's words, so startling only a fortnight ago, mellowed in Gilda's heart. "Auntie, Conn has asked me to marry him."

With a sigh, Tavia sank to the foot of the bed. "Have ye said aught to yer parents? They are neither blind nor daft."

"Nae. I told him I dinnae want to marry him."

Tavia sent her a piercing look. "'Tis not what it looked like a moment ago."

"Weel, mayhap I had a change of heart."

"Do ye love him, lass?"

Gilda pulled the protesting babe from one breast and presented him with the other. Crooning softly to mollify him, she pondered Tavia's question. Did she love Conn? What had changed in such a short amount of time?

"I cannae say, Tavia. I certainly dinnae love him as I did Ryan." Her voice caught and she bit her lip to control its tremor. "My feelings for Conn are verra different. Seeing him with William, the look on his face—I know he would love him like his own bairn."

Gilda lifted her chin and stared in challenge at the old woman. "I know it isnae easy to get a man to take another's child."

Tavia rose to her feet, hands on her thighs to assist the move as her joints creaked audibly. She shuffled to Gilda's side and draped her hands across her shoulders, hugging her tight against her bony chest.

"Och, lass, dinnae judge every man by Laird Macraig's standard. He cannae see what a beautiful child he lost that day. Only the woman who would have brought his clan much wealth and land and prestige. Young MacLaurey seems a much different sort."

Gilda patted Tavia's hand. "I know, Tavia. That is what draws me to him. I believe William and I could have a good life with him."

"Weel, ye dinnae have to make a decision today. Ye need to talk to yer ma and yer da before ye say aught to young MacLaurey. They are well aware of his visits and likely wish for ye to bring up the subject."

"I would like to get to know Conn a bit better." She gazed down at her son, his mouth now lax on her breast as he drifted off to sleep. "I will talk to Ma and Da soon."

Finn clung to Conn's arm as he balanced his feet on the rungs of his chair, peering at William as the babe opened and closed his tiny hands.

"He's not much fun yet, Conn," the lad confided. "But me and Jamie will teach him a thing or two when he gets older."

Conn laughed at the firm assurance in the boy's face. "I am sure ye will, Finn. Are ye a help to yer sister with young William right now?"

Jamie and Finn exchanged looks and Finn stepped down, away from Conn's close scrutiny. "We have been verra good to stay out of her way," he declared.

Jamie bobbed his head. "Aye. We dinnae get into trouble anymore." His cheeks reddened. "Much."

"What is there to help with?" Finn frowned as he considered the bairn. "All he does is eat and sleep."

"And poo!" Jamie snickered behind his hands.

Finn looked abashed. "I dinnae want *that* job!" Both lads scrunched their noses and Conn bit back his laughter. He cast a sideways glance to Gilda who watched the exchange, amusement in her eyes.

"Have ye brought yer sister flowers? Watched young William sleep so she can do other things? Ye know the bairn keeps her verra busy."

The twins dipped their heads in unison. "Aye. She doesnae have time to go to the beach with us anymore."

"Or pick berries."

Finn rolled his eyes at his brother. "*Amadan.* The berries willnae be ripe for another month."

Jamie shoved Finn. "They will, too!"

Finn pushed Jamie with a shout. "Willnae!"

"Lads!" Their da's admonition brought instant, albeit reluctant, obedience. Heads down, they shuffled their feet on the stone floor, slanting promising looks at each other that the argument was far from over.

Conn studied William, still studying his fingers with puzzled intent. "They dinnae bother him?"

Gilda rose and moved to his side, leaning over his shoulder. "Nae. He is already used to their antics."

At the sound of his ma's voice, William grinned and pumped his arms and legs.

"'Tis near his bedtime. I will take him up."

"I would like to put him to bed, if ye dinnae mind?"

Gilda smiled. "Can ye sing?"

"I can hum a bit off-key."

"Perfect. Walk slowly and croon. He will likely be asleep afore ye reach the cradle."

Conn rather doubted the bairn would be asleep that quickly, but he did as she prompted him. A lullaby? He wasn't sure he knew any songs that didn't start off, *There was a young lass who...* Hardly appropriate.

A grin touched his lips and he began to hum. "Bee baw babbity, babbity, babbity. Bee baw babbity, a lassie or a wee laddie?"

Gilda laughed softly. "A little nonsense song for young William?"

"I dinnae suppose ye wanted me singing him a song I picked up at a pub."

"Och, nae as a bairn. We will save those for when he is grown, aye?"

They made their way up the staircase in unison and he heard Gilda's voice, soft and sweet.

"*Baloo baleerie, baloo baleerie.*
Baloo baleerie, baloo balee.
Gang awa' peerie faeries, gang awa' peerie faeries.
Gang awa' peerie faeries, from our home now.
Doon come the bonny angels, doon come the bonny angels.
Doon come the bonny angels, to our home now.
Sleep soft, my baby, sleep soft, my baby.
Sleep soft, my baby, in our home now."

Conn laid William, already asleep, in his crib, tucking a loosened piece of silver birch trim out of his reach. The bark kept away faeries and goblins, and he did not want harm to come to the babe.

Gilda nodded in approval. "Ye handle him well, Conn. Ye might think ye had raised a bairn or two."

"None I could lay claim to as my own." He gently pulled the soft wool blanket over William's chest. Taking Gilda's hand, he led her to the seat at the window.

"Ye know how much I love the lad. I cannae believe how much he resembles his da." He shook his head ruefully. "'Tis likely ye will have yer hands full with this one."

Gilda leaned against the stone at her back, happiness tugging the corners of her lips. "He already is a demanding lad." Her face softened and she stared at a point beyond his shoulder. "But when he isnae demanding to be fed or changed, or is tired, he is so sweet."

Conn heard the wistfulness in her voice. "Aye. There are things I wish were different, too. But we cannae change the past."

He took her hand and her delicate fingers curved around his. "Gilda, will ye and young William become a part of my future?"

Chapter Twenty-Six

Ferlie eyed the mares appreciatively. Even beneath the torches they were magnificent. "I wish I had time to see them in daylight. But my ship leaves at dawn and I must be on it."

Bray leaned over the half-wall of the stable. "Which do ye prefer? The chestnut or the dainty white mare?"

"The little mare has spirit. A bonnie lass. But the chestnut is sleek and well-built. I have never seen anything like them."

"No. They are bred almost exclusively by monks in Spain. It is rare to find one outside their walls and quite unusual to obtain permission to bring them here." Bray chuckled. "*Mon père* has interesting friends in interesting places."

The white mare shook her head, her long, flowing mane sliding over her neck like a heavy, silken veil. She picked her way across the stall, hooves making crinkling sounds in the deep, fresh hay. Nudging Ferlie's hand with her nose, she snorted.

He laughed. "She expects gifts, aye?"

"I could beggar myself supplying her with treats." Bray reached into a nearby tin and retrieved a small apple. "These are from our orchard. Small and a bit tart, but they are good in cooking. Here, give it to her."

Ferlie held the piece of fruit to the mare and she nibbled it daintily from his flattened palm. Biting down on it, she jiggled her head up and down until the apple broke in half. With great relish, she chewed the first piece then searched Ferlie's hand for the second. Saliva mingled with slivers of apple peel as she nudged him impatiently.

"She isnae much of a lady, despite her looks, is she?" He could not keep the pleasure from his voice.

Bray grinned. "She is yours, *mon ami*. I will have a man prepare a space for her on your ship. She will be ready to leave in the morning."

Eyes wide, Ferlie could only stare at Bray. His hand strayed to the mare's thick forelock, his fingers twined amid the coarse strands. He shook his head.

"Nae. 'Tis too soon for her to travel again, even if I could accept yer offer. I cannae."

"*Mon père, l'capitaine,* bade me make one of these a gift to you. We will see to it she is well cared for on your journey home."

Ferlie's insides swirled. *Yer journey home, young Macraig. Yer journey home.* Another ship. Another horse. Another time. Home.

"Are you well, *mon ami*?"

Bray's concern pierced the fragmented memories. Ferlie gave himself a mental shake. "My memories of home arenae clear."

"I understand. They will, mayhap, return in time." He turned back to the matter at hand. "I hope you will take *la petite jument*. She will make a fine broodmare one day. And give you much pleasure as well."

Ferlie understood Bray's and the captain's desire to see him well equipped on his journey. He had brought them safely to the end of theirs, against staggering odds and amid great peril. They merely wished to assure themselves they had done what they could to aid him in return.

"I wish for no reward, and I have no way to purchase her from ye—"

Bray waved aside his words. "Our houses will always be open to one another." Emotion darkened his eyes. "There is no way I can ever repay you for what you did for my family. The mare is but a mere token of our friendship. Please accept the gift."

Finally Ferlie acquiesced. He stroked the mare's satiny neck. Lantern light turned her coat a creamy gold. "Does she have a name?"

"Her name is *Chance*. That is French for 'luck.'"

Ferlie tossed his head back, laughter spilling from his throat. "'Tis a match, then. Mayhap between the two of us, 'luck' will mean something."

A low rumble reached their ears. Both men glanced out the open doorway of the stable. On the horizon, lightning split the sky. The flame in the lantern guttered and nearly went out as a freshening breeze slipped through the building. Long moments later, thunder rumbled again.

"You are lucky, *mon ami*. The ship will sail tomorrow no matter the weather."

Unpleasant memories of storms at seas crossed Ferlie's mind. He wasn't so certain luck was with him yet.

Laird MacLaurey's eyes bulged and his face mottled an unpleasant pattern of dark and light red. He rose to his feet and pinned Conn with a glare.

"Ye *amadan*! Have ye completely gone off yer heid? Ye will be laird here, one day. Ye will marry close to home, a lass of our clan bloodlines, one who understands our ways. Not a widow who brings a bairn and uncertainty with her."

Conn returned his father's look with grim determination. "Ye are overreacting, Da. Gilda is a lovely young woman. Surely ye dinnae hold her parentage against her?"

The laird waved a hand dismissingly. "Och, she is as much Ranald's daughter as if he sired her." He stared at his papers arranged on the desk before him, not meeting Conn's gaze.

Conn felt dismissed, but he pressed on, leaning forward for emphasis. "What is on yer mind?"

"There is Lord Wyndham's daughter—"

"Ye havenae signed a betrothal without my knowledge, have ye?" Anger rose and he bristled. "We have had this discussion before."

Laird MacLaurey raised a hand in supplication. "'Tis a wish her da and I—"

"The two of ye can wish all ye want. I will pick my own bride."

His father angled his hard gaze at Conn. "Ye would bring the woman who disgraced yer sister here? To live?"

Too intent on his own pleasures, Conn hadn't considered that particular perspective. Then again, he was aware his da had accepted an offer of marriage for Mairead who prepared for an alliance with a chieftain to the east. She would leave Corfin Castle long before Gilda could arrive.

"Da, Mairead will be wed and away in a matter of weeks. I

wouldnae bring Gilda here until after. She still needs time to recover from young William's birth."

Laird MacLaurey slammed a fist on the desktop. "That bairn would inherit Macraig lands and ours as well should ye sire no sons of yer own. Ye would hand us over to a lad of Macraig and pirate blood?"

"I will raise him as a MacLaurey."

Shaking his head violently, his da denied Conn's claim. "I willnae hear of it. The woman challenges my pride and yer sister's honor. The bairn upsets the rule of the clan. If ye raised him as a MacLaurey, he would expect to be laird here one day. That cannae be his future."

Conn regarded his father's words carefully. Struck by the possibility of being able to raise Ryan's son, he had not looked to the bairn's future as a man. His da was right. He must never let William forget he was Ryan's son. It would be up to him to see to it the lad knew his heritage and understood he would rule Ard Castle one day, not the MacLaurey lands. And it would be his pleasant task to see to it a MacLaurey son followed him as laird.

"I will love him as my own, but ensure he knows his birthright. This, I can do."

For long moments Laird MacLaurey battled with Conn's proposition. Several times he started to speak, and each time he stopped. At last he shook his head, disappointment etched across his features.

"What of the lass?"

Conn stared at his da uncertainly. "What do ye mean?"

"The lad would grow up loving ye. Of that I have no doubt. But what of Gilda? In her heart, whom does she love?"

Land was a faint smudge on the horizon. In another hour, they would lose sight of it completely as they left the coast of Wales for Larne's harbor on the coast of Ireland. Ferlie stood at the bow, weary after three weeks at sea. Anticipation for their next port of call was hard to muster, even though it brought him that much closer to home.

He squared his shoulders against the fading sights behind him and scanned the open waters, sunlight flashing on the waves as they kicked up brisk and hard against the ship's hull.

Dear God, be good to me; the sea is so wide, and my boat is so small. The prayer whispered effortlessly from somewhere deep within him. A part of his past. A fisherman's prayer?

That would put an end to the idea I am part of Laird Macraig's brood. He snorted, more than sure such thoughts were but wishful on Greum's side. *Unless I was birthed on the wrong side of a Highland plaide.* That was much more likely. Personally, he did not care who sired him. He only wished to find a home and someone who remembered him.

Red hair, adoring eyes—gray, full of laughter, twinkling with delight. He closed his eyes, savoring the sweetness of the vision in his mind. Sunlight sparked strands of gold glimmering against vivid embers. Heavy curls tossed across burnished ivory skin, supple and warm to the touch. An aura of mist behind the sweet face crept inward, dissolving the memory.

No! His eyes flew open, met with the vast aloneness of the sea. Overhead, gulls banked and dipped, their cries harsh on the wind. If the weather held, 'twould be only a few days until he was back on Scottish soil. Salt air whipped around him, tugging at his clothing, wrapping loosened tendrils of hair about his face. Absently, he dragged the strands away.

"Sir, we will be in Larne tomorrow. Ye'd best get a good night's rest."

Ferlie turned toward the first mate. "Aye. Staring ahead doesnae make the land approach faster, does it?"

"Nae. Not as I've noticed." The man's rueful voice caught in the wind and was torn away. "May as well sleep now. This swell foretells a storm."

"No *pirr* to gently fill our sails?" One side of Ferlie's mouth quirked upward. Already the slap of water against the hull grew more pronounced, the pitch steeper as the ship rode higher and higher waves.

"Nae, more of a *rumballiach*—a fickle wind that will hopefully not be at cross-purposes with our journey."

"I will check on *Chance*. I fear she tires of the long journey, and this *jaup* may sour her sweet temper."

"We all eagerly anticipate a night ashore, I assure ye." The man laughed and jerked his head toward the makeshift stall. "'Twill take more than choppy seas to sour yer beast. I wish my wife were as sweet-tempered and easily pleased. But yer mare is a noble animal and I would not wish her to come to harm during the rough passage."

"She is a rare creature, and I cannae thank the good captain enough for her."

"My friend, Captain Rousseau owes ye and Greum not only his life, but those of his wife and daughters." He gripped Ferlie's arm. "He is a man of honor, and will never be able to repay that debt."

Emotion tugged inside Ferlie, warm and deep. "I wouldnae be here were it not for him. He treated me well, as more than a friend in his home. But I am eager to be back in Scotland."

"We should spend a day offloading and taking on new cargo. 'Twill put us at Ayr a day after that."

"I have been studying yer maps with the captain. Greum and I will head inland once we disembark. He insists we pay a visit to the Macraig clan just along the coast."

"I wish ye well on yer journey. Every man should know his past."

"'Tis something I must pursue."

No reply came from the first mate, and Ferlie felt the deep silence between them. Memory loss was difficult to explain, even more difficult for others to understand. Part of Ferlie was missing—that much was simple. Explaining how it gutted him, made him feel only partly alive, was something that defeated his words. He longed desperately for a way to understand who he was, how he had gotten where he was—a way to point himself to the future. He felt like a rudderless ship bereft of even the meanest navigational skills, needing a welcome port to call home.

With a short nod of understanding between them, Ferlie turned his steps to the partitioned area that housed his mare. Half-walls stood bolted securely with an oiled tarp attached several feet above the mare's head, keeping her out of the sun's harsh light, yet allowing the fresh air to swirl through. His eyes scanned the lean-to behind the makeshift stable. Wisps of hay drifted out onto the deck, but the bin still contained a good bit of fresh hay. He'd ordered it refilled at each port as well as a complete mucking and refurbishing of the straw in the stall. Despite the deckhand's muttered complaints, Ferlie had insisted the straw freshened daily. Even in the short time he'd owned the dainty mare, he was besotted with her.

Chance crossed the roomy box and hung her head over the chest-high wall. Ferlie smiled. Already she'd learned her master's footstep, and they formed a close bond. He ruffled her long forelock and she tossed her head, nickering softly.

Ferlie inspected the stall, approving the crisp, fresh straw. "How do ye fare, lass? I dinnae like the feel of the wind kicking up. I fear we are in for a bit of weather before we make Larne."

Reaching in his shirt, he retrieved an apple core he'd saved from his supper. He watched in fascination as the mare delicately plucked the proffered fruit from his hand, her thick lips tickling his palm.

"As much as I like the way we are named alike, I dinnae think 'Chance' rolls well from a Scotsman's tongue. I have thought it over and believe I will change it a wee bit to 'Shona.' 'Tis a sweet lass' name and I dinnae think our friend Bray will mind."

Shona swallowed her treat and nuzzled him, looking for more, clearly unconcerned with her name change. Ferlie stroked her satin neck, her skin warm and soft beneath her heavy mane. The ship rolled beneath their feet as it crested a wave.

The mare stomped a hoof.

"Easy, lass. I cannae make the storm go away. Our ship is sturdily built. We must wait it out." Crooning to her, he continued to rub her glossy hide. The waves built steadily and the ship rocked harder, hitting the bottom of the waves with a solid thwack. The timbers creaked and groaned, men's shouts rang out as they rushed about their duties. Shona nickered again, louder, her head up, eyes wide and intent.

"Shush, lass." Ferlie stroked her head. Her ears flicked at the sound of his voice. "So, ye like it better when I talk to ye? Something other than the storm to think about, aye?" He hummed softly and the mare calmed.

Rain broke over their heads and Ferlie stepped inside the makeshift stall, though the tarp proved poor protection from the windswept water. He clung to the mare's halter, anxious lest she panic and injure herself.

"'Twill be only a bit further, lass. We will see the lights of the harbor soon."

Lightning split the sky and Shona jerked away in a half-rear, tossing her head as her feet slipped in the wet straw. Ferlie settled her with a firm hand and soothing words. She placed the flat of her forehead against his chest, her body trembling.

"Dinnae complain about my singing voice, and I'll sing ye a song my nurse sang to me as a wee bairn."

Shona shuddered, her legs braced apart against the swell of the ship, but her ears twitched as his voice soothed her with a simple lullaby.

"*Baloo baleerie, baloo baleerie. Baloo baleerie, baloo balee.*

Gang awa' peerie faeries, gang awa' peerie faeries. Gang awa' peerie faeries, from our home now."

Chapter Twenty-seven

$\mathcal{G}$ilda noticed the sparkle of silver among the rich red strands of her mother's hair. Her ma smoothed a palm over the escaped curls framing her face, her grey eyes dark and troubled.

There is much to worry her when Da is not here. Gilda frowned. Mayhap Jamie and Finn should be fostered soon. Another jolt of conscience ran through her. *Will and I are likely a source of her worry as well.*

"I am not saying ye *cannae* marry him, Gilda. Have ye truly thought about this?"

She saw the concern on her ma's face. "I am only telling ye how I feel about Conn and that he has asked me to marry him. 'Tis not something that is going to happen tomorrow. I will talk to Da when he returns from Troon. King Robert cannae keep him there forever, aye?"

Her ma peered around distractedly and stepped to a chair, patting the cushion of the one next to it in invitation. "Sit with me a moment, Gilda. Tell me what is in yer heart."

Gilda seated herself beside her ma, turning so she angled close to her. "I know the MacLaurey clan doesnae border our lands, but it isnae so far that an alliance with them wouldnae be helpful. Mayhap Niall and the twins, and even wee Sara will marry into neighboring clans." She laid a comforting hand on her ma's. "Morven isnae so far away."

"Och, 'tis not the distance, Gilda, though my heart would be lighter were ye settled closer. Once ye are married with a home and family of yer own, 'twill be difficult for ye to visit no matter where ye live." She pulled her hand from beneath Gilda's and clasped it, giving it a quick tug. "Ye were married to Ryan—"

"So briefly, Ma. I scarcely felt wed, and certainly wasnae in charge of my home."

"Listen to me, Gilda. Ye were wed and have a son. Will is the heir to the Macraig lairdship. If ye marry Conn MacLaurey, what will happen?"

Gilda sagged in her chair. The happiness she'd carried with Conn's loving words evaporated in a whoosh of reality. "If Conn adopted him, Will would inherit Morven."

"I doubt Laird MacLaurey will be happy with such."

"Nor would Laird Macraig. I still dinnae like him trying to use Will to manipulate the rest of us."

"The Macraig is a verra sad man, *a stor*. He has made decisions he felt he needed to, but they werenae always for the best, and they have shaped his life. He is alone except for Lissa, now, and though he doesnae approve of ye, Will is his only link to his son."

Gilda sighed. "Aye. I feel sorry for him, but he should learn to love. He makes everyone around him struggle to please him, and 'tis never enough."

"I understand not wanting to raise Will at Ard around Laird Macraig, though he must get to know his clan and their ways. If ye marry Conn, ye take Will away from his birthright."

Hot tears stung Gilda's eyes. "Do ye think I should never marry, never have a husband or other children? Other women arenae asked to remain widows all their lives!" Gilda bit her lip to stem the bitter words and hurt churning inside.

"Other women arenae mother to the clan heir. I am not saying ye cannae remarry. Only, ye must consider all the consequences."

"I dinnae consider the consequences when I married Ryan." Tears threatened to build and she held the words in her heart, scarcely able to breathe. "I loved him so much! I couldnae imagine life without him. And now…"

"Och, Gilda. 'Tis not yer fault he died so young. Please think on this until yer da comes home. I want both ye and Will to be happy. Truly I do."

Gilda nodded past the bleakness she felt inside. Her ma rose from her chair, a sad smile on her face. Settling a quick kiss to the top of Gilda's head, she bustled from the room, leaving Gilda alone with her thoughts.

Long moments passed as Gilda stared at the open window across the room. Beyond the thick rock walls lay treasured memories of her childhood. Waves crashed on the rocks far below and the sound reminded her of the white shells which fascinated her as a child, drawing her to the beach. The memory pulled her gaze to the mantle above the fireplace where a handful of white shells still resided. Her old, tattered cubbie in the corner glinted with the residue of mineral shards and finely ground shell.

Angel shells. She drew in a quick breath as another memory surfaced. *Is grandda an angel?* Warmth filled her. Though he had died when she was a small child, he had been so loving and kind to her. She wanted that for Will, not harsh words from a man so embittered with his own past.

I was looking for faerie *shells.* Gilda's lips curved fondly. The first time she'd met Ranald, he'd appeared as a hero to her, striding through the waves that had caught her unawares, trapping her on a rock away from shore. With calm assurance, he'd plucked her from the rock and whisked her back to the beach. Though she'd lost her shoes and disobeyed the rule against going near the water without an adult, he'd not scolded her. *Well, only a wee bit.*

Oh, how she wanted the same memories for her son. Braw, fair men ready to praise and correct in equal measure. Kind, indulgent women to laugh at his boyhood mischief and care for his skint knees with a kiss and a hug. She wanted Will to grow up loved, knowing the difference between leading and controlling, between honor and disgrace.

What will his fate be if Conn raises him as his own? Gilda stood and walked hesitantly to the window. She leaned against the open frame, the sun full on her face. She closed her eyes, feeling the warmth, breathing the sea-tainted air.

I dinnae want him to feel less a son. How to raise him as Conn's son, and yet not? Ranald never treated me as less than his daughter— but I never stood to inherit Scaurness.

With a frustrated sigh, Gilda turned her back to the window and slouched against the stone, her arms hugging her waist. Would it be best for Will if she didn't remarry? Her heart twisted. She couldn't love again as she did Ryan. It still hurt.

Tears sprang from her eyes and she did not stop them as they slid faster and faster down her cheeks.

Gilda eyed the two men as each bobbed his head and endured her gaze. Tall, strong, stern and fully armed, the men appeared menacing, even standing still.

She turned to Finlay. "Is it truly necessary for me to have a guard to visit Tavia?"

The look he gave her was sympathetic, but he nodded, dashing her hopes for time to herself. "Ye know ye need to be protected. Ye are the laird's daughter and mother to young William, the Macraig heir. I promised yer da ye would have a guard wherever ye went."

"A guard?" She stared pointedly at the two soldiers. "I count two."

Finlay's face took on a long-suffering appearance as he lifted one brow and his lips threatened a frown. "Sweetling, dinnae *fash* with me. I've known ye since Ranald pulled ye from the water, yer hair in snarls and yer shoes lost to the selkies. Ye have me wrapped around yer little finger, but I willnae risk yer safety away from the castle." He jerked his head at the other two men. "Yon lads will be discrete. Ye will hardly know they are there."

Gilda rolled her eyes, knowing she would not win an argument with her da's captain. "They take up entirely too much space not to notice them. I suppose they could be useful, though."

Both men stared straight ahead, though Gilda was certain one shuddered, as though resigned to the task of playing fetch-carry for whatever she brought back from the healer's cottage.

"I will be back later this afternoon. Hopefully before young William awakes from his nap."

Finlay beamed at her. "The lad is growing. Two months old and holding his head up well. He has a strong grip, too."

Gilda's smile wavered. "Aye. He is a braw lad. He looks a lot like his da."

Finlay placed a comforting hand on her shoulder. "His da would be proud of him, lass."

"Aye." She took a deep breath. "I must head to the beach if I am to make it back in a couple of hours." Accepting his help to mount, she reined her mare toward the castle gates.

Urged by the longing for a bit of freedom, she kicked Fia into a gallop across the field to the head of the trail leading down to the beach. Ignoring the soldiers who flanked her at a slight distance, she clung to her mare's back, relishing the crisp wind in her face, the snap of Fia's mane across her hands, and the surging muscles of the horse beneath her. She slowed the mare to a safer pace as they plunged down the rocky path, then sped across the beach to Tavia's cottage, nestled against the stark cliffs beneath the castle.

Slipping lightly from Fia's saddle, Gilda stumbled as her feet hit the ground. Surprised at the tremor in her leg muscles, she straightened, smoothing her skirts as she reached for her basket. By the time she untied the wicker cubbie, her legs were steady and she gave a cheery wave to the soldiers who quickly posted themselves at each end of the cove.

"Auntie! Auntie Tavia, I'm here! And see what Cook sent you!"

The cottage door opened and Tavia's wizened face peered out. "Come inside, lass," she bade Gilda. "Leave yer guards outside."

Gilda slipped inside and placed her basket on the table. Instantly the sights and smells familiar since early childhood calmed her, and she breathed deeply of the mingled scents of dried herbs, a simmering fish stew, and the milk goat tethered in her stall beneath the eaves.

She flopped into the nearest chair and began emptying the basket's contents. "Cook sent ye bread, some meat pies, and pastries."

Tavia slid another chair out next to Gilda and sank onto its seat. "Of course Cook sent pastries. Likely there is an extra one in there for ye as well."

Gilda laughed. "Verra likely. She knows me too well."

Tavia was silent and Gilda looked up sharply. "Auntie? Are ye well?"

A quick glance told her the old woman seemed smaller, older, more tired. Her hearty, no-nonsense manner had always made the tiny healer appear larger than life, and even the most dour man in Scaurness did her bidding. Today, the ancient woman seemed to have shrunk, her small frame barely supporting her wrinkled, leathery skin and stringy muscles. And when had her grey-streaked hair turned white?

Piercing blue eyes met hers and for a moment held Gilda's fears at bay.

"*A stor*, I have lived longer than most women and certainly most men. I was yer ma's nurse and her ma's before her. I have had the keeping of ye more times than I can count. Mayhap I appear a wee bit tired today?"

"Mayhap ye need someone to help ye, Auntie."

Tavia placed a feather-light hand on Gilda's. "In this tiny cottage? I can care for it quite nicely, and another body just clutters up the place. Thank ye, lass, but I dinnae need help. Young Agnes and I can fend for ourselves." She gave the goat a grimace. "Though, mayhap one of yer soldiers could replace the straw in her stall while he's here. Useful things, guards," she mused as she rose and gave the stew over the fire a quick stir with a wooden spoon.

Gilda laughed, only partly reassured with Tavia's words. "I will send one of them in. I must run up to the berry patch and collect whatever is ripe for Cook's pastries."

Tavia waved her away with a flick of her spoon and Gilda grabbed her cubbie and headed outside. The soldiers exchanged glances at Gilda's request.

"Nae, milady. We will both help Tavia when we return. One guard with ye away from the castle isnae enough."

Gilda did not argue, sensing no way to change their resolve. Humming, she strolled down the beach, her basket dangling from one hand, the guards trailing behind.

As she reached the edge of Macrory land, she peered over her shoulder, wondering if her guards would object if she edged a wee bit over the line to the berry patches beyond the border. Deciding not to risk their immediate censure, she angled away from the beach into the brush. Perhaps they would not be so vigilant if she approached the previously forbidden bushes from the thicket. Asking forgiveness would go farther than asking permission. And she was a Macraig now, no matter she called Scaurness home.

She edged deeper into the brambles, picking berries and dropping them into her basket. The afternoon sun beat down and her dress began to cling to her back and shoulders uncomfortably as the dense undergrowth kept the ocean's breeze at bay. She wiped her brow with the back of her hand and pressed deeper into the thicket.

Ow! Jerking her hand back, she stuck her finger in her mouth, soothing the injured digit. Drawing it forth, she eyed the pricked spot critically before moving to the next bush.

That must be enough for today. 'Tis too hot to hunt for more. Turning carefully to avoid snagging her gown on the prickly branches, Gilda tramped back through the foliage toward the beach. Both guards glowered at her when she broke through the bramble, but visibly relaxed when they realized she was safe.

"I realize ye dinnae fit well diving in the thicket. But that also means I am quite safe there. And think of Cook's pastries at supper tonight!"

"Milady, ye need to stay closer next time."

The older soldier's stern words chaffed Gilda's patience, but at least he mentioned 'next time.' She motioned to a large boulder overlooking a narrow ravine. "I am going to rest a bit on yon rock. 'Tis a lovely view and the breeze will cool me."

Leaving the two men to do as they wished, she flounced up the slope to the outcropping. Seating herself on the rock, she settled her skirts around her, drawing up her legs and leaning her cheek on her knees. She scooped her hair to one side, allowing the breeze to caress the back of her neck.

She sat there quite still for several minutes, watching a hunting hawk hanging high in the clear blue sky. A rabbit hopped hesitantly across an outcropping part way down the ravine, and just a bit further, on a sunny ledge, a young cub gamboled near an older wolf that stared across the narrow rift right at Gilda.

Her skin chilled in sudden apprehension and she turned a bit to view both guards standing nearby, each keeping a watchful eye on the beach and sparse woodland. She slid her gaze back to the wolf, curious to have it observe her so fearlessly.

The wolf lifted its right paw, and recognition dawned. *'Tis my wolf! And he has a wee cub!* Happiness flooded through Gilda as she watched the cub roll and tumble. The older wolf's jaws slacked open and his tongue lolled to the side as he panted lightly in the heat.

I agree, lad. 'Tis an unusually sweltrie *day. Ye have a bonnie cub, and ye seem to be taking good care of him. Teach him to stay clear of traps. I have a bairn of my own and cannae be spending my time taking care of ye.*

A smile tilted her lips as she remembered the day she met the wolf—and Ryan. "I am verra pleased to see ye safe and sound and leading a happy life," she murmured aloud, as though the beast could hear. "That, my friend, is what I want. A happy life. And I think I know what to do."

Chapter Twenty-eight

$\mathscr{G}$ilda fisted her hands on her hips and gave the room a final look. A large, sturdy bag with a rope handle perched atop the bed, crammed full of baby blankets and clothing and other bits and bobs she might need quick access to on their trip to Ard Castle. A small trunk sat on the floor, its space divided between a few of her gowns and other clothing, and the rest of Will's baby items.

Satisfied, she tipped the chest's lid closed and pulled the bag off the bed, cinching its neck tight. She slipped the rope over her shoulder and held her arms out to Tavia.

"I can carry Will. Have one of the men carry the chest down."

"I can do it!" Finn shouted as he grabbed the sturdy handles.

"No! I will!" Jamie cried, pouncing on his twin to knock him aside. He spread his arms wide, trying to grasp both handles, but his span was too short.

Finn shoved him away and squatted close, hugging the trunk to his chest. His reach was no better than Jamie's, and his face reddened as he tugged ineffectually at the weighty box.

"A pox on the both of ye wee scunners! Grab one handle each and work together, for the love of St. Andrew! And Finley will have yer hides if ye drop it."

Tavia handed Will into Gilda's arms. "The two of them are enough to turn a body's hair an early gray."

Riona entered the room. "Och, there they are. I thought I heard a *stramash* in here." She gave the twins a stern look which they ignored as they hoisted the trunk between them. Muscles straining, backs arched against the weight, they held the chest a few inches above the ground.

"We are helping Gilda!" Jamie informed his ma on a pant of exertion. Finn beamed, his face still red.

"Och, dinnae hurt yerselves or the chest. I can have one of the men carry it down," Riona pointed out.

"We can do it."

"I dinnae want help." Finn glared at his brother. "Pick up yer end. 'Tis dragging."

Jamie squinted at his end of the trunk. "'Tisn't."

"'Tis."

"Lads!" The Macrory captain's voice cut through the bickering and the twins fell silent. Gilda rolled her eyes as she jostled Will in her arms.

With a warning scowl at the lads, Finley turned his attention to her. "Are ye ready, lass?"

"Aye. I dinnae plan to be gone long." She glanced at the baby who settled as the twins' noise subsided. "Will is old enough to travel to Ard, and I dinnae wish to deny the laird a bit of time with his grandson."

Finley rested a hand on her shoulder. "'Tis generous of ye, lass. I know he isnae an easy man to deal with. Lissa will be glad for yer visit."

"I am looking forward to seeing her. She is a wee bit short of friends at Ard. And I like her."

"Ow! Ye smashed me against the door!" A thud echoed as Finn dropped his end of the trunk. Unable to hold the chest without help, Jamie dropped his end as well.

"Look what ye did!"

"Ye crushed my hand!"

"Dinnae!"

Finn shoved his fist beneath his brother's nose. "See!"

Finley pulled the cloth bag from Gilda's shoulder and strode to the doorway. Hefting the chest to his shoulder, he thrust the bag into Finn's startled grip. "Away with ye. Carry yer sister's bag."

The boys hurried behind him, the hapless bag thumping across the floor as they dragged it between them.

Gilda turned sympathetic eyes on her ma. "Take care of yerself. They are enough to try the patience of a saint."

"They will foster soon, and I do believe I shall miss them."

With a dubious look at her ma, Gilda carried Will from the room.

A small wagon awaited her outside, her mare tethered to the back of it. Six outriders flanked the cart. Finley loaded her chest in the back and took the cloth bag from the twins before they could dash it against the sideboards. Gilda leaned into her ma's warm hug, then kissed Tavia's papery cheek, offering hers in return.

"Enjoy yer visit, lass, and dinnae *fash* yerself." Finley clapped a gentle hand on her shoulder. "Duncan and Archie will stay at Ard with ye. Should ye need anything, let them know."

Gilda nodded solemnly. "I thank ye. Will and I will be fine. I dinnae plan to stay longer than a sennight."

Finley took Will from her, rocking him gently in his arms before he handed the baby to Riona. "Get settled in the wagon. I dinnae want ye traveling in the dark." He handed her into the seat, then returned Will to her grasp. She arranged his blanket about his face as the wagon rolled forward. Waving goodbye, Finn and Jamie bounced off each other as they leapt excitedly in the air.

"Watch out for wolves, Gilda!"

Gilda grinned as she remembered the playful antics of the young cub she'd seen, and the thrill of knowing the wolf she had rescued was doing so well.

"And pirates!"

Her smile vanished. Darkness crowded her vision as though the sun had suddenly plunged behind a cloud, and a chill shivered down her spine. Suddenly the pungent aroma of fresh blood assaulted her, and Acair the pirate's dead gaze filled her sight. She gasped to recall the horror, as the slick, sucking sound of Conn's sword as he pulled it from the pirate's chest shrieked through her ears. The whine of an injured wolf panted in the background, and she recoiled from the cloying scent of heavy underbrush and rich, moist soil.

Gilda clung tightly to Will and he mewled in protest. Her hands trembled and a sour taste rose in her throat, spilling into her mouth. She gulped, trying to drag air into lungs tight with dread.

"M'lady? Are ye sick?"

Duncan's warm hand settled over hers, and she stared at it, the black hairs, thick and wiry, springing from the tanned skin. With an effort, Gilda dragged her gaze away.

"Nae. I am a wee bit cold, 'tis all."

She ignored Duncan's puzzled look and pulled her plaide close about her, shutting her eyes against the memory of the horrific day Ryan, the love of her life and her son's father, had died.

Ferlie eyed the ship's hull in disgust. Beside him, Shona snorted and sidled nervously as the timbers creaked and groaned.

"How long will it take to get that repaired?"

The ship's mate jerked his gaze from the damaged planks. "Och, ye'd be better off finding another ship to get ye to Ayr. But in this weather, 'tis doubtful any will be setting sail before a couple of days at least."

Frowning, Ferlie peered at the overcast sky, squinting against the spray kicked up by the rising wind. Shona stomped a forefoot and shied at the hollow sound of the wooden dock. Ferlie tightened his grip on her lead rope and rested a comforting hand on her muzzle. The ship bounced and grated against the pier. Shona laid back her ears and nipped the edge of his palm.

"Witch!" He snatched his hand back, taking a quick inventory of his fingers. "I will see this beast to her quarters and return to talk to the captain. Is there anything ye need from town?"

Shaking his head, the man moved away, directing the offloading of the ship, likely glad to see Ferlie taking care of himself and one less thing to cause him worry.

Shona danced sideways down the length of the dock, ears flattened against the sounds of the ships and crews. Ferlie spoke soothingly to the mare.

"Enough is enough, aye? Only one more leg to our journey and I will give ye free rein to run."

Greum hurried to catch up, his peculiar rolling gait reminding Ferlie the wizened old man had suffered his share of sailing woes.

"'Tis right glad I'll be to see Scotland's shores again," Greum muttered from deep within the cowls of his cloak. His eyes sparked, reflecting the flickering torchlight along the quay. A gust of wind roared off the sea, pushing him against the mare's shoulder. He hopped a step away, regaining his balance, and huddled deeper in his plaide. Rain began to spatter the already slippery wooden planks.

Ferlie raised his voice over the noise. "Go to the tavern. I will settle the mare and be inside anon."

Greum lodged neither argument nor complaint as he headed for shelter and a roaring fire.

A bit of coin Captain Rousseau had gifted him to help along his journey secured Shona a bag of feed and a snug stall away from the worst of the wind. Leaving her munching contentedly on her oats, Ferlie charged across the rain-swept yard, and into the inn.

He closed the door behind him, shutting out most of the sounds of the gale, and hung his cloak on a wooden peg on the wall. The noise from the main room was a cheerful contrast to the weather outside, and the glow of the fire drew him in. A harried serving girl spared him a glance as she moved among the tables full of tattered sailors and weather-worn travelers grounded by the storm. Across the room, he spotted Greum and veered in his direction.

He slid onto the bench next to the older man. "Any chance you were able to find us a place to sleep tonight?"

Greum finished a deep drink of his mug, wiping the back of his hand across frothy lips. "Nae. But we can bide the night by the fire. Too many people already here to get a private room." He wiped his mouth with the back of his hand. "But the ale is good and there will be food as fast as wee Mairi can serve it."

Ferlie peered about the room. Catching wee Mairi's eye, he held up a coin. She gave a jerk of her head, and moments later placed a trencher of stew and a plate of bread on the table. The warm aroma reminded Ferlie he hadn't eaten since early morning, and he dug in.

"Here is a bit of ale, me fella."

A tankard appeared at his elbow and Ferlie met wee Mairi's gaze. A silent invitation played about her lips and she pressed against him, her breasts nearly spilling from her low-cut bodice. He grinned, but a nagging feeling of doubt slid through him, and he declined her offer. Placing another small coin in her hand, he waved her away.

Greum wiped up the last of broth with a hunk of bread, then pushed back from the table with a rumbling belch. He thumped his chest and slumped against the wall at his back.

"'Twas a right good meal for all it was shared with this *manky* group."

Ferlie followed his gaze as it wandered about the rough men at the tables, their damp clothing giving off various, rather offensive aromas in the warm, crowded room. For the first time, he was aware of his own rather pungent odor; a combination of hard work, the stables, and infrequent rinses with sea water.

"I dinnae suppose one overworked serving lass can provide a couple of travelers with a bath?"

Greum picked a partially masticated particle from between two of his teeth with the edge of a fingernail. "Nae. There isnae an unused space to put a tub, even if I were of a mind to shuck my breeks amid this rabble."

After weeks at sea, the warm, crowded room began to seem oppressive. Ferlie pushed his trencher to the center of the table amid the rest of the clutter. "I think I will step to the doorway for a bit of fresh air."

"Mind ye, dinnae be long. I cannae hold ye a sleeping spot once this lot decides to turn in."

Ferlie acknowledged the warning with a shrug as he rose to his feet. Weaving carefully amid the packed tables, he arrived in the front hall without incident. He opened the door with care, pleased to note a lull in the storm. No moon or stars shone through the heavy clouds, and it was certain they would endure another drenching rain soon, but for the moment, the stiff wind was cool on his face and the overhanging roof above the door kept the steady, light drizzle at bay.

He stepped to the edge of a pool of light cast through the tavern's window and breathed deeply, shedding the stifling heat of too many bodies packed too close together.

To his left, the stables were a dark stain against the darker night. Across the mud-churned street, torchlight blinked blearily beneath a dripping eave. The door beside the torch opened and three men exited into the street, pulling their plaides tight across their shoulders as they prepared to cross to the tavern. The men were of differing ages, older to younger, their multi-colored cloaks marking them as Scotsmen.

The younger man was bare-headed, his bright golden hair glinting in the flickering light. He was tall and lanky, and primarily notable for the petulant scowl on his face. The elder of the three was a bull of a man, thick-necked and powerful. His balding pate glistened with moisture, and his fierce eyes stared at Ferlie from beneath bushy eyebrows that shot upward in a surprised motion.

The man's arm sliced through the air at chest height, blocking the other two men's forward progress. They jolted to a stop, angry words against being held to the middle of the street in the rain. The bulky man's voice rumbled from deep within his barrel chest.

"Sweet Virgin's tits! 'Tis the Macraig's son!"

Chapter Twenty-nine

Ferlie recoiled from the force of the man's accusatory tone. He drew back into the shadows but the Scotsman barreled his way forward and grasped him by the shoulders, dragging him once again into the feeble glow. Ferlie shrugged off his grip but did not retreat again.

Eyes squinted to mere slits, the man peered at him intently, his gaze settling on his face. At last he gave a grunt of satisfaction and jerked his head.

"Aye. No doubt about it. Ye are Macraig's son." He fisted his hands on his hips, feet spaced beneath him to balance his stout, muscular weight. His chin jutted forward. "Whereaboots have ye been, lad?"

Ferlie's gaze darted from one man to the other. The middle-aged man's countenance was calmly interested, but the younger's scowl deepened and he leaned forward aggressively, his height overshadowing Ferlie by a couple of inches.

Giving the golden boy a quelling look, Ferlie faced the question. "I am recently arrived from France, sir. Might I ask what business it is of yours?"

"Ye stole m' bride!" The blond youth took a menacing step forward, his fists clenched at his sides, his outburst startling Ferlie. The older man halted him with a slicing movement of his hand.

"She wasnae the lass for ye, Boyd. *Haud yer wheesht.*"

Boyd's scowl twisted into a jeer and he jerked his head at Ferlie. "Aye. Yer da dinnae think her good enough for ye, neither." He snorted, scorn evident in the tilt of his head and the way his gaze slid down his crooked nose. "He still doesnae."

Ferlie drew himself up, tired of not understanding. "Enough! Who are ye?"

The bull-necked man puffed his chest. "Are ye daft, lad? I am Laird Maclellan and this is my son, Boyd. Yon is my brother, Drustan. Gilda's da, Laird Macrory, and I had all but signed the betrothal documents when she ran off with ye."

"Aye, and 'tis a good thing they werenae signed. M'da would—"

Ferlie scarcely heard Boyd's scornful, bragging words.

Gilda.

His knees threatened to buckle and his breath came harsh to his chest. Visions of enticing lips beneath gray eyes framed with red curls flashed before him. In rapid succession memories poured through his head. Bare legs peeking from her tucked-up skirt on the beach, a smoldering kiss in a moonlit garden, naked skin beneath his hands, golden in the firelight. Gilda's sweet voice.

I willnae marry Boyd.

I want to be yer wife, mo chroi.

Gilda...

Graim thu, Ryan. I love you.

Ryan.

"Ryan, lad. Ye dinnae look so good. Are ye ailin'?"

Through the roaring in his ears, Ryan heard the concern in Laird Maclellan's voice and he took a deep breath, pulling himself together.

Boyd spoke first. "I dinnae think he's daft, Da. He likely stayed away so he dinnae have to put up with the Macrory bastard."

Anger raged through him, and Ryan whirled on Boyd. "What did ye say?"

"I said ye are likely sorry ye married the Macrory bastard."

Ryan's fist flew, catching Boyd off-guard. He staggered back a pace, his hand to his jaw. His eyes flashed and with a roar, he launched himself at Ryan, grappling him about his middle, shoving him backward. Ryan's breath left him in a whoosh as Boyd's arms forced air from his lungs. His feet slipped in the mud and they both went down, rolling and struggling to gain footing and the upper hand.

Boyd straddled Ryan's hips, using his weight to hold him in place. Pinning one of Ryan's arms in his meaty grip, he loosed a punch at his head. As the blow descended, Ryan bucked his hips upward and shoved his body to the side, throwing Boyd off balance.

Ryan snaked an arm upward as they rolled, taking the brunt of the blows from Boyd's fist against his shoulder, using the force to roll the larger man beneath him.

Someone grabbed him from behind, hauling him off the young Maclellan. He struggled to free himself, but more hands caught at him and pulled him back. Boyd scrabbled backward in the mud and quickly regained his feet. He flexed his arm and darted forward, but his da stepped between them.

"Enough! Ye both disgrace yerselves. Hie back to the inn and clean that muck off ye."

"He swung first!" Boyd wiped the back of his skinned knuckles across his jaw, his eyes full of resentment.

"Ye dinnae have to call the lass a bastard," the laird replied with heat. "Insolent wee *scunner*."

Boyd spat on the ground. "Doesnae matter. He's welcome to her." He sneered. "If she doesnae marry the MacLaurey lad first."

Ryan tore himself away from the restraining hands and pushed his way through the crowd, and made his way to the wharf. Returning to the inn an hour later, he spied Greum and waved to him to follow. Without a word, Ryan led him through a back door and through the narrow streets to the stable.

"Who have ye been fightin' with, lad?"

Ryan ignored the critical edge to Greum's voice. "Laird Maclellan's son needed to be reminded of his manners."

"What does Laird Maclellan's son have to do with ye?"

"It seems he believed Laird Macraig's son took something he considered his."

Ryan opened the neck of his leine and poured a bucket of cold water over his head, washing away the worst of the mud plastered in his hair. Shrugging out of his filthy leine, he set it aside and used the remainder of the water to finish his ablutions.

Greum's eyes widened. "Ye are Laird Macraig's son?"

Turning his shirt wrong side out, he used the cleaner surface to dry himself off. He shrugged in answer to Greum's question and shoved his arms into a cleaner leine from his bag he'd left earlier in Shona's stall.

Meager light from a single lantern resting on a wooden shelf in the stable barely pierced the gloom. Lacking a looking glass, he could not tell how he'd fared at Boyd's hands, but the left side of his face was tender to the touch, and he was certain he sported a scrape and bruise or two. He would arrive home looking much the worse for the wear.

"I have no doubt Boyd Maclellan and his da spoke truth. They recognized me." He lifted his gaze to Greum's. "*I* recognize me."

Clapping his hands with glee, Greum settled back on his stool. "'Twill be fine to see ye welcomed home, lad! I hate to see the storm delay ye, but another couple of days willnae change things."

"I dinnae plan on waiting."

"But the storm, lad! There willnae be a ship in yon harbor willing to set sail in this!"

Ryan shoved his meager belongings deep in his cloth bag and yanked the drawstring closed. "I have already spoken to the captain of a *birlinn* headed for Scotland. He is agreeable to leaving within the hour."

"But, the storm!"

Heaving the strap of his bag over his shoulder, Ryan paused, giving Greum an impatient look. "The crossing will take only a few hours. I have missed much this past year, my friend. I have a lady wife who pines for me. My father and sister also believe me dead. Would ye have me wait longer to tell them I dinnae perish?"

Greum's jaw clenched. "A shipwreck could still make it true."

"Aye. But now my memory is returned, I cannae wait to be home. I find I miss my sweet wife." He could not keep the pleased look from his face and Greum sighed.

"I hope ye willnae take it amiss if I dinnae join ye on this journey?"

Ryan patted the old man's shoulder, aware of his fear of being shipwrecked. "I am sorry to leave ye at this point, my friend, but I understand. Ye must follow as soon as ye feel able. Ard Castle will always welcome ye."

With a slow nod, Greum acknowledged Ryan's words. "I pray ye safe journey. I would like to meet this lass who holds yer heart. She must be devoted to ye and grieving terribly."

"She is a beautiful young woman. I can only imagine the toll this has taken on her. Her hair glowed as though lit with fiery embers, and her skin smooth as the finest cream." He winced. "If she has declined, 'twill be my fault. I would spend my life making her happy again."

Greum leapt to his feet and clapped Ryan on the shoulder. "Then, Godspeed, my friend. Yer lady waits for ye."

It had taken a hefty bribe and a ship's captain anxious to set foot on Scotland's soil and willing to risk the brewing weather, but they made the crossing from Larne just ahead of the next squall. The revelation of who he was spurred Ryan beyond caution, and he had been impatient to set sail. Much too impatient to even spend a moment longer with the angry, arrogant Maclellans, and he'd been glad to escape their 'talk' with little more than a few bruises and mucked clothing.

A lull in the storm had been enough to launch the ship, and though the night had been taxing as they rode the rough seas ahead of the next squall, morning dawned bright and clear. Ryan chose to ignore the dark clouds as they threatened to overtake them. He'd spent the hours keeping his own dark questions at bay.

How will I be received? Spending a year living with pirates could make my character suspicious, mayhap an outcast even. Will people trust me? Will they even believe me? Will they accuse me of staying away on purpose?

He took a mental inventory of his appearance. Dirty, ragged, still too thin. Did he even look like the person they remembered? Would they recognize him?

Doubt crept in and he searched for other questions. At least he knew Da and Gilda still lived. Laird Maclellan would have said otherwise. And his wee sister, Lissa. A smile touched his lips. *She has such a sweet way about her. I wonder if Da has thought to her future yet?* She would make someone a fine wife one day.

Gilda. My wife. He remembered the passion in her, the exciting, fulfilling nights they'd shared. Too few of them. *Will she still grieve me? Will she still be at Ard Castle, or would she return to Scaurness?* His father wouldn't have been likely to have offered a reason for her to stay on, wife or not.

Widow, he corrected himself.

Morning light chased away the darkness and he gave himself over to the scenery before him.

"A bit of a sea *brack* following us, but worth the choppy seas to get us home." The captain's voice drifted over his shoulder.

Ryan tore his gaze from the sight of the misted mountains as they slipped down to the blue waters of the firth. "I thank ye. I know the risk to yer ship was great."

Eyes gleaming with avarice and challenge, the captain grinned a gap-toothed smile. "Och, I had no intention of becoming *shipwrackt*. This ship has proven herself against worse storms than this." He peered into the distance. "We should put to port soon. Yer da willnae deny us mooring space, will he? I dinnae want to be mistaken for a pirate ship."

"Nae. I will take my horse and go ashore as soon as we land. The men at the docks will know me."

The captain gave a grunt of acknowledgement and clapped Ryan on the shoulder. "Then I will leave ye to yerself whilst I manage the ship. 'Twas our pleasure to have ye on board."

Ryan nodded absently as they entered the bend that marked the beginning of Macraig land. The sight was familiar and a lump rose in his throat. A year of no memories, and suddenly he was home!

The realization squeezed his chest. *Gilda. I've been gone a year. Has she thought to put aside her mourning?* He remembered Boyd Maclellan's spiteful words. *And marry Conn?*

He scratched his head, unable to make sense of Boyd's statement. Conn did not like Gilda, and would have had reason to hate her, blame her for the dishonor to his sister, and left to see his sister home. *He would have blamed her for my death.*

Boyd cannae be right. There would be no reason for them to marry, no reason for them to have ever seen each other again. He remembered the night in the cave as they fled Scaurness and said their vows to each other. Gilda was sweet and innocent—and ready to be his wife in every way.

My 'death' would have crushed her. My sweet darling. Living with my da for the past year with no one but my wee sister for company. She will be overjoyed to see me. His blood warmed and his breeches became uncomfortably tight.

Tonight she would be his again.

Chapter Thirty

$\mathcal{G}$ilda stretched her arms over her head, letting slip a sigh of satisfaction. The days at Ard castle had flown by, made almost pleasurable by Laird Macraig's conspicuous absence in whatever room she happened to occupy at the time. He had inspected Will the day they'd arrived, his belligerent stare twisting with a grimace as Will opened his amber gaze to his grandfather's sight. With no more than a grunt of acceptance, Laird Macraig had since left the two of them strictly alone.

Lissa had been a welcome distraction, fussing over Will almost to the point of being a nuisance. But her love for the baby was obvious and Gilda could not bring herself to scold the lass for spoiling the bairn. Today, however, Lissa had snuffled and sneezed her regrets through a partly-opened door, revealing her illness and sadly unable to help with Will or attend the picnic on the beach they had planned.

Gilda sighed. *I suppose I could spend the day packing and leave for Scaurness in the morning.* One day earlier than planned, but with Lissa ill, there was little to keep her here.

Footsteps pounded in the hall and ended at her door. A gentle yet urgent knock sounded. Curious, Gilda opened the portal.

"M'lady, there is a young man here to see ye!" Keita's normally dour face broke into a smile. Gilda's eyebrows rose.

"Who is it, Keita?"

"Will's favorite uncle, of course," a deep voice sounded as Conn skirted the maid. Gilda flung her arms wide with delight and stepped into his embrace.

"I dinnae expect to find ye here. I must be back at Morven tomorrow and couldnae wait for ye at Scaurness."

"Och, I cannae keep Will away just because his grandda and I dinnae get along."

Her voice was light, cheerful. It was difficult to hide her happiness at seeing Conn. She motioned him inside the room and toward the sleeping bairn. Conn took a step forward and paused. Keita's dour, untrusting look returned, causing Gilda to wonder what she thought Conn planned.

"He is here to visit Will, not ravish me," she scolded. Conn coughed and Keita's face reddened. With her nose tilted in the air, the maid pivoted on her heel and stalked down the hall.

Laughter burst from Gilda as she led Conn across the bedroom to the cradle lined with silver birch bark to keep evil spirits and faeries at bay.

Amber eyes blinked sleepily at them, tracking from one face to the other. A toothless grin split Will's face and he kicked his feet beneath the blanket, waving his chubby hands in the air.

"So, ye are awake, my lad?" Gilda tucked the bairn into her arms and turned to Conn, offering the chance to hold Will. With eager hands, he took the bairn and lifted him into the air. Will chuckled and thrust a fist into his mouth.

Gilda sighed. "Ye best give him back to me before he realizes how hungry he is." Her face brightened. "We were going to break our fast on the beach, but Lissa isnae feeling well. Would ye go with us?"

"Aye. I can linger the day." He handed Will back as the bairn began to chew vigorously on his fist. "I will meet ye in the great hall when ye both are ready."

He cleared the room, shutting the door behind him, and Gilda unlaced her bodice as she sang softly to her baby.

Feeding, burping and a change completed, Gilda made quick work of getting a basket of food together. Duncan and Archie, as well as Conn's men, would act as guards, and Gilda bade the cook to include plenty of food for all. She settled Will against her in a heavy cloth sling after she climbed aboard Fia, and, taking the reins, began the sedate walk to the beach.

Later, Gilda's heart swelled with contentment as she watched Conn and Will together. Conn lay on an elbow, propped above the bairn, and dangled a late-summer flower above his face. The baby's amber eyes tracked the slow movements and his fists alternately fanned the air and retreated to his mouth.

"Ye are so good with him."

Conn glanced up, the foolish smile with which he'd entertained Will lingering on his face.

"Ye know how much I enjoy spending time with him." His look turned serious. "And ye."

Gilda dropped her gaze and fingered a tiny flower poking through the grass at her side. Her forefinger traced the silken petals and down the hairy stem. The air was bright with morning sunshine, and the thin canvas stretched over them and anchored by four slender poles, flapped gently in the breeze. The soldiers formed a distant perimeter around them, giving both privacy and protection. Beyond the wiry salt grass, waves broke on the shore, a repetitive, lulling sound giving Gilda reassurance and courage.

"Do ye often think of that day, last year—" She could not finish the question, but Conn nodded. He rolled to a seated position and draped one forearm across his knee, twirling the flower between two fingers as Will cooed.

"Aye. 'Tis not so frequent now, but for months not a day went past I dinnae wonder what I could have done differently, how things would have changed—if it had been me killed that day instead of him."

Gilda lightly touched Conn's upper arm in sympathy. "I used to blame myself for wanting an outing that day. As I dinnae lure us out to help the pirates attack, and truly dinnae know they had returned, I finally had to admit 'twas not my fault."

"Gilda, 'twas never yer fault."

"I know." She pressed a hand to her heart. "In here, I know. Up here?" Her finger pointed to her head. "'Twas not so easy to understand."

Conn paused thoughtfully then turned his attention to Will, who appeared to be studying the undulating canvas overhead with awed intensity. The baby's rosebud lips puckered in an 'O' of delight and he chortled happily.

"I am amazed every time I see him," Conn murmured.

Gilda swallowed past a sudden lump in her throat. "He needs a father, Conn."

Conn glanced up sharply. "What are ye saying, Gilda?"

She shot him a teasing look. "I cannae be a mother *and* father to him, ye know."

"Are ye ready to be my wife, then?"

Gilda hesitated. *Was* she ready to be Conn's wife? *He doesnae stir me as Ryan did.* But would there ever be another man such as her true love? Did she want to live with Conn, love him, bear his children? She was no longer a starry-eyed girl. She knew full well what Conn asked of her.

It could be sweet between us. Is that enough?

Somberly, she nodded. "Aye."

"Do ye love me?"

Again, Gilda looked for the truth in her answer. Would Conn settle for her dedication to their marriage, her companionship and her acceptance of him in their bed? *Oh, Conn, I cannae love ye as I did Ryan.*

"I love how ye love Will. I love how ye make me feel wanted and safe." She worried her lower lip. "I dinnae know if I love ye like ye want. But I would do all in my power to be sure ye never regretted marrying me."

Conn stared into the distance. "I thought if I loved ye, if ye let me love ye, it would be enough. But I want ye to love me, too." He turned an intense gaze to her. "Do ye still love Ryan?"

A tremor shot through Gilda and she closed her eyes, fiercely holding the memories at bay. His face had faded in her mind, the look and smell and touch of him slowly becoming a mere ghost of the past. But the space in her heart only he inhabited was still empty, still tender.

At last she opened her eyes. "There will always be a place inside that remembers him. Seeing Will every day keeps that alive. I dinnae know how to change that."

Conn scooted across the few inches that separated them and pulled her against him. It was the first time in more than a year she'd been held by a man, one who wanted to be her husband, her lover. Her breath quickened and heat swirled through her, banishing the emptiness inside. As his lips met hers, she slid her arms around his neck and curved her body to his.

With a groan, he cupped her face in his hands and ended the kiss, slowly pulling his lips away. He rested his forehead against hers, his breathing a rasping echo of Gilda's own.

"I thought our lives would fit, regardless if ye loved me or not. I am not sure that is true anymore. I have loved Will since the day he was born, but I also love ye, Gilda. God help me if I hear Ryan's name on yer lips while loving ye."

Cold doubt washed over her. *Am I making a mistake?* "What if—"

Conn touched his finger to her lips, silencing her.

"Let me help ye forget him, Gilda. I dinnae want him to come between us."

His next kiss stirred her, warmed her.

And for a moment, she believed he could make her forget Ryan forever.

Conn brushed a final kiss against Gilda's temple and rose to his feet. She tilted her head in question.

"What is it?"

He gave her a reassuring look. "A *birlinn* approaches the dock. I would not have thought any would chance the weather. The seas have been choppy for several days. Likely a storm brews up the Channel."

A chill shivered down Gilda's spine. "Think ye 'tis a pirate ship?" She attempted to make the question lighthearted, but her voice broke, betraying her sudden fear.

"Och, nae. Dinnae fash yerself. There are soldiers at the dock. They will be watchful."

Gilda tried to steady her heart as it raced in her chest. She forced herself to take slow, even breaths, but it left her light-headed, and her throat was dry. She rose to her feet.

"I believe 'tis time to take Will back to Ard. We will likely travel home to Scaurness tomorrow since Lissa is not feeling well." She began gathering the remains of their meal, tossing food and cloths in the large wicker cubbie.

"Here. Let me give ye a hand." Conn reached across the basket to help, but his movement startled Gilda and she knocked against the lid. It fell with a thud, rapping her fingers still gripping the edge.

"Oh!" She jerked her hand free, thrusting the throbbing fingers to her lips as tears sprang to her eyes.

"Gilda! I am sorry. Let me see."

"'Tis not your fault," she murmured, her voice high and tight in her ears. But she let him hold her injured hand in his, inspecting the light red line across her knuckles. "I am more startled than hurt."

He lifted her hand and gently kissed the back of her fingers, one at a time. By the time he finished, Gilda's heart rate was racing more from pleasure than fright.

"The thought of pirates still upsets ye?"

"Aye. I thought it had passed, but when I left Scaurness, one of the twins shouted for me to beware of pirates. For several moments, it was as if it were happening all over again. I could see, hear, smell everything."

Conn glanced past her to the dock. "I believe the *birlinn* is carrying sea sales and likely the last until after the storm. Mayhap a walk to the pier, seeing the normal shipping would help put yer fears to rest?"

Gilda chewed her lip and cast a doubtful look at Will who had managed to kick a foot free of his blanket and grab his toes. He seemed content to pull his foot back and forth, and Gilda took a deep breath, steeling her nerve.

"Aye. A walk would do us all some good. Mayhap I will get a glimpse of some of the goods before they are sent up to the castle."

"Looking for cloth for a new gown? Mayhap a wedding gown?" Conn's teasing grin sparked an answering one from Gilda.

"Ye will want to talk to my da, but, aye. I will need cloth for my wedding gown."

Shona displayed her displeasure at the rough sea crossing by nipping the first lad who tried to enter her makeshift stall, and turning her back on the second, adding an ill-tempered swish of her tail in warning.

A large wooden chest, no longer secure after the tossing waves, suddenly crashed to the deck, spilling its contents as its slats burst apart. Bottles scattered across the planks with the sound of rolling thunder and Shona shied at the rumbling noise, tossing her head as she lifted her forefeet off the floor of her stall.

"Steady, lass." Ryan watched as her ears twitched in his direction. She shook her long mane and stamped a hoof irritably. "Let the lads sort out the mess and we will be off this ship. Ye dinnae want to be risking a cut leg on one of those broken bottles."

The ship's captain stalked past, anger showing as he berated the hapless lads clearing the deck. The sweet odor of claret permeated the air as it bled from the broken bottles across the wooden planks. Within a few moments, the salvaged flasks were packed away amid fresh straw, and the remaining shards swept away.

Ryan slipped the leather halter over Shona's head and led her from the stall. She butted his back with her forehead in her eagerness to leave the ship, and he took a skip step forward. "Wheesht, lass. I am sorry for the delay, but I will have ye saddled in a trice and give ye a bit of a run." He raised a hand to his brow, shielding the sun. "Looks like we will need to be careful of the people headed to the docks. Likely the captain will do well with his sea sales today."

A lad met him in a covered area just off the dock and handed him Shona's saddle and bridle. With a nod of thanks, Ryan tossed the lad a coin and quickly tacked up the mare. She danced on the end of her reins, obviously eager to put distance between herself and the ship. With a grin for her antics, he stepped lightly into the stirrup and swung aboard.

"Give yer muscles a bit of time to warm up and get used to dry land." His hand firm on the reins, he guided her through the crowded path up the beach. His heart quickened its beat and his head grew light with anticipation. He'd cleaned up as best he could in the moments before the ship docked, and managed to change into a moderately fresh leine. A complete transformation from ship voyager to laird's son would have to wait. Announcing his return from the dead would likely be a long, joyful event.

What would Gilda think? What would she do? He imagined her now, a year of mourning behind her. *It must have been verra rough on the lass. I doubt she's smiled much in the past months. My poor, sweet Gilda.* She had likely wasted away, devastated, no appetite to speak of. He'd heard of women whose hair had turned prematurely gray after they'd endured such a traumatic event. Would her beautiful hair have faded?

He reined Shona away from a cart full of produce and settled her beneath a canvas overhang in front of a tiny tavern as he took in the activity around him. The scene was much the same as the day he'd arrived home more than a year ago, how he had left Conn nursing a sick stomach and traveled along the beach searching for memories.

And found Gilda.

Sunlight glinted off thick red curls as a woman walked in his direction. Her face was tilted away as she listened to the man beside her. His hair shone gold and his attention turned to the bundle she carried in her arms. He took it from her, lifting it in the air. A section of cloth fell away, revealing a bairn who waved chubby fists at him.

Ryan smiled. He could imagine a scene such as this with himself and Gilda in a year or so. A twinge of envy twisted inside as he contemplated the time he and his sweet wife had lost.

The man and woman tossed back their heads, laughing. Recognition flooded in an icy wash through Ryan's veins. 'Twas no chance couple out for a stroll on the beach.

This was Conn and Gilda—and their bairn!

Chapter Thirty-one

$\mathcal{G}$ilda laughed as Conn tickled the baby's chin, earning a gurgling coo as Will waved his chubby fists. *Conn is so good to him. He will be good for both of us. I have made the right decision.*

The words flooded her heart, piercing her with warmth and conviction. *Da will be back in a few days and we will start arrangements then. It has been more than a year since the pirate attack. So much has happened. I know he will give us his blessing.*

She felt radiant and lighthearted, happy and excited in overwhelming measure. Conn tucked Will against him and Gilda slid a hand beneath his elbow, placing her other palm lightly on his forearm. The look of approval from Conn set her spirits to humming. With a lightness she'd not felt in far too long, Gilda gave her attention to the activity on the dock.

Only one *birlinn* sat docked. The other boats were fishing vessels, in with the morning's catch. Seagulls crowded the sky above them, screeching their hunger and greed. Everywhere, people hurried about on foot, carrying various wares and goods in bags, baskets, casks, chests and barrels. The creak of a wagon warned her of its approach and she clung tighter to Conn's arm as she stepped out of harm's way.

Just ahead, a man on a beautiful white horse approached, following the only path from the wharf to the village. The horse picked its way through the throng of people, front feet flashing, mane rippling like a banner in the breeze. Gilda's gaze slid from the magnificent animal to the man on its back, his dark hair shoulder-length and unbound, his face—

Gilda's vision swirled and her feet faltered. She couldn't draw breath and a gasp of distress slipped from her. At her side, Conn spoke, but his words made no sense to her. He pried her fingers from his arm and thrust Will's bundled form into her arms.

Mindlessly, she pulled the baby tight against her chest. He began to cry and a vague reality forced itself past her daze. Without breaking her gaze away from the rider of the horse, she loosened her grip on the bairn, and he snuffled against her breast.

She could not bring herself to name the man before her. It was too impossible for him to be here, yet he was, his hooded look betraying no emotion, though his lips were chiseled in a straight, stern line. A droning sound grew in her head and she swayed on her feet.

Conn gripped her arm, moving her protectively behind him. "Gilda?"

His voice sounded muffled and distant. She bit her lip against the burst of hysteria rising in her throat. Time passed—an instant or a year, she could not say, as the crowd ebbed and flowed around them, and the man on the horse never wavered. Conn stepped forward and left her abandoned, her emotions naked and vulnerable.

He grabbed the horse's reins and jerked her to a stop. "Ryan?" His other hand trembled as he lifted it, almost touched the man's leg. "St. Andrew's Balls, man! Say something to her!" Anger whipped through his voice, but the man on the horse still showed no emotion.

At last he lifted a hand, reining his horse to the side. "My apologies for startling ye. I will let *my* family know I am home, and give the three of ye a chance to recover." With a tap of his heels to his horse's flanks, he moved around them and turned up the path at a brisk trot.

Conn stared after Ryan, hands fisted on his hips, but Gilda could not have moved if her life depended on it. People shouted and chattered around her, but they could have spouted nonsense for all the words meant to her.

He looked at me with hatred. What have I done?

Conn took Will from her boneless arms. The babe grunted against the transfer, but settled quickly. "Gilda, lass. Speak to me."

Hours seemed to pass before she moved herself to answer his question. Feeling bewildered, stunned, lost and rejected, she slid her gaze from the spot Ryan's horse had occupied moments before to Conn's face.

"Is he truly Ryan?"

Conn drew a finger gently across her cheek. "Aye. Ryan has returned."

Gilda blinked. "Where has he been?"

"I dinnae know, lass. We are sure to find out soon."

The memory of Ryan's cold look twisted her insides and she whispered, "Why does he hate me?"

Shona bucked her hindquarters in complaint as Ryan dug his heels into her flanks, urging her forward. He rolled automatically with the movement, taking scant note of the mare's flattened ears as she chewed the bit between her teeth.

His mind replayed the touching scene of his wife and Conn—and the bairn between them. He ground his teeth against the shouting denial churning through his chest. All his memories of Gilda, thoughts of her despair, her pining and her decline—his hurry to return to her, to assuage her grief—all was for nothing. She certainly hadn't spent more than a week or two grieving him. He did a rapid mental calculation. The bairn couldn't be more than a couple of months old. Which meant she'd wasted no time before seeking solace with his best friend.

So, this is what Boyd meant when he said she'd likely marry the MacLaurey heir. Heat rushed through him, forcing air from his lungs like the hottest furnace. Sweat broke on his brow, and he felt physically ill.

Shona's gait quickened into a canter and he welcomed the rush of cool air on his face as he turned his attention to the guards at the castle gates—and away from the young woman who had just torn out his heart.

There was no recognition from the men at the wall, but the gates were open for the villagers' travel to and from the beach, and Ryan rode in unchallenged. He pulled Shona to a halt and dismounted, handing her reins to a stable lad who led her away.

He stared at the bailey walls, tall and stark and familiar. People surged around him, paying him no particular attention. With a shrug, he entered the great room's open doors, his shadow falling inside the hall of his birth.

A middle-aged man approached him.

"Might I help ye?"

"Ye dinnae know me?"

The man looked him over, a puzzled look on his face. "Nae," he ventured, his voice not quite sure.

"Then I shall require my father to verify his son has returned."

Recognition dawned and the man's jaw fell slack, his eyes bulging wide in his suddenly pale face. His hands fluttered up, having no job but to pantomime his complete surprise. Even heart-weary and bone-tired, Ryan couldn't resist a chuckle. Their conversation drew attention, and voices around them pitched to a curious murmur.

"'Tis the laird's son!"

"Impossible..."

"...dead..."

Ryan grimaced at the words, knowing all believed him dead this past year. A flurry of activity at the entry to the hallway near the laird's chamber captured his attention, and he saw a tall, robed man enter the room, his hair gray and sparse, his hands spread wide as though questioning the commotion in the hall. *Da.* Though more stooped than he remembered, and his hair nearly white, it was Laird Macraig.

Squaring his shoulders, he strode across the room, full aware of the words uttered behind raised hands.

Why? When? Where? How? He kept his shoulders squared, wondering how they'd respond to his answers. What they would think of him once they learned he'd lived the past year with the hated pirates.

A flurry of crimson cloth flew at him and he caught the bundle of tears and flailing arms.

"Ryan!" Lissa clung to him with the strength of ten, her sobs wetting the front of his shirt. His name rolled brokenly from her lips over and over, and he was at last moved to set her from him.

"Aye, Lissa, I am home."

Her sobs faded into hiccups and snuffles, and he gazed at her face, swollen eyes, tear-streaked cheeks, and thought them beautiful.

"Why are ye in yer robe, lass? Are ye in the habit now of sleeping late?"

"She is ailing, sir." Keita placed her hands on Lissa's shoulders. "Naught but a summer chill, but she shouldnae be out of bed."

Ryan placed a kiss on Lissa's forehead. "Aye. Ye are feverish. Hie yerself back to bed and *corrie doon* beneath yer blankets. I will be here when ye wake."

"Ryan, I have so much to tell you!" Her excitement ended on a rasping cough and Ryan nodded to Keita to return her to her room. Lissa flung an anguished, entreating look over her shoulder as the older woman led her away. "Ye will be here? Ye willnae leave?"

He smiled reassuringly. "I will be here."

His heart warmed by his sister's reception, he turned to the uncertainty of his father. They were at odds when they last saw each other.

Around him, people waited expectantly. Murmurs still raced around the hall, echoes of the same questions and speculations.

Where has he been?

What happened?

What kept him away?

How is it he returns?

Ryan completed the distance to his sire and stood before him.

"Hello, Da. I am home."

The elder Macraig's eyes reddened, his face twisted.

Is he not glad to see me? Ryan's resolve faltered. Laird Macraig's hands moved helplessly before him. At last he spoke.

"My son? Is it truly ye?"

Ryan's heart twisted at the hesitant sound of his da's voice. More than months had aged the man before him. Loss and grief had taken its toll. Ryan's eyes misted.

"I am home, Da. I am truly home."

His da gripped his arms with claw-like force. "Where have ye been?" His gaze turned frantic as he inspected him head to toes. "What happened to ye?"

Ryan glanced to either side, aware of the eager ears surrounding him. "I would tell ye of it in private, sir."

Drawing back, his da gave him a thunderous look. "Why did ye not send word? Do ye have any idea what ye have put us through?"

Ryan sighed. "May we speak in private?" He returned his da's look with a steely gaze of his own.

Laird Macraig dropped his hands and stepped back. "Aye. Clean yerself up and come to my chamber." He sent one more look over Ryan. "I need a glass of whisky."

Gilda cast a frantic look up the narrow road to Ard Castle. "I cannae return there. I want to go home!"

Conn recoiled with the force of her words and touched her shoulder with a soothing gesture. She jerked as though stung, her eyes wide with anguish, her skin devoid of color.

"I am sorry, Gilda. I dinnae know why he acted the way he did. I am sure he doesnae hate ye."

Gilda clasped the bairn tightly to her chest, rocking back and forth. Her distress unnerved him, made him feel helpless, useless. And afraid.

Would she ever feel as strongly about me? It was glaringly apparent, given the choice between himself and Ryan, whom Gilda would choose. But it seemed just as apparent Ryan no longer cared for her or wanted to have anything to do with her.

"Please, Conn? I want to leave now. I must go."

"What about yer things?"

"I dinnae care. They can be sent to me later."

"I will have the men escort ye back to Scaurness." He lightly touched her pale, cold cheek with the backs of his fingers. "I need to speak to Ryan."

Her eyes flew to his face. Her demeanor remained firm. "I will go to Tavia's cottage for a day or two. I am not expected back at Scaurness yet." Tears sprang unchecked down her face. "I need to be alone."

Conn had not the heart to argue with her. "Aye. Tavia can help with the bairn. I will tell the men."

Gilda made her way back to the picnic site where the horses were tethered. Conn jerked his chin to the four men who had walked to the dock with them and they closed ranks behind her. His heart thudded dully in his chest.

What is best for her and the bairn? Do I denounce Ryan and give her time to come back to me? How long will it take her to get over his loss a second time? Especially his cold rejection?

Anger began to simmer inside. He watched a guard grab Gilda's arm as she stumbled. Another gently took the bairn from her and she wiped a sleeve across her face before picking up her skirts and continuing along the trail. Regardless of her feelings for Ryan, his heart went out to her, his arms ached to comfort her. Conn clenched his fists, his thoughts grim.

Ryan had better have a damned good reason for treating her like this.

Chapter Thirty-two

Conn stormed the width of the great hall and mounted the stairs three at a time. The staircase curved upward, its thick stone walls encasing him as he followed the treads to the third storey. Lissa's maid, Keita pulled up short as they met at the head of the stairs. A watery smile lit her face.

"M'lord Ryan is home!"

Conn tamed his grimace to acknowledge the woman's happiness. "Aye. I saw him on his way from the dock. I would like a moment to speak with him."

Her face fell. "I dinnae think he wants to speak to anyone just now. He is closeted in his room. He shut his door quite firmly."

Venting his opinion of Ryan's reticence in an expletive he managed to keep under his breath, Conn strode to the paneled portal and, not bothering to knock, opened the door. Ryan paused in his ablutions, then, without even a shrug in acknowledgment, returned to his bath.

Conn pivoted angrily and snatched a chair from its position beside the hearth. Dragging it noisily across the wooden floor, he settled it between Ryan and the door and plopped himself down in it to wait. Ryan leaned his head against the wooden rim and closed his eyes.

Battling back his rising impatience as silence ensued, Conn cautiously opened the conversation. "Lissa's maid seemed glad to see ye."

Ryan grunted his answer.

"Have ye spoken to yer da yet? I am sure he is thrilled his heir has returned."

Silence met this observation.

"Where have ye been? I think that is a good place to start."

"I died and came back to life as a pirate."

Conn bolted up in his chair. "Ye what?"

"I have lived the last year as a pirate, Conn. What do ye think the clan and my da will make of that?"

"I dinnae think they will blame ye."

"Blame me?" Ryan gave a harsh laugh. "Mayhap not. But ever forget it? Doubtful."

Conn digested the news thoughtfully. "Ye were taken prisoner, then? But why did they not ransom ye?"

Ryan's fingers gripped the edge of the tub and his knuckles whitened. For a moment Conn was sorry he'd asked the question.

"From what I was able to piece together, their leader was killed and they had little banding them together beyond the need to survive. They found me floating in the water a small distance down the coast and pulled me out of the waves as a matter of course. Apparently they needed slave labor to fill in where they had lost men."

"Slave—you dinnae tell them who ye were? Were ye afraid they would kill ye?"

"I was often afraid they would kill me. But, no, I dinnae tell them who I was." He leaned forward and turned his face to Conn, moving his hair behind his left ear. "That verra large scar is what is left of a head wound that caused me to lose my memory. I only learned who I was a day ago."

Conn slumped back into his chair, his head whirling with disbelief. Ryan's story was simply incredible and he wasn't sure whether to heartily welcome him home or give him quiet and space to recover. He stole a glance at his friend, unwilling for Ryan to think he stared. His shoulders were muscled and lean, his skin darkly bronzed. But if he looked closely, white lines of scarring crossed the portion of his back he could see above the edge of the tub, and his shoulder blades were far too prominent. Conn shuddered to imagine the rest of the scar that crossed his head.

Ryan's next words took him off guard. "Why did ye not marry her?"

He thinks Gilda's unmarried state is my fault? He scowled, remembering Ryan's cold dismissal of her by the dock.

Pulling his anger in check, Conn bit out his words, striving for civility. "I almost did. I asked her twice, if ye want to know." Shrugging, he added, "I dinnae realize ye were alive at the time."

"She turned ye down." Ryan's voice was almost flat, emotionless, but Conn sensed the thin line of anger riding just below the surface.

"She was still in love with ye! Though I cannae for the life of me see why."

"Och, aye. I could see how much she once loved me."

Conn clenched his fists to keep from smashing the sneer from his friend's face. 'Twas not Gilda's fault she'd been too stunned to greet him with the joy Ryan had obviously expected. He'd been dead to her for a year, for pity's sake!

"If ye dinnae want her, just say so. She had only this morning agreed to be my wife. With ye gone over a year, she has every right to do so. Ye were never formally married before a priest, so yer vows willnae hold ye if ye want out."

"Ye would like that, aye?"

Conn bolted out of his chair and stormed to the edge of the tub, shoving back the desire to haul Ryan out of the water and beat some sense into him.

"I dinnae know what yer problem is. That lass grieved far longer for ye than was good for her. Then young William was born and she grew up a lot, became stronger—a young woman to be proud of. She has fought long and hard to overcome the nightmares of guilt she had of the day ye died—disappeared. Ye can either give her the respect she deserves, or go to hell! And I dinnae care which!"

He stared at Ryan for a long moment, but his friend made no move. Conn threw his hands in the air in disgust. "Och, wallow in yer self-pity for all I care. But ye'd best make yer mind up soon, for I'll not be put off by yer bull-headedness!" Spinning about with furious energy, he crossed the room in long, angry strides and flung open the door. Muttering dire consequences under his breath, he stormed down the stairs.

Tavia paused, tasting spoon at her lips, as a pounding at her door sounded. She set the long wooden utensil on the hearth and dusted her hands on her apron as she crossed the tiny room. Worry creased her forehead as she pondered the significance of a visit to her wee house.

She'd long since trained a healer for the clan, and other than the laird's own family, the new healer was usually sufficient.

She yanked the door open and peered into the bright midday sunlight. In the backlighting from the darkened cottage to the brilliant sun reflecting off the water of the firth, her goddaughter looked ghastly.

Tavia hurried to usher her inside. "Wheesht, lass! Ye look as though ye've seen a ghost! Sit down. I will take the bairn."

In short, commanding movements, she whisked a chair out for Gilda to sit, slipped young William from her arms and perched him on her hip. Peering up at the guards at the doorway, she shooed them away.

"Not enough room inside for that many braw men, and thank goodness for that. They only get in the way." She poured hot water from a steaming kettle over a spoonful of dried herbs. She stirred it slowly then set the mug on the table in front of Gilda. "This will put a wee bit of color in yer cheeks, lass."

Gilda forced her lips into a tight line of thanks and Tavia could think of no clear reason for it.

"Tell me what has upset ye, *a stor*. Has something happened at Ard Castle?"

Gilda wrapped her hands around the mug. "Aye."

Mustering patience, Tavia placed Will on a blanket in a large basket near the hearth and returned to the chair next to Gilda. She slid a hand across her shoulders, noting the tension and the way the lass flinched at her touch.

"Has someone hurt ye?"

Gilda shook her head violently. "Not my body. My heart."

"Conn MacLaurey, the wee *scunner*!" Tavia exploded.

Gilda placed a restraining hand atop Tavia's. "Nae. 'Tis nothing Conn has done." She tilted her face and Tavia wilted at the despair written in the tear streaks on her too-pale cheeks.

"Ryan Macraig is home."

It took a few moments for Gilda's words to register, and Tavia could tell how hard it was for her to say them. Gilda leaned back in her chair and crossed her arms, wrapping them about her waist as though shielding herself.

"Lass, tell me what happened."

Gilda stared at the mug of brewed herbs before her in silence.

Tavia searched for something to say. "This has come as quite a shock. I know how much in love the two of ye were—"

"He doesnae want Will!" The words burst from Gilda's mouth even as her hand flew to her lips, a horrified look on her face.

"Och, Gilda, that cannae be true." But despair slashed every line of Gilda's body and Tavia folded her into a tight embrace.

Slowly, Gilda began to speak. "Conn arrived at Ard Castle this morning. Lissa and I had planned to take Will out on the beach for a picnic, but she wasnae feeling well, so Conn went with us instead."

She took a shuddering breath. "As we finished, a *birlinn* docked and I was frightened—remembered the pirate attack a year ago. Conn thought it would be good if I walked to the beach, faced my fears." She fell silent and Tavia waited for her to regain her composure.

"A man on a beautiful white horse rode up the path. In a few moments he was close enough for me to recognize him." Her voice dropped to an agitated whisper. "'Twas Ryan."

"Did he see ye?"

"Aye. He saw me. He stared, no, he sneered at me! His eyes went from me to Will and back, and he sneered at me! As though he couldnae believe I had a bairn!"

Tavia placed a fond kiss on Gilda's temple and smoothed the fiery curls back from her face. "I imagine he was startled to see ye."

"He hates me. I saw it on his face. Why does he hate me?"

Tavia shook her head, swallowing against the tears clogging her throat. "I dinnae know, *a stor*. I dinnae know."

Ryan stood at his open window, surveying the land from his vantage point. Every dip and rise, every tree and stone were as familiar to him as his life's own blood. Conn's words still ran rampant through his mind. He sought peace, a refuge from the terrifying months with the pirates. Gilda had suffered, too, and he tried to wrap his thoughts around why she would turn to Conn at such a time. He had faced death more than once, and watched too many people die to continue to blame her for needing comfort in another man's arms. She had thought him dead, after all.

He scowled. Conn had not handled the situation well. He knew better than to take advantage of a young girl's distress. For that, he would consider thrashing him later. But for now, he needed to know if he and Gilda had a chance for a life together.

I could raise the bairn to know his da, to give him security and a good life. I could adopt him as my heir if I had no other. Though I dinnae know if Conn would agree.

He shoved his hand across his forehead in frustration. *She is the love of my heart. I would let her go if she was set against me. But if there is a chance, any at all...*

His da and the clan awaited him downstairs. But he would not face them without answers. Keita told him Gilda had not returned to the castle and Conn had ordered her things sent on to Scaurness.

Draping a plaide about his shoulders, Ryan slipped down the stairs unseen and hurried to the stables.

In the act of saddling his own horse, Conn was startled to see Ryan enter the stable. He stepped to the door of the stall as Ryan led his mare down the aisle.

"A nice-looking mare ye have. I dinnae think I have seen one so fine."

"A Frenchman I met gave her to me. I will tell ye the story sometime."

Conn leaned his forearms across the top of the half-door. "Where are ye going?"

Ryan finished saddling his horse quickly and swung into the saddle.

"I am going to talk to Gilda."

"She said she was going to stay with Tavia for a day or so."

Ryan pulled his mare's head around and gave Conn a long assessing look. "I thank ye." Putting his heels to his horse's sides, he sent her out the door into the evening.

Conn called after him. "Young Will is a good lad. Ye will like him."

Ryan did not answer.

Chapter Thirty-three

Gilda stared groggily at her mug. In the corner of the room Will slept, tucked in his blanket on the cot. Tavia had left them to check on a woman near birthing in the village, and she'd tried to nap as well, but, as tired as she was, both emotionally and physically, sleep would not come. Staring at the thatched ceiling, she'd waited until Will's eyes closed, then slipped quietly from the narrow bed.

She jumped at the rap on the door frame, nearly knocking over the table in her haste to stop whoever it was from making so much noise and waken her sleeping son. She jerked the door open, rocking back on her heels in disbelief.

Framed in the doorway, his shoulders taking up most of the open space, Ryan stood before her. His build was stronger, yet leaner than before, his hair tied neatly back, but still longer than she remembered. Deeply tanned skin contrasted vividly against his white leine, but his amber eyes glowed fiercely from his familiar face.

In spite of the shuttered look he gave her, her heart lurched longingly.

Dead over a year and he still makes my heart tremble. The admission brought an irreverent tilt to her lips which she quickly raised a hand to conceal.

Recovering her poise, she recalled his earlier dismissal of her and Will and put her hand to the door, intent on closing it.

He pressed his side of the door with spread fingertips, stopping her. "May I come in?"

His voice rumbled through her, recalling passion, and her heart warred with her head. She peeked past him and was reassured to see the guards only a few feet away. Without enthusiasm, she stepped back, motioning him inside.

"Aye, but please keep yer voice low. I dinnae want ye to wake Will."

His eyes slid from hers at the mention of the bairn, and Gilda's efforts at politeness slipped a notch. Her jaw clenched as she offered him a chair.

"Would ye sit?"

Ryan gave her a sharp look, but she maintained her calm as she seated herself across the table from him. He touched the table with a forefinger, drawing an invisible design on its surface. Gilda waited for him to break the silence.

"I believe we got off on the wrong foot earlier."

"Och, well, I was a wee bit surprised to see ye on yer fine horse at the dock." Gilda could not hold back her sarcasm at Ryan's poor opening statement, and was satisfied to see him wince.

But his voice remained even. "I am sorry for that. I can only tell you about these past months and hope ye understand."

Gilda's eyes widened and her voice dropped to a whisper, her hand at her throat. "I dinnae want to hear!" She cringed at Ryan's wounded look, and she battled down the fear stirring inside. "Ye dinnae know the nightmares I had after the pirates—"

"I am sorry, *a stor*. I dinnae mean to cause ye more distress. Will ye not hear me?"

Not immune to his endearment, she hesitated, biting back the insistent *No!* roaring through her head. She pleated the fabric of her skirt with trembling fingers then leapt to her feet and added hot water to her mug. The soothing aroma of herbs wafted in the air and she took a small sip of the liquid. Cradling the cup between her hands, she nodded. "Aye."

"The day the pirates came, I sent Conn to protect ye and the other girls—get ye to the castle and out of harm's way. We were outnumbered, and I prayed reinforcements from the castle would arrive in time. We just had to hold them off until Conn got ye to safety. Soldiers arrived and we fought the pirates back to the cliffs, but the battle was fierce. I took a blow to the head and that was the last I remembered for a very long time."

Gilda eyed him, puzzled. "What happened?"

"I fell over the cliff and floated down the coastline. The pirates fled our beach and picked me up as they sailed away sometime later."

"Why did they not ransom ye? Why did we not hear?"

"My wound was severe, Gilda. There was no one who recognized me. I learned later their leader was dead. When I finally woke, I dinnae remember who I was."

Gilda rose slowly and paced the small room. He'd been alone and unable to remember his name. Visions of Acair's death leaped through her memory. The sound of the wolf's snarls, the pirate's anguished cry. The sight of the sword Conn slid through his chest.

A nameless emotion seared her insides, leaving her breathless and cold. She startled as a hand clasped her shoulder and she whirled to meet Ryan's gaze.

"Will ye not sit with me?"

She nodded and followed him back to the table. Catching her chair by its rungs with his foot, he slid it next to his. Gilda sank slowly onto the woven seat and jerked as his thigh brushed hers. Ryan cleared his throat, a surprised look on his face as Gilda edged away.

"I lived with the pirates, Gilda. I saw many things I dinnae like, but couldnae change. They kept me as a slave for many months, shackled, starved. They made their living plundering foundered ships, and I hated every moment.

"One day they pulled an old man from the battered remains of his small boat and tossed him below decks to either live or die. I nursed him back to health as best I could, and he gave me the first clue to who I was. He said my eyes marked me as a Macraig."

His words stirred Gilda from her dread of his story. "Aye! Ye and Lissa both have the same eyes." She started to rise. "Even—"

Ryan caught her hand. "Please let me finish."

She glanced over to where Will lay sleeping and reluctantly dropped back into her seat. He did not release her hand, and she found the warmth of his palm stirred pleasant memories. A smile tugged at the corners of her mouth and Ryan tightened his hold.

"Not long afterward, Greum and I decided to escape. The pirates had stumbled across another sinking ship and planned to take its treasures and send the rest to the bottom. I managed to convince the ship's captain I was there to help him, and Greum loosed the grapples. Together, we turned the tables on the pirates, leaving them on the sinking ship and taking over theirs. By then, we were near the coast of France.

"Captain Rousseau's wife and daughters had been on board the ship and were verra distressed, so we took them home. I was their guest for a week or so while he arranged passage for Greum and me back to Scotland. Our trip was long, but uneventful.

"On the last leg of the journey, we were held up by bad weather in Ireland, and I met Laird Maclellan and his son, Boyd. They recognized me and that was the first I knew my name. I bribed a ship's captain to leave immediately, and arrived here this morning."

Something in the bland, impersonal way he spoke, told her he left out many details she had little desire to know. She finally understood why he had stayed away so long, and why no word came to them to tell them he lived. Perhaps she did not need to know exactly what had happened to create the gaunt man she saw before her, and she mulled over his story.

She gazed upon the sharp lines of his face, cheekbones prominent, his skin reddened from sun and wind. Fine lines stretched from the corners of his eyes. His fingers wound through hers, lean and strong. There was a look of sadness about him, resoluteness replacing the carefree young man he'd once been.

"Conn talked to me a lot about ye. Told me stories about ye and him as lads. It was hard to get over ye, but he helped."

His hands gripped hers almost painfully and she flinched in surprise. His brow furrowed angrily and muscles twitched in his jaw as he clearly ground his teeth.

"Please dinnae be angry! He has been wonderful to me."

"And how wonderful was that?" His mocking words taunted her and she snatched her hands away.

"Ye are jealous! How can ye possibly have the right to be jealous?"

He exhaled a long breath and scrubbed his face with his hands. "I dinnae know, Gilda, but I am. And 'tis tearing me apart."

The agonized look on his face pulled at her heart. "Conn has been a dear friend this past year. He couldnae visit much, but he made a point of doing so after he found out I was with child. He was there the day Will was born, and has been so good to the bairn."

"I can imagine." His words scraped past clenched teeth.

"He really loves Will."

Ryan's snort of derision astounded Gilda. She rounded on him angrily. "What is wrong with ye? I loved ye so much, but ye werenae here for me, and I am sorry I couldnae be there for ye." Tears burned her eyes and she jabbed at them furiously with the heels of her hands.

Ryan picked up a cloth spread across the back of his chair and gently wiped her cheeks. "I am sorry, Gilda. When my memory returned, all I could think of was ye and how good we were together. As soon as I knew I rushed home to ye. I wasnae counting on seeing ye and Conn together—and the bairn."

Small, snuffling noises came from the bed in the corner of the room, and Gilda broke away. She lifted Will, cuddling him against her, her mind a whirlwind of thought as she tried to jostle him back to sleep. Tiny fists waved sleepily in the air and his face scrunched tight.

Ryan peered over her shoulder. "He is a braw lad."

His voice was quiet, but her heart swelled. *I never thought he would see his son! Oh, how I longed for this.* Swallowing the lump in her throat, she touched Will's fist. Instantly his tiny fingers wrapped around hers and his eyes opened wide. She was struck anew at how much he resembled his father, his night-dark hair framing his amber eyes.

"Whose child is this?" Ryan suddenly demanded.

Gilda hesitated, flustered by his tone. "What?"

Ryan grasped her shoulders and forced her to face him. "His father, who is he?"

Gilda's heart tripled its beat, fluttering uselessly in her chest as she realized he hadn't known. Hadn't suspected.

She gasped, "You are." Then she found her breath again and fresh anger blazed.

Her palm made resounding contact with his face, showing a white imprint on his cheek before it flared bright red. "How dare ye? How dare ye think I slept with Conn mere days after ye disappeared! I was devastated! I would never have done that." Numb with shock, she stared at him. He had paled noticeably beneath his tan and looked so ghastly Gilda almost lifted a hand to soothe him before she remembered how angry she was.

He held out his palms in a gesture of surrender, then let them drop to his sides. "I cannae believe what an *amadan* I have been. If there is anything I can do to make ye forgive me, I will do it, *a stor*. Anything at all."

"Explain to me how you could think Will could be Conn's son."

Ryan shrugged ruefully. "I dinnae think we had been marrit long enough and was so blinded by jealousy, I couldnae think straight. When I saw the three of ye walking down the path and at first dinnae know who ye were. But ye were exactly what I wanted for us. For you and me, Gilda. A family. And then I saw Conn apparently had already taken what I wanted and made my dream come true for himself." He drew a deep breath. "I was an ass."

"Aye. A big ass."

Will began to cry and Gilda gave Ryan an apologetic look. "I must feed him."

"I want to stay."

With a hesitant shrug, Gilda unlaced her bodice and slid it over one shoulder, baring her breast. Will latched on hungrily and began nursing. Ryan caught her elbow and guided her to the edge of the cot, helping her to sit. He perched on the edge of the nearby chair, fascination on his face. Heat twisted inside her to have him watch her feed their son.

"Would ye tell me of it?" he asked. "The time before he was born?"

Her voice softened as she gently rocked the bairn. "Yer da couldnae stand the sight of me and I came back to Scaurness to live. I had my family, and occasionally Lissa would visit. But ye werenae there. I was carrying yer bairn and ye werenae there. It was such a relief when he was born and everyone told me how much he looked like ye. I had a part of ye with me again. A part I could hold and cuddle and love. He has meant everything to me."

Will turned his head away from her breast and stuck his fist in his mouth. Gilda smiled. "He usually is a fierce eater. He will be hungry again soon." She pulled her bodice closed and lifted him to her shoulder.

"May I?"

"What?"

"I would like to hold him."

She turned the bairn and placed him in Ryan's arms. For a long moment the two stared at each other, mirror images, older and younger.

"Ye need to burp him."

"Aye." He placed Will against his shoulder and patted his back gently. Gilda slipped a cloth beneath the bairn's face. After a moment, he let out a very satisfying belch. He chuckled and drooled, his head bobbing as babes do.

Ryan grinned.

Gilda felt an answering smile begin from her heart and touch her lips and sincerely hoped she didn't resemble a besotted idiot. She reached for the bairn, but Ryan caught her waist and pulled her against him. Before she knew what he was doing, his lips met hers, devouring her in a kiss that left her breathless. She returned his passion, wrapping her arms about his neck, partly to get as close to him as possible, part to counter the trembling in her knees.

Will fussed, trapped as he was between them, and they reluctantly ended the kiss, giving the bairn a bit of breathing space.

"I should have gotten off my horse and kissed ye like that when I saw ye this morning." He softly kissed her cheek. "My arms have been empty too long, *a stor*. Even when I dinnae know who I was, I remembered yer hair, yer skin, yer voice. Yesterday, I remembered yer name."

Gilda began to weep. Great, gut-wrenching sobs threatened to pull her apart. Ryan held her against him and she felt him shudder.

"I am sorry, Gilda."

"I am glad ye are home!" She gulped, sniffing back her tears. Her heart seemed to somersault in her chest.

"Aye. Ye are my home. Ye and Will are all I need. I want to watch all our children play and grow."

"All? I just gave birth to this one!"

Ryan laughed and Gilda thrilled to the sound.

"Will ye marry me, Gilda?"

"In front of a priest and everything?"

"Aye. In front of a priest and everything."

"I will marry ye, Ryan Macraig." She lifted an eyebrow, a merry glint in her eyes. "And mayhap see about those children ye say ye want."

Epilogue

$\mathcal{R}$yan faced Conn over the windy moor. He'd sent a runner ahead to ask Conn to meet him here. He didn't want to be haring off all the way to Morven after his friend on his wedding day. At least, he hoped Conn still considered him a friend.

Conn's face gave away nothing as Ryan recounted the previous week's revelations.

"I could pummel ye right here for thinking such a thing of Gilda." Conn squared off in tangible fury.

"Aye. And it appears ye would be right to do so." Ryan spread his hands wide. "I dinnae deserve her after what I put her through, but for some reason, bless the sweet saints, she has consented to marry me."

Conn made a disgusted sound. "Och, she is in love with ye, though I dinnae know why."

Ryan grinned, relieved Conn did not seem inclined to follow through with his promise of a beating. "Nor do I, my friend. Her da has given us his blessing. We are to wed today. Are ye and I still friends?"

With a long look, Conn clapped his hand to Ryan's shoulder. "We are brothers, aye?"

"Aye. We've been brothers since the day I placed a spider next to Mairead's platter at supper."

A grin split Conn's face at the memory. "We've shared everything since then. Lessons, games, pranks, beatings." His hand drifted unconsciously to his arse as though the last was recent enough to remember.

Ryan's smile faded. "We willnae share my wife."

"Nae. We willnae share yer pretty wife. I may come play with yer son from time to time. He is a braw lad and should have more than his disreputable father to look up to."

"Agreed." Ryan took a step back to the grove where they'd tethered their horses. "What will ye do now?"

Conn ran a hand admiringly down Shona's neck and across her shoulder. "Och, I have a yen to own a horse or two like yer mare. She is a *lichtsome* lass."

"Aye, she is a delight, though a bit mettlesome at times." He ruffled her mane affectionately and Shona tossed her head. "Vain lass."

"Ye say she is from Spain?"

"She is an Iberian horse. I can give ye a letter of introduction to my friend, Captain Rousseau. His son, Bray, traveled there to purchase this mare and others. I am sure they would be happy to receive ye and help ye find one or two of yer own."

"That sounds a good bit better than the betrothal Da is threatening me with. Mayhap a long trip to France and Spain will give me some breathing room."

"A betrothal?"

Conn shrugged. "I dinnae think he was entirely pleased with the possibility Will would inherit Morven. He thought I planned to marry too far from the clan. He wants me to marry a young widow who brings land next to ours."

"It could be worse."

Conn cocked his head. "I saw how much ye loved Gilda and how much ye still do. I dinnae want an empty marriage."

"Then be safe, my friend. Come back to Ard when ye return from Spain. Gilda and I would like to see ye again soon."

Conn swung into his saddle and directed his horse down the trail, his soldiers falling in behind him as they disappeared into the trees.

With a feeling of overwhelming gratitude, Ryan picked up his reins and mounted.

The stone kirk was festive with pink and white heather wound with ribbon, and bright flames danced on the wicks of a hundred candles. Ryan faced Gilda before the priest in front of an enormous crowd. Gilda's da and ma stood to his left, the twins pinned on either side, their scowling faces red, their eyes downcast. Doubtless they expected punishment for some mischief when they returned home. For now they were accounted for and silent.

On his other side Laird Macraig waited, his consent given, and perhaps, at last, even his approval. Closest was Lissa who beamed at them over the bairn she carried in her arms. Will gurgled and cooed as he kicked his legs and Ryan's heart swelled as he turned his attention back to his bride.

He took one of her hands in his and brought it to his cheek.

"Gilda Macrory, *thabharfainn fuil mo chroí duit.*" *I give you the blood of my heart.*

"Ryan Macraig, t*ugaim mo chroí duit go deo.*" *I give my heart to you, forever.*

"I pledge my love to ye, Gilda, and everything that I own. I promise to honor ye above all others, and we will remain, forevermore, equals in our marriage. This is my vow to ye."

Gilda glowed happily. "I pledge my love to ye, Ryan Macraig, and everything that I am. I will honor ye above all others, and it will be into yer eyes I smile each morning. I will love and cherish ye through this life and into the next."

"*A stor*, ye have given me a son. I am humbled by yer love and care, and amazed ye are willing to trust yer heart to me. Nothing I own now or ever will, could measure greater."

Gilda leaned forward for his kiss. Her lips grazed his ear. "We have more bairns to discuss, aye?"

"Aye."

There were definitely greater things to come.

A Note to my Readers

I hadn't meant to let a 4-year-old little girl come so close to taking over the prequel to this story in The Highlander's Reluctant Bride, but she was the obvious choice when looking for the heroine for the next book. Thanks to everyone who asked for her story—I hope it was everything you expected.

Look for Connor's story, coming next in *The Highlander's Outlaw Bride*.

Other books by Cathy MacRae

The Highlander's Bride series:

The Highlander's Accidental Bride (book 1)

The Highlander's Reluctant Bride (book 2)

The Highlander's Tempestuous Bride (book 3)

The Highlander's Outlaw Bride (book 4)

Enjoy an excerpt from

THE HIGHLANDER'S
Outlaw Bride

CATHY MACRAE

Prologue

1386, the Scottish Highlands

Brianna glared at her da, hands fisted on her hips, the belligerent thrust to his chin mirroring her own. "I willnae marry. Ye can burn that contract as easily as sign it."

"Ye will marry, and ye will wed whomever I choose."

"Ye put all of Wyndham into the contract. Wyndham belongs to Jamie. I want to stay here and take care of ye both. I cannae do that if I marry."

Lord Wyndham dropped his gaze and pivoted on his heel, his heavy cloak billowing about his legs. He pulled the wool close about him. "Yer brother is weak—has been since he was born. He willnae live to inherit."

His biter voice tore at Brianna's heart and she slipped behind him, an arm about his waist. "I know how ye've grieved since ma died, but 'twas five years ago." She eyed the whisky flask on his desk, already half-drained at this early hour. Rare was the afternoon that saw her sire sober.

"Though Jamie was born much too early, he has grown into a good lad. He cannot help being sickly. I know he will grow out of it soon."

"Ye are over optimistic, daughter. And headstrong and disobedient." Her da broke from her embrace and stalked to his chair behind his desk. "We have too much trouble on our borders and Laird MacLaurey has offered his help if we combine our lands."

Again, Brianna's hands propped on her hips, frustration boiling to the surface. "And by that he means I am to marry his son. Weel, I dinnae like it. Connor is a skirt-chasing rogue by all accounts and lost his heart to Laird Macrory's daughter. He isnae likely to be happy finding himself betrothed to me!"

She knelt beside his chair and placed a hand on his. "Besides, he is in France nursing his broken heart and who knows when he will return? Will his da honor his word to help us whilst his son traipses around the continent?"

Lord Wyndham eyed the whisky flask and licked his lips. His hand trembled. "We need the help. Reivers have struck us too many times. Our people willnae eat this winter if we cannae protect our cattle."

Brianna bit her lip. 'Twas her da's inability to stay sober that affected them most. She knew her ma's death at Jamie's birth had hit him hard, and his bouts of drinking had gotten worse, not better since. When he could be roused to remember his duty as lord of Wyndham, he would bluster and rail, swearing vengeance on those who stole from his people. But, in the end, he did nothing. Except drink himself into a deeper stupor.

"There has to be another way. Gavin and I—"

Her da smacked the desktop with a ferocious stroke of his palm and Brianna flinched in surprise. "Ye are a lady and willnae consort with the soldiers!"

"But, da—"

"Dinnae disobey me, daughter! We will obtain help from Morven and ye will wed the MacLaurey heir." He waved his hands in the air. "Be gone! Away to yer sewing and leave me in peace!"

Gathering her dignity, Brianna strode to the door and into the hallway. The clink of the flask reached her ears as she closed the door.

About the Author

Cathy MacRae enjoys combining her loves of Scotland and happy-ever-afters. When not writing, she finds herself in the garden, playing with the dogs, or cooking.

She also enjoys hearing from readers. You can read more about Cathy and her writing on at http://www.cathymacraeauthor.com and email her at cathymacrae@cathymacraeauthor.com.

Information on upcoming books and projects are listed under 'News', and you will find lots of writing-related blogs under the 'Bits 'n Bobs' tab, including author interviews and book releases for fellow authors, as well as some fun posts on Scotland.

Look under 'Wonderful Wednesdays' for bits on gardening, corgis, and the newest member of the family, Freki. See how she came up with the name and watch Freki grow up amid two very short-legged dogs.

Made in the USA
Las Vegas, NV
16 August 2024

93947710R00155